ATTACHED
AT
THE HIP

ATTACHED AT THE HIP

CHRISTINE RICCIO

WEDNESDAY BOOKS
NEW YORK

First published in the United States by Wednesday Books, an imprint of St. Martin's Publishing Group

www.wednesdaybooks.com

Designed by Jen Edwards

All emojis designed by OpenMoji—the open-source emoji and icon project. License: CC BY-SA 4.0

The Library of Congress Cataloging-in-Publication Data is available upon request.

ISBN 978-1-250-76009-8 (hardcover)
ISBN 978-1-250-76010-4 (ebook)

Our books may be purchased in bulk for promotional, educational, or business use. Please contact your local bookseller or the Macmillan Corporate and Premium Sales Department at 1-800-221-7945, extension 5442, or by email at MacmillanSpecialMarkets@macmillan.com.

First Edition: 2024

10 9 8 7 6 5 4 3 2 1

FOR THE KAT(S) OF MY LIFE:

Schwan, who accidentally older-sistered me in
  integral ways when I was floundering.

Tastic, the best/wisest/most fun critique partner
  a banana could ask for.

&

[-ie] McCormick-Huhn, my soul sestra.

ATTACHED
AT
THE HIP

1

Hi, I'm Orie, And

DAY 1

I am on a beach in Fiji about to be voluntarily marooned on an island to prove a point.

I'm here alone. I don't do things alone. I don't take pictures alone. I don't eat alone. I don't go to the movies alone. I barely shower alone—my dog insists on being in the room with me.

The producer examines the orange clipboard she's holding. Wild red hair billows around her face, tangling in her headset. A cameraman looms over her shoulder, his giant professional-grade lens aimed straight at my face. I shift over the rock I've been positioned on. I'm so anxious, I can't feel my hands. I keep looking down to make sure they're still there. (They are.)

Yes, I auditioned for this. But did I think it would actually pan out? No. Not in a million years. Why would it? Nothing else in my life has. I thought I would fall madly in love with my best friend and get married straight out of high school. I thought I would be excited to graduate college. I thought AcroYoga would just be a fun activity I do to spend time with my sister. I thought by this point I'd be . . . living happily ever after.

I've always pictured Happily Ever After as a linear spectrum, and somehow, I'd deluded myself into thinking I was feet away from the finish line. If you stand at Happily Ever After, spin around, and squint really hard, I'm that moving dot in the distance you can't quite make out, waving frantically from atop a rock in the middle of the ocean. Happily Ever After is a space station, and I'm Blake Lively in that random movie with the shark.

I'm supposed to introduce myself to the camera when I'm ready. I'm still debating what to say. *Hi, I'm Orie, and I spent the last ten days alone in a hotel room, scream-singing pop punk songs from 2004.*

The films I grew up on make weaving a happy life look so much easier than it actually is. The random person the protagonist bumps into within the first twenty minutes is always their *perfect* match, and within two hours, all their problems are solved, and would you look at that, they're also getting married. I spent my childhood striving for that. I consciously placed myself in a romance trope. I followed the beats. It didn't work.

2

Lectures with Lark

DAY −90 | THREE MONTHS EARLIER

The screech is out of my control. It spews out of me like steam from a screaming teapot. I'm possessed by pure, unadulterated, body-function-freezing terror for twenty-three seconds before my mom comes tearing down the stairs and bursts into my bathroom.

"Jesus, Orie, where is it?" she bleats, exhausted.

I point to where the evil, possibly blood-sucking demon spider is hovering over the toilet, waiting to drop down and murder me when I least expect it.

My mom grabs two tissues and smashes it midair before the thing even registers the need to flee. I exhale, my hands falling from their en garde positions, smashing up against my cheeks à la *Home Alone.*

"Thank you," I squeak.

Mom sighs, drops the carcass in the toilet, and flushes it. "You have to stop doing that."

"You don't understand. They're out to get me, Mother." I watch as she instinctively starts picking up in here, refolding my towel, straightening out my various skin products. "They have an elaborate plan to steal my first-born child, turn her against me, and send her back to kill me in my sleep."

"The spiders want your specific child?" She's crouched next to the tub now, going through my shower products, shaking them to see what's empty that she can purge from the area.

I lean against the sink. "Yeah, they left a threatening note in the shower steam once. They're very impressed with my AcroYoga. A child with my skills could be the new Spider-Man."

Mom smiles, chucks an old bottle of conditioner into the trash, and stands up. "Well, you don't have any children, so there's nothing to fear."

She walks out of the bathroom. I follow her into the den where she folds the blanket sprawled out on the couch.

"They're on a quest to lay eggs in my makeup. It's an elaborate plot to gain access to my insides and control me via my organs like kids do in the biology episodes of cartoons."

"What if the makeup eggs turn *you* into Spider-Man?" She artfully drapes the blanket and heads into my room.

"Don't be ridiculous, Mom. They would never give me that kind of advantage. They wish me compromised."

Mom snorts, straightening out my comforter. "Orie, you're gonna give me a heart attack. You have to stop screaming."

"You say that like I'm doing it on purpose. I don't want to do it, but I'm like a werewolf, and spiders are the moon. I'm overcome with guttural fear. Can we get a bug guy back down here?"

"Orie—"

"Please? It's definitely been over three months. I'll pay for it. Lark and I have a pretty steady flow of income now. I can pay for it."

Mom takes a seat on my bed, frowning as she catches sight of the chair in the corner of my room currently buried under a mountain of the colorful new yoga sets I tried on for a sponsorship today. She pulls back the front of her strawberry bob, yanks the band off her wrist, and secures her hair into a tiny bun. "Aren't you supposed to be outside with Lark and Dad?"

"I am!" I start backing out the bedroom door. "I just have to pee. Now that you've slayed the Antichrist, I can do that in peace. Thank you for your service."

"Go."

"Okay, hold it!" Dad urges, kneeling with his camera in his Levi's and light blue button-up. He's concentrating on the shot, face pressed up against his DSLR as he focuses through the viewfinder, the setting sun bouncing off his white hair.

Rob Lennox is an artsy guy. He's an uber-passionate creative, constantly raving about his latest ideas and inspirations, and as far as dads go, he's pretty great. He fully supports our obsessions. This man sat next to me on the couch and watched an infinite number of *Hannah Montana* episodes through my elementary school years. He took me to Miley Cyrus concerts. He played her CDs in his car. I was shocked when I learned that other kids' dads didn't also know all the words to "The Best of Both Worlds."

My mom's pretty great, too. I'm one of the rare modern-day young adult humans with still-married parents. Mom and Dad are soul mates— real-life proof that romance books are accurate. She's open and patient but disciplined when she needs to be, and she brings those traits out in all of us. Dad's eager, impulsive, buzzing with energy and innovations. He builds us up, and Mom calms us down. Dad works nights and weekends; she works normal hours during the week. They're the perfect team.

"Hold it!" Dad says again.

"We are holding it." I press out from my precarious base position supporting Lark as she arches over my extended legs. "My eyes are burning!" My back presses against a cold blanket of grass, and my arms quake with the strain of the pose. It's a warm day for October, but not quite warm enough for skintight athletic wear.

Lark shakes slightly. It's rough holding these for more than fifteen seconds.

"Why are your eyes burning?" Lark hisses.

"I don't know. I think some of my glitter must have shifted."

"One more second, just want to try one last angle," Dad shouts from farther down the driveway.

"How many times do I have to lecture you about wearing *glitter* during a shoot?" Lark huffs.

"I like when my eye makeup is shimmery in our pictures, and our followers like it. I did a poll."

"You're not going to see our eye makeup in this pose!"

"I'm not wearing my glasses, so you'll see it enough to think, *ooh*, cool, she matched her eye makeup to her outfit."

"Got it!" Dad strolls back toward us.

We are blessed to have a former photographer father to shoot our sponsored content.

For years AcroYoga (acrobatic yoga) was a thing the two of us did for fun. I used the word "content" ironically, and Lark handled the @LennoxSisters AcroYoga Instagram on her own. But seemingly overnight five months ago, it became our job. We went from 70,000 followers to 670,000 within a matter of weeks.

We do these short sister-sister flow videos; imagine AcroYoga as a dance. Lark choreographs a two-minute yoga routine to a popular song, we do it, and she posts it. One of our more impressive flow videos, set to the new Taylor Swift song, went viral. Then all our other sister-sister AcroYoga flow reels started to gain traction. Before we knew it, we had half a million people watching. I'm still trying to wrap my head around it.

Before this summer, Lark would pick up a sponsorship for us here or there, but nothing like the companies and opportunities popping up in our emails now. She's been lining things up for us, one after another, week after week, leading all the way up to Christmas. It's been a strange combination of thrilling and terrifying. I never imagined I would be flying out to different cities to host yoga retreats as part of my job.

Lark gracefully dismounts off my feet and folds over her legs to open up her lower back. I shift onto my knees and into an arch to stretch out my pecs.

My sister's five foot nine and willowy. Her chestnut pin-straight hair is always pulled into a perfect high ponytail. I got Mom's strawberry-blond hair, which is fun, but it doesn't tame easily like Lark's. Mine needs product and tender blow-drying care so as not to become a nonsense nest of frizz.

And Lark's got these big green doe eyes that trip everyone up. People can't help but fall in love with her. Through high school, there was always this disconnect when people learned I was her little sister. The compact athletic girl, full of hard angles, who enjoys constantly switching out her glasses and wearing over-the-top colorful glitter makeup to school every day is related to the popular, graceful, perfect president of the senior class? I was the tryhard. Lark was the innately cool smart girl who everyone wanted to date.

But these last few years, that imbalance has shifted. Since we embarked on this AcroYoga journey and started to grow *together*—I've felt less "less than" and more like an equal member of a team. An integral part of a valuable duo. People like *both of us.* People follow my individual Instagram on top of our sister account. It's been so incredibly validating to be considered just as crucial and viable a human specimen as she is after feeling subpar for so long.

"That was beautiful, girls. I'm going to get these onto the computer!" Dad crunches over dead leaves as he heads back in the house through the sliding glass door to the basement.

"Thanks, Dad!" Lark and I say in unison.

I'm fairly certain Lark is my parents' favorite, and I can't blame them. She'd probably be my favorite, too. She's so on top of her shit. She decides things, and then before you know it, those things are happening. And she's not just doing the things she decided on; she's killing the things. *She's a finisher.*

Lark turns to me. "Earlier, I sent over a Drive link of your new reel for the Nike campaign. Did you get it yet?"

I roll back onto my shoulders and lift my legs in the air, prepping for plow pose. "Oh thanks! I haven't seen it yet. I was at Wes's this morning, but I'll download it as soon as we go back in."

Wes should be here soon. He's grabbing Lark, my dad, and me iced coffee from the Tea Shop on his way over to join us for dinner.

Lark stands and grabs my ankles. She lifts them until I'm in a full handstand. "Or . . ." She hesitates for a moment.

"Yeah," I say, upside down.

Lark exhales. "Are you ever going to dig into an editing program so you can put these things together yourself?"

"The reels? I thought you liked editing?" I step out of the handstand and rise to full height so I can look Lark in the eye. I'm only three inches shorter than her, but I feel much smaller when she asks pointed passive-aggressive questions like this. Lark is a complete control freak. She's never expressed any interest in sharing that particular workload.

"I do, but we're getting busier, and it's become . . . a lot to do all our individual account reels and TikToks and handle our shared one. You're depending on me for everything."

"I'm . . . depending on you?" I cross my arms. "You never asked me to do anything."

"Don't get upset."

I bark out a humorless laugh. "I'm not upset. I'm calm!" I focus on the clouds above her head and blow out a breath.

If I know Lark, and I do, she's about to lead me into a seemingly random argument about something she's been stewing about for weeks. We almost never argue, but when we do, it usually starts with Lark saying *don't get upset* and ends with me in tears.

Lark never gets outwardly emotional. She's cool, calm, and collected, even when she's mad. When she's angry, anxious, scared, or hurt, she can be cutting, witty, logical, and pensive. Meanwhile, cast me into any heightened emotion, and I'm incoherent, weepy, loud, and sweaty.

Lark serves me an exasperated look. "Do you think we can have an adult discussion about your role in our business?"

I shove my hands onto my hips. "I don't depend on you for everything."

"Okay, sorry, correction, you depend on me *and* everyone else for everything. You're a codependent person, Orie."

Hurt slices through my chest. *Wow.* "What's that supposed to mean?"

"You can't do anything yourself! You literally don't do anything without Wes, Mom, Dad, me, or our audience holding your hand."

I stare at her, speechless for a moment, before pivoting and power walking toward the house. I tug the sliding glass door open and shove it closed behind me. My toes curl into our fluffy basement rug as I try to calm my nervous system. *Must remain chill so I can speak like an intelligent member of the human race.*

Our sandy wheaten terrier, Stanley, comes barreling down the steps to greet me. I manage to give him a few pets before the glass door slides open again, and Lark comes in.

"I read by myself!" I spout defensively.

Lark sighs behind me. "Yeah, the books Mom brings you."

Damn, I didn't think she'd be able to swing that around.

I spin to face her. "Well, Mom gets free books. Why wouldn't I read those?"

"You never go get your own books!"

"How would I know which to buy? There are so many options, Lark! Why would I waste my money on one I might not like! Mom knows which ones are good."

Lark smacks a hand to her face. "You could use that thing we work on—the internet."

"I trust Mom."

"Ugh, Orie! You're missing the point. You have this job because I needed an AcroYoga partner, and I'm our manager, so you continue to have this job because I manage it for us. You still live with Mom and Dad, so you don't have to pay rent—"

I throw my hand up. "I do pay rent!"

She crosses her arms. "How much?"

An annoyed sound escapes my throat. "An amount."

A very reasonable $400 a month because Mom wants me to save money for my own place and won't let me pay a normal rent, even though *I'm fairly certain* they could use the money. The restaurant's not doing well. It's closed for the winter, and Dad is concentrating more on photography, which is not normal. I've been offering to start paying them a price-appropriate rent every month since graduation, and Mom continues to turn me down.

Lark rolls her eyes. "Mom still does your laundry and picks up after you. Dad cooks your meals. You're still on the family cell phone plan. You use their internet. Wes brings you coffee every day and goes with you literally everywhere—"

"I don't have a car!"

"And you don't have your license!" she snaps.

I flail my arms about. "Where is this coming from, Lark? How is this relevant?"

"You can't go anywhere without another person! And I edit your video content on top of fielding all our emails. What do you do for this business, Orie?"

I gape at her, feeling like she just punched me in the throat. "I'm sorry, what do I *do for this business*? What are you trying to say? I'm here! I'm always on time. I'm your base! I follow the exercise regime you set up! I go to the gym to weight train twice a week with Wes, on top of all our practices, so we can do cooler poses! I . . . plan out the outfits for all our shoots!"

"You send me five options and make me choose. And when I don't choose, you take a poll on Stories. You're *incapable* of making your own decisions."

I shrug angrily. "They like being involved in our decisions, Lark!"

Lark backs into the large gray sectional hugging the wall that's been a staple in the house since we were kids. She collapses onto it, looking drained.

I walk over and blink at her maniacally. "Lark, I do everything you tell me to."

"That's the problem, Orie," she mumbles.

"You want me to disagree with what you tell me to do?"

"No! Oh my god." She drops her head into her hands.

I perch carefully on the couch a few feet away from her. "I don't get it. Is this all because of my glitter?"

Lark abruptly straightens, pushing her palms into her thighs. "No! I'm not saying don't do what I ask. I'm just saying it'd be nice if you took a less passive role in our work. You're already passive in every other aspect of your life!"

I make an involuntary nasal, offended noise. Lark takes out her phone and starts tapping to avoid looking at me.

I don't know what to say. I'll think of the perfect response in an hour, once all this confusion stops raging through my limbs.

After a moment, I poke her in the arm. "Mom and Dad like having me here. I'm saving money for the future."

She drops the phone from her face. "How long do you think they want you to stay here?"

Wow. "Forever, if I wanted! Mom's been saying that since we were babies."

"And what future?" Lark interrupts. "The one where you, what? Marry Wes despite not being in love with him?"

I gasp.

"Have his babies and grow old AcroYoga influencing? What about your English degree? Didn't you plan on using that?" She gestures to the three bookcases taking up the entire far wall. It's full of Mom's and my extensive collection of favorites. Lark cleared her books out when she got her own place two years ago. "Did you read all these to influence people about how to lead a healthy lifestyle? I'm the nutritionist, Orie. This is stuff I like to talk about. This AcroYoga health stuff is a thing *I wanted*. You graduated months ago now. What the hell did *you want* to do? What plan have you tabled?"

What plan have I what?

"I don't know! What is this, some weird random intervention? I'm planning to be happy! What's wrong with getting married and having babies? Mom and Dad were high school—"

"Sweethearts," she interjects. "Yeah, I'm aware, Orie."

"They got married and had babies, and they're disgustingly happy."

"You and Wes are not high school sweethearts! If you're not into it anymore, you have to break up with him. Things can't always just stay the same!"

"*You* think I should break up with Wes?" The words wheeze out of me. Lark and Wes have always gotten along so well.

"If you don't want to be with him, then obviously, yes, you should!"

My eyes fall to the braided silver band around my right ring finger. The promise ring Wes gave me before we went off to college. He was ready for a commitment. But I still didn't feel *it*.

You're familiar with *it*: the rom-com movie, romance novel, all-consuming *it*.

I've gone through many a spiral regarding my lack of *it* feelings for Wes. But maybe I'm just not a person who feels *it* feelings! Maybe what I have with Wes is the best a relationship will ever get for me. Am I gonna throw that away? Wes understands me. He supports me.

I clear my throat, struggling to remain tear free. "Wes is my best friend. We've been together for so long. If we break up, it would all be a waste."

"A waste?" Lark shakes her head. "That's not how relationships work. Staying together just for the sake of staying together is the waste, Orie."

And I'm crying.

My self-esteem is bleeding. I need to extricate myself from this conversation. Recover my ability to think. Formulate a well-thought-out response. I stumble off the couch and back up in the general direction of my bedroom. "I'm not codependent."

Lark rolls her eyes. "Keep telling yourself that, Orielle."

Wow.

"Hey!" Dad calls down from the top of the steps. "Dinner's ready! Timer for the lasagna just went off. Wes is here helping me set the table."

Lark and I stare at each other. She's completely maintained her composure: self-assured, leaning against the couch, legs crossed, arms crossed, in her purple corset-style yoga top with turquoise accents and matching leggings. As I suspected, she's clearly been thinking about this for a while. I inhale a sharp breath.

"What?" she demands.

I clear my throat again. "Are *you* . . . breaking up with *me*?"

Lark rolls her eyes again. "I'm your sister. I can't break up with you."

"Do you not want me to be your yoga partner anymore?" I clarify sheepishly.

Lark exhales. "That's not what I'm saying. But Mel *has* been doing AcroYoga with me on the side for a while now, and she's gotten pretty good."

She doesn't want to work with me anymore. But I've been a perfect partner. We put so much time into this—I've gotten so good at it. We're a team!

"I—wha—are you—?" I press my hands against my temples. "Lark. We've been building an audience for five years together . . . You want to replace me with your girlfriend?" I shake my head, incredulous. "Isn't Mel busy teaching fifth grade? Doesn't she like teaching? How long have you been planning this? I don't understand what I did! Are you sure this isn't because of the editing thing?" My voice cracks. "I can learn to edit. I'll learn, I guess! Can you help me learn? Or, wait, maybe Wes can help me!"

Lark closes her eyes. "No, Or, that's not it . . ."

I pinwheel my arms like a cartoon character about to fall off a ledge. "Then what is it?"

Lark shifts to better look me in the eyes as I pace a hole through the carpet. "I want you to have your own life, not just fall into the one I've set up for you. You're done with college now; you don't have to keep doing this for me."

Tears slip down my face. Is Mel stronger than I am? Does she think a couple will be more marketable than a sister duo?

A smile has the nerve to slip up Lark's cheeks.

"Are you really smiling at me right now?" I yelp.

"I'm sorry. I was going to wait to announce this over dinner, not mid–random weird fight but . . . Mel's not just my girlfriend; she's actually my fiancée now."

I stop short, a blaze of happiness chasing away every other emotion as I gawk at Lark.

Mel and Lark are engaged!

I suck in a shaky breath and point at her accusingly. "I'm really hurt right now, but also, I'm so happy for you two, and I want to know the story of exactly how this happened, play by play. But right now, I need to go have a cry in my room. I'll be late for dinner. Please make sure Mom and Dad save me a plate because I'm starving, and I've been craving that lasagna all day." I take a step back. "Can you tell Wes to come down-stairs—?"

I can practically see the *There she goes again, being codependent* thought take shape through Lark's shoulder tension.

"No," I course correct. "Tell Wes I'll be up in ten minutes. Tell him to stay upstairs." I sprint to my room six feet away. "Stanley!" I hiss. Stanley hops off the couch and trots into my room. I slam the door shut behind us.

"Orie." Lark sighs on the other side of the wood. "I'm not trying to be mean. I just want you to chase what you want for yourself!"

I am an independent person! I will now cry without anyone around to watch it happen. Look at me go.

I chuck myself onto the bed with an irritated growl. Stanley hops up and lies down next to me, licking my hand. I flop onto my back, pull out my phone, and sob-scroll through Instagram. I stop on Wes's latest post and double tap. It's a reel about his new gaming chair.

Wes asked me out in eighth grade. It had felt inevitable at the time: We'd already been neighbors and best friends since kindergarten. Before that, I was invisible at school. I was the girl who was bullied for the most boring reasons: red splotches on my face and reading during study hall. Then Wes asked me to be his girlfriend, and I became *Wes's girlfriend*. It's weird how being someone's girlfriend can reframe the world's perception of you. Wes's middle-school heartthrob status rescued me from oblivion. Back then people would wonder (aloud, mere feet away) why he would ask out *a girl like me*. I knew it was because he knew me, inside and out. Wes saw the obsessive book-reading, movie-worshiping person that I was and *wanted me*.

On our one-month anniversary, he tried to recreate that *Friends* episode with Ross and Rachel in the planetarium in his bedroom. That night, he straight-up told me he wanted to marry me after we graduated high school and start a family together after college. *A thirteen-year-old boy said these things to me.* Then he told me he had loved me since we were seven years old, and I'd smeared half a jar of peanut butter on his head to get the gum out of his hair. A second-grade asshole, Keith, had spit it on him in gym.

I remember that moment so vividly. My face went flush. My heart felt like the cheap pink ball attached via flimsy white string to a thin wooden paddle, soaring up into my throat only to be jerked back down into my chest.

A boy loved me, and I never in my wildest dreams thought that would happen so soon. In all the books I had read, the girls were fifteen or sixteen, at least, before they meet their love interests. All I could think in the moment was *Wow, this is such a great story. We met at five. We started dating at thirteen. We're going to have an epic romance. The kind they make movies about. The kind with quotes you remember for the rest of your life like* When Harry Met Sally *or* Mean Girls.

So, I told him I loved him, too, even though I wasn't sure what loving someone felt like. I wasn't sure what I felt qualified as romantic. He pulled out a jar of peanut butter and two spoons. We toasted our globs to Keith, his second-grade bully, and the rest is history. To this day, we eat peanut butter on our anniversary. He's always been so sure about me. So enthusiastic about our future family. *Such a romantic.*

I swipe at the tears falling down my cheeks and continue doomscrolling.

An announcement post catches my eye, and I pause, my thumb pressing into the screen. It's about the TV show *Survivor*. I follow a million *Survivor* accounts on Instagram, so the fact this is *Survivor*-related isn't what snags my attention. It's the word "casting."

When we were younger, Lark and I would always talk about auditioning for *Survivor* together, getting on a "Blood vs. Water" season, where you go on with a family member.

They're currently casting for the new *Survivor* season. They're accepting audition videos through the end of the month when the current season's finale will air.

The phrase "incapable of making decisions alone" rattles against my skull.

3

The Call

I could be reading the climactic scene of *The Vanishing Half* right now, but Wes has his tongue down my throat. I shouldn't want to read over having my boyfriend's tongue down my throat. I shouldn't be thinking about this at all right now. *Right?* It's a really good book. I had to put it down when he got here twenty minutes ago. I wonder if there's a movie in the works. I'll have to google it later.

I've never stopped to think about how weird it was that I thought about things like this every time we kissed until Lark's passive-aggressive lecture last month.

Or maybe I've thought about it and brushed it aside.

I think maybe I've spent ten years pretending nothing between Wes and me was weird because the prospect of breaking up with him terrifies me.

Lark and I haven't had a *real* talk since last month. I don't know what the deal is with Mel replacing me, but we've been going along with our influencer stuff as usual. Nothing's changed with our @LennoxSisters account. Lark hasn't brought it up again.

But I can't stop thinking about the insults she flung at me. They carousel around my brain on a loop. I can't help that I like doing things with other people. Other people are better at things than I am! What's so wrong with that? Is enjoying company a crime?

I also can't stop thinking about how every time Wes and I make out now, his tongue feels like a probe, and I feel like an alien, completely foreign to the earthly act of kissing.

Wes slips his hands under my shirt and pulls it off. I'm hungry. When will it not be weird for me to suggest going upstairs for a snack? He drifts his hand down the quote collection tattooed over my left shoulder blade and upper waist. It's a smidge sensitive right now; I got a new one last week. I was flipping through my quote notebook, and one was so relevant, it leapt off the page and smacked me in the face. I showed Mom, and she liked it, too, so we got in the car, and she drove me to my tattoo place.

I think I do have to break up with Wes. Lark was right, and it makes all the other things she said bother me exponentially more than they did when she'd first said them. Cutting comments are supposed to fade, not gain traction over time.

Breaking up with Wes feels like the responsible thing to do.

Reasons to Break Up with Wes

1. I don't love him.
2. I don't feel anything when we're physical together. (I don't know that I ever have.)
3. I'd rather find a snack than make out.
4. He doesn't read.
5. These past six months, he's felt about 100,000 miles away. (Which doesn't make sense since we see each other every day, and right now, I'm literally in his lap. He's still doing all the good boyfriend things he's always done, but something feels off about his demeanor? I don't know. Maybe I'm projecting.)

Reasons Not to Break Up with Wes

1. He watches movies with me. (Lark doesn't like movies.)
2. He drives me places.
3. His friendship.
4. His helpfulness.

This is a sad list. The saddest reason being the one I couldn't garner the will to actually put down: I don't feel like his girlfriend. I've always kind of felt more like an actor hired to play his girlfriend.

I am messed up. That's a messed-up thought.

My stomach rumbles. We're still making out. There's a knock at the door. I jolt backward and hop off of him.

"Come in!" I yell eagerly.

"Whoa, Or," Wes counters, disappointed.

I've never liked the nickname Or. Orie is already a nickname. I'd really like to not be shaved down to a conjunction, and the most confused conjunction at that. "And" is inclusive. "But" is obnoxious. "Or" is just confused. It's indecisive. It hits too close to home.

Wes hastily pulls on his shirt. Wow, I didn't even realize he took it off.

Lark pokes her head into the room. "Oh god, did I interrupt something?"

"Kind of," Wes breathes quietly as I swipe an arm across my mouth.

"All good, what's up?" I exclaim. Lark glances from me in my bra to Wes now sitting awkwardly with his legs pulled up.

She lowers her brow. "Dad's ready to shoot. Put on the new blue outfit."

I smile. "Aye, aye, sis. I'll be out in five minutes." I salute her. Lark rolls her eyes and retreats, closing the door.

Wes sighs. "I thought we were going to have some time together, you know? It's been . . . a while since we had time alone. I miss you." I know by "time alone" he doesn't actually mean time alone. He means since we've been . . . intimate.

I take in Wes for a second, willing myself to feel *something*. He has great hazel eyes. Tanned olive skin. Dark floppy hair. Toothy smile. He's so cute, and he's a wonderful human.

I've always clung to the idea that our love story is legendary. Adorable! We're Orie and Wes, childhood friends to lovers! But after weeks of processing and reprocessing what Lark said, I've come to the gross realization that our story was never cute.

Our love story is that situation when you hear someone call you by the wrong name, and in the moment you think, *Whatever, no biggie, I'll let it slide.* And then the next time they say it wrong, you're mid-important thought, and you don't want to break the flow of conversation, so you let it slide again. And then, before you know it, you've known them for five years and now it's too late. *You can't tell them you never actually loved them—because you're in too deep.* You've built an entire fake reality upon this tiny neglected correction. If you tell them now, you shake the foundation of your whole relationship in a way that will undoubtedly send fathomless unfixable cracks into the trust you've forged over the years.

I turn away from his face, seemingly random tears welling up as I spiral down the breakup rabbit hole. I plop myself in front of my vanity to touch up my base makeup and add some fun eye art to match the blue yoga outfit.

"I'm sorry! I forgot Lark scheduled this shoot, but we can hang out after," I offer. "Do you want to have dinner here? Dad's making his short rib stew." My go-to move to compensate for lack of intimacy is a dinner invite. Dad makes a mean dinner. It's not nothing.

Wes appears in the mirror behind me, something like . . . sorrow settling into his sweet boyish features. It hurts my heart. "You okay?" I ask.

"Yeah, I'm fine. I'll be back for dinner." He pulls on a small smile. "I'm going to run to the Tea Shop for a coffee and a croissant. You want anything?"

My eyes meet his. "Yes, thank you so much! Can you grab me a croissant, too? And a tea with milk and sugar?"

He leans forward over my shoulder. "You got it."

I meet his lips with a quick peck. "Thanks, Wes!"

As he slips out of the room, my phone starts to ring. I snatch it up off my mattress.

"Hello?" I greet.

"Hi, my name's Don; I'm from *Survivor* casting. We loved your audition tape. Do you have time for a chat?"

If you've never seen *Survivor,* you're probably wondering what the deal is with my obsession. You may have the wrong idea. *Survivor*'s not a show for people who enjoy and/or are good at being survivalists. I would never watch that. The majority of people on the show are regular humans looking to go on some sort of life journey and, hopefully, win $1 million along the way.

Survivor's all about relationships. It's a chess game on an island. You have to forge strong bonds with as many people in the game as possible so every person likes you enough to keep you around. Every three days, someone gets voted off the island. The last two people standing plead their case for $1 million, and then all the people who were eliminated get to vote *for* the million-dollar prizewinner. Voting people off in a manner that keeps them wanting to turn around and give you $1 million is an art in itself. It's a constant social balancing act, and all the while you compete in awesome challenges for food rewards and other fun stuff. It's full of drama, strategy, twists, and intrigue. *I love it.*

I feel like a struck tuning fork as I wander robotically out into the yard where my dad and Lark are shooting. I think my soul is actually vibrating.

My father lowers the camera to smile at me as I approach. "Look who finally decided to join us!"

Lark seesaws out of a standing split to glare at me. "Orie! We've been waiting for thirty minutes. I switched outfits and did an entire solo shoot without you! Who the hell were you on the phone with?"

"*Survivor* casting," I say, dumbstruck.

"What do you mean *Survivor* casting?" Lark snaps as she crosses her arms.

Dad's scrolling through the pictures on his DSLR. His head pops up. "*Survivor* casting?"

"I applied for *Survivor* last month."

"You?! Applied for *Survivor*?" Lark says.

I nod. "I was upset about how you said I never did things independently and desperate to prove you wrong, so I applied all by myself for both of us. I submitted us as a sister team."

She blinks at me. "You applied for both of us?"

"I made an audition tape for the two of us, edited it, and sent it in . . . and they loved it."

Dad throws his arms in the air. "What! Honey! That's spectacular! All that prep from elementary school is finally going to pay off." He laughs in disbelief.

Lark's eyes bulge. "We're going on *Survivor*?" I can hear her barely contained excitement.

I shake my head. "I—I wanted us to do it together. I don't want to do it alone, but they only want me."

Lark stalks across the yard to where I'm standing. She grabs my elbow tightly. "Orie, you have to do it."

We haven't talked about applying together in years, but we still watch *Survivor* together every week. She comes over, and we sit on the couch with popcorn and scream things at the TV like the lifetime unofficial cohosts we've been since we were kids.

"But what about our socials? What about all our upcoming campaigns? What about the retreats we're booked to host in January? I need to be there with you. We're a team. If you can't go, I shouldn't go. I don't want to go by myself. I can't."

Lark groans. "What did you tell the casting guy?"

"I asked if I could call him back in ten minutes."

"Go call him back and tell him you'll do it, Orie!"

"You've always said I'd be terrible at *Survivor* alone!"

"Yeah, whatever. *That doesn't mean don't do it* if you're cast!" she scolds. "I'll figure out the campaigns, and Mel can sub for you at the retreat!"

"But I get really hungry!"

"I know! Whatever. You'll figure it out!" Lark presses.

I glance over at Dad. He nods his approval. "You should do it, sweetheart."

"I would have to leave in two months," I say nervously. "Right after New Year's."

"That gives us two months to prep." Lark drags me by the elbow toward the house. "Come on, you're calling the guy back."

I let her lead me back through the sliding door and into my room. She picks up my phone where I abandoned it on the bed, hands it to me, and stands there with her arms crossed.

I dial them back. Tell them yes. Before we hang up they relay a final caveat: contestants must enter this season single, which is strange. I can't help but think the universe has overheard my drama and is backing Lark's argument to break up with Wes. I accept the terms.

Casting emails over all the paperwork. I immediately fill everything out, answer a million questions about myself, take the contestant compatibility quiz, and sign all the contracts—

Before I have any more time to think this through.

Before I actually have the chance to panic.

Lark sits on the floor against my door working on her phone like a human roadblock while I race through it all, sweating like a fiend the entire way.

I'm . . . going to be on *Survivor*. Alone.

4

Sixty Days Later

DAY 1

"Do you see yourself winning the game?" the producer asks. She's sitting across from me in a tan jumpsuit with a cinched waist. I glance over at the camera. They've been rolling for three minutes. Thus far, I've been stating my name and hometown in a variety of different ways so they have "options in editing."

Do I see myself winning the game?

I thread my numb fingers together. "No, not exactly, uh, I don't know."

It's been:

Ten days since I arrived in Fiji [all Wi-Fi-less].

Eleven days since my relationship with Wes imploded [the breakup did not go as planned].

And twelve days since my family officially went into crisis [a freeze frame of my dad's haggard expression is living rent-free on the backs of my eyelids].

After landing in Fiji, I was immediately transported via van to a hotel room where I endured ten endless miserable days in "mandatory pregame isolation."

I spent the first two days of my quarantine crying about my relationship, the second two spiraling about the fact that I'm here without Lark, and the next three worrying about my parents' marriage. On the eighth day, I realized with a jolt of terror that now my family actually *really needs* this prize money. And I spent days nine and ten feeling like the most oblivious person on planet Earth—for a multitude of reasons, the prime one being how long it took for the money realization to hit. I squeeze my eyes shut.

My bangs waft around in the breeze, tickling my forehead. I got bangs two days before my flight. Hours before the emergency family meeting. Lark recommended it to make me look especially approachable (you want everyone to trust you in *Survivor*). I took a poll on Instagram to see if our audience thought bangs were a good idea. They approved; so, I went for it.

And I'm wearing my glasses. Lark said that these, too, would make me more approachable. She's not wrong. When I wear my contacts at the grocery store (I always go with Dad; we divide and conquer) no one talks to me. But when I wear my glasses, it's like I'm suddenly everyone's long-lost friend. I get compliments and questions, people make small talk—it's fascinating.

The wild-haired producer presses her lips together expectantly. She's holding out hope for a more thorough response to *Do you see yourself winning?*

I glance nervously from her to the camera. "Hypothetically, I know how to win the game. I've watched over forty seasons. But hypothetically knowing how to do something and actually doing it are two very different things. I hypothetically know how to drive, you know. I took driver's ed, I passed the written test, but that doesn't mean I'm actually competent. The first time I got in the car with my mom, she had parked it facing the road in our driveway. I pressed down on the gas with the car in reverse, and I . . . ran her Prius right into the garage door."

I am a menace. I will never live that down, and I haven't gotten behind the wheel since. With Wes living next door, there's been no need for me to endanger the world with my hypothetical driving skills.

The producer looks like she's trying not to explode with joy. "Can you tell us more about yourself?"

I pull my right fingers back with my left ones, nervously stretching my wrists so my hands have something to do. "Um, I like eating food. My dad's a chef."

The producer nods at me with her lips pressed together.

She really just asked me to describe myself to America, and I told her *I LIKE EATING FOOD*. Like a mandatory bodily function is my defining characteristic.

"Uh." I search my brain for another tidbit. "I'm an AcroYoga influencer. I make acrobatic yoga content with my sister. And I love words."

"Can you elaborate on words?" she asks.

I bob my chin, anxiety mouth taking the wheel. "Yeah, book quotes, lyrics. And movies, and fairy-tale love."

The producer unleashes a predatory leprechaun smile. "Fairy-tale love?"

"I mean, like, true love. Like, rom-com love. My parents have it. I love reading about it and watching people fall in love in movies, and I hope I get . . . to experience it, too."

There's a long beat of silence. I glance down at my legs self-consciously. The leggings I'm wearing are bright gold. Lark and I picked out the outfit together. The idea was to be cute but also super memorable to viewers. The gold really pops. Wardrobe asked for five different options, and they chose my number one: knee-high polka-dot socks over my favorite yellow-gold yoga set with my yellow-framed wayfarer glasses.

I won't be able to do my usual bold makeup out here to complete the look, but I did get lash extensions last week, so at least I'd have something to make me feel less . . . exposed.

"Hey," the producer says. I look up into her gold eyes, now brimming with empathy. "I admire that; it's really hard to not get cynical about love."

"Thanks," I say quietly.

"How long have you been watching *Survivor*?" the producer asks slowly.

I clasp my hands together. "I was eight years old when I watched my first season, and afterward, I asked Santa for flint and fire lessons for Christmas."

The producer flips through some paperwork on her clipboard. "Are you single? Do you think you'll find love out here?"

I try to laugh and end up choking on my own spit. "I don't know."

I glance down at my formerly promise-ring-laden finger. "I mean, I do know I single. I mean, I single. I mean, I am." I cycle through a coughing fit. "I am single. I'm single."

The woman's brows have disappeared up her forehead. "You okay?"

I bob my head repeatedly. "I'm great. I'm newly single, and I'm great. My ex, who I'd been dating for the last ten years, let it slip that he emotionally cheated on me right as I was getting on the plane to come here, so I'm a little ahhh! But more like, oooh, freedom! You know. It's . . . I was going to break up with him anyway," I finish, tagging on a big smile. "So, it's fine. I'm great. It's just—I've never been single in my adult life, so. It's. Uh, it's . . . an adjustment. It's an adjustment."

"Fantastic." The producer grins.

"I'm open to love," I blurt. "And flirting." I glance at the camera and try to wink. I can't do it without also closing the other eye, so I just dramatically blink. Great. "I haven't done a lot of flirting, but I've read and watched a lot of flirtatious dialogue. So, uh, hypothetically, I should be a master of flirting."

The producer covers her face with her clipboard to try and hide a snort. *Oh god.*

I should never be allowed in public without Lark to monitor my every word. Never. This was a terrible, terrible idea.

"Amazing!" the woman coos. The cameraman relaxes into a casual seat as she taps her phone.

My shoulders drop back to an acceptable distance from my ears. I didn't even realize they were up there. There's a strong chance I've looked like a petrified dramatically blinking ostrich this entire time.

The producer looks up again. "So, Orie—"

Crap. Lark and I also talked about names. A lot of the memorable *Survivor* players have unusual nicknames. Lark recommended coming up with one so that if I did do poorly, at least I'd still make my mark with an interesting name.

I interrupt the producer with an uncomfortably loud throat-clearing noise.

"You okay?" she asks carefully.

I shake my hands out. "Yeah! Sorry, can you actually call me Piccadilly? I've been wanting to try out a new nickname."

The producer looks at the ground for a moment. "You know that's longer than your actual name?"

"Yeah, but I still like it!" I explain.

"Picca-dilly," she tests. "That's, like, a stop on the London subway, right?"

I nod eagerly. "Yeah, the Tube! The London subway, it's called the Tube."

The producer grins. "I can dig that. Come to think of it, I'm inspired. Don't call me Jamie; with you, I'm Leicester Square."

I smile at her. "Nice to meet you, Leicester Square!"

She chuckles. "Give me a second to check with the rest of production."

Leicester Square types out a text and sends it into the ether. A moment later, her phone buzzes with a response. Her bottom lip juts out in annoyance. "Shit. I'm sorry. Since you're known on socials and such as *Orie*, production needs to be using your actual name for recognition purposes. It was in the contract."

My shoulders slump. "Oh."

"But you can ask your castmates to call you Piccadilly if you want," she adds.

I nod, fiddling with my fingers again. I guess I'll try it. If I can get enough people to call me that, maybe the show will do it, too. Orie is a unique-ish name, but it's not *Piccadilly*.

Leicester Square clears her throat. "Also, I need to clarify, before we actually get you started and placed in the game today, you're not competing on *Survivor*."

My eyes slide over to the camera. "Wait. What?"

5

Thirty Seconds Later

DAY 1

"But I am . . . ?" I glance over at the camera guy. The red light is on. He's still rolling.

Of course I'm on *Survivor*. I was cast and flown out to Fiji! Wardrobe chose my outfit. We just did an entrance interview . . . She must be making some kind of weird joke.

"You've been cast for the first season of a *Survivor* spin-off show. It's a romance-based social experiment to test the strength of different types of human relationships against the backdrop of a million-dollar prize."

My head tilts. "Wha . . . ?" My voice does a weird slurry bob down into speechlessness. "Am I on a . . . dating show?"

She smiles. "A dating show of sorts. Yes."

I blink at her, trying to process that. Not *Survivor*. *A dating show?* "What are the rules? Is there a game synopsis?"

I've never been on real, adult, get-to-know-you dates.

"We're going to need you to put this on for placement." She hands me a yellow blindfold.

I hold it away from my body between pinched fingers. "What placement?"

"And put these in." She pulls earplugs from her pocket. I take them with my free hand. "Your location and starting circumstance are confidential.

This game begins differently. It's more intimate, so you can quickly forge meaningful bonds. Kind of like a *Survivor* take on speed dating."

A Survivor *take on speed dating?* Am I about to be "placed" on a date?

"You read the contract, right?" Leicester Square asks.

I bob my chin. "Of course . . ."

Of course I didn't. I signed everything in a trance without looking back.

Hi, my name is Orie, and I'm a giant idiot.

"There's a whole section about spin-off shows," she continues. "It talks about how they might inform you last minute that you'll be competing on a new show with a similar premise? They like to throw in the element of surprise with reality TV. Makes things more dramatic. I wish we could have told you during your isolation. The higher-ups wanted it all on tape."

I stare blankly at the blindfold in my hand. Am I, indeed, the most oblivious person on Earth?

A fresh wave of anxiety hurtles through me. *This is why I had to be single.* I think I'm having a hot flash.

Leicester Square chuckles. "Orie, you're going to be great! Don't worry, none of the other contestants were aware they'd be on this particular show until today. I mean, they did seem to know there was a slight chance they'd be put on a spin-off show, but it's still a curveball. This is a completely new show. You're not alone in feeling caught off guard. Everyone thought they had been cast for *Survivor.*

"There are ten contestants. You'll be out here for twenty-four days. There will be challenges and elimination cycles and twists. You'll need to depend on strong partnerships to get to the end. You may find love, you may find friendship, and, if you're lucky, you'll win the money, too."

I may find love.

"There's a lot of *Survivor*-like skills involved," she continues. "Our tag line is: Connect, Commit, Conquer. We played around with a few titles, one being *Friendship, Money, Love* or *FML,* if that gives you any more context."

I blink at her. "I'm on a dating show you considered titling *FML?*"

She laughs. "The blindfold won't bite, and we'll be with you every step of the way. If you need anything, I'm always going to be around, okay? Feel free to ask for me. I watched your casting tape. I follow you on Instagram! You're adorable. I'm a fan, and I genuinely think you're going to enjoy this. A PA and I will be leading you, extremely carefully, to your starting point. A doctor will be within shouting distance at all times. There's literally a doctor right over there as we speak." She points into woods toward a blue crew tent. "You'll always have at least one cameraperson with you."

I glance up at the cameraman next to her.

"When you're not in a confessional interview, do your best to pretend the cameras don't exist," she adds quickly. "You will have a mic pack on you twenty-four-seven. You're allowed to turn it off when you're using the bathroom, and you can flip it off once a day if you need to have a private discussion that is not game related. It will flip back on automatically after fifteen minutes. The switch is on the top; it's super easy."

I nod. "Okay."

The producer claps. "I think that's it. You good?"

Am I good? Not particularly. But this is a family affair now. *We* need this. I NEED TO BE GOOD.

I had to fill out that extensive compatibility quiz and answer all those questions about myself . . .

They were looking for potential suitors.

I pop in the earplugs and secure the blindfold over my eyes.

6

Hello

DAY 1

I've been positioned lying on my back in what feels like a bed of leaves. A PA removed my earplugs. It's quiet. I can hear the ocean. Birds. Leicester Square instructed me not to touch the blindfold until someone told me to. I resist the urge to tear it away. There's a lot of sweat happening between my back and the leaves. My anxiety is so obnoxious. It can't just torture me silently; it has to turn me into a wet carrot.

I feel a little like I thought I was being sent to the moon, got on the rocket, and was told mid-launch I'm actually on an uncharted speed-dating-themed mission to Pluto.

The dating part temporarily distracted me from the *Pluto* part. Lying here, blind to my surroundings, that's all I can think about. I have *absolutely* no idea what's about to happen. No clue what this game entails. *I'm off to Pluto alone.*

I squeeze my blindfolded eyes shut. I have to calm down. Be cool. Collected. Logical. The producer said this was a *Survivor* spin-off, so *I know* it includes *Survivor*-like things. *I know* how to win a *Survivor*-like game. I need to keep my emotions under control. Keep my responses calculated but natural and open.

They very well may have thrown me right into *a date.* In mere moments, I may have to be chill and flirty and funny and—my throat feels tight.

I focus on the sound of the ocean until the sensation passes. It's warm out. Humid. My high pony is smushed up against the back of my head. I spent so much time on that thing this morning.

With Wes, I never had to worry about being cool or flirty. I didn't care. *Maybe that was part of the issue.*

Out here, no one has any idea who I am. I get to shape that from scratch. I need to channel Lark. Choose my words wisely. Roll with the twists. They're part of the journey. And they make for good TV.

What do I know so far? Friendship. Money. Love. This is a social experiment. We're probably going to have to choose between the three? Maybe?

Why did we have to be blindfolded?

There's going to be some surprise. Before we set off on the trek to this spot, they put some sort of utility belt around my waist. It feels like a harness but without the irritating half that wraps through your legs and squeezes the life from your upper thighs.

"Okay," says the quiet voice of the PA.

I suck in a sharp breath, my heart thudding frantically.

"You may remove your blindfolds."

I shove the fabric off my face, and the world burns white. Some sort of paper scroll bounces against my wrist as the blindfold snags on my bangs. I reach into my sports bra for my glasses and slap them back on. Trees and sky slowly come into focus overhead.

There's a rustle.

I bolt upright. Leaves and debris come up with me, fused to my back. I swipe at them frantically. Sweaty leaf back is not cute, *not cute*!

A camera guy crouches in the trees ten feet away. I stare at him, gazing right down the barrel. Crap.

"Sorry!" I spout reflexively.

I glance down and catch sight of the belt they have on me. It's made of a light black material, and there's a hefty yellow rope hanging off of it via a carabiner leading around my back. I follow it with my eyes, twisting to look over my shoulder—

"GAHH!" I leap into a squat.

There's a guy sitting four feet away with a blindfold around his neck staring at me. I glance down at my hip, eyes tracing the rope across the ground to the man's hip on the other end of it. It's an eight-foot-ish-long rope latched to a metal carabiner on his harness.

We're attached via rope? We are *attached*. We're *tied together*. Is this a date thing? Is this a challenge? Did they dump us right into some sort of challenge where we're tied together? Maybe it's a date-slash-challenge?

The guy clears his throat. When I finally muster the courage to meet his gaze, my eyes basically flop out of my head.

He raises his hand in a motionless wave. "Hi."

7

Locker Associates

I'm as chatty as the average person. I say things. But I can't manage to say any of those things to Remy Orlando Lasorsa. Our lockers have been next to each other for four years, and I haven't said more to him than "Hi."

I think one time I said "LOL" when I couldn't get my locker open three times in a row, and he stood there watching me struggle. Truly, a conversational breakthrough.

It's not like Remy's tried to initiate discussions. He just smiles at me like we share a secret and walks away. Maybe I can't speak to him because he's one of the most attractive people I've ever-not-really met. But it's most likely because I have a Wes.

Wes is my boyfriend. I do not, under any circumstances, want to hurt Wes Diaz, so I can't even bring myself to talk to Remy Orlando Lasorsa. It feels like a betrayal.

Wes is gorgeous and wanted by every single person in the grade. I have no business entertaining a crush.

Remy's tallish and muscular with a square face. He has these freckles across his sun-tanned nose and cheeks that give him this adorable boyish look that I find irresistible. He's hilarious in class, which would usually mark him as obnoxious, but he's so entertaining that no one cares. He's the guy in the back randomly blurting out snarky commentary, and what he says is so clever, we all forgive the interruption. Even the teacher. She loves him. Math class would be 50 percent less enjoyable without his presence.

Around Remy, my body says: *Take me now, hot mystery boy who doesn't post anything on Instagram but follows all the* Survivor *players I follow.*

We follow each other on Instagram, Remy and I. When I see Remy like *Survivor* players' posts, I get butterflies. We're practically Romeo and Juliet, bound by loyalty to Wes (he and Remy are on the swim team together) and social anxiety.

Remy and I communicate in smiles. When he smiles at me, I feel like I'm made of strawberry Jell-O and sunshine. *Shaky, but warm.*

In his presence, I am a borderline problematic young adult love interest cliché. These feelings are nonsensical! But I can smell the destiny wafting off of him. DESTINY HAS A SMELL, AND IT'S REMY ORLANDO LASORSA.

The two of us are currently in third-period chem staring ahead at the whiteboard. Mr. Rose is running down the lab partnerships for the day. When he announces, "Orie Lennox with Remy Orlando Lasorsa," my heart spasms.

I glance over at Remy's desk two rows away from mine. We're both in the front of our desk columns in this class. He meets my eyes, smiles at me, and I just know: this is it. This is our real-life Bella and Edward moment! It's happening!

The two of us stand to relocate for the lab assignment. We silently rearrange two desks in the back of the room to sit side by side. Time to dive into conversation.

Me: Hi.
Remy: Hi.

Pause.

Me: Hey.
Remy: Hey.

Pause.

    Me: Ahoy.
    Remy: Aloha.

Pause. Shuffle papers.

    Me: Ciao.
    Remy: Bonjour.
    Me: Bonjour.
    Remy: Bonjour.
    Me: Bonjour.
    Remy: Bonjour.

He smiles. I laugh and look down at my desk.

We're practically singing together! We just flirted. I think we both just confirmed the two-sided nature of this non-relationship relationship.

The rest of the class chatters around us as they work through the lab questions with their partners. We say nothing to each other for three hundred full seconds. We left off on "bonjour."

I know something we can talk about: the *Survivor* finale aired last night. I know he must have watched it because of Instagram, but I can't make my mouth open to talk about it. But we'd probably both love to talk about it.

"*Survivor?*" I articulate at second 330. Remy looks up from his chem sheet and smiles at me again. My brain refreshes back into strawberry Jell-O. Damn it.

We fill out the lab separately for thirty-five minutes and hand over separate, completed papers to our teacher at the end of the period.

The next day, we get our graded labs back. We've both received Cs for having different answers and clearly not completing the assignment together.

8

FML

DAY 1

I blink at the contestant roped to my hip, trying to piece this together. "You look like someone from my high school."

He tilts his head. "I am someone from your high school."

I laugh nervously. "No, you're not." He can't be. How would he be here? How could they know? They don't know. *How would this random new show know about REMY ORLANDO LASORSA?*

"Yes, you're Orie Lennox; our lockers were next to each other for four years. We follow each other on Instagram. We got a C on a chem lab once. You said hi to me, like, five times."

I get up and stumble backward. "Remy Orlando Lasorsa, *YOU* said hi to *me*, like, five times!" The rope between us pulls taut, and Remy is yanked forward. He stands up, walking in my direction as I continue to step backward over leaves and branches.

I do not like being roped to another human. I do not like it. "I go by Piccadilly now! What are you doing here?"

"Probably the same thing you're doing here?"

I stop moving. Is he taller? I think he's taller. Remy stands before me, hands on his hips, arms flexing in all their muscular glory. He wasn't like this in high school. He was normal-teenager-who-swims muscular, now he looks like a teenager on *Riverdale*. He's wearing a button-up, collared, long-sleeved black dress shirt tucked into black slacks? That's what he chose to be marooned on an island in!

My forehead scrunches. "What are you wearing?"

He looks down at himself, completely unruffled. "Clothes."

His brown hair is still close cropped and spiked up in the front. He looks annoyingly put together and . . . business casual? I'm suddenly extremely self-conscious in my gold workout set and yellow-framed glasses. Should I have worn all black?

No, he's the ridiculous one! We're on an island!

How is he here?!

"This isn't fair!" I squawk randomly. "This feels illegal! Two people from the same town shouldn't be cast for the same season of anything!"

"I live in California now." He shrugs. "Maybe us knowing each other is part of this game."

I rip the blindfold off my forehead and toss it to the side. He's right. It has to be. It has to be part of it. Speed-dating mission to Pluto featuring your high school crush. I rake my fingers through my bangs and stalk toward the ocean. "STOP YELLING. THIS IS GOING TO BE FINE."

"You're yelling," Remy says.

"I JUST NEED A SECOND," I tell him.

Warm, clear blue island water washes over my feet as I approach the ocean. I glance over my shoulder to find Remy's tan freckled face a foot away and startle. "Don't follow me!"

"Orie, we're literally attached to each other."

Oh yeah.

I heave a breath. "Piccadilly! Call me Piccadilly!" I slosh into the water, exhaling and inhaling giant gusts of air until the waves are lapping up against my thighs. The ocean is calming. *Calm down.* I concentrate on the feel of the water against my skin. Close my eyes.

This is unbelievable. The only person who even barely knows about Remy is Lark. Lark was my emergency contact on my paperwork. Did they interview Lark? They could have.

Do all the contestants know the person they're paired with? Leicester Square said there are ten of us. Are they all past high school crushes?

I can't concentrate around this boy. I can't start fresh with him. He already has preconceived notions! And now he looks like . . . a womanizer you'd find at a club.

WHO WEARS BLACK SLACKS AND A BUTTON-UP TO BE MAROONED ON AN ISLAND?

I glance at Remy. He's unbuttoning his shirt to reveal a chiseled eight-pack physique.

"What are you doing!" I yelp.

He shoots me a bewildered look, folding his shirt. "We're in the ocean, Orie—"

"PICCA-DILLY."

"I'm up to my knees in water in a pair of slacks. It'd be nice to keep at least one article of clothing dry."

"Why the heck did you wear slacks to an island?"

"I wanted to look professional."

I throw my hands into the air. "FOR THE OCEAN?" The scroll tied to my wrist whacks me in the face. "Ow!" The edge slices a tiny paper cut up my right cheek. I press my hand against it, already feeling exhausted. I don't know if I can do this. I'm already so hungry. I feel so . . .

Remy tosses his shirt, now folded into a neat store-display-worthy square, onto the beach.

Frazzled. I feel frazzled.

"We should probably read our scrolls," Remy reasons. He removes his from his wrist. I snatch mine off as well and turn away from his distracting torso.

I'm usually not distracted by torsos. It's rare and very confusing as to why one is distracting and another is not. Remy's torso is calling out to my eye sockets; they're itching to slide back in his direction against my will. *Do not do it.*

I look back at him. *Damn it.* "Do you work at Abercrombie or something?"

"I work for a producer."

I slit my eyes at him. He must mean a DJ. "Like, in a club?" I ask.

"Like, in Hollywood," he clarifies.

My mouth flops open. "Like, you're a club promoter in Hollywood?"

"Like, I work for a guy who makes movies in Hollywood," he corrects.

I *pfft* in disbelief. "*You* work behind the scenes on movies in Hollywood?"

"That is what I said."

"So, you're like, trying to be an actor," I clarify loudly. Everything coming out of my mouth is loud.

"No . . . a producer."

"In Hollywood?" My voice squawks up an octave.

"Yes?" he says.

"I like movies," I blurt.

He cocks a brow. "Okay?"

"If you work for a producer, why do you look like that?" I ask as diplomatically as possible.

"Like what?"

I gesture to his abdomen area. "Come on, you know, *like that.*"

He glances down at his abs in confusion. "I do CrossFit."

I narrow my eyes. "Why?"

"For fitness?"

I cross my arms. "What do you do for the producer?"

Why am I aggressively interrogating Remy Orlando Lasorsa on a beach in the South Pacific?

"I'm interning for him while I get my master's in film production at UCLA. I organize his calls, messages, read scripts, sit in on meetings, get his coffee. That sort of thing."

I blink at him. "You're getting your master's at UCLA?" *And it doesn't look like I'm stopping anytime soon.*

He smiles. "Are you just going to repeat everything I say?"

"You're the one who repeats what I say, Remy Orlando Lasorsa!" This is not going well.

I glance around at the two cameramen who are now floating nearby, filming every embarrassing thing I say. This is going to be on national television.

Remy waves a hand like I've zoned out. "Are we going to read the scrolls?"

I shake out my limbs and flatten out the scroll. FOCUS.

WELCOME TO *ATTACHED AT THE HIP*!

"It's called *Attatched at the Hip*?" I blurt.

Remy glances up. "Guess that explains the rope."

"*Congratulations on your first partnership!*" I blurt again.

Remy raises his brow. "Are we reading this aloud? Do you want to take turns?"

I look up at him. "Do you think we should take turns?"

"Sure." He grins down at the page. "*The two of you must survive to earn the chance to thrive.*"

I feel, rather than see, the camera come closer. "*You have seventy-two hours together before you'll be untethered* . . . What the hell? Not seventy-two hours straight?"

Remy eyes me over his paper. "Uh, I think that's why it's called *Attached at the Hip.*" A small wave laps at my legs.

I vaguely register the cameraman repositioning again to get a good shot of my reaction. "Oh, ohhhhhh. Oh no."

Seventy-two hours is decidedly *NOT* speed dating. That is the opposite of speed dating. That is SLOW-MOTION DATING.

Remy continues to read aloud behind me. "*For sustenance, you'll need to scavenge. Day three will bring the second challenge.*"

I'm going to smell and grow hairy armpits in front of Remy Orlando Lasorsa?

"*One of ten won't make it to day four.*"

Am I going to have to poop attached to REMY ORLANDO LASORSA?

"*Set up, bond, and strategize; you'll need partnerships to reach the million-dollar prize.*"

I'm going to have to URINATE EIGHT FEET AWAY FROM REMY ORLANDO LASORSA?

"*Your first test will be judged at sundown. Get started; the beach is your playground.*"

I sink into the water, tugging Remy forward an extra foot and further soaking his preposterous slacks. I leave my hands out so as not to wet the scroll. I already don't remember anything Remy just said. I glance down at it.

CONGRATULATIONS ON YOUR FIRST PARTNERSHIP!

THE TWO OF YOU MUST SURVIVE TO EARN THE CHANCE TO THRIVE. YOU HAVE SEVENTY-TWO HOURS TOGETHER BEFORE YOU'LL BE UNTETHERED. FOR SUSTENANCE YOU'LL NEED TO SCAVENGE. DAY THREE WILL BRING THE SECOND CHALLENGE.

ONE OF TEN WON'T MAKE IT TO DAY FOUR.

SET UP, BOND, AND STRATEGIZE; YOU'LL NEED STRONG PARTNERSHIPS TO REACH THE MILLION-DOLLAR PRIZE. YOUR FIRST TEST WILL BE JUDGED AT SUNDOWN. GET STARTED; THE BEACH IS YOUR PLAYGROUND.

THE SHELTER MUST BE BUILT SOMEWHERE WITHIN THE CONFINES OF YOUR MAP. THERE'S A MACHETE, TWO BAGS, FLINT, TWO CANTEENS, TWO FIRST AID KITS, A MAP TO WATER, AND A POT AT THE BASE OF THE MARKED TREE ALONG THE FOREST LINE.

WITH THE EXCEPTION OF CONFESSIONAL RECORDINGS, WHERE YOU WILL BE ACCOMPANIED AND SUPERVISED BY A PRODUCER—THEY'LL BE IN BLUE SHIRTS—YOU MUST REMAIN TETHERED TO EACH OTHER AT ALL TIMES, OR YOU WILL BE ELIMINATED.

YOU MAY TURN OFF YOUR MIC:

1. FOR BATHROOM PURPOSES
2. FOR A FIFTEEN-MINUTE LENGTH OF TIME, ONCE A DAY, TO HOLD A PRIVATE CONVERSATION. THEY ARE PROGRAMMED TO FLIP BACK ON AUTOMATICALLY AFTER FIFTEEN MINUTES.

24 DAYS. 10 STRANGERS. 1 MILLION DOLLARS.

CONNECT. COMMIT. CONQUER.

FIRST TEST: BUILD AN SOS THAT DOESN'T SAY "SOS"

AT SUNDOWN A COPTER WILL JUDGE

THERE ARE FIVE PAIRS. TWO PAIRS WILL WIN A PICNIC REWARD.

HOP TO IT, CREW. YOU SHAN'T BE BORED.

I'm going to die out here.

I am going to die of constipation on national television.

And then I will rise again to die of embarrassment.

And I'm going to have to do it all in front of a very fit version of Remy Orlando Lasorsa.

How does he work for a producer? He's never talked about movies.

To be fair, we've never talked about anything.

We could have talked about movies in high school! At our lockers. Or *Survivor*. Or storytelling. Does he read, too? Are we some sort of fated perfect match? Did the show have him take the same compatibility test?

"What do you think our SOS sign should say?" Remy asks casually as a wave crests higher against his thighs.

Why am I looking at his thighs?

My eyes flick up to his face. What would Lark think the sign should say? Lark would tell me I need to stop spiraling; I have a challenge to conquer. *You're on a reality game show. Pull it together.*

As I stand up from the water, my eyes snag on Remy's neck. He's wearing a puka shell necklace. *Is he serious?*

I heave in a dramatic breath. "Can you put on a shirt?"

Remy frowns. "You're not wearing a shirt."

I glance down at my yoga set. "So? I'm in a sports bra; my boobs aren't out."

A small wave breaks against my legs as I make my way around him and up the beach. I grab his button-up from the sand and toss it to him.

He catches it, staring at me like I have three heads. "I don't . . . have boobs," he comments as he follows me toward the tree line.

I walk backward for a moment, brandishing a finger in the general direction of his chest. "These are your boobs. They're bigger than mine, Remy. I have small, compact gymnast boobs."

Why am I talking about boobs?

He gestures to his chest. "These are my pecs."

"They have nipples."

"But these are muscle."

I whip around. "You think I have no muscle on my chest?"

Remy blinks. "What are we talking about right now? Are you afraid of nipples?"

I stumble over a dip in the sand. "Why are mine called boobs, and yours are pecs? Why do *my* pecs get a silly name, and yours are taken seriously? Those *are* boobs!"

Remy shoves his arms through the sleeves of his shirt. "I don't know if we should be talking about your boobs on television—"

"You want to talk about my boobs in private?" *Kill me. Kill me now.*

"Orie." His eyes dart around nervously. "I don't need to talk about your boobs—"

"What's wrong with my boobs!" I screech. *SOMEBODY STOP ME.*

Remy runs his hands down his cheeks, scared now. "Nothing, you have great boobs! They're great boobs!"

My face burns. From the corner of my eye, I catch the camerapeople relocating to get the best angles on this conversation.

I just terrorized Remy Orlando Lasorsa into complimenting my boobs.

We're silent for a long moment, staring at each other, wide-eyed, as my cheeks go beet red.

I SHOULD NOT. BE ALLOWED. TO SPEAK. ON NATIONAL. TELEVISION.

"Should we start the challenge?" I squeak.

Remy closes his eyes and nods. "What do you think our sign should say?"

I shake out my arms and focus on a spot in the sand.

An SOS sign that doesn't say "SOS." I've watched this sort of challenge run enough times on *Survivor.* It's usually judged during the day, not at sunset. We can take advantage of that. And Leicester Square . . . Leicester Square dropped me the perfect phrase.

"Do you have any ideas?" I prompt.

"Nothing off the top of my head."

"Do you feel any which way about the acronym 'FML'?"

ATTACHED AT THE HIP—PILOT
OPENING MONOLOUGE: TRANSCRIPT

Steadicam tracks host Jamie Federov as she walks along the waterline.

JAMIE

Welcome to the first season of *Attached at the Hip*, a new romantic twist on the classic *Survivor* game we all know and love! Think speed dating, but marooned on an island in the South Pacific.

For months before we cast this show, we did research on relationships and compatibility. We isolated key variables, traits, and commonalities that set the stage for a strong match.

And then we dove into the *Survivor* applicant pool to find our season-one cast. Our team dug in, cross-referencing personality types, interests, life events, and relationship histories. Every castmate is romantically compatible with at least three other castmates in the game, and everyone out here is platonically matched. I've gone through every social post, talked to family members, and tracked down missed connections, meticulously crafting the perfect relationship storm. We're in for a wild ride.

This is a social experiment to test the strength of human relationships, in extreme circumstances, against the backdrop of $1 million. What will win out in the end? The strongest friendship? A budding romance? Or will greed be the victor here?

9

Snail Dating

DAY 1

We created a masterpiece, and now we're dying. It's been hours. I don't know how many. I'm not fluent in sun clock yet.

A drone camera has been buzzing over us all afternoon. We've been grinding methodically over the sand in silence for what feels like eons.

Thirty seconds ago, we collapsed side by side, snow-angel style, on the sand next to our enormous FML-shaped trench.

It's safe to say I'm dehydrated and starving. We're both extremely sweaty and covered in dirt. I probably look like an ancient doll that was thrown into the back of a garbage truck, covered in a layer of trash, removed, tied to the back of the truck via rope, and dragged through a pit of loosely packed mud.

We have not peed. We have not eaten. We went into full robot competitive mode and didn't stop until we got it done.

Remy's business-casual outfit now looks especially ridiculous. His neat, close-cropped, stands-straight-up chestnut hair is *slightly* disheveled. His button-up has taken a beating; the mud smears are giving it a whole new vibe.

We need to find water. There's a well on our map. We maybe should have hunted that down before digging a gargantuan FML-shaped hole and spending hours under the sun filling it with a meticulous blend of firewood, kindling, and tinder. At least we prepped a campfire. We're ready for water boiling once said water is acquired.

Sand scratches at my cheek as I turn my head in Remy's direction. "So what's your favorite color?"

Remy lifts his head from the ground to cock a bushy brow at me. "What?"

He's completely gassed. He did all the heavy lifting and the wood chopping. I don't trust myself with our machete. I've never chopped wood, and it looks dangerous.

"Favorite color," I breathe, rising out of the sand to hang my torso over my knees and clutch my temple.

"Macaroni," Remy responds. "Why?"

I lift my head. "Macaroni isn't a color . . ."

"It's in the sixty-four box of Crayola crayons. It's a color."

"That doesn't count as a color."

He shrugs. "Sure it does. Your outfit is macaroni. It suits you."

My stomach groans. I close my eyes, trying to quell the hanger building in my chest.

Remy sits up. "Is this you . . . trying to bond?"

"Yes, Remy. I'm trying to get to know you. The producer said this is supposed to be . . . like a date."

"What's your favorite color?" he asks back.

I sigh. "It changes from day to day, I guess. There're so many nice colors."

"Well, what is it today?"

I glance at his outfit, annoyed by his non-color answer. "Business casual."

My feet crunch over a billion twigs as we hike our way to water. According to the map we were gifted, this trail will end at a picturesque, ancient-looking stone well.

My mouth is dryer than boxed pasta, my lips are burning from Blistex withdrawal, and I can't stop imagining what a future would look like with Remy Orlando Lasorsa.

He's wearing puka shells. He thought business casual was a good choice of island wear. His favorite color is *macaroni*. The red flags just keep coming. And yet—here I am mentally planning the first dance at our wedding (a waltz) as I follow him through the jungle.

This is what I get for reading too many romance novels.

We're making our way around an enormous outcropping of rock. The trail snakes around a giant boulder with a two-foot-wide opening across the entire length of the stone that starts about five feet off the ground. It looks like the decapitated head of an old toothless man with his mouth open. Or a gigantic, out-of-place, airplane-style overhead compartment that someone left haphazardly ajar. I wonder how much space is inside.

Remy stops for a second, breathing hard as he studies our cloth map. We've gone ten minutes walking in complete silence. I'm still sweating like a frozen water bottle on a hot day. I wipe the back of my hand across my forehead. How is there any liquid left in my veins?

I glare at Remy's black clothes. "If the color I'm wearing is macaroni, what do you call what you're wearing? Olive?"

He looks up, and gestures to his clothes. "This is black. Are you colorblind?" He wraps the map back up and trudges forward.

I follow. A cameraman walks awkwardly beside us in the brush. "No, I meant. Olives—like the food," I explain.

"Olives are a grayish green. That's why the color olive is a shade of green."

"No, I meant, I was talking about, like, the other ones. Never mind."

He throws a bemused smile over his shoulder. "Wait, are you trying to be cute?"

Ugh. "No! I was—nothing! I was curious about your color-naming system. Forget it!" Somebody tape my mouth shut before I bury myself alive in shame. "What was your favorite year of school?"

We make our way over a broken tree. "Random. I guess tenth grade," he says, "when I made varsity swimming. You?"

"Seventh grade. I had the same exact schedule as my best friend, Kaitlyn, and it made every class so much fun."

"I remember her. You still hang out?"

"She's down in Florida. Moved there for college, and she lives there now."

Remy takes out the machete to slash at a plant that's only vaguely in the way of the trail. "That sucks. Wasn't she, like, your only friend in high school other than Diaz?"

I glance down at my sneakers. What's the cool way to say *Yes, I only had one friend in high school outside of my boyfriend*?

I settle on, "Yeah, I guess." I spent too much time with Wes to have many friends. He didn't have many, either.

"You still talk?" Remy asks.

"To Kaitlyn? Yeah. I mean, not as often. She's really busy. She's in medical school, but we talk, like, once a month or so on the phone." The urge to call her right now hits me like a physical ache. I haven't spoken to her in . . . over three months.

Has Lark become my best friend? Am I one of those people now who doesn't have friends, just blood relatives?

Remy stops short, and I run right into his back like a wind-up toy with no control over its appendages. "Oh my god, sorry!" I clear my throat, removing myself.

His back is so . . . firm?

STOP BEING ATTRACTED TO A BACK.

I stumble away as he swings around with his perfect, square, chiseled jaw.

SERIOUSLY STOP. He's a class-A "f-boy" who thinks pasta is a color. If someone like Wes could emotionally cheat on me, someone like Remy would betray me in a millisecond.

Remy tilts his head. "You still with Diaz?"

My throat squeezes uncomfortably. "No. No, broke up. Single now. Are you?"

"Am I with Diaz?"

"No! Are you?" I micro-shake my head. "I— Are you with person? Other. Do you have person? Romantically?"

"Do I have person romantically?"

I roll my eyes. "You know what I'm saying!"

He cracks a smile and turns away, continuing toward the well. "Yeah, but it's fun to watch you forget how to use the English language."

My mouth falls open.

I stomp after him before the rope can snag. "You didn't answer the question!"

Remy meets my eyes as we come to a halt next to our water well. I lock my arms across my chest expectantly.

"I am not with person," he says.

The part of me planning our wedding starts picking out our children's names.

But—of course he's single. We had to be in order to come on the show! Dumb question. He probably doesn't even "do relationships." I bet he has "commitment issues." I stare at him, unsure of what to say next. He stares back, *amused*?

Annoyance clangs through me as I realize Remy's real eyelashes are almost as good as the ones I paid for.

I turn my attention to the well. It's covered with a two-inch-thick circular wooden slab. "So, how do we open this?"

Remy shoves the wood, and it flies off like it's made of Styrofoam. The well is filled to the brim with water. Something twisted up in my chest decompresses. *Water good.* My body feels like a raisin, but I should be back to grape status by the end of the day.

10

Twilight

DAY 1

Our flame-filled FML sign bathes the beach in a flurry of glorious red-and-orange light. We kind of killed it. I can't contain the screech of victory that claws its way out of me as a parachuted box labeled CARE PACKAGE in large painted yellow letters falls from the helicopter roaring overhead.

We won. We're one of two teams that won! We're going to eat! In a game we know nothing about, we did something right!

Earlier, Remy got the fire going. (It took him ten minutes.) We then used the campfire to set the FML trenches ablaze, and five minutes later, the first helicopter whizzed by.

The prize box lands with a splash some forty feet out in the ocean. Without discussing it, Remy and I jog toward the water, a cameraman tailing us. I avert my gaze as Remy throws off his shirt.

The cool water feels like a balm on my exhausted body. I throw it onto my arms, rubbing at the dirt that caked there while we dug up the trenches.

"Are you, like, super religious or something?" Remy asks as the ocean reaches our thighs.

I look over. There it is. The eight-pack. I avert my gaze again. "Religious?"

"You seem scandalized by partial nudity."

I guffaw as we swish into deeper water. Mid-stomach now. "Remy, I'm not scandalized, I'm just . . . sensitive to naked skin." *Great save.*

The water grazes my neck, *and we're clear.* Abs gone. Distraction avoided. I fall into a leisurely sidestroke.

"You're showing naked skin," Remy replies.

I'm still in my sports bra and leggings. It may have been a mistake to wear the leggings into the water now with the sun below the horizon. How am I going to dry these? On a stick over the fire?

"What are your hobbies, Remy?" That's a date question. We should be exchanging date questions, not inquiring about my aversion to his partial nudity. I switch to an above-water breaststroke, and Remy matches it.

"I guess going to the gym," he starts.

"Sure," I say.

"Hitting the beach," he continues, "doin' laun—"

I come to an abrupt swimming standstill. "Do not say laundry."

Remy stops a foot away, treading water. The corner of his mouth curls up. "Laundry." He launches back into the breaststroke.

I groan and swim after him. "REMY. NO."

"I enjoy doing laundry with my grandma. Is that a crime?" He grins. "GTL is a cliché for a reason."

"GTL" is an acronym from the trashy, highly memed early 2010s show *Jersey Shore.* All the male cast members were obsessed with going to the gym (G), tanning (T), and laundry (L).

"Remy. I don't think you know what a hobby is. Laundry isn't a hobby. It's a hygienic necessity."

"If you enjoy doing it in your free time, it's a hobby," he says.

We dive under a small wave and pop back up on the other side. "Tanning gives you skin cancer."

"Not self-tanner," he counters.

"You do not do self-tanner," I insist.

"Yeah, I do. Like you said, sun tanning is terrible for your skin. I use the self-tanner, and I wear sunblock."

"Wow."

"What can I say? I enjoy rocking a sun-kissed glow," he says cockily.

Double wow.

"I feel like 'the gym' is too often used as a personality-defining hobby. Should it really count? We have to do it, or we die. Is breathing a hobby?"

"Orie, CrossFit is a hobby," he states.

"Are you *really* not gonna call me Piccadilly?" I complain.

"I don't know what a 'pikka-dillee' is," he says flatly.

"Do you know about the Tube?"

"The fallopian tube?" he says.

I suck in a flustered breath. "No."

We've reached the box. It's a big wooden thing with two leather handles nailed into it. The phrases ATTACHED AT THE HIP and CHALLENGE 1 WINNERS are burned into the side. Remy and I each grab a handle and start the journey back, tugging it along toward land.

We swim in silence for a minute before he says, "So what are your hobbies, *Orie?*"

I turn to snap at him and miss a crest of ocean water coming at us. It slaps into my now-open mouth. Remy watches as I cycle through a coughing fit, clinging to the box for dear life as water dribbles down my chin like toddler drool mid-tantrum.

"My hobbies!" I croak, slowly regaining control of my lung function. "Are reading. I love reading; it's my number one. I love movies. I do reviews on my—" I pause as another wave rolls through, submerging my mouth and nose. "I do reviews on my Instagram stories every night. I typically watch a movie a day. Usually before bed. And I do AcroYoga with my sister."

"I like movies," Remy says, mimicking me from earlier. I cut him yet another irritated look, and his lips curl into a pleased smile.

My toes graze the soft sand of the ocean floor. We're almost back to the beach.

"So you didn't answer before; are you religious?" Remy asks again.

I bristle. "No, Remy, are you religious?"

Remy snorts. "I'm not religious."

"Great. Let's move on from that."

The water level's dropping quickly now as we close in on the shore. I pull off my glasses (slowing our progress) and clean them the best I can before we carry our box up the final stretch of wet sand. It's a losing battle, trying to dry these things on my wet yoga clothes. After a thirty-second struggle, scrubbing them vigorously against my thighs and sports bra, they're just as wet and smudged as they were before I tried to wash them in the first place.

I shove them back on my face to find Remy frowning at me. It's the sort of frown you pull to counteract an uncontrollable urge to laugh.

"Are you laughing at me?" I accuse as I straighten the frames.

He laughs. "No, I think you're really cute."

I frown at him. "*You* think I'm cute?" Remy follows my lead as I re-grab a leather handle and continue toward land.

"Yes, I do," he says.

"No, you don't."

He squints at me. "Yeah, I do."

"Cute like a child?" Without the buoyancy of the water, the box is very heavy. We speed up, power walking, until we reach the campfire, where Remy nods and we drop it into the sand.

He's watching me as he settles his hands on his hips, salt water streaming off him. I feel like I'm caught in the slow-motion moment of a music video. "Cute like a grown woman who is sexy and cute."

I stare at him for a beat, heart jackhammering in my throat, unsure how to respond.

Should I reciprocate that statement? DO I SAY THANK YOU? Is it a trap? Is this like in Mean Girls *when she says, "You're, like, really pretty," and then Cady says, "Thank you," and Regina's like, "So you agree? You think you're really pretty?"*

I wish this were a text. I wish I could screenshot this entire, weird, disjointed conversation and send it to Lark, and then draft a response, and get her notes before sending it back to Remy.

I throw my arms around aimlessly. "I, uh, well, y-you, too."

He smirks. "What?"

"You." I nod. "Yeah." I cough. "Can we open this?" I knock on the care package.

The sun has completely disappeared now, and we're both ravenous and sopping wet. Without further discussion, Remy grabs our machete and uses it to pry open the box.

We lay out the contents:

    1 blanket
    1 pillow
    2 toothbrushes (YAY)
    2 small tubes of toothpaste
    1 bottle of wine
    6 bananas
    8 slices of cheese
    2 turkey sandwiches
    1 first aid kit
    1 blazer (Remy's, apparently)
    1 gold sweatshirt (mine)

Shivering, I whip my sweatshirt off the sand and pull it on over my head.

"You should probably take your wet clothes off so you don't freeze," Remy says.

I hide behind a palm tree to peel off my wet leggings and sports bra, rearranging my mic pack as needed. Luckily, my sweatshirt is oversized and falls mid-thigh, so I don't feel too naked. The yellow connecting rope between us snakes out from under the fabric like a misplaced tail.

Remy takes off his wet pants, revealing striped black, purple, and yellow underwear. I look away as my brain conjures an image of us together, tossing ropes up and down at a gym.

Why am I imagining us doing CrossFit? Is that even CrossFit? I don't know what CrossFit is. I shake my head around.

"What's wrong with you?" Remy asks.

I glance over at him, annoyed. "I—just—nothing."

We hang our wet things over a tree before settling across from each other on our new blanket to eat in silence. I happily devour the most delicious turkey sandwich I've ever had the joy to taste.

My mind wanders to the game aspect of all this. Do we have to successfully date to move forward? I wonder if this is one of those shows where if you're not part of a pair, you're eliminated.

I can't get a clear read on Remy. Does he *like* me? Or is he just one of those flirty guys who says "you're cute" to everyone? Do I *like* him? I can't tell.

When we're done eating, I grab my leggings off the tree, tie them to a stick, and settle next to the fire, holding them over the flame.

"So," Remy starts. I look over to find his silvery eyes alight with a playful new spark. "You do movie reviews. What genre's your favorite?"

A smile leaps up my face. "My favorite type to review is book-to-movie adaptations. I love doing in-depth analysis of how they're different, what the book brought that the movie didn't, what the movie offered that the book maybe didn't. When they're done well, I mean, there's nothing like it! A perfect book-to-movie adaptation feels miraculous when you're watching it. Like they extracted your imagination, photographed your thoughts, and built them into reality. It's mind-boggling in the most enchanting way."

Remy pokes at our fire with a spare piece of wood, grinning. "I'm gonna have to start reading more just so I can experience that."

I take a swig from my water canteen. "What's your favorite movie genre, producer's assistant Remy Orlando Lasorsa?"

The fire crackles as Remy plays with the stubble on his chin, rubbing it with the back of his hand. "You use my full name a whole lot."

I shrug. "Well, you have one of those names."

"What names?"

"One of those names that's super fun to say all together. Like a stage name. Your parents did a great job; the *Orlando* really makes it pop."

If I'm not mistaken, Remy's cheeks flush. He smiles down at his lap. "I really dig superhero movies. I know at this point a lot of people are burned out and over it, but I love 'em."

I love them, too. I smile at him, pulling my legs to my chest. "Which one's your favorite?"

His grin splits big and wide. "Hands down, *Iron Man.*"

Without consciously deciding to, my fingers reach over my shoulder to trace the area where, under my sweatshirt, it says I LOVE YOU 3000.

"That's a good one," I agree. "Did you read the comics?"

He nods. "I did."

My eyebrows shoot up. "You did?"

The crush in me roars with pleasure. *HE CAN READ. Our wedding waltz will be to "Cruel Summer" by Taylor Swift. We'll raise our kids in Seattle, so they're sure to be open-minded and progressive. We'll get a dog and name him Tony.*

"Yeah, don't be so surprised."

"You just don't seem like the comic-book-reading type."

He serves me a hard look. "Maybe stop trying to fit me into a type. I'm a person, Orie, not a caricature."

I snort, cheeks burning. "I'm sorry; it's really hard to take that statement seriously when you're wearing a puka shell necklace."

Remy stares at me across the fire, a smirk growing out of the corner of his mouth. "Come on," he says. "Puka shell necklaces are fire." He reaches behind his neck and starts fiddling with it.

This man just used the word *fire* as an adjective.

"Come here," he says.

I blink at him. "What?"

Remy sighs and scoots around the fire until he's sitting just slightly behind me. He maneuvers his arms up and over my head.

"What are you—?" My skin heats as his biceps brush over my shoulders. His puka shells skate over my clavicle and up my neck as he fastens them onto me. They're warm.

I glance over my shoulder and freeze when I find his face *there*, silver eyes sparkling. A delighted fizzy feeling settles low in my stomach as he holds my gaze. Then he gets up and moves back to his previous spot.

I stare at the necklace in disbelief, trying to find the words to re-roast it while Remy smolders at me from across the fire, but I have no words. I am a speechless giddy blob.

"You look hot," he says.

I'm in an oversized sweatshirt without pants, holding my leggings on a stick over the fire, now feat. puka shells. I *do not look hot.* I proceed to stare at him. What do I do now? What's the proper response when he says things like this? Do I say: *You, too, are hot?* Do I tell him I had a crush on him all through high school? Is that super uncool? Does this mean he likes me? Or is this all a ploy to get with me? Do I care if it is?

"I have to pee," I blurt.

11

There Is No Bathroom

NIGHT 1

Remy grins. "Ditto." Remy also has to pee.

I push my wet hair behind my ears as we stand up. "Cool. Sounds like a recipe for ro-*mance*."

Remy makes a choking sound. "Doesn't get much more romantic than peeing eight feet apart."

"Except, well pooping," I add automatically.

Remy's eyes bulge.

I drop my gaze to the sand as we start down the beach. I just said pooping. *DON'T EVER SAY POOPING.*

"Fuck, I didn't think about that yet," he says belatedly.

My lips flop open. "How have you not thought about that? It's the first thing I thought about when I saw you."

"The first thing you thought about when you saw me was pooping?"

"Not, like, pooping because I saw you."

"Have you had to poop since you saw me?"

"No! No pooping! I never had to poop!"

"You've never had to poop," he says dryly.

"I poop," I clarify.

"I hope so."

"Dear god, Remy."

"So you are religious," he quips.

"REMY!" I snap.

"Do you currently have to poop?"

I side-eye him. "I am never pooping again."

"Let me know how that goes for you."

Remy comes to a stop next to a small line of four-foot-high bushes. *I just flirted about poop. On television.*

He gestures to the brush. "This looks like a good divider."

I watch as Remy crosses over the bush barrier and turns away from me. *Oh my god.* He's already peeing. I jerk down into a squat and stare at the ground.

I'm just supposed to pee now. With him right there. Behind these tiny bushes.

"You can still see me!" It's dark, but there's moonlight. We can still see things!

"I'm not looking, Orie. I'm peeing."

"You'll be able to hear me," I clarify.

"Can you not hear me peeing right now?"

"I can, but I'd rather you not hear *me* peeing, if that's possible."

Remy's peeing stops. "How would you like to make that happen?"

"Can you sing something?" I request hesitantly.

"What's something?"

"Just anything!" I urge.

"When I was! A young boy!"

Wow. My Chemical Romance.

"My father! Took me into the city—"

"Really? This?" I interrupt.

He pauses. "Is this not adequate pissing music?"

"It's just a little intense—"

"To see a marching band!"

I get it done.

I hug myself, trying not to shiver as we return to our campsite. The fire's still burning, but it's low. We need to feed it. I grab some of the extra wood we have off to the side and throw it on before collapsing onto our blanket.

Remy settles inches away from me. I can feel the heat radiating off him. I wonder if he likes words.

I fiddle with a stick before looking up at him. "Do you have a favorite word, Remy?"

He angles himself toward me and grins. "Like 'fuck'?"

I huff a disappointed sigh. "No, not like fuck. Of course you would say fuck."

Remy's brow furrows. "Of course I would say fuck?"

"Never mind." I turn myself back toward the fire.

"Tell me."

I poke the flames with my stick. "It's not a nice thing to say, and I don't want to hurt your feelings."

"Orie, we're gonna be tied together for three days. Tell me so we can move past it."

"Nothing, it's just, you look like one of those womanizer f-boys, so of course your favorite word would be 'fuck.'" When I glance over, his eyebrows are practically levitating over his forehead. "Remy! We're on an island dating show! And we've clearly been paired as a match. I'm just confused!"

He holds my eyes. "You're judging me by how I look?"

I run my hands down my face, panic zipping through me. "No! I mean, I don't know, Remy, a little? Can you blame me? It's not just your looks. You said you love gymming, tanning, and laundry. That sounds like a type, and I'm kinda emotionally delicate at the moment, and I don't want to get involved with someone who chronically hurts people by never calling them back. So, if that's you, I don't want this to go anywhere."

I press my palms into my eyeballs. That was not the right thing to say. *I need a phone. I need to obsessively transcribe our conversations for Lark and get her thoughts!*

"Orie." Remy's voice is soft when he speaks again. I drop my hands, and he's closer, right in front of me, eyes shining in the flickering firelight. "Just because I take care of myself doesn't mean I'm some brainless meathead douchebag. I don't want to hurt you." The words sound genuinely heartfelt.

I close my eyes, shame blooming in my chest. "I'm sorry. I know you're not *brainless*. We were in the same honor classes," I mumble.

"I want to get to know you—you weird, yellow-glasses-wearing, athletic nerd."

I snort, flopping forward over my legs. "I know you're trying to snap judge me based on how I look, but I am a glasses-wearing athletic ner—" There's a *thwop* as something hits my arm. All four of our eyeballs dart toward it.

Water.

We watch as it slowly soaks into the fabric of my sweatshirt. A drop lands on Remy's nose. My head. His hand.

Thunder groans in the distance.

I meet Remy's eyes. "Oh no."

"Shit."

I leap up and grab our wooden box, yanking it closer. Remy sees my line of thought and starts chucking our things into it. The blanket, the pillow, our food, the wine, our packs, the flint. I rip my damp leggings off the stick and throw them in. I almost whip off my sweatshirt, too, so it stays dry, before remembering I don't even have a sports bra on underneath this. *Shit.* Remy throws the top onto the box.

"What should we do?" I ask, desperate, as the rain starts coming down harder. The sound of it falling goes from soothing to abrasive in a matter of seconds.

"Look for shelter in the woods!" Remy instructs. We each grab a handle and run toward the forest.

Water slams into us now. I yank our other wet clothes off their "drying" branch and toss them on my shoulder as we sprint for the trail.

I gasp as a solution slaps me in the face.

Remy looks over at me. "What?"

"The rock thing!" I yell over the rain.

"Rock thing?"

12

The Rock Thing

NIGHT 1

The rain chases us through the trees. It's dark and frigid as we fumble down the trail toward the well at a frantic pace. I nick my elbows on trees and stumble over branches, but nothing matters except getting out of the downpour.

The boulder rises before us faster than I remember, a pitch-dark silhouette against the gray night. We throw down the box. I use it to step up to the yawning mouth in the stone, hoist myself horizontally, and slide into the low opening on my stomach. The stone is freezing against my soaking sweatshirt. It feels like ice pressed against my chest as I pull up my second leg. I shimmy sideways, farther into the pocket.

The rain is a rising drumbeat as Remy lifts our box up to the opening. It barely fits under the overhang. I drag it backward as much as I can without pulling our connecting rope taut, and then shove it aside with my legs, cringing as it scrapes over the rock like nails on a chalkboard.

I throw a tentative hand up over my head, trying to test the rock's height past the initial mouth of the cavern. A foot or so in, it opens up. Sitting down, I can completely lift my arm and not touch the "ceiling." I crawl back toward the rain as Remy heaves himself up. I grab his arm, anchoring him as he gets horizontal and rolls into the cave.

Neither of us moves for a minute. Remy lies on his back, breathing hard. Staring out at the storm, my eyes snag on a light twenty feet away, out in the trees. There's a cameraperson out there filming us, a tiny spotlight in the night.

I scoot farther into the crevasse, away from the downpour's roar. The darkness level quickly intensifies—like we've entered a sensory deprivation bubble. The cave is at least five feet deep.

Anything could be in here and we wouldn't know. I stretch about, probing blindly with my legs, and realize with vague surprise that I'm shivering violently. Everything is *so cold.* Dread seeps up into my gut. *There are no towels. There is no blow-dryer. There is no heat.* Remy drops a blind hand on my shoulder, and I jolt.

"H-heyy," he says through shivers.

"Hiiiiiii," I reply back, shaking.

An image of us as Rose and Jack from *Titanic* runs through my mind.

"You can. Get warm. With the blanket. I have. My blazer." Remy shivers. "Probably. Should take off. Wet clothes."

I'm already only in a sweatshirt, my mic pack, and my underwear. "Is. Everything. Going to be dry. Inside the box?" I ask.

"It has. A varnish. It'ssss waterproof," Remy explains. I hear rather than see Remy's shirt splat onto the stone next to us.

"This is k-kind of l-like *T-titanic,*" I share aloud.

Remy snorts. "N-no. It's really n-not."

I shiver-laugh, pull off my sopping sweatshirt, and toss it in the general direction that I chucked our wet clothes from earlier. I twist around in the dark with an arm across my boobs as Remy pulls off the top of the box. It clatters onto the stone.

A moment later, Remy's holding the blanket out to me, his warm arm bumping into my elbow. I quickly wrap it over my shoulders, tugging the scratchy fabric tight under my neck.

Immediately, my muscle tension levels drop at least 10 percent. I hear Remy's blazer slip over his arms, and then . . . the scrape of skin on stone.

Remy's . . . brushing his hands over the floor? Our rope drags as he moves around.

"You drop something?" I ask into the abyss.

"I think there might be enough dry debris around in here for a small fire."

"Oh, good idea."

That's pretty fearless . . . feeling around for stuff in a cave *in the dark*. I bob around with my fingers for our box, grinning as they brush against the wood. I tug it closer until I can easily flail my hand around inside it.

After a moment, my fingers triumphantly close around our flint. I extricate it and feel around for the spot between us where I can hear Remy gathering a small pile of twigs and . . . leaves? It's too dark to identify what sort of nature odds and ends he's gathered from this rock crevasse. I hope to god it doesn't include anything that's alive.

I fasten the blanket around my chest like a towel and reach out in Remy's general direction. I could let Remy make the fire, but his flint technique had been pretty abrasive in the light. He may break it in the dark. (And/or take a long time trying to get it started.)

"Can I have the machete?" I ask quietly.

"Why?" Remy's voice echoes slightly from wherever he's splayed out.

"Fire?" I say back.

"You're going to try to make the fire, with the giant knife you wouldn't even touch earlier in the daylight, in the dark?"

"I don't have to," I say softly. "You want to try?"

Movement. I think he shook his head. "I could, but you can try first."

"Okay, you keep looking for more tinder. I'll give it a go."

"Be careful." Remy's hand lands on my arm. He slides his thumb from the inside of my forearm down to my palm, leaving a trail of blazing goose bumps in its wake. Then he presses the butt of the machete into my hand.

I clear my throat. "Okay, maybe . . . back up," I tell him as I set down the machete. I hear him scoot and feel the rope extend.

I use my fingers to feel about and organize our materials.

I set the flint on the tinder hovering protectively over the pile Remy's acquired and carefully position the machete so as not to slice my fingers or damage the flint. Then I dig in, shaving off what should be an appropriate amount of magnesium.

Within a minute, I have a spark.

"Holy shit," Remy breathes in the flash of light. I catch a snapshot of him exploring the other end of the cave with his palm.

A minute later, I have a tiny fire.

"Fuck," Remy says softly. Soft orange light flickers across his shocked, freckled face.

"You have more stuff from that corner? It's gonna eat this up in minutes."

Remy looks from the fire to me, clutching a new batch of gross nature stuff, stunned. "That was . . . really quick."

I shrug.

I haven't chopped wood with a machete, but I've practiced making fire with Lark.

For years.

In a million different possible *Survivor*-esque scenarios.

Including blindfolded.

It's the only thing I can always dependably best her at.

Light shivers against the cavern, not enough to properly illuminate the space, but enough for us to see each other. Enough to know there's not an anaconda rearing to attack in the corner. (No, I don't know what actual species of snakes are out here in Fiji.)

We've gathered enough debris to keep a minuscule fire going. I feel very thankful to this cave for hoarding an adequate amount of twigs and leafy crap.

An angsty-looking Remy watches the storm. The low light is making him look extra sharp and dramatic in his shirtless blazer getup. Somehow, his hair hasn't budged. Meanwhile, my bangs are skewed in every direction known to man because I keep shoving them out of my face.

Bangs were *a horrible idea*. Why, as a society, can we never remember bangs are *always* a horrible idea? Never, ever endorse anyone's whim for bangs! I don't care about the visual benefits—they're *not worth it*.

Remy and I have been silent for a while, and it's getting awkward.

"This feels less *Survivor* and way more *Hunger Games*," I open shakily.

"Does everything you ever experience trigger a pop-culture reference?"

Excuse me? I can't tell if he's being insulting, sarcastic, or asking a genuine question because I can't read his eyes. The lighting's too low, and he's watching the rain.

"No. Yes. I don't know. I find it fun to make connections between the things I like and things happening in my real life." My neck pulls taut. "It helps start something called 'conversation.' Maybe you've heard of it."

Remy shifts toward me. "Tell me more about this 'con-ver-sation'?"

If I wasn't half-naked and freezing in a cave, I might have laughed. I scoot sideways, tucking the blanket under my butt. "It happens when people exchange more than one word apiece, back and forth. Smiles don't count. The word 'hi' doesn't count."

"Hi doesn't count?"

"No, hi is a greeting, not a conversation."

"What else ya got?"

I purse my lips skeptically. "'Yes, and'-ing a cute icebreaker comment and/or question: good. Cutting off the speaker with an insult: bad."

Remy punctuates my statement with three slow claps. "Life-changing notes, Orie. Honestly, you should teach a class."

I smile, weirdly pleased with myself. "You're welcome."

He nods. "Yeah, this is all groundbreaking and not at all hypocritical advice."

My jaw clenches. "Well, anxiety gives me brain freeze, Remy. But I do my best to keep conversation moving."

His eyes narrow. "Do I give you anxiety?"

I cross my arms over my blanket dress. "New things give me anxiety."

We stare at the fire for a few beats.

"You want to have some fun?" Remy asks.

"What kind of—?" I catch the glint of a thin gold chain on his neck and point. "You have a *second* necklace?"

He holds it up with a hand: a small gold cross.

I gape. "You literally said you weren't religious!"

"I'm not. I'm Italian—there's a difference," he says, reaching into our box.

What's Italian for eye roll? "What kind of fun?" I ask.

Remy pulls out the wine. "Drinking game?"

I blow out an exhausted breath. "Of course you'd—"

Remy's brows jump to his hairline as he cuts me off. "Of course I'd—what? You got another judgmental tidbit you'd like to share?"

I smother a surprised chuckle, squeezing my eyes shut. "No, never mind, fine. Sounds great. I read that alcohol helped the people in the water after the *Titanic* sank stay alive longer because it kept them warm!"

"Yep! Because being cold in a cave on a tropical island is the same as freezing to death next to an iceberg in the Atlantic," he says cheerily.

"Just open the wine, Remy."

"'Never have I ever'?" he suggests, lip curling into a grin.

I snort. I've never actually played this game, only watched it go down in different TV shows. "Sure, an icebreaker! A great way to practice the art of conversation."

He snickers as he twists the top off the wine. "Wow, she called 'never have I ever' an icebreaker."

"That's what it is!"

He sighs. "Listen, nerd—"

Actual laughter bursts out of me.

Remy grins as he sets the bottle down between us. "An icebreaker is an awkward activity you engage in during freshman college orientation. 'Never have I ever' is a party game."

I stare at the wine, trying not to smile too hard. "Are you going to start?" I prompt.

He settles into a seat against the "wall" opposite the cavern's mouth. "Sure. Are we playing where we hold up a certain number of fingers, and the person who puts them all down first loses?"

I hold up five fingers. "Sure."

Remy holds up his hand. "Never have I ever . . . had a favorite word."

"Woooow." I put down a finger, grab the wine bottle, and take a swig. It's sour. I suck my cheeks together as the warmth slips down my throat.

"I shoot to win, Orie Lennox."

"Bleh," I respond, mostly referencing the wine.

"You gotta share the favorite word," he says simply.

"Well, I have a lot of favorites."

"All right, woman, share one."

I throw up a hand and let it fall. "Afoot."

"A. Foot?" He glances down at his bare feet.

"Afoot!"

"A . . . foot?" he repeats, confused.

"Not a foot. AFOOT!"

"Do you mean like, a foot?" Remy holds out his hands to mime the measurement of a foot.

I start cackling. "AFOOT, REMY."

Remy chuckles, as confused as ever because there is no distinct difference between the pronunciation of "afoot" and "a foot," and I fold forward, silently shaking from this unexpected realization.

"As in, *the game is afoot*! From Sherlock Holmes! I have it tattooed on my shoulder."

"Ahhhh." He settles back against the wall, snickering. "Afoot! I mean, hey, to each her own, but I stand by 'fuck' as a great word. You can use it anywhere to mean anything at any time."

"The f-word is the simplest, most cliché, boring favorite word of all time, Remy."

"What about 'the'?"

"'The' what?" I ask.

"If 'the' was my favorite word, I think that's more boring and simple than 'fuck.'"

I roll my eyes. "Fine, 'the' is more boring than 'fuck,' but it's not more cliché. If you said 'the,' I'd be like, why 'the'? And then you could have word wooed me with some deep pretentious musing."

"'Word wooed'?" he repeats gleefully.

"All right, my turn!" I push the wine bottle toward him. "Never have I ever done CrossFit."

Remy puts down a finger and takes a swig of wine. "Low blow."

"You did this to yourself."

Remy passes the bottle to me. "Never have I ever gotten a tattoo."

"Remy," I scold. I put down a second finger and take another chug. I'm already feeling it a bit because *all I've eaten today is a turkey sandwich*.

He shrugs. "You've got a lot of tattoos."

I shrug in return and feed some debris to the fire. "I like a lot of words. They slip into my bloodstream and inspire me to keep putting one foot in front of the other when nothing else can."

Remy's lips fold into an amused pout. "Are they all just words you like?"

"Quotes." I clear my throat, a floaty undercurrent of warmth running through me. "All right, f-boy! Never have I ever kissed more than one person!"

Remy laughs taking the wine bottle. "At once or in one night?"

"At all."

He throws back a swig. "What do you mean at all?"

"I mean, I've only ever kissed one person."

"What? How? Why?" he says, aghast.

"How!" I bleat. "I'm still a youth! I had a boyfriend! That's what happens when you've been in a relationship since age thirteen! You only kiss that person!"

"What about after you broke up?"

"We *just* broke up at the airport before the game started!"

"This game?"

"Yes, this game!"

"You've only ever kissed Diaz?"

"Yes! That is what I'm saying. Put a finger down, Lasorsa!"

Remy puts a finger down.

"I knew it!" I say, pointing at him triumphantly.

Remy serves me a dry look. "Not too big of a stretch to assume I've kissed more than one person, Orie."

I lean back on my hands, peering at him. "Textbook f-boy, Remy Orlando Lasorsa."

Remy holds my eyes with his twinkly silver ones. "Are you drunk?" he asks in disbelief.

"Nooo, just tipsy."

"What exactly do you think a textbook f-boy is?" he asks.

"Someone who sleeps with girls for money!"

"That's a sex worker."

Crap, I am a little drunk. I snort. "I mean, I didn't mean that. Someone who says things so girls sleep with them!"

He cocks one brow. "Everyone attracted to women says things so girls sleep with them."

"You know what I mean!"

"I really don't." He grins. "Have you enjoyed kissing Diaz and only Diaz for the last ten years?"

I snort, letting humor fill the anxious void yawning in my gut. "That's the kicker. I never really did. I wasn't attracted to him, and I've been in denial about it for an entire decade! Almost half my life."

Remy's eyes light up. "You weren't attracted to Diaz? That guy is hot!"

I keel over, cackling so I won't cry. "He is super hot!" I throw a hand up and let it fall. "The chemistry just wasn't there for me. I think I was more into *the idea* of having a boyfriend back when we first started dating, and things spiraled out of control from there."

"Are you attracted to me?" Remy asks.

I blink, mouth frozen in the remnant of a laugh. "I. Ye-yeah."

Ye-yeah. No biggie. Just spent the day casually planning our wedding.

I turn to stare at the fire, sobering a bit with embarrassment.

"So you've never had a good kiss," Remy says beside me.

I shake my head. "Never had one where I wasn't simultaneously doing an in-depth analysis of the mechanics between our mouths."

The flames flicker as a cold breeze whistles through the rock. I swing my gaze back to Remy with forced enthusiasm. "Truth or dare?"

Remy smirks. "You mean 'never have I ever.'"

"Switching it up; truth or dare?" I ask again.

He studies me for a moment. "Truth."

I sit up taller. "Okay, Remy Orlando Lasorsa. Tell me, why, exactly, are you here?"

The humor in his eyes douses so fast, I immediately regret asking the question. *Crap.*

Five long seconds pass with him staring off into the darkness.

I shift uncomfortably. "Sorry, I didn't mean to upset you."

He exhales, tension billowing out of him. "No, it's whatever. I'm here because I was invited on the show, obviously, and because my dad's a dick."

A loud clap of thunder rumbles over the island. We both glance out toward the rain.

"Are you . . . running away from him?"

Remy huffs something like a laugh. "Nah. I already live on the other side of the country. It's a bit of a saga." He grabs the wine and meets my eyes over the bottle as he takes a swig. "I've always loved *Survivor,* but I'm out here playing for my little sister. She's been talking about going to UCLA and doing their film program since she was in fourth grade. It's always been the dream school for both of us."

"I didn't even know you had a sister."

"Yeah, her name's Jerri. She's five years younger than me." He pauses, grinning. "We had this old video camera growing up, and we were constantly making stupid little commercials and reenacting movie scenes. We've always had this pipe dream of being a sibling movie-making team. I would produce; she would direct. We've literally been planning our careers since we were prepubescent.

"And I got my half of it. I went to UCLA for film, and I have a scholarship for the master's program I'm in. I live off campus with my grandma, and the plan was for Jerri to come live with us in the fall when she starts her undergrad. She just got accepted into UCLA early decision with a partial scholarship."

He rubs his stubble with the back of his hand. "The day after she was accepted, we found out that my dad had recently gambled away her entire college fund on a football game."

I suck in a sharp breath, my stomach slipping into my colon. "Wait, *what*?"

His eyes fall to his lap. "He gambled away her college fund."

A frown etches into my lips. "No, I heard. I just . . . Is your dad . . . does he have a gambling problem?"

"Yeah."

"Can you turn off your mic?" My voice comes out as a breathy wisp. I reach back to flip my switch. Remy moves to switch his off as well.

"We're good," he says.

I clear my throat. "Wha . . . I . . . ." I pause, gathering myself. "My dad has a gambling issue."

Remy squints at me. "I think a lot of people do—"

"No, Remy. Like, a serious issue. Just like your dad." I wince as the freeze frame of my father pulses behind my eyes. "*How* does the show know?"

"The show?"

"The show must know, right? Do you think they know? Is that why we're paired?" Fear scuttles through me, a rogue bug moving too fast for me to squash. How could they know? "I just found out—" My esophagus tightens. I put a hand to my throat.

Remy grabs my forearm. "Whoa, hey. Can you breathe?"

I nod. Take a forced breath and blow it out too quickly. Repeat the process.

"You okay?" Remy asks.

"Yeah, I—" I glance around for cameras. There are none. We're in a cave alone during a downpour. "I *just* found out the week we flew to Fiji. About my dad. He's a gambling addict, and—and an alcoholic. He's been sober for twenty years, and he relapsed right before I left."

Remy's face goes slack. He sits back against the wall.

"My sister and I are both grown adults, and our parents never told us." I throw my legs out in front of me, my feet coming to rest inches away from Remy's hip. He reaches out and gently squishes my foot. It's oddly comforting.

"My parents sat Lark and I on the couch the night before my flight to let us know my dad's going to rehab." I fiddle with my fingers. "My dad, he's a chef. He owns—he owned a restaurant, and he lost it. Gambling. He lost an entire restaurant. He told me it was *closed for the winter.*

"I barely questioned it at the time, and now my parents are suddenly in a ton of debt. And rehab's expensive on top of everything he lost, and I-I never even thought about why my dad didn't drink. Neither of my parents drink! I just thought they didn't drink. It's always been the norm. I've been so stupid."

It could be a coincidence that both of us have parents who are struggling. *But how could it be a coincidence?*

"Orie, if they hid it from you, there's no way you could have known," Remy says quietly.

I take a beat to dam up the waterworks burning behind my eyes. "Did you know about your dad?"

Remy nods. "He's had fuckups before this. I went to a few GA meetings with him back in high school."

We sit in silence for a minute. "That's cool that you were able to support him that way."

Remy bobs his head from side to side. "I'm sorry about your dad. If you just found out about him, I doubt the show 'knows.' It's probably just a coincidence."

I gnaw at my lip. Addiction is a common struggle. *But this is weird.* What are the chances we're both freshly dealing with such a big gambling-related loss?

I flip my mic back on, and Remy reaches back to flip his as well.

"Thanks," I say quietly. "That's really cool that you're trying to help your sister go to her dream school."

He lifts a shoulder and lets it drop. "She's my best friend."

I smile. "Will I get to meet her after this?"

He rubs his stubble and chuckles. "Obviously! I think you two would hit it off."

I nod, the last of my energy puttering out. Exhaustion is a weight on my already-sore limbs. I feed the fire some of the last remaining debris.

"We should probably try to sleep," I suggest. "We're going to run out of tinder soon. The fire will be out within the hour. If you want, we can share the blanket."

Remy's mouth flips up. "Thanks."

"Yeah, uh, we'll probably need each other for warmth," I add awkwardly.

He nods. "Before we sleep, I need to do something."

I glance nervously out at the still-pouring rain. "What? Bathroom?"

He chuckles, glancing down and shaking his head. "No. Come here."

My nose scrunches up. "Come . . . where?"

"Can you come over here?" he says.

Remy's three feet away from me. *I'm already here.*

"Why?" I ask.

"Can you just come closer, please?" he says.

I raise my brow. "Why?"

He laughs. "I wanna tell you something."

"Tell me, then."

"Without being picked up by the mic."

"Why don't we turn them back off?"

Remy exhales, flustered. "We're only supposed to turn it off once a day unless we're going to the bathroom."

I sigh, pull my knees to the side, and scoot closer. I stop a foot away. "What is it?" I ask quietly.

Remy takes my chin and pulls my face to his. His lips crash into mine, hot and intentional. For a moment, I go boneless.

My brain temporarily implodes with the triumph of a million unfulfilled high school wishes miraculously coming to fruition. He tastes like the beach and wine and . . . winning? Stubble scrapes my cheek as we reposition. His tongue slips past mine. His hand rakes into my hair as he amplifies the kiss. I pull him closer, fingers anchoring in the lapel of his blazer as a trail of heat burns straight down to my core. This kiss is a religious experience.

We break apart.

Remy smiles, his eyes flashing with satisfaction as he studies my face. I'm up on my knees now, practically on top of him, holding on to his blazer. I let it go.

I feel like someone lit a sparkler and stuffed it into my stomach.

"You kissed me," I say stupidly.

"Didn't want you to have to go another day with Diaz as your only reference."

I nod—way too naked in my blanket dress to process this. "Oh, cool. Okay."

I turn toward my pile of damp clothes and fish out my sports bra.

13

Sleep, Question Mark

NIGHT 1

The fire's gone out.

We've cocooned ourselves in the blanket back to back. I've been staring out into the rain for hours.

An inconvenient giddiness is bubbling inside me. I don't know if I'll ever sleep again. Remy's entire body is pressed up against my back. Remy Orlando Lasorsa kissed me. And it was exceptional.

I need to dissect this with Lark. I won't be able to rest until I've talked this out from every angle. I can't just kiss another person for the first time in ten years and not talk about it with anyone after! I'm actually going to lose my mind.

Remy shifts behind me.

"Remy?" I ask quietly toward the rain.

"Yeah?"

"Are you up?"

He laughs. "Yeah. Are you cold?"

I swallow. "Yeah, a bit."

"Same. You okay with me turning around?"

"Yeah. That's cool," I tell him quickly.

Remy shifts so he's in position to be the big spoon. His arm comes around my waist, and he pulls me against him. An electric current zips up and down my spine.

"Better?" he mumbles.

"Yeah." Yeah, I'm definitely not falling asleep now.

I lie in a constant state of awareness, willing my body to calm and failing. I can't stop analyzing the day. Reliving the moment he said I looked hot. When he grabbed my chin. How his mouth fit against mine. How much I want it to happen again.

I dissect and dissect and dissect, sparks of want running in circles across my limbs until I'm so worked up, it's all I can do to keep my eyes closed.

DAY 2—PRODUCER CONFESSIONAL NOTES (CONT.)
ORIE LENNOX & REMY ORLANDO LASORSA—CONFESSIONAL #1

TRANSCRIPT OF EDIT

Rain beats down on each contestant, interviewed separately against a tree in the forest.

PRODUCER Z

You and Orie had a little back-and-forth about snap judgments. Can you discuss that?

REMY

People love to judge me by the way I look, and it's tired. We're human, and we all have layers. I'm more than a gym rat. I'm a person who graduated from UCLA. I'm an older brother. I'm an aspiring producer. No one is just one thing. I know we all know that, but it never stops people from making ridiculous assumptions.

PRODUCER Z

Is there romance in the air?

REMY

[smiles bashfully] Who knows! There might be something stirring.

———

PRODUCER Z

Do you have feelings for Remy?

ORIE

[blushes] I maybe possibly had a giant secret crush on Remy all through high school. It's so weird to see him

again. We went to school together! Which must mean everyone on the show must have some connection to their partners. I'm on to this game.

PRODUCER Z

Are you optimistic for romance?

ORIE

I'm trying to keep my heart open, so if the right person comes along, they can come in.

14

First Bath

DAY 2

The rain has dulled to a light shower, and we're taking advantage of it.

I splash into the ocean in my sports bra and underwear, and Remy joins in just the latter. He asked if I'd be up for a bath since he felt "kind of gross" going to bed without his nightly shower and skincare routine. I readily agreed, thrilled to feel a little less like the least outdoorsy person who ever lived.

The ocean *feels* like a bath compared to what's hitting us from the sky. "This is actually nice!"

"I told you it would be!" He grins. "Baths are my everything. There's nothing like a man bath after a hard set at the gym."

I laugh and lean down to scoop some sand to use as a makeshift loofah. I gently coat my biceps and scrub at my arms. Remy starts to scrub himself down as well. I turn away, gazing out at the water, trying to create some modicum of privacy.

Things have been smiley and quiet in the cave since the kiss last night. Other than cuddling to sleep, we haven't intentionally touched since, and I've become a ball of jitters trying to figure out what that means.

"So, Orie," Remy asks playfully behind me, "what's it like being a famous up-and-coming influencer? Have you been traveling the world and shit?"

Delight balloons in my chest. *He knows things about me?* I spin to smile at him as I'm working on my neck and find him using sand to exfoliate his face. "How do you know I'm an up-and-coming influencer?"

Remy rolls his eyes. "Come on. We follow each other on Instagram."

Giddy energy ping-pongs across my rib cage at the idea of him following my content. "You *never post anything*. I didn't realize you even still used the app."

"Well, I do."

"Well, you're a creepy lurker. Post something!" I splash him.

An almost imperceptible smirk appears at the right corner of his mouth; the only tell is a tiny little dimple I've only just noticed. "You got it. One shirtless mirror selfie coming right up."

"REMY." I splash him again.

A pleased smile settles onto his face. "That's pretty damn cool, though, the influencer thing. Do you love it?"

I study my hands, floating in the water. "Yeah, it's cool. It's not . . . my dream job, but I like being around my sister, and I think it's beautiful— being a puzzle piece in a greater piece of art. Making things as a team."

His purses his lips, shifting closer. "I think we make a fucking good team." He grins. "If we weren't on a reality show stranded on an island, I'd ask you out today."

I blink at him, trying to restrain the teenage thrill aching to gallop through me in reaction to that statement. "Ask me out . . . like, on a date?"

He dunks his head under the water and comes up like a male mermaid, brushing his hair back before shooting me a hundred-watt smile. "Do you really feel the need to clarify that? Yes, like, on a date."

Y'all, we did it. Remy wants to date me. I WONDER HOW FAR IN AD-VANCE I'D NEED TO PURCHASE A SIDE-BY-SIDE PLOT SO WHEN WE DIE WE CAN BE BURIED TOGETHER.

I smash my overeager lips into a line. Clear my throat. "You know, I actually know a place we can go after this. Great food, up off the trail, hidden in this giant boulder."

The rain has ramped back up to a steady pour. Everything's wet now, so we won't be able to make a fire once the sun sets tonight. It's just going to be dark.

Remy and I sit across from each other situated around the spot where our fire burned last night. Remy has donned his mud-stained button-up and still-wet slacks. The fanciest thing I have is my damp yoga set so . . . I'm in my damp yoga set. I did desperately try to finger-comb my hair. It feels . . . very floofy.

Remy's arranged our canteens with the tops off in front of both our "meals" (a banana each). He retrieves our pot full of rain from the ground outside the cave and refills our water bottles.

I'm starving, but the *what's happening between us* excitement that's been pumping through me since last night has curbed my "lack of food" frustration. I'm hungry, but it's easy to shift my thoughts away from the discomfort to Remy. To what our kids might look like. What our first off-island date might entail. What it'll be like the next time we touch.

"So," he starts as we sip our rainwater. "If you don't want to make AcroYoga influencing your career, what do you want to do?"

I glance up at the cave ceiling, rolling the question around my mind for the millionth time, hoping something finally pops. As usual, I come up empty.

"I don't know." I sigh. "I do know I'm really lucky to have . . . what I have. Being the 'Lennox Sisters,' I mean. It's a great gig; it's just not my passion project."

Remy picks up his banana and peels it slowly, the technical way where you pinch the bottom rather than cracking off the top. "What *is* your passion project?"

I turn my banana upside down and open it his way. "I don't know— that's the thing! I'm kind of at a loss of what my passion project should be."

Remy slits his silver eyes, humor singing through his serious expression. "A passion isn't something that should be; it's something that you *want* to be."

I shrug. "I just don't really know what to want to be. None of the career classics have caught my attention."

Remy purses his lips. "What did you major in?"

"English," I mumble.

"So you want to be a writer?" Remy discerns.

I shake my head. "I don't have the hunger to be a novelist."

He leans sideways onto his forearm and takes a skeptical bite of his banana. "The hunger?"

"Yeah, you have to really want to write books to write a book. But books are my oasis. They're my ultimate happy place. I don't want anything to spoil that. When you turn something into your job, you have to start looking at it more critically. I want opening a book to always feel like coming home." I take my first bite of banana and savor it, like it's a complicated, layered, homemade dish and not the one piece of fruit we'll eat today.

He arches a brow. "What about movies?"

"What about them?"

"You *like* them. Do you want to work on movies?"

I laugh. "I can't work on movies."

"Why not? Are they also your oasis?" he asks cheekily.

I snort. "No, I really like breaking them down and looking at them more critically. It's fun."

"So why can't you?" Remy presses.

"What, work on movies? Write movies?"

Remy nods.

"Because. I live on the East Coast, and I'm not qualified!"

"You know you're allowed to leave the East Coast."

"I could never leave my family. I couldn't function without them. And I've never written a script before."

He looks me up and down. "You seem to be functioning right now."

"Am I, Remy? I'm stranded on an island, hiding in a semi-cave during a downpour with no dry clothes and a limited amount of bananas, with some guy from high school."

He holds a hand to his heart in mock offense. "Some guy from high school?"

"You know what I mean! I'm not thriving."

"We won our first challenge," he says. "We found shelter. We have food, water. I think as far as *Attached at the Hip* goes, *we are thriving.*"

I shake my head. "That's not a job I can actually work toward."

Remy abruptly sits up. "I have connections in the business. That's how I got my internship. I can get you in front of the right people to pitch, help you get started."

"Really?" I ask hesitantly. "But I've never written a script. I wouldn't know where to start."

Remy shrugs. "That's what books are for. And I want to be a producer; I could help you shape a script. That's what producers do. I would help you get your foot in the door."

An image of Remy looking stupidly handsome in some blue suit that makes his silver eyes look amazing comes together in my head. Him going out of his way to vouch for me. To wedge open the right door so I can stuff my foot inside.

But when I walk through the door, I freeze up: all my carefully planned words crumbling to dust, melting into each other, getting lost en route from my brain to my mouth. That same door gets slammed right back in my face, and Remy pays the price.

"Maybe we could work together," Remy continues. "You and me and Jerri! Start our own company. We'll need a writer."

But—if I was working *with* Remy, if I was just the writer, maybe that would look different. Maybe I would write the pitch, but they could pitch it. I wouldn't be there to ruin it. I'd be behind the scenes, making sure my anxiety wouldn't get in the way of the success of whatever project we're working on.

"You think Jerri would actually be into that?" I fiddle with my banana peel.

"Are you kidding? She's gonna love you." Remy grins.

Seeds of hope burrow deep inside my chest. What if Remy and I started legitimately dating? If Remy and I won the game together? If I had someone solid in California? Someone who could help me make things happen? Maybe with him on my side I could . . . want to be a screenwriter?

Remy shifts, moving to sit in his favorite spot, leaning against the cave wall. "Orie. We could run this game."

I laugh.

"I'm serious," he says, smiling.

I put the banana peel aside and lean back on my palms, stretching my legs out in front of me. "Remy Orlando Lasorsa, are you proposing an official alliance?"

15

Alliance

DAY 2

"I would love to get to the end of this game with you, Orie Lennox." The words are low, husky.

My cheeks heat, and I swallow hard, possibilities sprawling out before me. He wants to run this game together. This is good.

Does this mean we'd be doing that as a couple? Or as game partners? Or both?

Does it matter? You always say yes to an alliance on Survivor, *you need a strong core alliance to get to the end.*

I *need* to get to the end of this game. My parents *need the money.* And, *with Remy* . . . I would have a real chance. He's super fit and should do really well in physical challenges. Together, surely, we'll be able to outmaneuver the other players. We'd be a power couple. As long as no one turns us against each other, we'll have a great shot.

Remy's palm comes down over my calf, and my skin heats. His thumb rubs circles along the inside of my ankle, scattering my thoughts. Tugging my eyes up his clothed torso. I want to explore him. Am I allowed to explore him?

Secure the alliance, Orielle.

I cough and stare into my canteen. "The whole deal? We go to final two? We win this game together?"

When I look up, Remy pins me with his gaze. My heart rate shoots up. "The whole deal." He reaches out to shake my hand.

I smush my smile into a business-appropriate purse as I scooch forward and give it a firm shake. Remy's hands are warm and peppered with blisters from all the chopping he did yesterday with the machete. He holds tight to my fingers and lifts my arm, confidently guiding me closer. I oblige, lips stretching into a full grin as he maneuvers me into his lap.

I'm on Remy Orlando Lasorsa's lap!

I drape my arms over his shoulders, admiring those long, curling lashes. "What should we call our alliance?"

Remy glides his fingers up my arm, down over my tattooed shoulder, and along my waist, gaze roving over me as he goes along. My thoughts jellify as his palm closes over my hip.

"AP Chem," he says, his eyes dragging back up to mine.

"Why?" I ask. He smiles like it's an inside joke, and I lean forward, touching my nose to his. "Tell me."

He tips forward, lips brushing my cheek. "Because we've got AP-level chemistry."

I feel like an electric fence that just came back online. I'm amazed to find my brain is still functioning enough to respond. "That's a good line, even for an f-boy."

He closes the last bit of space, fitting our lips together in a smooth, gentle kiss. The sparkler from the other night reignites.

When we break apart, he reaches out and straightens my glasses, now slightly askew. I slide my hand down his neck and fiddle with his mud-stained black shirt. "May I open this?"

Remy's lips condense into an amused purse. "You may."

I work the buttons apart until I can study his torso. This boy looks like a statue.

He shivers as I run the tips of my fingers over his pecs.

A surprised smile slips up my cheek. "You're soft!"

"Thanks?"

"With all that muscle, I was expecting you to feel like the bottom of a pool or something."

"The bottom of a *pool*? I'm not made of concrete."

I eye him wryly. "You say that like it's obvious."

He chuckles and tugs me closer.

This kiss is not gentle. It's hungry. Breathless. My arms tighten around his neck as his fingers glide up the sides of my stomach, play with the band of my sports bra, slip under and around the ridge it's carved into my skin, a teasing caress that sets my brain spinning.

Kissing Remy is infinitely different from kissing Wes.

With Wes, I was performing an expected task. A necessary chore. I was *performing*—physically present, but mentally wandering between it and one to five other trains of thought.

Right now, I'm consumed: heat building under my skin, sweet tendrils of electricity corkscrewing through my veins. I don't have room for other trains of thought.

I twitch as something tickles my right foot. Remy seems to have a slight preoccupation with feet. But it doesn't feel like a hand. His free hand is . . . on my hip.

My eyes snap open and cut to the right. Two inches from my foot is a tarantula the size of a dessert plate.

An inhuman shriek explodes out of me as I scramble up, trying to escape Remy's lap—my knee slams into something.

"Ah!" Remy—it slammed into Remy.

Terror has me in a chokehold as I try to stand, hit my head on the ceiling of the cave, collapse back onto the ground, and barrel-roll toward the exit wailing a mash-up of profanities—*TARANTULA,* and *SLAUGHTER ITTTT*—while Remy utters the f-word on a repeating loop.

A TARANTULA WAS ON MY FOOT. A TARANTULA TOUCHED ME.

And then, I'm falling.

Uh-oh.

Rain pelts at my back as the rope snaps taut, yanking my hip right before I can belly flop into the mud puddle outside our rock. Our pot full of rainwater rests inches from my feet. I grab it, dump out the water, and fling it across the cave floor to Remy.

"WEAPON!" I instruct.

He snatches the pot and slams it down over the Antichrist.

I bruised Remy's chin. There's a wicked black-and-blue forming on his handsome jaw. He squats next to me in the rain as I push a small clod of dirt over the tiny hole I dug to bury Satan so his spider friends don't find the body.

"This is not how I pictured our date ending," Remy says, humor lacing his voice.

I put a stone over the tarantula's grave. "I'm sorry again about your chin." I turn to meet his eyes. "I have an illogically intense fear of bugs."

A tiny smirk appears on his lips. "I noticed." Somehow, the water dripping down his face looks sexy. It's annoying. Especially when I feel like a tissue that accidentally went through the washing machine.

Together, we straighten up. Remy pulls me close, setting an arm around my shoulders. "Don't worry, Orie Lennox. I'll protect you."

Warmth floods my chest. "Thank you." I wrap my arm around his waist as we make our way back toward the cave. "And I promise I'll stand a safe distance away and throw you tools to murder whatever it is you end up protecting me from."

DAY 3—PRODUCER CONFESSIONAL NOTES
ORIE LENNOX—CONFESSIONAL #2

TRANSCRIPT OF EDIT

Rain beats down on Orie. She sits on a rocky outcrop with the forest behind her.

> ### ORIE
> At home, I LOVE RAIN. When there's a roof over my head, GIVE ME ALL THE RAIN. It's an excuse to read all day. But out here [shakes head], it's hard to imagine how hopeless you start to feel when you just can't get dry. I HAVE NEVER truly, properly appreciated dry socks until now.

> ### JAMIE
> How are things going with Remy?

> ### ORIE
> [shy smile] Honestly, right now I feel like I'm on page eleven of my own real-life rom-com. I'm all giggles and butterflies.

> ### PRODUCER Z
> Page eleven?

> ### ORIE
> Page eleven of a rom-com script. Like a romantic comedy! You know. The beginning part when the couple first meets—the chemistry is hypnotic, and everything is wonderful.

16

First Challenge

DAY 3

The silence of a world without rain almost brings me to tears. The sky ran out of water.

For a second, Remy and I exchange a look of disbelief. Then I roll out of the cave, a wild, unbridled happiness exploding through me.

"We did it! We survived the rain!" I yell to the forest.

I made it three days in pouring rain. Freezing, *in a cave,* in the dark! Drinking rainwater and eating small pieces of banana!

I barely complained because I didn't want to annoy Remy.

I know I'm only three days in, and this may sound really sad, but I've never been so proud of myself.

The sun is shining, and I say this with the utmost earnestness: it's spectacular. Muscles I didn't even know I was holding unclench.

On the boat ride here, I curled up in the sun patch on the deck like a puppy, shifting around to follow it whenever it moved.

We've been ferried to another island and shepherded to a beach covered in a colorful obstacle course that appears to end in a puzzle. Classic *Survivor* challenge setup. Camerapeople, boom mic operators, and other crew sprinkle the area.

It's becoming very apparent, now that I'm standing and sizing up an obstacle course, that I'm hungry. A famous question posed by Katy Perry comes to mind: *Do you ever feel like a plastic bag?*

I am currently the plastic bag. I may very well be blown over by the next gust of wind.

"All right!" Leicester Square, the producer who did my entrance interview, claps. She stands opposite us all, her bright orange-red curls billowing in the faint breeze. She's dressed in a tan collared shirt and khaki shorts. The other producer, a young (late twenties?), handsome brown-skinned man with a great head of hair stands at her side in a similar getup.

They're probably our hosts. I've been talking to *our hosts*! Leicester Square is our host! *I don't even remember her real name.*

Remy and I have been lined up on a colorful mat facing away from the ocean, next to our castmates: a diverse group of eight young, attractive humans. On *Survivor*, you usually get a cast that spans all ages, but here, no one looks older than twenty-something.

Closest to me is a young (probably late teens), eager-looking, dark-skinned Black girl with braided hair pulled into a high ponytail. She's tethered to a youngish, pale, athletic-looking Asian guy with a man bun. They're both very attractive. And strong. Everyone looks pretty strong. There's a pair of two tall guys in baseball caps who look especially buff. Jocks? A white guy with short dark hair in a Yankees hat, and a Black guy with shoulder-length locs in a Mets cap. I hope they're just baseball fans and not actual professional players.

"Good morning, everyone!" Leicester Square cheers. My head snaps back to her. "Take a look around at the season one cast of CBN's newest show, *Attached at the Hip*!"

We clap and glance around nervously. I make eye contact with the partnership closest to us. Man Bun nods. Young Girl smiles.

"My name's Jamie; this is Zarar—"

"You can call me Z," he interjects.

"And we're your hosts, babes! You're in for a wild ride, and we're very excited. *Attached at the Hip* is a social experiment all about relationships. As you can see, there are only ten of you. Each of you was chosen specifically to match with *this cast*. You *are all* compatible in different ways. And you are *romantically* compatible with at least three contestants. We did our research. The question is: Who is who? How will a potential love match change your game? How far does friendship stretch? Do relationships mean anything in the end when there's money on the line?"

She holds on to the silence, making eye contact with each of us. "If you find love, will you be brave enough to look it in the eye? Embrace it? Will you trust your instincts or your greed?" She smiles like the Cheshire cat, reveling in how vague her statements are. "A lot of people, including me, are cynics. Greed typically wins. But we still want to believe that people are better than that. Hypothetically, if we found a perfect match, we would treasure that seed. Collaborate civilly. Share.

"So, I went out of my way to find you all potential perfect matches. You all know one person here already. A missed romantic connection. Someone you shared strong chemistry with, but for one reason or another, didn't end up with. And you're all cross-matched with two other contestants. Everyone will find connections out here."

Jamie paces the length of our lineup. "And just like in a relationship, anything can happen in this game. The routine will continue to shift. We will throw new circumstances and new predicaments at you to keep you on your toes. At the end of this, either one or two people can walk away with the million-dollar prize." She rubs her hands together. "It's time for your first group challenge."

One *or two* people? Remy and I exchange a look as the group of us cheers for this news.

Z steps forward. "If you look out in front of us here, you'll see an interesting-looking course. It's made up of unique fencelike obstacles randomly scattered about that form a bit of a maze. There are five colored tables spaced out within the maze. At each table will be a bag of puzzle pieces for each pair.

"One of you will be blindfolded, and one of you will act as a caller, directing your partner through the maze to each of the five bags and back to your assigned puzzle station. You can only grab one bag at a time, so the blindfolded member will have to make five trips. Once you have all five, the runner can remove their blindfold, and the caller must run to grab their team flag twenty feet away. Once the caller has the flag, the runner can open the puzzle pieces and complete the puzzle. First team to show a finished puzzle wins."

Zarar points to the ropes tying each of us to our partners. "You will be untethered for this challenge. Your caller will have to remain by the puzzle station while the blindfolded member runs for the pieces, and then the caller will remain on the mat by your team flag while the blindfolded member completes the puzzle. The last pair to finish today will be vulnerable to elimination. Jamie, how does elimination work?"

Jamie smiles. "The elimination process will be different every cycle. Today, at the conclusion of the challenge, one player from the losing team will be voted out of the game."

There's a general intake of worried breath among the ten of us.

Jamie continues, "After the elimination, the partnerships will be shuffled. The players on the winning team will get first choice of new partner. Second-place team gets second choice, and so on and so forth. You will be with your new partner for the next three days. You cannot choose the partner you're currently partnered with for back-to-back cycles. You must switch.

"On top of getting first choice, each player on the first-place team will be gifted a care package to bring back to their new camp and share with their *new* partner."

Zarar steps forward again. "This week, one person will obviously be left out of the choosing ceremony because after elimination, we'll be left with an odd number of players. The leftover person will be sent to exile. In exile, you will sleep on a beach alone until the next challenge. You will most definitely be at a social disadvantage, but there are certain freedoms and opportunities available to you when you are unattached."

My head is spinning.

"Are we all clear?" Jamie asks.

Are we?

17

Blindfolds

DAY 3

Remy is the caller. I'm the blindfolded runner. He's been positioned on a stool next to our puzzle station: a glorified table. I wait, braced with a hand on said table facing the maze, poised to leap into action. There are five colored barrels with puzzle bags on them dispersed among the array of obstacles. It's up to Remy to get me safely back and forth five times, as fast as possible, without getting me hurt in the process. A yellow band has been fastened over the top half of my face so tightly I couldn't open my eyes if I wanted to.

I trained for puzzles, so obviously I was going to be the runner. And I feel like I'm made of air right now, so hypothetically, I shouldn't get too hurt even if I do run into and/or trip over a random waist-high fence.

I trust Remy.

"All right, all right, all right!" Jamie's voice booms excitedly from alongside the course. "On your marks. Get set. Start!"

All five callers immediately start bellowing demands. I pause, trying to make sense of the chaotic chorus of FORWARD, FORWARD, LEFT, A LITTLE BACK, STOP, FORWARD! HELLO! I home in on Remy's voice, Remy's warm, scratchy timbre.

"*Orie*. Forward and to the right, walk on a diagonal." After a second, he repeats the same thing, like a GPS, waiting for me to move. So I do. I move in five-step increments and wait for his voice to reach me again.

Jamie's yelling over absolutely everyone, narrating the competition for viewers. And maybe for us, too, shouting about who's doing poorly, who's in first, and who's bringing up the rear. But there're so many other voices, I can't make sense of anything once I lose Remy's. It's sensory overload. So I block them out, find Remy, and concentrate.

The first time I accidentally ram into a fence, it hits me square in the stomach, knocking the wind out of me. Remy apologizes. And from then on, I'm more prepared. I put my hands out strategically at different heights and directions. I move slow. I follow Remy's voice. I find a puzzle bag. I follow his voice back to our table. We work methodically. I stay calm, ignoring Jamie's commentary until I've dropped all five bags onto our table.

Then I explode.

I rip off the blindfold. In front of me, Remy sprints for the colored mat with our flag. He grabs it.

"YOU'RE GOOD TO PUZZLE, ORIE!" Jamie yells.

I gaze down the line of puzzle stations as I'm yanking open my bags and dumping the pieces on the table. Yankees Cap is heading back with his final bag. Next to me, Man Bun's ripping off his blindfold. His partner is sprinting for their flag. Man Bun glances at me, his eyes laser-focused, and I shoot him a confident smile. This puzzle is mine.

"Don't get too excited," he says. "I'm gonna win this."

"Cocky much." I dump my last bag and dive in.

It's an oval, thirty pieces, probably *the show logo*. I quickly lock in the edges.

"OSPREY, YOU'RE GOOD TO PUZZLE," screams Jamie.

"I'm not being cocky," Man Bun says next to me. "I'm just stating a fact. I'm excellent at puzzles."

Irritation sizzles through me as I whip together the pieces. "I eat puzzles for breakfast, Man Bun." I steal a glance his way, slowing for a moment as I take in the amount of progress he's already made. His hands are speeding from piece to piece.

He doesn't look up, doesn't smile, doesn't break focus. *Shit.* I snap back to my own work.

"That's your first mistake, Glasses," he responds belatedly. "Puzzles aren't food."

I keep my eyes trained on the logo coming together before me. "That's where you're wrong, Man Bun. Not all food is for your mouth; puzzles are food for the brain."

I only have seven pieces left. Six. Five. Adrenaline's screaming through my veins. "That was deep. Are you a philosopher?" he asks.

I tamp down the urge to tell him to shut up. He's distracting me. *Don't respond!*

"That's comical; are you a clown?" I blurt.

Way to go.

"Somebody call a custodian—there's some shit-talking happening over here," Jamie announces. "Clown shots have been fired. We've got a show-down between Orie and Osprey."

Osprey. His name is Osprey. I only have three pieces. TWO PIECES. Remy cheers for me from his spot on the mat.

I *slam* the last piece into the oval.

"Jamie, done!" Osprey yells next to me.

My heart stops.

"OSPREY AND KENNEDI HAVE IT!" Jamie yells.

18

Elimination

DAY 3

Remy and I take a second. My jaw's still clenched as we're lined back up to stand opposite Jamie and Z. *I had that damn puzzle.*

Third place goes to Leo and Rick (the baseball guys). Fourth to Trina (white, short, curvy, blond, pixie cut) and Priya (tall, athletic Indian woman with long locs). A young Asian girl, Mai, and a white nerdy-looking, early-twenties guy, Quintin, end up in fifth place.

"All right," Jamie announces, rubbing her hands together excitedly. "The time hath come for our first elimination vote. Quintin and Mai, if you could please come stand here."

Quintin and Mai exit our lineup to stand next to Jamie and Z. They both look like they may vomit.

"Today's vote is with your hands," Jamie continues. "It's public."

Someone to my left whispers an *oof.*

"Because no one really knows any of the other players yet, how your fellow castmates vote will be your first gauge of their character," Jamie explains. "When prompted, you will raise a hand to vote for the player you wish to see eliminated today. Before the vote, both Mai and Quintin will get a moment to plead their cases to stay."

Quintin starts. He talks about how he's smart and loyal and would love to make some friends out here. He's not a very good speaker. His statements are too full of "ums," "likes," and hesitations to bring any emotional pull.

Mai, on the other hand, is eloquent and heartfelt. She talks about her internship at the United Nations. Her quest to get her PhD, her student debt, how this money could change her life, and how she wants to change the world. She's passionate. It's very moving.

The question here is: Do we leave a player in the game with such a great story and such a natural ability to speak to an audience, or does that very trait make her too big of a threat to win in the end?

I know the logical answer. I've watched too many seasons of *Survivor* not to know. She's a huge threat. She's smart, she's pretty, she's a great speaker. If left in the game, she can easily win if given the opportunity to make a speech. Quintin, on the other hand, can probably be used as a pawn to help one of us get to the end. It's always advantageous to leave malleable people in the game.

But I already like Mai. I want to be her friend based solely on that three-minute monologue. I want to vote out Quintin. But voting Quintin would be playing with my heart and not my head.

"All in favor of Quintin leaving the game today?" Zarar prompts.

My pulse pounds in my ears as I throw up my arm and look around. Osprey's partner, Kennedi, has her arm up as well. No one else has raised their hand.

"All in favor of Mai leaving the game?" Jamie asks.

Everyone else's hands go up. My face falls, as does Mai's. This is brutal.

"Mai," Jamie says sorrowfully. "I'm so sorry. The decision has been made."

Zarar escorts Mai into a boat waiting near the beach. We all watch quietly as she's driven away. Her adventure has been cut so short.

A bug-eyed Quintin rejoins our lineup.

"Okay, Kennedi and Osprey, join me over here?" Jamie prompts.

Four production assistants appear carrying two large wooden care packages. One is set at Osprey's feet. One at Kennedi's. Kennedi's grinning from ear to ear, glowing with excitement.

"Congratulations to our challenge winners!" Z says. We all politely applaud.

"The two of you will have the honor of leading our first choosing ceremony," Jamie explains.

"Our winning pair will get first choice of partners for the next cycle. And we'll work our way down with the second-place team choosing next," Z continues.

"Who chooses first of these two?" Trina points to Osprey and Kennedi.

"They'll rock, paper, scissors for that honor," Jamie says.

Osprey and Kennedi rock, paper, scissors for first pick, and Kennedi wins.

"Kennedi, you get first choice," Jamie says.

Kennedi's gaze trails the lineup slowly and lands on me.

I cock my head in surprise, eyes sliding from left to right to make sure I'm not hallucinating.

"Orie," Kennedi says firmly.

Jamie claps. "Orie! Come on over. Look at you getting picked first!"

I stumble over to stand next to Kennedi. Remy catches my eye as I go. He shoots me an *it's gonna be fine* smile. Z picks up a purple rope and tethers me to Kennedi.

Osprey (Man Bun) chooses Leo (Yankees Cap). If I got to pick today, I was thinking either Leo (Yankees Cap) or Rick (Mets Cap).

Remy steps up. He'll probably take Rick. *He should take Rick.*

"Priya," Remy calls.

Tall, strong, body-builder-esque Priya steps out to Remy. Priya is gorgeous. Does Remy think Priya is gorgeous? Of course he does. How could anyone not? All of these people are so attractive.

I wonder if Priya does CrossFit. She probably does. It's fine.

Priya's former partner, Trina, picks Quintin.

Rick is left out of the choosing ceremony.

"Rick!" Jamie calls. "You have not been chosen, but you are still in this game. You will spend the next three days in exile."

KENNEDI JACOBS ENTRANCE INTERVIEW TRANSCRIPT

JAMIE

Can you introduce yourself?

KENNEDI

Hi! My name is Kennedi. I'm eighteen, and I'm from Boston.
You might be thinking I look like some sort of marooned
beauty queen, and if you are, you're abso-[censored]-lutely
correct. You're looking at last year's Miss Massachusetts
Teen USA.

My parents have been signing me up for pageants since
I was three years old. My mom was Miss Massachusetts.
She's obsessed with the whole ordeal.

I, hands down, have what it takes to win this game.
Charisma, smarts, sportsmanship—I've got 'em, and I'm
ready to use 'em.

I think I'm the youngest contestant out here, so everyone's
going to underestimate me. I'm a parkour athlete. [Insert
parkour footage from Kennedi's socials.] It started as my
special talent when I was a preteen. Now I have millions of
followers on TikTok and Instagram. I've done commercials
for Adidas. Brand deals for all sorts of athletic wear. I am
a physical and mental threat. I'm here to win.

JAMIE

Are you concerned at all about getting targeted early
because you're such a threat?

KENNEDI

I'm the wolf in sheep's clothing, as everyone loves to say.

I'm an upbeat, positive young woman, and no one's going
to expect me to be cutthroat.

JAMIE

But you're going to be?

KENNEDI

I love people, but out here, I'm in a game for a million
dollars. I'll be whatever I have to be to win. I'm blowing off
part of my senior year to be here. I'm not going to let this
time go to waste.

JAMIE

Are you sad about that?

KENNEDI

Nope! I'm a competitor; this is gonna be fun. Before I was
asked to be on the show, I hadn't seen any *Survivor*—
but now, I've seen every episode. And I know this isn't
technically *Survivor,* it's a spin-off, but it's close enough. I'm
gonna rock it.

DAY 1—PRODUCER CONFESSIONAL NOTES
KENNEDI JACOBS—CONFESSIONAL #1

TRANSCRIPT OF EDIT

Kennedi sits along the waterline before sundown, the ocean behind her.

KENNEDI

WHAT THE [censored] IS OSPREY SUZUKI DOING ON
THIS SHOW?

PRODUCER Z

Who is he to you?

KENNEDI

Osprey is my East Coast parkour nemesis. He's beaten
me out for the number-one spot at the last four coed
championships. He's a snarky son of a [censored].

PRODUCER Z

Do you talk? Are you . . . friends?

KENNEDI

We periodically exchange insults publicly on Twitter. Does
that qualify us as friends?

19

Partner #2

Relief spills over me when I catch the remnants of my giant FML sign on the beach Kennedi and I are being dropped at. We won't have to learn the landscape of a new area. We already have a cave, a blanket, and a pillow!

The two of us step out of the boat into the shallow water, heaving Kennedi's care package between us.

"Was this your beach?" Kennedi asks.

I nod.

"FML, huh?" she asks as we jog ten more steps from the sea before dropping the box.

"It means fuck my life," I explain, hands braced on my hips as I catch my breath.

"Yeah, I know it," she says, grinning. "We went with a more classic HELP."

"Did you win?"

"Nope. Did you?"

I nod. "Yeah, we have a blanket and pillow that should still be—" I catch sight of a pile near the forest line. "Oh!" The pillow, blanket, box, and our original survival tools—machete, pot, flint, et cetera—are up near the trees. Reset for us as we start this new cycle.

We drag everything to the campfire area Remy and I made our first day here.

"You didn't make any sort of shelter?" Kennedi asks. She has a strikingly symmetrical face and soft, disarming light brown eyes.

I tell her about the pseudo cave as we open the prize box.

 1 tarp
 1 blanket (great)
 1 pillow (nice)
 1 sleeve of crackers
 1 first aid kit
 1 bottle of wine (cool)
 6 eggs (WOW)
 4 slices of bread
 4 slices of cheese
 2 apples
 2 matches
 1 pack of raw bacon on ice (holy crap)

Kennedi is all warm enthusiastic energy. I like her immediately.

"So what do you think of all this? Are you a big fan of *Survivor*?" I ask cheerily.

"No, I've never seen it." Kennedi blows out a breath as we trudge back down the trail with a heavy pot full of water. "I love a challenge, though, and casting reached out to me. I have a significant social presence and I'm Miss Massachusetts Teen USA; they must have thought I'd fit well with the cast."

"Oh wow, so you're new to this *Survivor* world?"

"Yeah! I'm a quick learner, though. Are you a big *Survivor* fan?"

"Yeah, kind of, I've always wanted to play." I shake the rope between us. "I'm definitely still getting used to the *Attached at the Hip* of it all. I was super anxious around my first partner."

"Your first partner was really hot. What was his name? Remy?"

I laugh. "Yeah, he's, ugh, yeah." I find myself at a loss for words, my face going beet red. I look away into the brush to hide my flush.

"Are you two hooking up?" Kennedi asks.

My neck burns. You never want to confirm you're hooking up with someone on a show like this. Then you get *seen* as a power couple, and power couples are seen as *too* powerful, and then you get voted off the game. "He went to my high school, but we didn't know each other back then. I'm assuming you know Osprey?"

"Yeah, he went to my high school! Graduated a few years ahead of me. We were on the cheerleading team together. The guy's all focus and no fun. What's Remy like?"

What's Remy like? Strong, sexy, supportive. Unexpectedly fun. I wonder how things are going with him and Priya. I wonder if Priya is one of his three romantic matches. Will they connect like we connected? Will I unravel if they do? I glance at Kennedi. "He's . . . ugh, we ended up getting along better than I expected."

DAY 3—PRODUCER CONFESSIONAL NOTES
KENNEDI JACOBS—CONFESSIONAL #3

TRANSCRIPT OF EDIT

Kennedi sits near the mouth of the forest, greenery behind her.

KENNEDI

She is so in love with this Remy guy.

PRODUCER Z

Why did you choose Orie?

KENNEDI

Orie looks like a cross between a butterfly and a golden retriever. I want that energy in an alliance.

PRODUCER Z

How's it going so far?

KENNEDI

She's sweet. I know she's older than me, but she's got this innocence about her. I'm gonna be the little sister she never had by the end of this seventy-two-hour bonding session. I'll lure her in with some girl talk. Share something near and dear. Give her a secret. Hopefully, lower her guard so she shares multiple secrets with me.

She's all heart. Heart can be used to help me get to the end of the game. I can win over a heart. It's the people like Osprey who are super logical and hyper-focused on the endgame you have to really look out for.

Osprey doesn't trust me. I can make Orie trust me. She's likable, so I'll have to get rid of her at some point—I need to be the most likable to win—but I think we can go far together.

20

Bonding

DAY 3

We huddle over the firepit, inhaling the intoxicating scent of bacon. It smells like a hug. The mere presence of bacon is ebbing the tension from my muscles.

The sun's setting. The sky is a mess of pinks and purples as it dips below the horizon.

Kennedi sighs and tosses her braids over her shoulder. "Anything fun you'd like to do these next three days? Other than survive?"

I clear my throat, looking up from the food. "I'd like to poop because, dear god, I couldn't do it attached to Remy."

Kennedi snickers, hissing into her chest.

"Did you poop with Osprey!" I squawk.

"No, I did not. I am most assuredly constipated! Let's get that shit on the itinerary." Kennedi pretends to take a notebook out of her pocket and mimes scribbling in it. "We'll make an event of it, sing some relaxing music, hold hands for emotional support. We will leave here in seventy-two hours cleared out and ready to rumble."

I snort, and we fall into a short comfortable silence, staring reverently at the slowly cooking meat.

"Were you and Osprey ever . . . romantic?" I ask. I'm dying to know what their dynamic is like.

"Nah," she says casually. "He's got a bit of a stick up his ass, and I can't roll with that. When the time comes, we should vote him out. He's too focused on the win."

I'm quiet for a moment processing this, thinking of the jabs we exchanged. Of how he cost me the challenge. She's right. He needs to go.

"I've never actually been in a real relationship," Kennedi continues. "Have you?" She glances at me sidelong.

I swallow, my throat squeezing uncomfortably. "I . . . yeah. Just broke. Before this. I was about to. He, yeah. Cheat. Ed. Yeah." I go silent, hanging my head toward the bacon.

Kennedi touches my arm. Empathy shines in her big brown eyes. "That's terrible. I'm so sorry." She glances around, searching for a topic change. "I thought it was super cool of you to vote to keep Mai in the game today. It would be fan-freaking-tabulous to see a woman win this game."

A smile creeps back onto my face. "I would love to see a woman win this game."

"You have any interest in building an all-female alliance?" Kennedi raises her pristine, thick, angular brows.

"I would LOVE to build an all-female alliance!"

Kennedi flips the sizzling bacon with the machete on our makeshift stove. "Amazing. Honestly, you and I together, we're kind of unstoppable challenge-wise."

"Should we come up with an alliance name?"

"Of course we should." Kennedi unscrews the wine bottle top as I prep our bread with cheese for our bacon sandwiches. She flourishes her hands dramatically. "*Womentopia.*"

I snort, mimicking her hand gesture. "Womentopia, it is."

She skillfully removes the bacon with the knife and places it on the breads I prepped. It melts into the cheese. *It looks like heaven.*

"All right, later after we take our group shit, we'll choreograph our secret Womentopia handshake."

I snort as we dig in, staring out at the twilight watercolor gradient painted across the sky as the day flips over into night.

———

After eight minutes of blissful sandwich eating, Kennedi turns to me, green apple in hand, and crunches into it. Juice dribbles down her chin as she closes her eyes, savoring it for a moment. "Oh wow. That's amazing."

She tosses me the other apple. I catch it and set it in my lap, not sure I want to eat it quite yet when we have two more days to ration for. Instead, I pick up the wine. We've been sharing it between us.

Kennedi clears her throat. "So how many of these people can you potentially see yourself falling in love with? Are there three? Because for me, there's, like, one."

I freeze mid-swig, accidentally spilling wine down my neck. "What?" I put the bottle down.

"Come on, Orie. Jamie said we're all compatible in different ways, and three people are romantic matches. Just based on today, how many do you think?" Her eyes are sharp, attentive, as she assesses me.

Kennedi's really smart. I think she's trying to downplay how intelligent she is with her youthful happy energy. But you can see it right there in her face as she talks; it's like she's trying to hide a neon sign with a towel. It's not working.

"Do you think you can call me Piccadilly?" I ask, dubiously attempting to change the subject.

"What?" Kennedi laughs. "Answer the question."

I study her, watching the cogs turn as she watches me watch her, and fumble for an answer. "I-I don't know. I'm—I don't know. I don't think— I've never been in love before."

She narrows her eyes. "What does that have to do with *falling* in love? There's no gatekeeping. It's not one of those stupid exclusive social platforms you need to be invited to, to be a part of. Don't think about it too hard. There's only nine of us."

"Have you been in love?" I ask instead of answering. "You said you haven't been in a relationship, but that doesn't mean you haven't been in love."

Kennedi studies her apple. "Yeah, I have, but it was a classic schoolgirl *it can't ever happen* sort of love."

"Someone else from high school?" I prompt. "Are you—how old are you?"

"Eighteen," she says.

My eyes widen. "Are you . . . still in high school?"

"Technically, yes. This is technically the second half of my senior year."

"Whoa. What?"

"Yep," she says curtly.

"So you're currently in love with this person?"

She shrugs. "A little. She's a friend and the track coach."

My mouth falls open. "How old?"

"Twenty-one."

"Oh. I guess that's not too bad. She's only three years older than you."

"It's bad when you're still in high school," Kennedi laments.

I nod. "I'm sorry; that sucks. Is it reciprocated?"

"I think so, but there will be no acting on anything till I'm officially out of the school system."

I nod again. "Good! I mean, that still sucks, but it's probably for the best because she could get in trouble, right? I hope you two can eventually work it out, though." I suddenly swing my head to the cameras. "Oh my god, we're on camera!"

Kennedi laughs. "It's okay. I'm eighteen. Nothing's happened—it's fine. She's not even a track coach."

I blow out a relieved breath. "Oh, thank god."

"Who do you think you can fall in love with, Orie?"

"I don't know, maybe Remy?" I struggle to find anyone else to say. I don't know anyone yet.

But I should probably give more than one name so the focus isn't solely on Remy. "Maybe one of the baseball boys? They're cute, but I don't know. I think they're already in love. That's the vibe I was getting. They had good energy."

"I got the same vibe." Kennedi tears off another bite of her apple. "They're cute."

"Who do you think you could fall in love with?" I ask.

She beams at me, apple juice on her lips. "Priya! THAT WOMAN IS A GODDESS."

I gasp. "Why didn't you choose her!"

"Next time. I liked how you voted. I knew we'd click. You need more than a love interest to get through a game like this; you need a friend."

My eyes well up instantaneously. "You do need a friend," I agree, my voice cracking.

Kennedi pushes me. "No crying! Living on very limited resources has me on an emotional precipice, and I'm dehydrated. I can't afford to lose any water, and neither can you."

I chuckle (and kind of cry). "Thanks for picking me. You're very cool."

Something in her eyes softens. Her bottom lip juts out. "So how old do you think Priya is?"

"I'm thinking you have a thing for older women. She's at least twenty-five."

"Whatever. It's fine," Kennedi says with a confident smile. "I'll be nineteen soon."

"When's your birthday?" I ask.

"December."

It's January. I keel over laughing.

"So no other prospects? Absolutely no Osprey feels?"

She shakes her head. "Nada."

"Not Quintin?" I ask.

"I mean . . ." She bobs her head around, humor bubbling to the surface. "We probably could get him in Womentopia."

"Should I try and induct him next cycle?"

She smiles maniacally. "Yeah! You get him; I'll get Priya. We'll probably get Trina if we get Priya—they seemed tight. And what the hell, we can pull in Remy, too."

"Oh cool, we can invite Remy?" I snort, feeling punch-drunk now from exhaustion.

"Let's do it! We'll all take over the game together!" she yells.

I throw my hands up in agreement. "*THE* first all-female alliance with two male members!"

We fall together laughing.

Kennedi and I make camp in the cave with our blankets and pillows. Not to be dramatic, but it already feels like we've been friends for years.

My favorite part of sleepovers with Kaitlyn was always *this*: this time in between awake and asleep, when you shut off the lights, and you feel so safe and comfortable in the dark with said person that you're seized with the sudden urge to free the worries hiding in your heart because you know the person you're with will never judge you. They'll take your worries and defang them.

"Kennedi," I test quietly in the dark.

"Yeah."

"Can I tell you a secret?"

She laughs. "Okay."

I swallow. "This feels, like, anti–modern woman, but all I've ever wanted to do is fall in love."

"You are so cute. That's not anti-woman; that's just human," she says softly.

"But I don't think I'm . . . I'm starting to think that maybe I can't. Do it."

"Can't fall in love?" she asks.

"I don't know. Maybe. Maybe I'm missing that thing that makes the leap from . . . like to love, you know? Like I—I can't connect in that way."

Kennedi sighs. "Orie, you like spray love straight out of your eyes."

A snort flies out of me. "No, I don't!"

"Yeah, you've got these insane blue googly eyes that ooze compassion. You look like that girl from *La La Land*."

"That girl from *La La Land,* you mean *EMMA STONE*?"

"Yeah, her!"

"That's, like, the nicest thing anyone's ever said to me."

"You're welcome," she says smugly.

"But, I mean, like, falling in romantic love . . . I was with my boyfriend for ten years, and I never fell in love with him."

"Then why the hell did you stay with him!"

"I really wanted to be part of a love story and he . . . was offering one."

Kennedi chuckles. "It's not a love story if you don't have the love feelings, Orie!"

"I loved him platonically, and it made it really hard to tell him I didn't romantically." My heart constricts, reliving the moment I was about to break up with Wes for the hundredth time. I procrastinated having the conversation till the last possible moment. We were at the airport. Wes was dropping me off for the flight to Fiji. Before I could get the right words out, he announced that he was in love with someone else. I froze up like an old computer with too many windows open. He chased me to security asking if I would take a later flight so we could "talk it out" because he didn't want me to "leave mad."

I left mad.

"And this is the guy who emotionally cheated on you?" Kennedi confirms.

"Yeah."

"I think he realized you didn't love him."

I blow out a sad laugh. "I guess. But he was super attractive and super nice and did things for me all the time, and I love his family, and he loves mine. And I still didn't fall in love with him. I didn't feel things when we kissed or anything. Like, that doesn't make sense."

I think Kennedi is laughing.

"Are you laughing?!" I say, aghast.

"You're lucky I'm a really wise eighteen-year-old."

"You know I'm only twenty-three."

"Yeah, twenty-three is ancient."

I snort. "Do you have wisdom for me or not?"

"Orie. Love doesn't make sense. You can't force sparks and attraction. They just happen."

"Yeah, that's the thing, though . . . Like, I read about sparks and attraction in books, and I fall in love and get giddy for fictional characters over and over again, but I almost never feel that for actual human people."

"Almost never?"

"Well, I've only ever felt it for one person. It's very confusing. But because it had never happened before, it felt magical when it did. With Wes, I always felt like that Katy Perry lyric."

"Which lyric?" Kennedi asks.

"Like a dead battery."

She laughs again. "You're not a dead battery. Orie, sexuality is fluid . . . it doesn't have to be sensical. Number one: you don't need to have sex and sexual attraction to fall into romantic love if that doesn't feel good to you."

"Well, it did feel good with the one person I was talking about," I add quietly.

"Maybe you're on the ace spectrum. Maybe you need a strong emotional bond to feel those feelings. Maybe there's a specific quality that attracts you to someone, and you just haven't explored that part of you enough to pinpoint it yet. *Or maybe* you just happened to not be attracted to your ex. There are so many variables to sort through. Nothing's black and white; there are no rules or boxes you have to make yourself fit into! It sounds like you haven't done much experimenting. You kind of locked yourself in an attraction-less box by staying with a guy you didn't have feelings for, for a million years. Maybe you should take some time to investigate what makes you feel connected to people in a romantic way."

I take a second processing all that. "You know a lot about this stuff. We underestimate the knowledge of today's youth."

She laughs. "I like to know a lot about things I care about."

I stare out into the dark. "No one's ever . . . talked to me about that stuff."

"You could have googled it."

"I . . . never thought to google it. I've never even articulated it out loud." Panic twists my colon up like a wrung-out rag. "Oh my god, Kennedi."

"What?"

"They can hear us right now; our mics are on!"

"They won't air this. It's *problematic* to air such things without getting permission from the human being who's currently panicking about them airing this discussion." She says this very pointedly to the phantom listener on the other end of the mic, or future editor running through this footage.

I blow out a breath and blink up into the darkness.

"So." Kennedi pauses. "Who's this one person you've felt sexually attracted to thus far? It sounds like you've been intimate?"

"We've kissed," I say carefully.

"And that person's not your ex."

"Um . . . no."

"But you were with the ex for ten years."

Crap. "Yeah . . ." I cover my face with my hands.

"So, you kissed Remy? *The one person was Remy.* Oh my god, how was it!"

My face burns, but now that she knows, all the giddiness I've been feeling for Remy bubbles over instantaneously. "When we kissed, I felt like a firework! Like that Katy Perry song 'Firework.'"

Kennedi snickers. "What is it with you and fucking Katy Perry?"

"I don't know!" I squeal self-consciously. "She uses really nice accessible metaphors."

I can feel the rope moving as Kennedi's body convulses next to me.

"Kennedi! Are you laughing again! STOP LAUGHING." I start laughing.

Kennedi bleats a loud gleeful cackle, and I laugh even harder. Joy pinballs through me as I convulse on the floor of this rock, our friendship solidifying into a real, tangible thing as our voices echo around the cave.

"What's the first thing you remember that gave you butterflies about Remy?" Kennedi asks after we've calmed down.

My mind winds back to high school. It stops short on a particular moment. "It was . . . after I followed him on Instagram. When I saw that he liked a post from one of the *Survivor* accounts I follow. I kept scrolling, seeing his name pop out on every current post from the *Survivor* people I like—"

"You are such a loser," she interrupts.

"What?"

"It sounds like the backbone of your attraction came from the fact that he also loved a TV show you're obsessed with."

"Well," I start defensively, "Wes never loved reading, and he'd watch stuff with me, but wasn't very fun to talk to about those things afterward. He doesn't like to dig into stuff. I love having in-depth, ridiculously niche conversations about the ins and outs of things I like. I want to do that with my partner!"

Kennedi snorts. "For someone who does social media for a living, you sound pretty internet green."

"I know about the internet! And Reddit and all that! I just, I like hashing things out with people in my real life. I want to meet real people who I can physically hang out with who like the things I like."

"Well, according to Jamie, you're in luck; three of those people are here."

I consider that for a second. "I bet Quintin is one of mine."

"I bet Mai was one of mine." Kennedi sighs.

"I hope you get to talk to Priya."

We're quiet for a while, my mind whirring as I ruminate on our conversation.

"It's weird how learning one seemingly abstract detail about someone can completely change the way you see them," I say quietly. "With Remy, I mean, that *Survivor* thing has felt like an invisible tether between us for eight years. And now with every new piece of information I learn about his life that's somehow significant to me, another tether shoots out, strengthening that connection. In my head—I kinda see it like we're two sides of a corset slowly being laced up and tugged closer and closer together."

Kennedi laughs. "You're such a loser."

"Shut up, Kennedi!" I kick her shin in the dark.

"Did you have friends in high school?"

"Kennedi!" I gasp, then I snort. "I had two friends, you jerk. Who are you, the freaking homecoming queen?"

"Orie, I'm valedictorian, captain of the cheerleading team, and Miss Massachusetts Teen USA. What do you think?"

"You're kidding."

She giggles. "I'm not."

I take a moment to digest that. "Jesus, Kennedi, that sounds like a lot of pressure for an eighteen-year-old human. That's a lot for an any-age human."

She's quiet for a moment. "It is, but I love it."

Time flies by with Kennedi.

On day four, we invent the secret Womentopia handshake that we'll probably never ever do in public but is a spectacular distraction from slow-moving, slowly starving island life.

It starts with us walking toward each other from opposite ends of wherever we find ourselves and then by happenstance (but actually on purpose) our shoulders bump. Then we pull back, bump them again, clasp hands at eye level, and dance around that pinpoint in a circle, kicking our legs up and about yelling "WHOA! WHOA! WHOOOA!" like some invisible earthquake has rocked us into spontaneous circle dancing, and we've just decided to run with it.

It's more of a dance performance than a secret handshake. I point this out, so we also invent a secret-secret handshake. (It's only vaguely more discreet.)

On day five, we take our group poop. And by group, of course I mean Kennedi and me. We find the perfect, far-enough-away, kind-of-tall bushes-and-ferns spot. We each gather some big leaves and dig holes (bushes and ferns dividing us). Then we squat in our respective spots and hold the rope for emotional support.

After fifteen seconds of silence, Kennedi starts belting Katy Perry's "Teenage Dream." I fall into my empty hole, laughing, and insist we switch to something more relaxing.

"Does Katy sing anything relaxing?" Kennedi spurts.

"Let's do something less mainstream so our brains don't get so excited."

"Oh yeah, cause Katy Perry is too stimulating," Kennedi cracks.

"She is! We should sing Enya," I say.

"What's Enya?"

"She sings those spa ballads." I do my best to sing, "*Who can say where the road goes, where the day flows, only time!* Yeah, I only know, like, ten of the words."

"OH, THAT SONG!" Kennedi yells excitedly. "LA-LA-LA. LA-LA-LA-LA."

I join in. "LA-LA, LA-LA, ONLY TIME."

We belt nonsense together until we've successfully expelled our nerves. Slowly our voices lower until we've quieted to a nice, soft, steady Enya-themed hum.

The excursion is a success.

21

Wondering

DAY 6

I'm getting used to sleeping in a cave. On rock. It's wild. Last night, I slept for four consecutive hours without waking up.

I lead Kennedi and me in a morning yoga session on the beach, trying to quell the extreme amount of anxiety I'm feeling about reuniting with Remy.

I miss Remy.

If we were in the real world, we'd be texting through this time apart. I'd know what the last three days have been like. I'd know whether or not we can trust Priya as a part of AP Chem. I'd be able to tell him about Women-topia. It's weird to form these intense pressure-cooker bonds with someone for three days and then just be entirely cut off from them the next three.

Nowadays, in the real world, we're all always connected. To be disconnected is to be disinterested, so there's this innate feeling of rejection when you're separated, even though there's literally no way to stay in touch when you're not together for a cycle. It's a weird emotional paradox.

I wonder if Remy made out with Priya.

I wish either of us could pick each other today when they reshuffle the partnerships. And technically we can, but it would most definitely draw too much attention to our bond, and it would cut us off from being able to bond with two more people and bring them over to our side. We need people to like us, to want to vote with us, and not eliminate us if they get the chance.

The logical part of me knows this. The logical part of me is strategizing to bring home the prize money for my family. But the other part of me, the desperate romance groupie fangirl part, *really, really* wants to ignore logic and pick Remy.

Throughout this time apart, I've thought extensively about what our life would be like together. We'd go to the gym every morning. We'd alternate making the protein shakes when we got home. We'd take a bath together at least once a week. We'd brainstorm movie ideas. We'd live in *Los Angeles*. I'd settle into the nook area of the apartment we'd share to write while he went to work. I'd live in the movie capital of the *world*.

22

Keys

DAY 6

Our hosts, Jamie and Z, stand side by side in their tan outfits on a square white dock fifty feet off the coast. The nine of us are lined up on said dock across from them. Out on the water, ten feet away from us, are four twenty-foot-high floating rectangles, each with a ladder along the side to climb to the top. At the top, projected over the water via wooden beams, are four dangling buoyed keys.

"Your jumper will climb the wall," Z instructs, "leap off, grab the key, and swim to shore where they will hand off the key to their puzzler. The puzzler will take the key and dig in their assigned roped-off area for a treasure box. Once you unearth the box, unlock it with the key. Inside are thirty pieces to a large 3D puzzle. Carry them to the puzzle table and assemble. First team to finish wins. Both members of the first-place team will win a barbecue boat picnic to share with their new partner."

Gasps of excitement are exchanged among the nine of us in the contestant lineup.

Kennedi and I were the first to arrive to the challenge today. When Remy's boat pulled up a few minutes later, our eyes locked, and he shot me the most relieved *I've fucking missed you* smile. It was the text, the phone call, the affirmation I've been craving the last three days. Before he looked away, he winked. That stupid wink sent a spike of want through me that I'd never experienced before.

"The first-place team will again get first choice of new partner," Zarar says. "Second choice will go to Rick, who found an advantage in exile that allows him to forgo the challenge today and guarantees him a second-place partner pick. After Rick, the team that takes second will choose and so on and so forth."

Jamie steps forward, smiling. "The player not chosen at the ceremony this week *will be eliminated.*"

My stomach drops.

There's no vote. Whoever loses the schoolyard pick is going home.

"Any questions?" Jamie asks.

Drones circle us on the beach as we wait for Jamie to count us in. Out in the water, Kennedi, Leo, Remy, and Trina are primed to climb the ladder of the twenty-foot floating rectangles. Osprey, Priya, Quintin, and I are lined up in front of four three-by-three marked-off areas of the beach where we'll have to dig for treasure chests of puzzle pieces once our counterparts hand over the keys.

I can do this.

23

Dig

DAY 6

"GO!" Jamie yells. My muscles tense as the four jumpers launch into action.

Kennedi reaches the top of her wall first. Arms pumping, she sprints and throws herself off, snatching the key midair from where it dangles off the wooden beam.

"YEAH!!!" I scream from the beach as she plunges into the ocean. Remy slams into the water with his key a second later.

"KENNEDI IS NOT PLAYING AROUND!" Jamie calls. Her voice is amplified so we can all hear her, even on the beach.

Kennedi's swimming for me like her life depends on it, and Remy's on her tail. Behind them, Trina launches herself off the wall but doesn't get enough height to grab her key. She disappears into the water. Leo is hesitating up on his rectangle, hands braced on his thighs.

"YOU CAN DO IT!" a voice belts. My head snaps to the left: Osprey. Osprey's cheering Leo on.

Kennedi's almost to the beach—she staggers to her feet at the waterline and tosses me the key, breathing hard. I dive to catch it as Kennedi collapses onto the sand. The key lands in my palm, and I fumble to my feet, legs burning as I sprint back to my assigned square.

"ORIE HAS THE KEY TO HER CHEST. SHE'S HEADED TO DIG!" Jamie narrates.

I fall to my knees and plunge my arms into the hot sand, chucking it out of the way as fast as humanly possible.

"Remy tosses to Priya! Priya catches the keys, and just like that, we have a challenge!" Jamie belts.

Priya throws herself into the dig two stations down—the two of us frantically offsetting the dirt, scrambling around like gophers on drugs.

"TRINA'S BACK AT THE TOP OF THE WALL!" Jamie updates. "Leo is still frozen! TRINA jumps. She gets the key! Leo, you gotta go!"

A man's scream echoes behind me, followed by Osprey whooping in celebration.

Jamie wolf-whistles. "HELLS YES, THERE HE GOES. LEO HAS HIS KEY. EVERYONE'S IN IT!"

I'm overheating. I feel like I've been stuffed into an oven, and I'm cooking from the inside out. *Where is this goddamn chest?*

"AH!" Priya yelps. I glance over as she yanks a medium-sized purple treasure chest out of the dirt. That thing was deep.

Seconds later, Osprey slides into his digging area, right next to mine. He starts shoveling out sand with unbelievable efficiency. *Shit.*

I switch into overdrive, clawing at the dirt until my nails scrape wood. A fresh burst of energy floods my limbs as my fingers close around a metal handle. In one fluid motion, I yank a blue chest from the hole, snatch up my key, and stagger out toward my puzzle table.

Priya stands two stations down, playing around with her pieces, but she has nothing together yet. It's tough to build a 3D puzzle when you don't know what it's going to look like when it's finished. The pieces are red. What's red and relevant? I drop my chest onto the table, shove in the key, and throw the thing open.

The puzzle is probably in theme with the show. The show is called *Attached at the Hip*. Friendship, money, love, relationships—I'm betting on a heart. I dump out my pieces and start to build.

Back in the day, when Lark and I took our first fire lessons, we were also obsessed with puzzles. When we completed our course, Dad set up a *Survivor* day where the two of us went head-to-head. He put together a bunch of competitions for us to do in the backyard with some of our friends. It ended with two showdowns between Lark and me. I won the fire. Lark won the puzzle. Dad was forced to declare *Backyard Survivor* a tie.

"Orie, quickly catching up to Priya! AND Osprey has his chest! What a comeback! Osprey sprinting to his puzzle station."

I glance over as Osprey rams into his table, key already stuffed into the lock on his chest. There will be *no speaking this time*.

"We meet again," I blurt.

What is wrong with me?

I refocus on the puzzle, moving frantically now, flipping over pieces, testing them. Slotting them into place.

"This isn't us meeting, Glasses; we're competing," Osprey replies.

Bit by bit, an emoji-esque red heart manifests before me. There's a design on it. Two black silhouettes facing in opposite directions with a rope connecting them.

"Orie's is really coming together!" Jamie yells from a foot away. "But Osprey is working *fast*. He's passed Priya; he's right on her."

"What do you mean he's right on me?" I yell. I steal a glimpse at Osprey's heart. He's only a piece behind. "*What in the flying flueper*," I gasp, heart pounding double time.

"Orie! Don't look at him! YOU'RE A FIREWORK! YOU'VE GOT THIS!" Kennedi's voice comes from somewhere close. I grin, sweat falling off my forehead and onto the pieces I'm hovering over.

"You know flueper isn't a word," Osprey says.

"I know *flueper* isn't *a word*. We're not supposed to curse on the show." I connect two more pieces and slap them into place.

"OSPREY IN THE LEAD NOW!" Jamie shouts, a new sense of urgency in her voice. "He's only got seven pieces left!"

HOW DOES HE MOVE AT WARP SPEED?

"We're fine, Orie!" Kennedi yells.

"Shit, shit, shit, shit." The word falls out of me on repeat, my mouth a faucet flipped on and forgotten, all available focus pouring into the structure before me.

"You know, you're not supposed to curse on the show," Osprey says.

God-fucking-damn it.

"Orie with nine left now, Osprey still at seven! He's slowing!" Jamie narrates.

My hands never stop moving. *This win is mine.*

"Orie with eight! Seven! They're tied! Wait, Osprey finds another piece! He's down to six!" Jamie screeches.

"JAMIE, YOU'RE KILLING ME," I belt. I only have one piece left. I shove it down; it doesn't fit. I rotate it—

"JAMIE!" Osprey yells.

"Jamie!" I scream a millisecond later as my last piece drops into place.

Next to me Osprey's red heart is full and finished.

Jamie throws her hands up. "OSPREY AND LEO WIN THE BAR-BECUES! KENNEDI AND ORIE TAKE SECOND IN YET AN-OTHER INCEDIBLE SHOWDOWN BETWEEN THESE TWO PUZZLE MASTERS!"

I collapse over the table, dropping my head into my hands as tears well in my eyes. *Fuck.* A hand starts rubbing my back. Kennedi.

"I'm so sorry, Ken," I mumble into my palms.

She pulls me into a side hug. "Don't be. You did great."

Twice.

I've now lost a puzzle challenge twice. Two stations over, Priya finishes her heart.

"Remy and Priya with the third-place win! Which means, I'm sorry, Trina and Quintin, you are last place today."

24

Shuffled

DAY 6

Whoever isn't chosen in the ceremony today is automatically eliminated.

We stand before Jamie and Z: all of us now, including Rick. Rick, who lived alone on a beach the past three days and now gets to choose third behind the winning team (Osprey and Leo) because he found an advantage during that time by himself.

"Osprey and Leo, please step forward." Jamie directs them to stand in front of her. "You'll be treated to separate barbecue boat picnics, each with your new partners, so choose wisely."

Osprey wins rock, paper, scissors.

"All right, Osprey—first choice, who's it going to be?" Z asks, blue connection rope in hand.

My eyes widen as Osprey's gaze cuts to mine. "Orie."

I glance over my shoulder as if there's a ghost he's *actually* looking at standing at my back. "Wait, me?" I clarify.

He nods. "Yep, you."

My mouth falls open. *What?* I walk over to where Osprey is, and Z hooks us together. I glance at Remy. He drops me a very subtle *AP Chem till the end* nod. I glance at Kennedi. She widens her eyes in a *you be careful* glare.

Kennedi is afraid of Osprey. She sees him as an enormous threat. He *is* an enormous threat. Puzzles are one of my things, and I can't beat him. I need to try to get him on our side. He's clearly a talented competitor. I'd rather be with him than against him.

"Leo?" Z prompts him to choose second. Leo glances around at the remaining players. His eyes linger on Rick longer than anyone else. Rick gives him the slightest nod.

"Kennedi," he says.

Kennedi steps up next to Leo. Rick is next. He picks Priya. Remy is next, and he picks the blond pixie-cut woman, Trina, leaving Quintin without a partner.

"Quintin," Jamie says somberly. "I'm sorry. You have not been chosen, and thus, you have been eliminated."

There goes our plan to bring him into Womentopia. A boat pulls up to the dock immediately, and Quintin is escorted onto it.

"And then there were eight," Jamie says.

25

BBQ

DAY 6

Osprey smells like . . . a boys' locker room. He's covered in dirt and probably sweat. I study his arm, taking in the layers of grime caked on him.
Has this boy not bathed this entire time? We don't speak on the ride to our
picnic, but we do sit near each other. Hence the smell.

After twenty minutes' worth of bumping over choppy water, our
regular-sized speedboat pulls up to a yacht.

A PA escorts us up and around to the bow where a blanket, pillows, and
full spread of BBQ wings, ribs, chicken, fries, cheese, crackers, bread, and
pitchers of soda are laid out for us. When the smell of it hits me, I go weak
in the knees. Yes, I have been "living large" in terms of *Survivor* because I've
had some semblance of food each day, but it's still been way less than your
average daily recommended caloric intake. The constant hunger thrumming through me is a beast I've been desperately trying to tame. I'm slowly
getting better at not letting it control me.

Osprey drops onto the pillows, picks up a wing, and rips into it. I settle
in across from him, maximum distance for locker-room-smell purposes.
I down a wing myself before trying to open conversation. I thought of a
good opening line: *So are we meeting now?*

I grin to myself as I load up a plate with the works. "So are we
meeting—?"

"I'm not here to be seduced. I won't be seduced," he interrupts.

Excuse me?

I blink at him in disbelief. He doesn't notice because he's fully concentrating on the chicken he's devouring.

"Do I look like I'm about to seduce you?" I ask.

"I saw the way Remy was looking at you. You've seduced him."

I ardently object via the grumbly *pfft* noise that falls out of me. "I did *not* seduce Remy. That's a sexist assumption. And this is a speed-dating-esque spin-off of *Survivor*, so people liking each other is to be expecte—" I stop cold, catching the smug curve of Osprey's mouth. "What?" I demand.

"He seduced you?" He bites into a rib.

"No—"

"You have a goofy aura that doesn't match his vibe."

Goofy aura? My eyebrows slant together. "No one was seduced!" I snap. "You have a goofy aura!"

"I don't have any aura," Osprey says automatically. "I'm an excellent concealer of aura."

I drop the wing I have in my hand back down onto my plate. "Why did you pick me if you think I'm going to seduce you?"

"Figured we should get to know each other. You're clearly competent; you're coming in second in every challenge. Kennedi likes you." He picks up a chunk of cornbread and stuffs it into his mouth, his eyes rolling back for a moment.

I pour myself some Sprite and drink down a big gulp. The sugar hits like a drug, energizing me instantaneously. "How do you know Kennedi likes me?"

"She picked you last round, and y'all were buddy-buddy today like you've been friends since birth."

He has a point. "I thought you and Kennedi don't get along?"

"She's got good instincts. I don't trust her, but I trust them."

I narrow my eyes. "That makes no sense."

"Yes, it does. She's smart. That's why I don't trust her."

I study his evasive eyes as he downs the rib. They're a dark bay-water green. And he has guyliner eyelashes. They're so black and thick, it looks like he's wearing bottom eyeliner. Like a hot pirate. I will never stop being upset about how great boys' eyelashes are.

I haven't seen my reflection in six days. By this point, my pale face has most definitely gone full tomato. There's sunblock in our first aid kits, but when you're constantly outside and in the water, you're bound to slip up sometimes.

"How'd you and Kennedi meet again?" I ask. According to Kennedi, they were on a high school cheerleading team together.

He twists the top off a glass bottle of Coke and takes a long pull before putting it down. "Parkour. We've been vying for the first-place position in our last four competitions. We're always super close in point values. I've been beating her out by the slightest margin. But I'm getting older, and I have an injury; she's going to surpass me soon."

My brows scrunch. "Parkour? Like those videos where you jump on stuff with . . . style?"

"Except we do it professionally," he clarifies.

"People jump on and off stuff professionally?"

Osprey serves me hard look. "Orie—"

"You can call me Piccadilly."

"I *can* call you Piccadilly? Why would I do that?"

"Because that's also my name." I bite into a new piece of chicken.

"Your name is Orie and Piccadilly?" he asks skeptically.

"Correct. How do you make money?" I ask. "At parkour."

Osprey shrugs. "Like any other athlete. Sponsorships, commercials, online content."

Kennedi didn't mention parkour at all, but she does look like an intense athlete. And moves like an athlete. And competes like an athlete. But that could be from cheerleading.

Someone's lying.

"Is Osprey your *real* name?" I ask.

He jerks up a brow. "Is Orie Picadilly yours?"

I frown.

He throws a bunch of grilled broccoli onto his plate. "Osprey's my name. My dad loves birds."

I frown harder.

"Were you named after a London Tube stop?" he asks.

I scoop some Caesar salad onto my plate as I watch Osprey obliterate his broccoli. His dark hair is tied into a bun at the base of his neck, and two thin pieces have slipped forward, framing his face.

"No," I tell him. "I wasn't named after a London Tube stop."

Osprey finally looks up and makes solid eye contact. "So, who are you, Piccadilly?"

Whoa. His full attention is unexpectedly . . . piercing.

I struggle to swallow the leaves stuck in my suddenly desert-dry esophagus. "I-I'm, uh. I'm a grill from New Jersey."

I bang on my chest and chug some water.

His mouth and eyes go flat. "You're a grill from New Jersey?"

"Girl. I'm a girl from New Jersey. I do AcroYoga." I try to clear my throat.

"Are you okay?"

"You answer first," I squeak out before chugging a glass of Sprite.

"Okay. I'm from Wilmington, Delaware. I was a national spelling bee champ. In eighth grade, I almost threw away my spelling career when I panicked and misspelled 'exercise' at a regional competition. It was and still is one of the most embarrassing moments of my life."

I snort. "How did you spell it?"

"E-X-E-R-C-I-Z-E. Which should honestly be how it's spelled. *I still stand by that,*" he says firmly.

I'm not sure if I'm allowed to laugh because he sounds very serious, so I hold it in.

"Anyway. Um, I went on to win the national spelling competition in high school . . ." He pauses for a second, swirling his water glass around. "I guess I kind of skipped the basics. My name's Osprey Suzuki. My dad's Japanese; my mom's white. Dad grew up in New Jersey; she grew up in Maryland; they met at a ski resort when they were eighteen, both went to college at University of Delaware. They were both in the ski club. They got married out of college, had me. Two years later had my brother; two years after that, had my sister. Yeah."

"Are your parents still together?" I ask.

He nods, warmth softening his features. "Yeah."

I smile. "Mine, too." An image of my parents standing opposite Lark and me pops into my head.

"You okay?" Osprey asks.

I snap back to the moment. "What? Fine."

"One second you were smiling like an idiot, the next you looked like you were about to cry. That was full emotional whiplash."

I shake my head. "I'm fine. I just miss them. It's hard being out here without anyone you really know." I huff a laugh. "Emotional whiplash."

Osprey studies me for another moment. He has a very angular face: high cheekbones and a chin that cuts down into a distinct *V*. And he has an earring? A tiny dangling silver cross. "You're smiling like an idiot again," he says.

"Because I think you made a *Twilight* reference."

He blows out an exhausted breath.

A downward-angled mustache is coming in over Osprey's lip. The outline's reminiscent of a capsized boat. An upside-down *V,* with the perfect amount of space left blank at the center: a mini foil to his spectacular *V*-shaped facial features. There's a small upside-down triangle of hair coming in under his bottom lip as well. It's all very neat and precise. He's a study in geometry.

"So you're the oldest," I say.

"Child? Yeah."

"You seem like an oldest child," I tell him.

"Why?"

I shrug. "You seem like a bit of a know-it-all."

He cocks his head to the side. Eyes narrowing. "All right, so who are you? Other than a grill, of course. From New Jersey."

A loud laugh barks out of me. I cover my mouth in surprise.

"I'm the younger sister," I say with a smile.

"Uh-huh, you seem like one."

"How?"

"You have an edge," he says knowingly. "The youngest is always sweet, but with an edge."

"Me? An edge? I have a long history of going with the flow with everything and everyone. Why do you think I have an edge?"

Osprey refills his plate with more wings. "Because you love *Survivor.*"

"How do you know I love *Survivor*?"

"You referenced it three minutes ago," he says pointedly.

I raise my eyebrows. "Just because I referenced it, I love it?"

"No one who doesn't love *Survivor* brings it up casually in conversation."

I stare at him for a moment, perplexed. "Do you love *Survivor*?"

"Of course. Why do you think I applied for *Survivor*?"

"What *Survivor* archetype would you be?" I ask.

"Probably superfan."

"I'd be the superfan," I say.

He shakes his head. "I don't think so."

"You don't *think so*? You've known me for twenty minutes."

"You can fit a variety of archetypes," he says, "whereas I fit into one, maybe two."

"Do you seriously think I'm a *Survivor* seductress? Look at me!" I gesture to my now dirty banana-yellow outfit and polka-dot socks. "I'm wearing glasses! I'm the nerd, Osprey."

"It's a little more nuanced than that."

"*It's a little more nuanced than that.*" I mimic him like a five-year-old without thinking and clamp a hand over my mouth, mortified.

"Clever," Osprey deadpans.

I drop my eyes to the pillows, embarrassed.

Osprey picks up another square of cornbread. "What do you do, Piccadilly?"

"I do AcroYoga," I tell the food.

I look up to find the hint of a smile in his eyes. "You said that already."

"I mean, I'm an AcroYoga influencer person. I do AcroYoga with my sister, like, on socials and in person at retreats and stuff."

He takes this in, nod-frowning in an acknowledging sort of way. "Interesting."

I don't ask why it's interesting. I eat a piece of cornbread and look out at the water. He's irritating.

"Five more minutes before we head to your new beach." The PA's voice floats over from the side of the boat.

"Are we allowed to take any of this with us?" Osprey asks.

He nods. "As much as you can carry on your person—no bags!"

Osprey and I hold a quick beat of eye contact before getting to work. I stuff bread and wings into my sports bra. We take the dinner napkins and fill them with ribs and chicken. Osprey fills his pockets with vegetables.

To my disappointment, the boat drops us at a new beach. Across the left side of the sand is an enormous HEY! made of rocks.

I blow out a sad sigh. I had assumed I'd be going back to the cave. I've gotten used to the safety of it. Being off the ground. Having something solid over my head, two sets of pillows and blankets. I haven't seen a spider since that second night. I think human-ing in there is keeping other wildlife away.

"This is my beach from last time," Osprey says as we step out onto the damp sand. I follow him up toward the forest line. "There's a shelter a little down the way. Leo and Rick are pretty handy. They built a whole raised sleeping area made of bamboo and palm fronds and stuff."

As we come around the curve of the beach, a prime-looking campfire and what looks like a professional-grade shelter come into view. There's a bed of bamboo up four feet off the ground, and it's covered with the blanket and pillow that I'm assuming Osprey brought from his care package last cycle. There's a full roof made of woven palm fronds and everything! And they made a real bench next to the campfire.

"Wow," I breathe, wonderstruck. "This is . . . wow." Leo and Rick are talented.

"Yeah, I was impressed as well," Osprey comments.

"I've been living in a pseudo-cave like a troll."

"Kennedi and I made a sad little tepee-esque tent thing that was not structurally sound. It fell apart during the first rainstorm. We found a rock overhang in the jungle to huddle under, but it was rough."

I put my bag and canteen on the bamboo bed along with my stash of napkin and sports-bra food. I rewrap everything and shove it in my bag.

"We should get some coconuts to go with dinner," Osprey suggests.

"Coconuts?" I ask.

In the six days I've spent here so far, I've yet to have to find a coconut. I've been spoiled with care packages and, thus, not forced to scavenge like normal *Survivor* contestants.

Osprey squats over the firepit. His ensemble is pretty simple compared to mine: black terrycloth pants and a dark gray T-shirt.

"Are you asking me what coconuts are?" he says flatly.

"No! I just, I haven't, I don't know—do we need them?"

"Our leftovers aren't going to keep without a refrigerator out in nature with bugs and wild animals. Tomorrow, we're going to want to eat some coconut, and maybe . . . try to find some sea life or fruit. There's a bunch of palm trees not too far from the beach, back where the SOS sign was set up."

I nod absently. "Oh, okay."

I'm so full right now, it's hard to come to terms with the fact that we might need . . . to eat coconuts.

Osprey and I stop in front of an unusually curved palm tree bent over the trees around it. About ten feet up, the palm tree arches over in between the branches of a thicker, brawny tree and grows outward to the left in the direction of the ocean. The last fifteen feet of its trunk are practically parallel with the ground. Honestly, the fact that it's standing up at all is a physics marvel. The coconuts Osprey wants are all the way at the top. (Or end? It feels like more of an end when it's horizontal.)

I glance up at the vertical half of the curved tree. "How do you expect to get the coconuts?"

"We're going to climb."

I shake my head. "Oh no, I could never climb this. It's, like, ten feet before you even reach the horizontalish part, and that part arches, and the beach slopes down. It's gotta be, like, twenty feet up!"

"You can at least try; we're on *Survivor.*"

"I didn't come on to *Survivor* to die. And we're not on *Survivor*!" I remind him.

"You're not going to die! Don't tell me you didn't come out here without thinking about all the things you might have to do to eat."

I shoot him a deadpan look. "Osprey, I cannot climb this."

"Classic youngest child," he says condescendingly as he feels around on the trunk and studies the bark.

"Excuse me?" I probe.

He bobs his head from side to side. "Little spoiled, little lazy."

26

Coconuts

DAY 6

"I'm spoiled and lazy because I don't want to climb a skinny, outrageously tall, sideways palm tree on an island where we're trying to survive, not die?" I burst out.

"All the youngest siblings don't want to do anything until it's absolutely necessary rather than being prepared, so when it's necessary, you have it done. You don't go out of your way to do things. You only do them when people specifically ask, keep tabs, and bug you to do things. And even then, you get annoyed."

Why does that sound a lot like things that Lark has said? "You barely know me."

"I'll go first; you stay behind me. Watch where I put my feet." Osprey runs a hand up the tree, caressing it.

"I'm going to slip and pull you down to your death. We're attached! This is reckless!"

He turns back to me, a childlike delight in his eyes. "This is going to be fun."

"Did you do this to Leo?"

"No, he's deathly afraid of heights, but we had my care package, so we were fine rationing for three days."

I'm not wearing my sweatshirt. I left it at camp. Probably a mistake to not bring it to *climb a tree.* The skin on my stomach is exposed.

Osprey puts a hand on my shoulder. His boys'-locker-room smell wafts over me. Oof.

"Trust me," he says. "This is just going to get harder the farther we get from food. We'll need our strength going into the next group challenge, and we don't have a care package to work out of. We have energy right now. This is the time to try."

He removes his arm. The second he turns away, I cringe. I know we're on an island, but this is extreme. "Osprey, why do you smell like you haven't bathed in a hundred years?"

To my surprise, he snorts. "Because I haven't."

I put down my pack at the base of the tree near Osprey's. "You haven't washed up in the ocean?"

"Nope." Osprey hops onto the trunk and takes a few steps up, hands casually clutching the bark, feet hugging the curve of the trunk.

"Wait, what? Why not?"

He's almost six feet up in seconds. When the rope pulls taut, he stops. "All right, London Tube Stop. Hop up."

There's about seven feet of upward climbing above him before we get to the area where the trunk starts to arch toward the sea.

"What if I fashion, like, a super tall step-stool thing, and then scoot it along on the ground as you climb?"

"Put your hands on the bark, and step up. You're strong; it's not going to be hard."

I put my hands on the tree. It's rough. I'll have to be careful not to scrape against it; it may cut my skin. I pull up my legs, copying exactly what I saw Osprey just do.

I grasp the trunk like it's an enormous rope that I'm tethered to and slowly work my way up. Osprey throws me a thumbs-up and keeps climbing. He's so sure-footed, moving like he does this every damn day. I know he's going slower for me so I can mimic his movements.

And wow. I'm doing it. We're *ascending* a palm tree. I can't stop to look around or down, or I will surely *stop* doing it. I can't believe we're foraging for coconuts way above ground when there are perfectly good sports-bra chicken wings in my bag.

I look down.

Shit.

There's our camera guy at the base of the tree, no doubt judging us, laughing with every new inch of progress we make away from the ground.

He looks *far away*. I squeeze my eyes shut for a moment, gripping the tree for dear life. "Osprey! This was a bad idea! If we fall, we can die! IF I FALL, WE'LL BOTH DIE."

Osprey's only a foot or two ahead of me. "We're ten feet off the ground; we're not gonna die."

"WE COULD DIE!"

"Keep moving!" he says firmly. "That's how you do something successfully. You can't leave time to panic."

"Too late. I've already panicked!" I grit my teeth and keep moving.

Within a minute, we've reached the arc where the tree starts to lean to the left and level out.

Osprey waits for me there. Now we can crouch on top of the tree rather than climbing *up it*. My breathing is ragged and tense. The coconuts are still at least ten feet away, *at least,* and the trunk leans out *over the beach.* Just free leaning! *Out!*

"All right," he says. "I'm gonna need you to follow just until I can reach the coconuts and then we can start back. Do *not* look down now. We're close."

Osprey has the nerve to *stand* on the tree trunk and take a few steps forward before sinking back into a squat.

"*Osprey!*" I hiss. "I am not walking! I will be scooting with one leg on either side of the trunk and safely getting there very, *very* slowly," I announce.

I start to scoot. He watches with a dry expression as I take an entire minute to cross the three feet he moved in one second.

"Oh, come on." Osprey sighs as he rises to move another four feet. I glare, refusing to go any faster; it's not safe.

We're now hanging over the downward sloping part of the beach, the gap between us and the ground getting wider by the scoot.

It takes us seven minutes to reach the spot where Osprey can *just barely* reach the coconuts. He unsheathes our machete from his belt and chops the first one off.

It falls, rolls down the hill, and into the ocean.

I shoot him an irritated look. "Wow."

"First pancake," he responds, undeterred.

The next one, he grips in his palm while he chops. It falls into his hand. He sits up and tosses it to me without warning.

"AHH!" I screech as it comes at my face. Instinct kicks in just in time—I whack it away. It goes flying, rolls down the hill, and into the water.

"OSPREY!" I yell.

He's busy chopping another. He gets it off, sits up, and tosses it in my direction.

This time I catch it, seething. "STOP THROWING WITHOUT WARNING."

"Toss it near the trunk!" he says in response. I suck in an irritated breath and toss the coconut in the direction of our bags with a growl.

He repeats the process, tossing me a second coconut, and then a third.

Is this what the next three days are going to be like? Am I to be bossed around and forced to do manual labor that's not actually 100 percent necessary for the sole purpose of preparedness?

I'm internally hemming and hawing as Osprey sheathes the machete and starts making his way back to me.

Two more days, and I can reunite with Remy. I wonder what Remy's doing right now.

"Are you in a fugue state?" Osprey's crouched right in front of me.

I blink at him. I've been staring at the bark under my hands. "No," I say defensively. I'm still straddling the trunk, facing him, one leg dangling on each side.

"You have to turn around now so we can get down."

I attempt to lift one of my legs and wobble dangerously off the side of the trunk. I drop it back down, eyes wide. "Nope! Nope, nope, nope. I'm gonna fall." I glance at the downward sloping mound of sand so many feet below us. "Oh no. Oh god. Oh no."

Osprey grabs my arm and grips it. "Don't look down. I'll spot you. Just bring your leg up carefully. Try to sit on one side of the trunk, like sidesaddle. Then you can maneuver around."

I squeeze my eyes shut. "Oh my god, Osprey, I'm going to kill you for thinking this was a good idea."

"You can try."

"This was asinine!" I open my eyes and whip up my leg. Fast. TOO FAST.

Everything slows in that adrenaline-spiking, oh-my-god-we're-about-to-fall-to-our-death-because-I-got-mad-and-whipped-my-leg-over-with-too-much-force kind of way.

Osprey is still holding my arm, but I moved the wrong leg for his arm to work as adequate leverage. We're both gonna fly over the side of the tree with this momentum.

Osprey's now saucer-wide eyes lock with mine. He reaches out and pushes me—SO I FALL EVEN FASTER—and he's propelled in the opposite direction.

WHAT THE FUCK IS HAPPENING? I'm definitely screaming. I'm tumbling out of a palm tree *screaming.* My head and throat jolt as I come to an abrupt painful stop, hovering *horizontally by my hip,* what looks like twenty feet off the ground.

THERE'S A CAMERAMAN RIGHT THERE, POINTING THE LENS STRAIGHT UP IN MY DIRECTION. CAPTURING MY DEATH!

And I'm swinging? I'm swinging! I turn my head to see a vertical Osprey coming right at me. My face is heading right for his stomach. I throw up my arms as we slam into each other.

"Gah!" I yelp as his gross, sweaty boy-socks scent gets all over me. He grabs my tether point with his free hand. As he does, I see he's using his other arm to hold on to our rope and keep himself upright.

Somehow, he tilts me upright. I grab the rope with one of my hands, mirroring what he's doing.

"Stop screaming," he says. I grab his stupid shirt with one of my hands and pull on it like a crazed criminal.

"YOU PUSHED ME OUT OF A TREE!" We start to spin together.

Osprey remains calm and points up. "You propelled us out of the tree, and I saved us."

I glance to where he's pointing. Our connecting rope is . . . thrown over the tree, one of us on either side of the trunk, dangling. As we rotate, it's braiding together like a twisted-up swing.

I can't feel anything right now, but I am most definitely going to have a burn from where this harness is choking the life out of my hips.

Once our momentum slows, we spin in the opposite direction as the two ends of the rope untangle. I hold fast to Osprey's shirt, so we don't fly away from each other.

After the longest twenty seconds of my life, the spinning finally stops.

"You're going to rip my shirt," he says flatly.

I bulge my eyes at him but concede to slowly let go. I glance nervously at our connection points. The carabiners are straining against the rope.

"I'd hardly call this saving us! We're twenty feet off the ground dangling from a weird, horizontal-leaning palm tree! I HOPE there's a second step to this plan."

"We're only fifteen feet from the ground."

"You don't know how many feet away we are!" I insist. The harness is digging into my waist. I grab the rope with a second hand, supporting my weight more with my arms. My side bumps into Osprey.

"Here's the plan," he says, somehow calmly. "You're going to climb up the rope on that side. I should be able to act as enough of a counterweight. Then you lie flat on top of the trunk and hold on with locked arms and legs as I climb up second."

I close my eyes and slow my breathing. "Okay. When should I climb?"'

"Now. Every second we stay like this, we're burning precious calories."

I snap open my eyes and focus on the rope connecting us. I'm only three feet or so away from the tree trunk.

"You can do it," Osprey says.

I use my core to bring my right hand up to the highest spot I can reach on the rope. "Oh god. Okay."

I exhale, let go with my left hand, and yank myself up, grabbing the rope above my initial holding point. There's so much adrenaline pumping through me. I'm only about a foot away from the trunk now.

I groan and let go with my right hand, using my abs and left arm to pull upward.

My right hand lands on the trunk. It takes all of my core and upper-body strength to swing myself up, but somehow I get my right leg over the tree.

The rope strains against my hip, towing me in Osprey's direction. I flop forward so I'm belly down, facing back toward our stuff, away from the water, and grip the bark with my arms and legs like a frightened bear, cheek turned to the left against the scratchy trunk.

HOLY. SHIT. "I. Did it," I breathe.

"Of course you did." The voice comes from under me. "All right, hold on. Ready?"

I grip as tight as I can, my arms just making it around the tree's circumference. I can't quite lock my hands together, but I can lock my ankles. "Go," I say.

Seconds later, his hand grips hard against my upper thigh. I suck in an unexpected breath as his fingers dig into my skin, using me as a handhold. "Sorry, shit, didn't think about this bit."

"It's fine. Get up however you need to," I grind out. My fingers slip a centimeter. I grip the bark harder. It cuts into my finger pads.

His other hand lands on my lower back.

"Jesus!" I groan.

He moves it lower to my butt area. "SORRY!"

"It's fine!" I yell, face pressing hard into the tree. "Just get up!"

Osprey shimmies himself up over me, his entire upper body now resting perpendicular to mine as he leans over my butt and thighs.

I blow out a loud breath. "Well, this is really not how I thought today was gonna go."

A sound barks out of him. I think it's a laugh. "Yeah, this wasn't the plan. I'm going to rotate so . . . um, I'm parallel to the branch."

"You really should have climbed up first," I say, smushed against the bark.

"I'm sorry." He manages to slide backward so he's straddling the tree behind me. "I was thinking about weight distribution on the climb up, not . . . not the logistics of me climbing up second . . . I feel like a dunce."

"You are a dunce," I squeeze out, finally sitting up. I wobble to the side. He catches me from behind, his hands gripping my waist, tightening on my bare skin.

I swallow, gripping the trunk again. "I'm okay."

Osprey drops his hands. "I think I should probably go down first and help you. I'll just have to leapfrog ov—" He stops mid-thought.

Dread hits me hard and fast. I'm facing away from him, so I have no idea what caused the stop. IS THERE A SNAKE OR SOMETHING?

"What, Osprey! Is there a deadly animal hovering over us? Is there a bug!"

"You . . . there's a *Divergent* quote on your back."

"Oh." My heart flips. "I . . . yeah, you know it?"

"And Emily Dickinson? . . . And *Titanic, Sherlock* . . . Cassandra Clare?"

I think I've stopped breathing. He knows five quotes from my collection? No one but my mom has ever placed so many. And so quickly.

He knows *I dwell in possibility*? Is it carved into his bones like it is in mine? I try to look back at him and almost lose my balance again. He re-grabs my waist.

This time, heat dances through me. I blink out at the forest.

"We should get down," he says quietly. "If you lean forward, I should be able to step over you pretty easily, then you can follow my lead."

We crawl around in the sand, gathering coconuts at the base of our palm tree and shoving them into our respective bags. The chicken wings unfortunately had to be relocated back into my poor, very stained, yellow sports bra.

I can't believe we made it out of that alive. I expected one of us to at least twist an ankle. We climbed a coconut tree while attached together, fell off, swung around like a demented human Christmas ornament, and survived to tell the tale.

I feel strangely invigorated.

I do have some mild scrapes . . . everywhere. And a hell of a rope burn around my hips. Osprey's covered in mild scrapes as well. We'll have to wash all these out so they don't get infected. The smallest cut can become life-threatening and nasty out here.

I grab another coconut and begin the task of shoving it into my over-crowded bag.

"*Divergent* is why I started parkour. I wanted to be Dauntless."

I freeze and look up at Osprey in surprise. "Really?"

He nods. "I broke my arm when I was seven jumping off a high dive at the community pool. I was midair when I decided I was too scared to jump, so I tried to reach back and catch the diving board as I fell. Instead of catching it, I awkwardly crashed into it on the way down. And something snapped." He says this lightheartedly, like it's small talk.

"It wasn't till my body flopped into the water that I felt anything. I basically accidentally drowned. I took in all this water in a raging panic. The lifeguard wasn't paying attention. It was one of those cliché teenager situations where he was talking to some girl when it happened. He jumped in late—saved me with CPR."

I gape at him.

Osprey casually nods. "Yeah, I was kind of afraid of everything after that, but I picked up *Divergent* as a preteen, and things started to change. It made me want to face the world head-on."

He picks up his bag and starts heading back toward our camp. My jaw is still hanging open. I'm still holding the last coconut I was trying to stuff into my bag. Our rope snags. I hop up and take off after him.

In the *Divergent* series, the characters have to perform in this simulation test where they face their greatest fears. The Dauntless characters are brave to the point of recklessness but also really inspiring. I remember feeling the same way after I read it.

"What were you afraid of?" I ask excitedly.

Osprey glances over his shoulder. "Too many things: heights, water, knives, fire. I hated candles, running, the ocean, flying, driving, skate-boarding, snowboarding, Florida—anything with any risk attached to it scared the shit out of me." He slows to walk at my pace. Presses his lips together. "*Fear doesn't shut you down; it wakes you up.* That's a powerful perspective shift."

That's the quote I have on my back. Those words blew through me when I read them. I was twelve. It was the first time words from a novel really dug in and grew roots in my psyche. I don't want fear to shut me down.

But it does. It cripples my voice. My thought processes. I can't spit out sane sentences or properly articulate my thoughts when I'm in any heightened emotional state.

But the quote still makes me feel stronger.

I clear my throat as we walk over the sand. "It's the first tattoo I got when I was sixteen," I say as we approach our camp. "It was the first time a set of words spoke to me in *that way,* that seeps into your bloodstream. Changes how you think about things."

For the first time in my presence, Osprey really smiles. It looks great on him. A genuine boyish wonder fills his eyes. "I love when they do that."

I can't not beam back. "Me, too."

27

Camp

DAY 6

I clutch the flint in my hand. I'm sitting a healthy distance away from Osprey on the bench Leo and Rick crafted next to their campfire. "Do you want to start the fire?"

"I think we should take turns," Osprey says. "Rock, paper, scissors for who starts?"

I win with paper and decide to let Osprey start it. He's good; he's got sparks within two minutes. We've got a roaring fire in five.

He sits back on the bench, legs straight out in front of him, admiring his handiwork for a moment before cutting his eyes to me. "Should we crack open a celebratory coconut?"

My lips twist into a hesitant grin. "Sure?"

He pulls one from his bag, unsheathes the machete, and offers them both to me.

"What?" I shift away, waving him off. "No, I'm good. You can hack it."

"No, I did the fire; you should do this."

"I can't," I tell him. "I'm going to slice off my finger. I didn't practice chopping open coconuts with the machete. Or chopping anything for that matter."

He shoots me a confused look. "Yeah, all right, you can practice right now."

"I don't even know how to properly hold it." I say this robotically because he doesn't seem to understand me.

"I will walk you through it," he says, mimicking my jolted robot voice.

I blow out an exhausted breath. "Osprey."

"Let's move off the bench; it'll be easier on the sand."

I follow him over onto the ground. He holds out the machete. I take it with a sigh.

"All right, loosen your grip," he says.

My brow shoots up. "Loosen it!" *Nobody wants a knife to go flying out of my hand; it will inevitably murder someone.*

"Loosen it, or else you'll get blisters and strain your hand."

"I don't know how to safely *loosen* my grip on a giant knife," I respond.

Osprey sighs and scoots closer. I hold my breath as he reaches over and pulls on my palm, un-tensing my hand, separating my fingers. His hands are strong. Calloused.

"Wrap your forefinger and your thumb around the base to meet," he says, watching as I follow his instructions. "And hold them together loosely. Let the other fingers rest, but not tightly, around the bottom. You want the knife to be able to move a bit without your hand doing all the work."

"How do you know this?" I ask, incredulous.

"*YOUTUBE,*" he says like it's the most obvious thing in the world.

I guess it is the most obvious thing in the world. I was way too focused on puzzles and fire to pay much attention to machete wielding, which I figured anyone else would be able to do for me.

"How old are you?" I ask. He can't be much older than me.

"Twenty-one," he says.

"WHAT! I'm older than you!"

He rolls his eyes. "How old are you?"

"Twenty-three," I lament.

"Yeah, I can see how that's upsetting; you're ancient."

Kennedi said that same thing, but with the implication that I was, indeed, ancient. Osprey said it sarcastically.

"You don't think I'm old?" I ask.

He looks up at me. "Seriously? Is this a serious question?"

I shrug, relaxing out of my squat in the sand. "Ever since graduation last year, I feel like I've been forcibly shoved out of the umbrella term: young adult."

Osprey's forehead scrunches in indignant disagreement. "You just graduated—you literally *are* a young adult. What else would you be?"

I fiddle nervously with my hands. "Well, I haven't found any *young adult* books with people my age."

Osprey shakes his head. "You're twenty-three; you can't even rent a car without an extra surcharge. By all real adult standards in this century, we're babies. Do you have your own place?"

"No."

"Are you settled into a career?"

"No."

"Are you married? Do you have kids?"

"No," I mumble.

"Do you live with your parents?"

"Yeah . . ."

"You're the most *young adult* young adult I can imagine fitting the words 'young adult.' We're the same age."

"Well, technically—"

He cuts me off. "Okay, take the coconut." He hands it to me. "Put it in front of you with the side that *wasn't* attached to the tree on the right. That's where you'll cut off the tip."

I follow his directions, placing the coconut with the tree end facing Osprey, and raise the knife.

"Don't swing yet!" he yelps.

A relieved breath spills out of Osprey as I lower the machete. "Okay, hold the tree end of the coconut and just practice for a second. Put the blade down at the tip on an angle facing *out* toward the sand so you get an idea of where and how you want to cut it. You'll slice on an angle, and then rotate the coconut till you get the entire outer shell off the tip area."

I fiddle with the machete, pushing it into the top of the coconut on an angle outward, toward the open sand. My chest tightens. "This feels dangerous, Osprey."

"You're cutting open a coconut, Piccadilly; it's not a cliff dive."

I shoot him a glare before refocusing on the coconut. I raise the machete again.

He throws up an arm. "Wait!"

And lower it.

"Take your left hand off it. You're not experienced enough yet to hold on to the coconut while you chop." I whip my hand off.

"Okay! You're good," Osprey says calmly. "Go for it. On an angle, remember."

I lift the machete aloft, staring down at my target, and bring it down. "GRAAAH!"

The blade slams into the sand next to the tip of the coconut. I glance over at Osprey. "Wow. Fail."

"Try again," Osprey says patiently.

I lift the knife, angle it, focus on the coconut. "GRAHHH!" It swishes through the air and hits the sand again. "Crap!" I growl. I jerk the machete up. Aim. "GRAAAAHHHH!"

Same result.

I turn to frown at Osprey. He's studying me with his deep green eyes like I'm a science experiment. "I feel like you might have some pent-up rage kicking around inside you."

My shoulders slump. "Why would you think that?"

"Because rage slips out of your mouth every time you swing the blade."

I let that percolate for a minute.

"It might be clouding your ability to actually focus on the goal," he says.

My eyes slide back to the coconut.

Osprey presses his lips together. "When I have some big issue or emotion bowling around inside, that's when I fuck up a run—and fall or hurt myself." He pushes a stray wisp of hair behind his ear. "Trying to suppress emotional stuff screws with your ability to focus your body and be in the moment."

I watch as he picks up a log from our pile of firewood. "When I'm dealing with something, my trainer makes me box it out in our gym." He replaces the coconut in front of me with the log. "Try taking a few swings at this instead for rage management."

"Rage. Management?" I repeat.

"Are you asking me for the definition of rage management?" he says flatly.

"No," I snap.

"With a log, you take a slightly different approach. Angle the machete left first, and then hit the same spot with it angled to the right. Keep alternating till you chop through it."

I fiddle with the machete. "Kinda like *Titanic*."

He shakes his head. "Much lower stakes."

The log's probably five inches in diameter. "What if the machete bounces off the wood and hits me in the face like that one time on *Survivor* Amazon?"

Osprey's lips shift into the tiniest smile. "Just go slow. That guy was chopping frantically; it didn't bounce. He ripped it out of the branch and hit himself in the face. And he was using the wrong grip."

I narrow my eyes, impressed he knows exactly what I'm talking about. With another growl, I bring the machete down into the log.

It makes a diagonal notch!

"Nice!" Osprey encourages.

Carefully, I remove the knife and bring it down again in the other direction. I don't hit my first notch exactly, but it's in the vicinity. A smile cracks across my face: notches that are roughly in the same vicinity! *Look at me go!*

I bring the knife down again. And again. And again. Growling all the way. There's a creak as the log finally breaks apart. I'm grinning like a mad woman as I raise the machete in victory. "I did it!"

I glance up at Osprey. He's smiling. *He has great teeth.*

"Fuck yeah," he says. "Feel better?"

I blow out a breath, assessing. "Actually, yeah." I'm breathing hard. "That was weirdly fun."

"Right? My mom always says—" He hesitates, eyeing me bashfully.

"What does she say?" I prompt.

"She says we have to feel our feelings so we don't become them. They creep up on us."

I close my eyes for a moment, committing the words to memory. "I like that. If I had a pen, I'd put it down in my quote collection notebook."

Osprey laughs; there's no sound other than a huff of breath as he rocks forward. Like joy came and punched him in the gut.

My smile stretches. "Are you laughing at my quote collection notebook?"

"No, I've just never heard of someone having a specific quote collection notebook."

"A lot of people do," I say.

"Name one."

"John Green."

He grins again. "I wish I knew if that was true."

"Your mom sounds emotionally wise. I'm gonna file that away for the day me and my notebook reunite."

Osprey and I share a smiley eye-contact moment before I realize what's happening and snap out of it.

"I DID THE COCONUT!" I cheer, a warm swirl of satisfaction settling over me as I offer Osprey my now drinkable triumph.

He takes it, smiling. "You didn't *do* the coconut. You *opened* the coconut." He tries a sip. "You *opened* the coconut, and it's . . . delectable."

Delectable? I cock my head, filing *that* away as he offers it back. We pass the coconut between us for a bit, gazing out at the ocean as we drink.

I sneak glances at Osprey. First the tattoo knowledge and now *delectable*. Who is this boy? He has such good posture. And he's so self-assured. And he's way too good at puzzles. And he—just caught me staring. Heat rushes across my clavicle.

Shit. Say something clever. "Delectable's a word for olds!"

Delectable's . . . a word . . . for olds?

Osprey squints at me for an extended moment, during which I physically resist the urge to bury my head in the sand.

"Wow," he finally says. "And I just laid out an entire argument defending your youth."

Nervous laughter bubbles out of me. "What, are you sensitive about being the ripe ancient age of twenty-one?"

He shrugs bashfully, his lips tilted up in a sad smile.

"Wait, you are?" I ask curiously.

"No, I just . . ." He takes a sip and passes me back the coconut. "You can only compete in parkour for so long before you just naturally aren't able to do the stuff as well because it takes such a toll on your body. Kind of like gymnastics. And recently, in that sense, I've started to feel old."

I study him for a moment. "Don't people do parkour, like, at all ages?"

"Technically, you can parkour at whatever age. But the longer you do it, the more you injure yourself, the harder it gets. I've been doing this obsessively since I was thirteen. And I have this knee injury that I keep neglecting. It's been getting worse. I need to stop training for, like, a year to try and get it better. Do a load of physical therapy."

"And you don't want to take a year off . . ."

He blows out a jaded laugh. "It's just not that simple. It's my job. It's what I post on my social platforms. I mean, there is other stuff I want to do. I don't want to compete in all these really physically taxing competitions forever. I'm prepping to retire from that aspect of the sport. I don't have to keep doing this at the level I'm doing it. But it's hard to let go of something that feels like such a big part of who you are."

I nod, empathy pooling in my chest.

"This is going to sound melodramatic," Osprey continues, "but when you become the best at something, you kind of want to believe you'll be the best forever? It's hard to make peace with the idea of someone coming in and taking that spot. But it's inevitable. It's coming for me. And its name is Kennedi." He snorts half-heartedly. "I'm still making my peace with it."

We sit in silence for a beat. I'm seized with the urge to rub his arm. I have my hand up and everything. I shouldn't, though, right? I lower it back down. And then I bring it back up.

"What are you doing with your hand?" he says, his eyes dropping to where my arm is indecisively moving up and down.

"I . . . was, um, trying to decide whether or not to comfort you with a rub on the arm . . . Should I?"

He eyes me skeptically. "You're welcome to, if you want."

After a prolonged beat of eye contact, I awkwardly drop my hand onto his shoulder, jolt it downward two inches, and hold for a second before jerking my hand back into my lap.

He stares at me, humor sneaking into the edge of his mouth. "Wow. Thank you for that tidal wave of comfort."

I bury my face in my palms. Exhale. Meet his eyes again. "You're not old, Osprey. You've got your whole life ahead of you. Me, on the other hand . . . twenty-three . . . I'm edging on senior citizen. Soon, I'll start being confused about youth slang—"

Osprey groan-laughs, cutting me off; it's a hearty noise that comes from the back of his throat. "Shut up. We're the same age, Tube Stop."

Tube Stop. I smile out at the water. "So, question: How do you know all the words on my back?"

28

Watercooler Talk

Osprey shrugs. "How do you?"

I roll my eyes. "How do I know my own tattoos?"

A close-lipped smile appears on his face. He looks into our now empty coconut. "Pass me the machete?"

I pass it.

"Once you finish the water, you can chop it in half and eat the meat." He places the coconut in front of him. In one clean sweep, he cleaves straight through and offers half to me. I watch as he picks the "meat" bit out of his half and eats some. His eyes flick up. "My parents own a book-shop. I've been spending the majority of my time in there since before I could read."

Mental gasp. "What! Which shop?"

He grins, leaning over to grab the log I chopped and toss it onto our fire. "Why? Do you think you know every independent bookshop in America?"

I pick some of the coconut meat out and try it. To my surprise, it's rather tasty. "No, but that doesn't mean I don't want to know what it's called."

"It's called I Like Books and I Cannot Lie."

A toothy smile splits my face. "That's not what it's called."

He closes his eyes and nods solemnly. "It is."

"I've seen that as a bookish meme; isn't it 'I like *big* books and I cannot lie'?"

"It is," he says seriously. "But my parents insist the word *big* in front of *books* will deter casual readers and young kids from coming into the store."

I keel forward, a weird, snakelike laugh hissing out of me.

"Yep," Osprey concedes knowingly. "What do your parents do?"

"My mom's actually an editor at Frollen & Reed."

Osprey sits up. "The publishing company?"

Osprey and I fall into a bookish discussion, the likes of which I've never had with another human IRL. He knows all the jargon, all the titles I bring up. He has his own two cents and commentary. We bounce back and forth discussing random reading-related topics for twenty minutes before I finally get to ask, "So what's your favorite book?" as I follow him into the jungle to refill our water supply.

"Too hard." Osprey laughs.

"How about one for each life era. Childhood, teen, and young adult," I suggest.

"Childhood is probably *Legend* by Marie Lu."

A light turns on in my chest. "That makes sense."

He narrows his eyes. "It makes sense?"

"Because you so wanted to be Day! The super cool, smart, can-climb-anything protagonist, duh."

He turns to me, perplexed. "Damn," he says, "I hadn't registered that." We trek around a sharp bend in the trail. "I've only ever talked about *Legend* right after I read it, and that was with my parents. I detailed the entire plot to them and then kind of moved on."

"Do your siblings read?"

"They went the opposite direction with the parents-owning-a-bookstore thing and decided they didn't want anything to do with it."

I *mmm* in agreement. "My sister reads the opposite of whatever I read, so I feel you. She doesn't like *fiction.* It's almost like she goes out of her way to not be interested in my interests. Like being associated with what I'm associated with will somehow taint her flawlessness."

Osprey turns again. "A lot of people don't like fiction, Tube Stop. Seventy-five percent of bookstore-goers come in looking for self-help or biography."

I roll my eyes. "Teen favorite?"

"*Divergent*," he says automatically.

We pull up to the water well. I feel like we teleported here, I've been so distracted by our conversation.

"Now favorite?" I ask.

"Maybe this is because I'm such a big fan of survivor tales, but I still *really, really* love *The Martian.* I first read it when I was, like, thirteen, but I've read it three times since."

I smile, stuffing my canteen into the water as Osprey fills up our pot. "Here, I can take care of your canteen if you're okay to carry the pot."

"Thanks." He nods and hands me his canteen.

We meander slowly back down the path, Osprey carefully maneuvering our cooking pot full of water so we don't lose any along the way. The sun's low in the sky, just about to dip for the day.

"All right, Piccadilly," he says. "Drop your three faves."

I watch the foliage going by under our feet. "I have such a hard time choosing favorites."

He shoots me an incredulous smile. "Are you serious? You made me choose; you have to pick."

"They're not like . . . highbrow."

A loud laugh barks out of him. "I just told you my favorites were two YA dystopians and *The Martian*—are those highbrow?"

I snort. "My childhood favorite is *Mark of Athena*—"

"Percy Jackson!"

"Yeah! Did you read those?"

"*Did I read those?*" He smirks at me, and I feel heat rising to my cheeks. More hair has fallen loose from his bun, framing his face. It looks . . . good.

I clear my throat. "When were you in London that you associate Piccadilly with the Tube stop?"

"I did a commercial out there for Nike last year. Stayed a few extra days because, well, London."

"Whoa! That's amazing."

"Yeah, it was really cool." We emerge from the forest and make our way to the campfire.

Again, I barely felt the walk. Osprey sets the pot atop this camp's boiling griddle. This griddle is of such high-quality craftsmanship, it, too, was obviously put together by Leo and Rick. They should start a carpentry business.

Osprey feeds our fire, and I add the water from our canteens to the pot.

"So is Piccadilly a nickname? Is that, like, what people actually call you at home, or is it just a thing you're trying to make happen on the show?" Osprey asks as I collapse onto the fire bench.

I like how our conversation stops and starts but never loses its place. Like there's an invisible bookmark we keep sliding in and out as we do other things.

I blow out a long breath, staring out at the darkening horizon. "I've been trying to make it happen out here on the show. I found myself getting caught up in spirals about how small my life was leading up to my flight out to Fiji.

"I kinda wanted to come out here and be *me, but better,* and the first step to reinventing myself felt like a cool new name. Orie is kind of different, but it's not different to me, you know? It's my same old name that everyone's always called me, and all the best *Survivor* players have a fun moniker.

"I read a book I really loved that takes place in London, and one of the Tube lines is the Piccadilly line and I thought it was snazzy. It'd be fun to be known as 'snazzy.'"

Osprey's mouth twists up as he sits next to me on the fire bench, leaving a healthy foot between us. He studies me for a moment. "Is Orie short for something?"

"Sure."

"What's your full name?"

I smile at him. "It's Tube Stop."

His head falls forward, hair fanning around the giant grin that cracks across his face. "All right, fine."

Osprey's kind of adorable.

We've relocated to the shelter with our newly boiled water and napkin stash of wings and cornbread from our earlier feast. The firelight dances over us. I still have a million things I want to ask Osprey. A million more bookish questions. Life questions. Relationship questions. I don't know where to start.

Before I can decide, he catches my eye. "You still owe me two book responses. Favorite teen and favorite now."

I finish a wing and add the bone to our little pile. "It's too hard."

He arches a brow. "No response, then no talking."

I frown. Across from me, his eyes spark victoriously.

"Fine." I swallow the food in my mouth. "Teen is probably this book called *Accidentally Abroad*. It's more obscure."

"Describe it?"

"It's a study-abroad romance. Duology. Yellow cover—"

"Oh! I think I've seen it: yellow cover with, like, a streetlamp?"

"Yes!"

"Interesting. I'm out of the romance loop, only ventured into that genre a couple times." Osprey finishes his last bite of cornbread.

"That's actually the London book I was talking about. I wanted to study abroad after I read it, but once I got to college, I felt like it was *too* much. Like I couldn't . . . go alone." Sadness roils through me. Wes didn't want to study abroad, and I was Lark's AcroYoga partner. "So I didn't go." I curl my legs to my chest. "And now—I've still never been out of the country. I let it slip by. I let so much time slip by because I was afraid of what would happen if I didn't do what everyone expected me to do." I swallow, staring out at the fire.

Osprey reaches out, rubs my shoulder once, and retracts his hand the same way I did earlier.

I snort.

"Just extending some comfort," he says.

"Thanks. It was wildly reassuring."

"You can go anywhere after this. And you've been out of the country. You're abroad! We're in Fiji."

A bleak laugh falls out of me. "Yeah. It's not quite the same as study abroad."

He raises a brow. "But it's not nothing."

"It is not nothing." A reluctant grin curves into my lips.

29

Trust

DAY 6

We lie together, but separate, under the blanket. We brushed our teeth and did a bathroom run. We never did take a bath. I'm worried about our scrapes. We put some hydrogen peroxide from our first aid kits on the cuts, but we're dirty. (Well, I'm dirty; Osprey's filthy.) Dirt is going to get in there. We need to wash. And now it's dark. We should wash first thing in the morning.

We're as far apart as two people sharing a pillow can be, but that's not quite far enough at the moment. The locker-room smell has intensified. I must smell, too, but it can't be this pungent yet! Kennedi and I had an ocean bath before the challenge today.

"Osprey," I say softly.

"Yeah."

"Why are you not bathing in the ocean?"

"Circle of trust?" he asks.

"We haven't established an official circle of trust." I turn onto my right side to look at him in the low light.

Why does he look like an Instagram model when he's lying on a pillow? He's staring up at the top of the shelter.

"Do you want to establish a circle?" he asks.

"Like, an alliance?" I prompt.

"Sure. What are you thinking?" He turns to look at me, and in reaction, I shift to study the roof.

"We could be the Paperback Party," I propose.

Osprey convulses beside me; the white of his smile bounces light in the dark. "That's not what I meant when I asked what you were thinking."

"You don't like a paperback?" I probe.

"That's just the most random alliance name of all time. I respect a paperback—it's light, it's flexible, and it's easy to travel with."

"Exactly!"

He sighs. "I meant, what's our agreement? We won't vote each other out? We'll pick each other when we get the chance?"

"We have each other's backs," I tell him.

He nods. "All right. So we'll leave that up for interpretation then?"

I smile. "I think having each other's backs is having each other's backs. It's self-explanatory. What do you think of all the other castaways?" I ask carefully. "What are your thoughts on Kennedi?"

Osprey sighs. "Kennedi is very athletic, she's very smart, she knows how to get people to do what she wants them to do. She's a huge threat to win the game. I think she needs to go sooner rather than later; she's definitely going to target me."

I chew on this for a moment. That lines up with what Kennedi said about Osprey. "I agree. She's a threat, but one I'd love to have on my team, you know?"

Osprey drops a quick nod. "Yeah. She's kind of the devil you know, whereas some of the other players are threats we can't anticipate."

"Would you be open to keeping her around longer and eliminating mystery threats first?"

Osprey returns to his back. "Sure."

I shift to my side. "Are you two . . . at all romantically involved?"

"No," he replies easily. "I think she prefers dating women?"

"Are you into women?"

"Yeah. I'm into anyone I'm into, sex and gender aren't really a factor."

A giddy jolt hits my heart. "Cool."

"What about Remy? Are you romantically involved?" he asks.

"No," I say quickly. "But I think he's a loyal person, though, good to work with in the game."

Osprey drops a *hmm*.

It's not a mundane *hmm*. It's an all-knowing *you said that way too fast, and I noticed* hmm.

"I haven't gotten a read on him yet," Osprey continues, "but he's definitely a physical threat."

"What about Leo?" I ask.

"I like him—trustworthy—but he's in a tight alliance with Rick, so if they get to the end, there's no turning them against each other."

That's what we call a power couple. It's only good to ally yourself with a power couple when you, too, are part of a power couple.

Osprey and I descend into silence, both of us gazing up at the woven palm fronds that make up the shelter roof.

"Wait a minute," I sputter. "You never told me about your absentee bath habits! We're in the circle now."

"I was hoping you forgot."

I snicker. "I'm not a big forgetter. You're making this way more suspenseful than it needs to be."

He releases a dramatic sigh. "I have a very healthy extreme respect . . . for the ocean."

I blink at the ceiling. "What do you mean?"

"I'm . . . afraid of the ocean. It's one of the things I haven't gotten past yet."

"I'm sorry; what do you mean?" I repeat.

"I mean, I have a very extensive fear of the ocean."

My eyebrows scrunch, and I shift again on the bamboo to lie on my side. "But you're on a reality show on a beach with the ocean."

He closes his eyes. "I know."

"But you're afraid of the ocean?" I ask.

"Yes."

"But we have to bathe in the ocean."

"I know."

"But you haven't bathed in what will be seven days."

"Yeah."

"Can you smell yourself?"

He nods. "Yep."

"Did you get wet from the rain?"

"A little, but we found an overhang. I didn't do any, like, scrubbing."

"Why not? That was your ocean loophole!"

He turns to meet my gaze, and this time I stay put. "I wasn't thinking about scrubbing at the time. I was a little too distracted by the freezing-rain-with-no-food-or-shelter thing we were dealing with. But part of the reason I wanted to come out here was to . . . finally, trial by fire, overcome it."

"But you haven't done any trialing?"

He shakes his head.

"I think we need to trial by fire at first light if we don't want our palm tree cuts to get infected and murder us. Also, and I say this with Paperback Party love, eventually you're going to smell so bad, people aren't going to want to be attached to you."

Osprey silently holds my eyes across the pillow. So I hold his back like we're playing some weird game of *don't speak, don't break eye contact* chicken. After thirty seconds, my heart starts to pound.

"Tomorrow," I finally say before turning away toward the ocean to sleep.

"Good night, Piccadilly."

I pull up my legs, curling into a little ball as I smile out into the night, warmth sloshing around inside me.

30

Trial by Fire

DAY 7

We get up at daybreak. I'm in my underwear and sports bra. Osprey's in his black boxers with his shirt thrown over his shoulder. We're at the edge of the crystal-clear water staring out at the sea.

Now that he's topless, I can see an even bigger cut on his upper arm that could easily become infected. We have to get in the dang water. He must have scraped his shoulder as he propelled himself over the tree trunk yesterday.

We've been standing in the same spot for twenty-five minutes. I'm starting to feel like an overbaked cookie in the morning sun. "Osprey. You saved our lives in the tree yesterday. Let me help you avoid septic shock."

"I don't think that's a thing."

I roll my eyes. "Something similar to that is a thing. Death or removal from the game due to infection *is a thing out here.* You've seen these shows!"

He presses his lips together, staring at the paradise blue water like it's a ring of fire I'm peer pressuring him to jump through.

"I'll be here the whole time—me, and the camera guy, and the crew out in the forest."

He exhales a billowing breath. "Sharks."

"I will stand in front of you so they'll eat me first, and you'll have time to escape."

"No, you won't," he says plainly.

I turn toward him, aghast. "I will! Osprey, we made an oath last night."

His eyebrows slant. It does great things for his face. There are so many angles. He's a study in triangles and how they can come together to create a human masterpiece.

"When did we make an oath?" His tone is skeptical.

"Hello, Paperback Party? Did that mean *nothing* to you?"

He narrows his eyes. "I wouldn't call that an oath."

"What would you call it, then?"

"We had a silly conversation."

"What do we have to do for you to take it as an oath? Should we slice open our palms and shake on it with blood? I never understand why people do that; it's a terrible place to slice. You need your hands ready to rock. Why not the back of your arm or, like, a thumb prick—"

"We don't have to mix our blood," he says stiffly. "That would only draw out the sharks faster."

I close my eyes, choking on the severity of his tone. I hold out my pinky. "I pinky promise I have your back."

He gravely hooks his pinky through mine.

I let the smile I want to wear pop on. "We are Paperback Party," I sing-talk. "We have each other's backs and protect each other from shark attacks. We don't do crack."

He watches me flatly. "You should do slam poetry."

"Thanks, maybe I will." I hold out my palm. "Hold my hand for emotional support."

He takes it.

"Just to be clear." I raise our hands between us. "This is not a ploy to seduce you."

His tight features break into a surprised laugh before rubber-banding back to fear. "You're all over the place."

I take a step forward, tugging Osprey toward the water. "What do you mean by that?"

The ocean washes over my feet as it laps calmly against the sand. Osprey closes his eyes and steps forward. "Shit." He exhales, looking up. "I mean, you're a bit of a kook."

I squeeze his hand. "You mean I'm quirky?"

"No. Kooky."

"Osprey. Are you saying the archetype you think I fill on the show is the weirdo?"

He nods. "Yes, that is definitely the archetype you're going to fill."

I take another step forward. Osprey follows with his eyes closed.

"I don't know about that," I counter.

He shakes his head. "You are so the weirdo, Piccadilly. Case in point: you've asked to be called Piccadilly."

"If I *am* the weirdo, I *better* be the lovable kind." I step forward again, and he steps without hesitating, his mouth twisted into a strained grimace.

"You are," he says quickly.

I bite back a grin, my shoulders shrugging up to my ears as I tug him another step. The water's up to our hips. "You can open your eyes; you're in."

He blows out a shallow breath, opens his eyes, and closes them again. "Yeah, no, I think I'm gonna pass out." He moves to step toward the beach.

I put a hand on his shoulder. "Hey, it's okay. Breathe. Let's just get you clean! It'll take five minutes."

Osprey presses his arms flat into his sides, like somehow if he stands straight enough, he'll magically teleport back to shore. When he opens his eyes again, I get a front-row view of the panic swallowing him up.

"Hey, Osprey, just look at me." His pupils cut to mine. A gush of courage floods my chest. "You've got this; you're doing the ocean."

His lip quirks the tiniest bit, but he doesn't try to correct my grammar. He squeezes his eyes shut again and sips in shallow breaths. He's completely locked up. I pull the black T-shirt off his shoulder.

"Is it okay if I help you?" I ask, reinspecting the thick layer of dirt on his arms.

"Please," he says quietly, his knuckles clenched and whitening like he's standing in a pool of acid.

I exhale my own long, slow breath and glance around. I think he's having a panic attack. "Inhale, Osprey." He does. "Okay, exhale." He does. "Okay, keep doing that for me? Count to four on the in and four on the out."

He obeys.

I dip down into the water and scoop up a batch of sand. Using Osprey's shirt as a washcloth, I work on his back, slowly scrubbing at the layers of grime. Bit by bit, it comes free, washing away into the ocean. I make my way to his shoulder blades. His neck. All with surgical precision so that my skin never touches his.

I'm glad his eyes are closed, or else, this might feel . . . intimate. And I—I like Remy.

I pay special mind to the scrapes that pepper his arms, being ultra-gentle, barely applying any pressure as I attempt to polish the area around the cut on his shoulder.

This is fine because we're not really touching.

This is platonic-friend washing.

My breathing is uneven, and my heart is pounding, but this isn't weird. It's not.

When I'm ready, I direct Osprey to sit down; to my surprise, he does. And then I dunk his head into the water. I feel like some weird cross between a Halloween nurse and John the Baptist.

He stays down, submerged to his neck, and I work my fingers through his hair, combing it out with my hands.

Maybe this does feel intimate. I don't think I'm breathing.

But Osprey's eyes stay closed. So, it's okay. He doesn't open them again until I'm done, and I tell him to. His breathing has slowed. His pupils find mine.

I don't know what just happened.

I thought this was going to be a funny face-your-fears adventure into the ocean where he washes off and I wash off and we laugh about how he was afraid of nothing and then we get out.

We stare at each other now, his eyes shooting flaming arrows into mine that scorch down my throat and settle in my gut where they fizzle and self-destruct.

My mouth is dry. We've been in here way longer than five minutes.

"Did you wash?" he asks.

I shake my head. He holds out his hand for the ocean-drenched T-shirt I'm clutching in my palm.

I open my mouth to tell him *I can do it myself.* But my mouth doesn't actually say the words because he's still looking at me—with those flaming arrow eyes—and I want him to do it.

Platonically probably. I don't like him romantically. Even though I really enjoy talking to him. And he seems to really understand me. And also I'm finding his torso extremely distracting, so I keep averting my eyes so I don't look at it.

Osprey dips down to acquire sand. Then he works it down over my shoulders, my arms. Gently, meticulously. The way I did to him.

I may have taken too long. Studied him too hard.

I can't believe I've been struck down by two distracting torsos in such a short span of time. Osprey isn't buff the way Remy is. He's lean, but he's structured lean. There's lots going on there.

He slowly pulls the hair tie out of my ponytail. A shiver whips through me. I watch as he glides it onto his own wrist. He guides me down into the water, and his hands slip up my neck. His fingers spread, combing up into my tangled mess of strawberry hair and massaging my scalp. An audible exhale escapes my lips.

The perpetual whirring torrent of my anxious inner monologue goes dark. If I had a fuse box, Osprey just reached in and flipped it off. For however long this moment lasts, my hamster wheel is still.

I come back online slowly as he pulls us up from the water. He gathers my hair and braids it back. Ties the hair tie at the bottom. It's a reverse French braid if I'm clocking it correctly.

What just happened?

"Thanks," I whisper without looking at him, uber casually, unsure of what to do next. Afraid to get caught in his ocean-green gaze because *Remy*.

Whatever spell has come over us breaks as I stumble away toward the beach without making eye contact.

Why does Osprey feel like a trap planted specifically for me to fall into?

31

Post-Bath

DAY 7

We sit on the bench next to our crackling fire sharing a new coconut, quietly drying off. I feel like I just lived a fever dream. Osprey's emerging-from-a-coma vibe is leading me to believe the feeling may be mutual.

"I'm afraid of bugs and driving," I blurt, like this will erase the weird magic of whatever passed between us during Bathgate.

He chuckles. "Driving, huh?"

"How do you know how to do this?" I point to my hair.

He shrugs. Osprey loves to shrug. His go-to is shrugging. And I can see why. He's really mastered it. When anyone else shrugs, it's kind of obnoxious. When he does it . . . it's, like, cool. "I have a younger sister, and I have long hair," he explains.

"Can I ask you another question?"

He leans forward, legs spread, resting his elbows on his knees. "You don't have to ask permission."

His hair is drying. It looks softer now, vaguely shiny. He's left it out of the man bun. It falls forward, and he tucks it behind his ear.

I blink at him. "How are you growing an extremely perfect, artistic Will Turner mustache and tiny underlip beard triangle?" I spent a lot of time staring at this during the bath.

Osprey tilts his head. "You know there's a razor in your first aid kit and a tiny mirror so we face shavers don't accidentally cut ourselves, get infections, and die."

I, in fact, had not noticed this razor. I waxed my entire body before this in the event razors did not exist. "Oh."

Osprey nods. "You know what we should do tomorrow?"

"What?"

"Get up early and do that thing where they hunt the giant crabs in the forest with long sharpened sticks."

"I don't think I can do that." My stomach grumbles as if it's a separate member of this conversation.

Osprey peers at me. "All we have right now for dinner is yet another coconut."

I am fading fast without protein. My arms are quaking, and my stomach feels hollow. "Okay."

We roll out of the bed before sunrise and wander into the jungle with our sticks. Osprey points out certain things to look for; he studied how to do this before coming out here.

We lift rocks and shift big pieces of debris, and when one enormous crab emerges from the dirt, we go wild. I come down with my sharpened stick and miss, my shaky arm not moving as fast as I wanted it to, but Osprey connects with his stake, piercing right through the shell.

It's hard to describe the joy I feel in that moment. The weird elation of knowing sometime in the next few hours, we will have meat. We throw this crab in our bag and are proceeding toward camp when I spot a chicken.

A wild chicken. Off ten feet away in the brush.

This is how I know New Jersey Orie has left the building.

I see that chicken, point, drop my stick, and run. Together, we leap over a fallen log, hustle through the brush, and when I'm the one gaining on the bird, I *dive*.

I dive for the chicken with no regard to the rope attached to Osprey or my own well-being. *I football-tackle a chicken.* Osprey must jump too because the rope doesn't jerk me back. I land hunched over the bird and snatch it up by the legs like I grew up on a farm and didn't only ever even attempt to catch a chicken while playing a mini game on Mario Party.

We name the chicken Fly. We fashion a rope out of jungle vine-y stuff and tie her to a tree near our camp. We're hoping Fly will lay an egg.

We cook the crab we caught. It's only one crab, but it's big, and it's protein. And it's delicious.

I feel strangely empowered by the fact that we're actually legit eating *off the land.* I lean my shoulder into Osprey, nudging him. My mood is lifting perceptibly with every tiny bite.

"So, when you maybe 'retire' from competitive parkour and get your knee back up and running," I say, breaking a piece of the crab shell apart, "what do you think you'll do after that?"

He takes a swig of water and exhales, his earring glinting in the fire-light. "I'll still do parkour and post stuff on socials and hopefully do campaigns for different companies, but I want to try and be a stunt man."

"Like in movies?"

"Yeah, or TV, or, you know, anything on film." He finishes off his piece of crab. "What do you want to do? Are you going to travel around conquering the AcroYoga world?"

I laugh. "I don't think one conquers the AcroYoga world; you dance with it. It's not a competition."

He smiles. "All right, are you going to dance with the AcroYoga world?"

I lift a noncommittal shoulder and chew another bite before answering, "I kind of want to do so many things that, instead of shooting for any of them, I've done nothing. And I've told myself I want to do nothing because all the things I've ever been interested in feel so out of reach and hard to access and get into . . . But now, I want to pick a thing."

"Good."

"But picking one difficult thing is scary because what if I put all my effort into it and commit years to trying to make it happen only to fail? And then I've wasted that time, and I don't have the luxury of wasting more time to try and put my effort into one of the other things I wanted to do, and then it turns out Lark was right: I *am* a codependent person who can't do anything herself, and I have to live with my parents forever."

Osprey blinks at me. "So you don't want to dance with AcroYoga?"

I shake my head. "Not as a career, no."

"Who's Lark?" he asks.

"My sister."

He tilts his head, pondering this. "You're not a codependent person who can't do anything herself, Piccadilly."

I sigh. "You don't know me well enough to say that. I kind of am."

"Just because you haven't done things yourself in the past doesn't mean you *can't*. You tackled a fucking chicken today so we wouldn't go hungry tonight. By yourself. I didn't even see the damn chicken."

I narrow my eyes at him.

He narrows his back. "What do you want to do?"

"I don't know."

"You know. You were just thinking it," he insists.

Now my eyes are practically closed via suspicious gaze. I'm starting to feel like Osprey has a weird proclivity for reading my thoughts.

I look down at his knees. He's shifted to face me. Both of them are pointed in my direction.

With Remy in my corner, the idea of pursuing screenwriting feels slightly less untouchable. I've been painting that future with a little more detail every day, growing more and more attached to the image. But it still feels too pipe-dreamy to admit to someone who isn't Remy. Someone who doesn't have ties to the industry. Someone who will see it as the unattainable starving-artist reach that it is.

Osprey nudges me gently. "I told you I was afraid of the ocean. That's the most embarrassing fun fact I could ever admit on national television. I didn't tell Kennedi. Or Leo. It was a Paperback Party exclusive. It's your turn."

I fiddle with my hands, my heart thrumming nervously against my rib cage. "Well, maybe, adapt books into screenplays. Or write . . . my own movie scripts."

I stare at him, waiting for a reaction. He just motions for me to continue. "And what else?" he prompts patiently.

"Um. Try to direct book-to-movie adaptations of stories I love?" I say quietly. "To make sure they're done right."

He smiles. "What else?"

"Edit reality shows like *Survivor* or whatever this is going to turn out to be? With shows like this, you really get to adapt everyone's arcs. Shape them. The editor's kind of the master of the final story; they pick what people are going to see, craft how they'll think about the contestants. It's fascinating thinking about how this will all play out in TV-show form." I glance over at the cameraman silently standing across the campfire.

"Anything else?"

I nod, feeling shy now. "Keep working with my sister on the side."

Osprey reaches out and quickly squeezes my knee. Heat shoots up my leg. Like in a movie when someone drops a match, and fire shoots down a driveway and into a house because—plot twist—when you weren't looking, it was doused in gasoline.

I ignore it, close my eyes, regroup. When I open them, Osprey is smiling. His pupils are once again fire-arrow focused on mine.

"Are you smiling because you think that's all ridiculous?" I ask.

"I'm smiling because I think that's awesome."

32

Challenge Three

DAY 9

Jamie keeps glancing over her shoulder, smirking at us. We're en route to today's challenge, and I guess it's not on the water.

Osprey and I were spooning when I opened my eyes today. *How does that even happen?* I always semi-laugh when I see that trope in rom-coms because *in real life that would never happen.*

EXCEPT WTF, THERE I WAS, LIVING IT.

I was so comfortable until I opened my eyes, registered the spooning, and proceeded to lose my mind. Instead of casually scooting over, I sat up, and tried to leave the shelter. I got out, took two quick running steps, the rope yanked, and I tripped, twisted, and fell face-first into the sand.

I told Osprey I was sleepwalking. I don't think he believed me.

Happy to report the cameraman was there filming all of it.

Today, I reunite with Remy! Today, we can pick each other! We haven't gotten to explicitly discuss it, but we did exchange some pretty intense smiles and nods at the last challenge that said things like: *God I really miss you; I wish we could pick each other this time but we have to get to know the other players a little more,* and *we'll pick each other next time.*

We emerge behind Jamie into a small clearing. Kennedi and Leo are there. Kennedi and I make eye contact.

"Octooopussss!" she yells in a construction-worker-hitting-on-someone voice as she shoots finger guns at Osprey and me.

I yell back, "Krill!" Kennedi and I look up at the sky, make eye contact on the way down, and then look at the ground—our "secret-secret" handshake.

Osprey trains his gaze on the landscape before us. "Was that a bit you two choreographed during your cycle?"

"Maybe."

"Did you come up with it?" he says under his breath.

Amusement dances through me. "Maybe."

His lip kicks up. "You did."

Producer Z escorts the next pair in: Remy and Trina, their faces expressionless for the cameras. When Remy catches my eye, he smiles like I've made his day. I smile back and raise my fingers in the tiniest *hi*.

If possible, he looks even better? He's deeply sun kissed, and his freckles are more pronounced and even more endearing. The sleeves of his button-up have been . . . ripped off? Like he's cosplaying as Bruce Banner, post-Hulk.

I put a hand to my neck and touch the puka shells there. He smiles wider.

Jamie ushers in the final pair, Priya and Rick.

I take a beat to study the challenge arena before me. It's small today. Very normal looking. There's a colorful, tall, narrow table set up in front of us. The crew and equipment are positioned in such a way that it's clear we'll be standing behind it. The table's set with four white plates covered by big colorful decorative food covers. Looks like we're eating—

My entire body goes cold.

I know what this looks like.

This is a food challenge.

"All right!' Jamie claps her hands at the front of the table. "Today you're competing as individuals, unhooked from one another and de-teamed. The rules are simple. You have to eat the dish put before you to advance to the next round. If you finish your dish and you want to tap in for someone else at the table, you may eat the dish *for* them if you wish, but if you don't also finish theirs, you will not advance. For the first round, you'll draw straws to see who's competing in group one and group two! The last person to finish in each group will be eliminated from the challenge. Then we'll move on to the next round.

"You must keep the dish down until after the round has finished. If any bit is regurgitated while the round is live, you must get it back down to advance. Z, what are we playing for today?"

Producer Z steps up. "There will be two winners today. They will be immune to the vote. Someone will be voted out, right here, after the challenge. Then we'll move straight into the choosing ceremony. Winners will choose first, and it will go on like that in descending order depending on how you place in the challenge."

"One person will not be chosen." Jamie grins. "That person will be sent to exile for the next three days."

Trina raises her hand. "Can you explain exile again?"

Z steps up. "During exile, you will be placed on a fresh beach. You must survive without a partner for the three-day cycle."

We all look around at one another. I make eye contact with Remy. Someone's being eliminated; someone's being sent to exile. I don't want either of them to be us.

Producer Z walks through, disconnecting our ropes. Osprey looks over at me as Z takes away our umbilical cord.

"It's been real, Tube Stop."

I grin. "See you on the other side, Man Bun."

I'm in the second group for round one. Anxiety builds in my gut like an abandoned Tetris game. I am not good at eating gross foods. My dad's a chef. I am quite fond of fairly pretentious foods.

Remy, Osprey, Priya, and Rick stand behind the table in group one.

"All right, lift your covers," Jamie instructs.

The four of them remove their food covers and cringe. I can't see what it is from here.

"For round one, we have a classic: boiled water roach."

I gag where I'm standing.

"Good, good, I need the protein," Remy comments.

Jamie laughs. "Yeah, lots of protein. They're very crispy, very juicy. I'm really glad I'm not involved today." She makes a face to camera. "They're all gonna want to brush their teeth after this." She turns back to the contestants. "First three people to show me an empty mouth are moving on. Ready?"

The group is silent, staring down at the bug.

"EAT!"

Osprey, Remy, and Rick throw the entire palm-sized roach into their mouths and clamp down. Green juice goes flying from the asses of all three bugs. The guys hunch forward as it dribbles all over their faces and plates.

Jamie coughs. "Oh wow, that's a lot of juice. Priya's taking a different approach, biting it in half. Working on the top chunk."

Remy, Osprey, and Rick are chomping vigorously. Priya's making all sorts of faces as she tries to get it down.

Rick's body convulses.

"Oh no!" Jamie narrates. "Rick's might be coming up. There's a bucket behind you if you need it."

He shakes his head no. But his expression says otherwise. Osprey opens his mouth and sticks out his tongue, followed a millisecond later by Remy.

"Osprey and Remy! Moving on!" Jamie yells. "Priya's got the whole thing in her mouth now. Rick still fighting to get it all down, but looking absolutely wrecked. Y'all can do it. Mind over matter!"

Priya throws up her arms and sticks out her tongue. Her mouth is empty!

"AND PRIYA DOES IT! SHE'S MOVING ON!" Jamie yells excitedly. "Rick, I'm sorry; you're out of this one." Mets Hat Rick turns around and spits his mouth full of roach into the bucket waiting behind him.

I make quick eye contact with Osprey. I must look ill because he raises his brows at me in a very *you can do this* sort of way. My eyes slide to Remy next to him. Remy winks at me. My cheeks heat.

"All right—Kennedi, Trina, Leo, Orie—you're up!" Jamie directs.

Production assistants appear and change out the group-one plates for four new covered ones.

Kennedi, Trina, Leo, and I stand behind the table now. I feel like I'm going to be sick.

"All right, folks, last one to finish doesn't go to the next round. Take off your covers."

I remove the protective top to reveal a dead three-inch roach on a white plate. I gag again.

Jamie walks down the lineup. "Orie and Trina look like they're gonna hurl, and they haven't even touched the roach. Kennedi looks ready to murder it. They're boiled! It's already dead. Leo looking calm as a cucumber. He's in the zone. Are we ready?"

No one says anything.

"COMMENCE!" Jamie yells.

I try to pick mine up, but my arm flails up into the air instead. "Gah!"

"Leo and Kennedi attacking it," Jamie announces. "Juice spewing everywhere."

I glance over at Kennedi to my left. Her eyes are twisted up in disgust, but she's chomping nonetheless, roach legs and bits going everywhere in her mouth.

"Leo! Moving on!" Jamie yells.

Oh my god. I try to pick up my roach again and drop it. UGH, IT'S GROSS. I DON'T WANT TO FEEL ITS SHELL.

"Kennedi! Moving on!" Jamie yells. "It's down to Trina and Orie, both of whom have yet to even put it in their mouths."

I glance at Trina next to me. She's staring down at the roach like she's going to cry.

"Trina, are you gonna eat it?" I ask quietly.

Trina doesn't answer.

"We've got one spot left—who's gonna take it? Will someone tag in? Are these women so comfortable in the game, they don't even think they need to try?" Jamie prods.

Ugh. I blow out a breath, reach down, and snatch up the bug. "EW!" My fingers physically don't want to hold it. The thing falls to the ground by my feet. "Noo!" I swoop down and pick it up. Drop it back onto the plate.

Jamie's talking, but I can't hear her anymore. Trina picks up her bug and drops it back onto her plate. I glance up at the other half of my castmates, watching us. We must look pathetic. Remy's biting his lip. I catch his eye. *DO IT!* he mouths.

"Come on, Orie! You can fucking do it!" Kennedi says next to me. "It tastes like crab!"

"COME ON, TRINA. YOU GOT IT, BABE!" Priya yells from the sidelines.

There's a crunch beside me as Trina bites into her roach, green juice spewing. She arcs over her plate, all of it falling out of her mouth, as she retches. *Shit.*

I glance back at Kennedi, wondering if there's a chance she'll eat this one, too. "Don't look at it, woman! Just bite and chew!" she demands.

Shit. Shit. Shit. I squeeze my eyes shut, grab the bug, bring it up to my mouth, and rip into it. Juice spews everywhere. I choke over the plate.

"DON'T YOU DARE SPIT IT OUT," Kennedi yells.

"Kennedi pulling Orie through this," Jamie narrates.

I hold my nose, chewing frantically. It's crunchy and mushy and—I gag again but keep it in.

"Oof, Trina is throwing her chewed-up roach back into her mouth over and over and letting it fall back onto her plate repeatedly," Jamie calls.

Don't think about it, don't think about it. It's chicken. *It's chicken.* By some miracle, I swallow.

"BLEH!" I shake out my body before stuffing the second half of the thing in my mouth without looking at it. Oh god, the legs. Oh god. EW, EW, EW.

"IT'S SCRAMBLED EGGS, ORIE. YOU'RE DOING IT," Kennedi screams.

Chew, chew, chew, chew, chew. I watch as a leg falls out of my mouth onto the plate. OH GOD.

"Trina's got it all in her mouth. Orie's got it all in her mouth. We have a showdown, folks. Who's going to swallow first! That sounded dirty, and I guess it kind of is—you're both chomping on a roach. There are literal guts dripping down your chin."

It's scrambled eggs. I swallow again, feeling like the entire bug is stuck in my esophagus and I barely have room to breathe.

"The leg!" Kennedi screams.

I glance over at Trina jumping up and down as she frantically chews like a boxer getting ready for a match. I throw the leg in my mouth. *Ew.* I've come this far. IT CANNOT BE FOR NAUGHT. It's protein.

I crunch down on it.

Swallow. Throw open my mouth.

Jamie's eyes bulge. "ORIE PULLS IT OUT! Girl, you are moving on! Wow! Trina, I'm so sorry, babe; you're out of the challenge."

Kennedi claps me on the back as I spin around to vomit into the bucket behind the table.

The PAs have reset the plates with new ones. Kennedi, Priya, Osprey, Leo, Remy, and I stand behind the table, ready for the next phase.

"Okay, round two!" Jamie announces. "The first three people to finish here will move on to the final course. Take off your plate covers."

A chorus of faint gasps and *oofs* echoes around me. I'm too afraid to look. I exhale a slow breath and whip off my cover. A screech rakes out of me as I stumble away from the table. A tarantula the size of my face spans the plate.

"A lot of reactions for the boiled tarantula," Jamie notes cheerily. "I'm told it's also going to taste like crab. And, or, digested insects. Lovely! Are we ready?"

"YES," Remy says from the end of the table.

Jamie grins at all of us. "Go!"

Immediately, I start to cry. I glance over at Remy who's already ripped off a big chunk of it. He's chewing like a machine. Osprey, Leo, and Priya, too.

"Everyone going at it except Orie. She's getting emotional. You gotta start to stay in the game, babe," Jamie says.

I can't even make myself touch it. "I can't do it," I mumble. "I can't."

"You can!" Kennedi screams as she rips off another piece, her jaw opening and closing to a dramatic degree, like she's trying to create a space for the thing in her mouth where her tongue won't have to interact with it.

I look desperately to Jamie. "If I eat this, the spiders will set a curse upon my family! All this spider's descendants will hunt me for the rest of time. I'll have to name my daughter Tarantula to break the spell, and then society will make fun of my daughter for the rest of time, and I'll know she's being protected from a horrifying spider-devouring demise, but I'll also feel terrible for eternity because it'll all come back to me making the inane, irresponsible decision to eat this and anger them in the first place!"

"Orie out here catastrophizing like nobody's business." Jamie glances down the line. "REMY MOVING ON!"

I glance down at my tarantula again and back away from the plate like it's coming for me.

"Orie still hasn't even touched hers! She's really worried about having to name her first child Tarantula as penance."

Remy appears next to me and rips off a giant piece of my spider with his teeth, gnashing it down. My chest convulses in an awkward laugh-sob. Remy's trying to keep me in it. I start crying harder.

"REMY! MAKING A HUGE STATEMENT STEPPING IN FOR ORIE, a second tarantula all up in his mouth," Jamie yells excitedly.

Down the table, Osprey sticks out his tongue. "OSPREY MOVING ON!" Jamie yells.

Remy is already three-quarters of the way done with my tarantula. I'm speechless. Remy (as me), Leo, and Kennedi are all working for third place.

"And Leo moving on!" Jamie announces. "Kennedi just a second too slow. Remy for Orie, wow, just one bite left. You do have to finish it if you want to move on, but you're still moving on."

"Thank you," I say quietly as Remy eats my last bite of tarantula leg.

"I got you," he breathes, before moving back to his spot at the table.

"Kennedi, Priya, Orie, I'm sorry, babes; you're out," Jamie instructs. "It's Remy, Leo, and Osprey moving on to the final round."

I'm still crying. I can't stop crying. What's wrong with me? Someone takes my arm and escorts me to the area where my eliminated castmates are gathering to watch the final showdown.

"Orie, tamp this down. It's okay." Kennedi's voice. I nod without looking at her as PAs set the table again.

Jamie starts the final round. Six live, thick, moving beetle grubs wiggle around on the plates. Two per finalist. *Triple gag.*

"All right, like we said, two of you will gain immunity today! One of you will not. These grubs are alive; they're juicy. They're nutritious. Ready? On your marks. Get set. Go."

Remy chucks the first wobbling fat worm into his mouth and . . . swallows.

"Holy. Okay, Remy just swallowed one whole. *Alive.* Leo's chomping the whole thing in his mouth. Osprey bit into his. Remy throwing in the second—are you gonna chew that?" Jamie coughs as Remy swallows a second live bug.

I heave in breath after deep breath. If Remy wins this, we're fine. Stop freaking crying. You tried. You ate a roach.

Remy opens his empty mouth.

"REMY WINS IMMUNITY, A BEAST," Jamie declares. "CAN YOU FEEL THOSE THINGS IN YOUR STOMACH! Osprey and Leo working on that last grub."

Leo swallows and sticks out his tongue.

"LEO WINS IMMUNITY."

Jamie and Z line us up in front of them. Z passes each of us a marker and a piece of parchment. I take mine carefully. I guess we're not raising our hands to vote this time.

"Okay," Jamie starts, "today, you can't vote for Leo or Remy. You have ten minutes to discuss among yourselves before you'll have to write down a name and put it in this bucket."

A PA runs out with a big heart-shaped cookie jar and a small coffee table. They place it in front of Jamie. My fingers tighten nervously around my marker.

Jamie smiles at us wickedly. "Go."

We all stand there dumbstruck for a moment.

"Timer is ticking, y'all, go!" Jamie repeats.

Kennedi moves first. She grabs my arm and pulls me aside. The second she does, chaos erupts between everyone else.

She's being way too obvious about our alliance.

"We have to vote Osprey!" she hisses. "I can see he got his fangs in you."

I shake my head. Fangs? "He said he's willing to work with us! Maybe we should vote Trina?"

"Trina's not a physical threat! And we want a woman to win the game! We can't vote a woman! Womentopia, Orie! We need the numbers! It's four-four right now. We have to go Rick or Osprey. Leo, honestly, is a great guy, and I think he's the type that's loyal to a fault. I think I've got him in Womentopia, but if we cut Rick today, Leo's not going to trust me. They're ex-boyfriends."

My stomach twists. "Please, I honestly think I have Osprey and not the other way around!" I tell her desperately.

I think Osprey does actually have my back, and I haven't even talked to Rick. I can't lose Osprey. "Please, let's do Rick!" I beg her.

Kennedi presses her lips together. "I mean." She blows out a long breath. "Damn it. Okay, maybe we can still get Leo on our side. We can explain the pickle we're in, and if we do get Rick out, Leo won't have his closest ally, and he'll be more likely to cling to other relationships, like the one I've made with him the past three days."

"Okay, so we're going to go Rick?" I whisper.

She nods. "Okay, you get Remy or Osprey on board, I'll get the girls, that's five. We can do this!"

She runs away from me to confer with Priya.

Osprey, who was talking to Priya, comes over to me. "Who does Kennedi want?" he asks quietly.

I glance from Kennedi and Priya to Remy who's in discourse with Leo and Rick. Trina's walking to join Priya and Kennedi.

"Kennedi wants Rick," I tell him. "Are you good with that?"

Osprey shakes his head, eyes spearing through me. "Priya and Trina are gunning for you, Tube Stop."

My stomach splits into two pieces and lands on my feet. "Oh god."

"They think you and Remy are too strong of a team, and they want to break up a power couple. Remy's got immunity, so you're on the chopping block. I think I've got a real bond with Rick and Leo, though. I might be able to get them to vote with me."

My heart taps double time. "Oh god. *Oh god.* Who do you think is more strongly advocating for me?"

"Trina. I don't think she likes Remy."

"Why not! Remy's a sweetheart!" I groan. "Did she even give him a chance?"

"She thinks he's too big of a threat, and she needs to weaken him—i.e., you."

"Will you vote Trina with me?" I hiss desperately.

Osprey nods. "Yes."

"FOUR MINUTES!" Z announces.

"Okay, you tell Leo and Rick! I'll get Remy," I bleat desperately. I run toward Remy, clutching my neck. It's slick and clammy.

I'm anxiety sweating.

I can't go home. I think I'm doing pretty well out here. I am. I'm doing well! I'm not done. My family needs this. And Remy's and my love story is just beginning! We're about to move into act two of our rom-com.

Remy sees me stumbling toward him and breaks away from Leo. Osprey pulls Leo's attention.

"Who are you thinking?" I ask Remy.

"Rick just told me Trina and Priya are pushing for you in order to weaken me; we've got to do Trina."

I nod, nerves eating me alive. "Yeah. Okay, good. Yes. Trina. You, me, Osprey, and the baseball boys for Trina gives us the numbers."

"Yeah, I think we're good; don't worry. I got you," he says, holding such intense eye contact that my insides start to glow with anticipation. I can't wait to be alone with him again.

"Okay," I whisper. Over to my left, Kennedi's still conferring with Trina and Priya, and now Osprey's in the mix. They're all nodding. I run over to grab her.

"TIME!" Jamie yells.

Kennedi catches my eye. She gives me a thumbs-up as we gather back in a line. She's still planning to vote Rick. I shake my head the slightest bit and mouth *Trina.* She shakes her head and mouths *NO! Rick! Trust me.*

I look over at Osprey. He mouths *Trina*.

Shit, shit, shit.

"Find a spot alone, record your vote, and drop it in the heart," Jamie instructs.

I huddle over my strip of paper on the far edge of the gross food table. I have to go Trina. She wants me out; she wants Remy out.

I can't vote Rick when Osprey says Rick is on our side! I want Womentopia to thrive, but not if that means I'm gonna be voted out! If Trina wants me or Remy eliminated, she won't stop until she has me or Remy eliminated. That's how games like this work. I've seen it time and time again.

My hand shakes as I write Trina's name. I fold the parchment, walk to the jar, and drop it in.

I bounce on my heels as Z lines us all back up to hear the results.

Trina and Priya are voting for me. But they would have had to convince Rick and Leo and someone else to turn on me. I don't think any of my alliances (AP Chem, Womentopia, or Paperback Party) would turn on me. I have all their backs.

The vote could be a tie. Which means, maybe we vote again like in *Survivor,* or maybe there's some other sort of tiebreaker in this game.

I don't know. I don't know. I don't know! Jamie wanders off with the heart for a moment, and Z stays, observing us.

Kennedi is on my left, and Remy is on my right. Kennedi smiles at me. I turn slightly to smile back, feeling like a piece of shit.

Jamie returns and sets the jar back on the tiny makeshift coffee table. She pulls out a parchment. "First vote." She turns it around to face us. "Rick."

I blow out a breath.

"Second vote." She pulls the second vote and turns it around. "Rick."

My stomach drops. *Did she get Priya and Trina to change their vote?*

"Third vote, Rick."

She did. She got Priya and Trina to vote with us.

Jamie pulls the next vote. Turns it around. "Fourth vote, Trina. Three votes Rick, one vote Trina."

Did I just fuck over Womentopia's first big move?

Jamie turns around the next vote. "Trina. Three votes Rick. Two votes Trina."

Jamie turns over the sixth vote. "Trina. We're tied, three votes Rick, three votes Trina."

I fucked over Womentopia.

She pulls the seventh vote. "Trina. Three votes Rick. Four votes Trina. One vote left. If we have a tie, the two players with equal votes will participate in a tie-breaking challenge. If not, the player voted out will be promptly escorted off the premises."

Jamie pulls the final vote, unfolds it. "Third player eliminated from season one of *Attached at the Hip* . . ." She turns it around. "Trina."

Kennedi tenses next to me. I feel her head turn in my direction. I don't have the courage to meet her eyes. I stare at Trina's name on my parchment. In my handwriting. She doesn't know it's my handwriting.

But she knows it's me.

Because Priya and Trina voted together. And she was counting on me to bring the other two votes, and I didn't.

I hope she doesn't hate me.

"Trina, you have been eliminated. Z will escort you off the island."

Trina steps out of the line and glares at us. I don't make eye contact. Hot searing shame floods my veins.

I hate upsetting people. How do I make this better? I want to go to the cave and sit with Remy. He'll know what to do. We'll regroup. It's going to be fine.

Z leads Trina away, and Jamie takes a step closer. "Okay." She smiles. "Congratulations! Things just got interesting. Lines have been drawn. Politics are in play. It's time for the choosing ceremony. Remy, please step forward. You're first today."

Remy steps up next to Jamie. His eyes sweep over us. I beam at him proudly. He smiles back, looks over at Jamie, and says: "Kennedi."

My heart does a double take. I glance from Kennedi to Remy. Kennedi doesn't look at me as she walks over.

He picked Kennedi?

The math plays out in my head as Jamie clips them together with a purple rope and directs them to the side. My lungs seize up.

Leo has to pick me. He has to pick me. What can I do to make him pick me? I stare at Leo. He's three people down the line, watching Jamie. I glare at his Yankees cap, trying to manifest telepathy. *Pick me, Leo. Pick Orie!*

"Leo, babe, you're up," Jamie says.

Leo takes his place next to Jamie. For a second our eyes meet. I smile sweetly at him. *PICK ME.*

He opens his mouth and says, "Rick."

Help.

Of course he'd pick Rick. They were a real-life couple. *He doesn't want Rick to go to exile a second time!*

"Osprey, you're up," Jamie announces.

Osprey steps forward. My head spins. I clutch my temples. *Osprey can't pick me. You can't partner with the same person back to back. He has to pick Priya.*

Osprey settles next to Jamie and shoots me a look. Not a sympathetic one. A lecture-y one. An encouraging, teacherly look that makes me want to shrink into a grain of sand and disappear into the center of the earth because no one's going to pick me. I am going to be the spare kid in gym class.

"We have a situation here!" Jamie says. "By default, Osprey is with Priya since he was with Orie last cycle. Orie, you are the unchosen."

Rub it in.

"How are you feeling about all this?" Jamie asks.

Sweaty. I feel like my innards are melting. I feel the camerapeople closing in like a cluster of heat lamps turning on at an outdoor restaurant.

I can't do this. I can't go to exile. I'm going to die. I'm going to starve. I'm going to lose my mind.

"Orie?" Jamie prompts.

I nod at Jamie. "I goor; I'm gro. I'm goot. Goot. Gort." I shake my head. "I'm gort! I'm GOOT." I shake out my arms. "God, good!"

THERE IT IS.

"Are you having a stroke?" Kennedi yells.

Jamie narrows her eyes. "Seriously, are you okay?"

"I am GOOD! I am good," I say loudly. "I am good," I say matter-of-factly.

"Are you?" Jamie says again.

"I am good!" I smile at her.

"Your face is scaring me." Jamie comes closer. "Do you want me to get medical?"

I shake my head no. "Leicester Square, I'm good!"

She searches my eyes. "Okay, I'll be escorting you to exile."

"Good! That's good!" I try to catch Remy's eye, but his gaze is firmly planted on his feet.

My throat constricts. Good. I'm good. I'm good. Breathe. One million dollars. One million dollars will keep my family from falling apart. One million dollars will let them keep the house. One million dollars will save us.

PAs enter the vicinity to escort the new pairs back out to their boats.

Jamie walks over to me. "Blink twice if your soul is being held hostage by an alien being."

"What?" I spurt.

"Thank god." She exhales. "You still know other words." Jamie puts an arm over my shoulders and squeezes my biceps. "It's gonna be okay."

I shake my head, tears burning the corners of my eyes. *No, it's not.*

TRANSCRIPT OF EDIT TO BE INSERTED DURING POST

JAMIE

Tell us what's happened.

ORIE

No one picked me at the choosing ceremony today.

JAMIE

How's exile been so far? Can you narrate your time?

ORIE

A boat dropped me off on this empty beach an hour ago
with this message in a bottle [holds up bottle]. I haven't
opened it yet. I've spent the first twenty minutes here
crying, stumbling around, gathering the tools to make a
fire. I have a flint and a machete and a pot. All the basics
I've had from the beginning. My canteen, all that. There's a
well.

[Orie nods, pressing her lips together. She tears up again.]

JAMIE

What's coming up?

ORIE

I think I know what happened with Remy. Today, Priya
and Trina were gunning for me because they think we're
a power couple, that we have too strong of a relationship,
and he couldn't add fuel to that fire or risk that image being
strengthened by picking me today. So, in hindsight, I mean,

he's doing what's best for our alliance. But I need to talk to him and make sure we're okay. I feel disconnected after six days apart with him being with other women. It's making me nauseous not being able to check in with each other.

JAMIE

What are your plans for the rest of the day?

ORIE

I . . . I guess I'm going to try to make some sort of shelter. [Tears start to well up again.] Try and find food. I'm so hungry.

JAMIE

Why don't you open your message now.

[Orie opens the message in a bottle. She unrolls it and reads it aloud.]

ORIE

Exile welcomes you. Adventure awaits you.

There's a limerick clue and a map.

Follow the map into the jungle; upon a rock you will a-stumble. Breach the top, and you will find a truly rare and valuable prize.

[long pause] Oh wow, an advantage?

JAMIE

You'll have to see.

ORIE

Are there any rules for when you're in exile?

JAMIE

Nothing out of the ordinary.

ORIE

Can I explore? Do I have to sleep fifty feet from this spot or whatever?

JAMIE

You have to spend the nighttime hours in this area and get water from your well, so I wouldn't go too far.

DAY 9—PRODUCER CONFESSIONAL NOTES
KENNEDI JACOBS—CONFESSIONAL #8

TRANSCRIPT OF EDIT

KENNEDI

Orie, of all people, screwed me over today. I worked my top-notch magic, completely spun Priya and Trina over to our side in a matter of *minutes*. MINUTES! After they were gunning so hard for ORIE. I SAVED HER ASS. And she screwed us over.

Orie thinks her connection with Remy is stronger and more valuable than her BFF-little-sister-she-never-had connection with me, which means that dude's gotta go.

Do I want to be livid and shun Orie? YES. Would that help my game? No. Orie lacks confidence. She was away from me and swayed by the other players because she can't make decisions herself. She needs to be directed. I just need to be there to direct her. I can still use her to my advantage here.

I know I'm sounding controlling, but I'm just playing the game.

PRODUCER Z

Do you think Orie's not smart enough to make her own decisions?

KENNEDI

I think Orie's too worried about hurting people's feelings and rocking the boat to make smart decisions. I need to be there to convince her feelings don't matter here.

PRODUCER Z

How are things going with you and Remy?

KENNEDI

Remy thinks he's Captain America. He's been droning on and on about how he had to sacrifice to further his and Orie's game by sending her to exile. He feels *"soooo bad."*

If you hated the idea so much, then you shouldn't have [censored] done it. There's always a choice, another path in games like these—you just have to be apt enough to find it.

If this guy brings up how he's doing this for his sister one more time, I'm going to slap him. How many times has he mentioned it in a confessional? *You're so noble.* Jesus Christ. Sit down.

33

All by Myself

DAY 9

This beach looks like every other beach: it has sand. There's no old sos sign here. No prebuilt shelter. No signs of previous life. Only the basic survival tools we're always given, my message in a bottle, and a map. I glance over at my new firepit. A cameraman hovers nearby.

Why couldn't I eat that spider for A MILLION DOLLARS? A *million* dollars, and I couldn't pick up a *dead spider* and eat it despite being hungrier than I've ever been in my life. I drag a hand down my face.

To think I was worried about being out here without makeup. About feeling naked. There are no damn mirrors, so after two days, you forget to even think about your appearance. I have absolutely no clue how disheveled I look, and honestly, I don't care. It doesn't matter.

What matters right now is the map to a game advantage. I have to get up and follow it. I need to keep trying. *I need to win.*

But I'm so hungry, and so sad—I feel like I'm made of noodles. Like I'm weak in the knees with loneliness. I wish Lark were here.

I close my eyes and imagine her next to me. It's not hard to predict what she'd say.

What are you doing! Get your ass to the advantage before the sun goes down. Chop, chop, Or!

I laugh to myself. I wonder how she's getting on without me on our socials. The longer I'm out here, the surer I become that I need to try and find my own thing.

Posting on Instagram and social media—it doesn't leave me feeling good about myself or accomplished in the way I want a career to make me feel.

For fun, it's great! And it's great for connecting with new people that you have things in common with! I love that. But I don't love being seen as a walking, talking advertisement. I don't love living in fear of the moment a mob of strangers may turn against me.

Lark was right, like she always is. That path is not mine. It was me piggybacking onto hers and hoping for the best.

I blow out a long breath, get my noodle legs under me, and stand. I secure the machete around my waist and pack everything a sad girl trekking alone through the jungle may need: flint, first aid kit, canteen, sweatshirt—the works.

The advantage map's a simple, elementary-looking thing with a long, classic, old-timey dotted line that winds around landmarks through an illustrated jungle.

I have quite the hike ahead of me.

I crunch over dead leaves as I follow the map line into the jungle. The cameraman walks noiselessly behind me.

Fifteen minutes into the journey I find a tall stick, one I can use for walking and turn into a stabby weapon like I did with Osprey to spear crabs.

Just thinking about that crab makes my stomach cramp. I should have eaten the goddamn tarantula. What am I going to do now? What if I have to resort to pulling up tree roots and eating termites off of them like that one guy in that one season of *Survivor*?

Ten minutes later, I come to an abrupt halt, blinking amid the greenery.

Fruit. There's a fruit tree! *Nature's McDonald's!* I hurry toward it.

Upon closer inspection, the fruit is, well, unreachable. My heart dips into the empty vacuum that is my stomach.

It's fifteen feet off the ground, and there are no branches to cling to along the way.

Cartoon Mulan climbing a massive wooden pillar outside her training camp pops into my head. She takes these two heavy weights on ribbons, locks them together to form a bandlike thing to loop around the pole, and uses it as leverage to help her climb to the top.

The bark of the tree isn't super smooth; it has ridges that could catch onto something like that.

I put down my stick, take off the machete belt, and remove the knife. This particular trunk isn't too wide. Maybe ten inches in diameter. I loop the belt around it and hold tight to either side. Then I raise it as high as I can on the tree, lean back, and place my feet against the trunk so I'm pressing into it, leaning on a diagonal.

I maneuver my legs higher, stepping up the trunk. Once I'm good and scrunched in a tight little sideways ball, I straighten my legs and thrust my arms and the belt *up,* hoping to gain purchase at a higher point.

There's a moment of weightlessness where I pray to the universe the belt will catch. I fall back into a lean, squeezing my eyes shut as I slide for an everlasting second before it finds a ridge and locks into place.

I exhale, heart pounding in my ears. *HELL YEAH.* One more round of scrunch into a little ball, spring up, and hope for the best with the belt should bring me within reach of the fruit.

My arms are shaking now, fingers clutching hard at the leather belt. Slipping a bit. I bring my feet up, carefully maneuvering into a new scrunched position. I make the mistake of looking down.

"Whoa—oh man," I breathe, closing my eyes. I am ten feet off the ground. I redirect my attention upward. The fruit. It's so close now.

I'm so hungry. I count to five. Exhale. And straighten, throwing my arms upward to find a new, higher groove.

My stomach drops before I do. The leather belt skids down the bark, my sneakered feet scraping uselessly against the trunk. My fingers slip from one side of the belt and—"Ugggghhhoh!"

My right foot smashes into the ground, and I slam onto my right arm and shoulder.

I lie still for a full minute as raw panic pulses through my veins. I fell out of a tree. AND I DIDN'T GET THE FRUIT.

I roll onto my back to make sure my arm is alive. It seems to be. Slowly, I try to get up to test my ankle. It works.

I didn't die. But I can't move on without the fruit. My eyes slide over to the tall stick lying two feet away in the dirt. I slap a palm to my face.

Why don't I ever THINK? WHY DIDN'T I TRY TO POKE THE FRUIT WITH MY BIG STICK?

I just jumped full force into the first random idea that flitted through my brain; now I'm going to look like a dunce on national television.

Why didn't I even think to *think* Wes might not be happy with me? Why would I assume I was the only one having second thoughts about the forever nature of our relationship?

I snatch the walking stick off the ground and hold it aloft as high as I can under the tree. I'm still over a foot away from the fruit.

I was with Wes *all the time,* and somehow, I missed that he was texting the girl who works at the Tea Shop for the last *five months.* He offered to go there and grab me tea *every day.*

I was so oblivious. I've been so *self-involved.*

I back up a few feet, run at the tree, and jump, gripping the stick like a spear. I stab at a fruit.

It makes light contact. I bend my knees as my feet slam back into the ground.

Why didn't I ever question why Dad *never drank?* Why have I never asked him about his teenage years? How did I not know my dad, my humanity guru and moral compass, had been arrested?

I back up and run at the tree again, this time holding the stick like a baseball bat. I swing as I'm airborne. The force of the fruit-stick collision reverberates down the wood. But nothing falls. My feet pound back into dirt.

I'm an adult; why wouldn't he ever open up to me! *Wouldn't it only make sense to warn me? Isn't addiction genetic?*

I back up again, panting now. Tears sting my eyes as I fumble into a different tree. I lean against it as my mind wind-tunnels back to the week I left.

To the rustling in my room in the middle of the night.

To the man standing over my bed, his hand in my purse hanging off the footboard. The paralyzing fear that seized my nervous system as I realized I was about to be murdered or worse. The sliding glass door outside my room must have been left unlocked. Or I must have forgotten to replace the rod I put in the slider.

The hand that slammed over my mouth when I screamed. The dirty green taste of cash on his fingers. The wild gush of tears that escaped before my eyes adjusted to the dark. The dizzying swirl of relief and confusion as I realized the man with his hand on my mouth was my father. Followed by the warring disconnect between who I know him to be and the scene unfolding before me.

The stumbling. The slurring. 4:08 A.M. burning into my retinas when I slid my eyes to the clock. The way he fell into the bedroom door, trying to escape, and belly flopped onto the carpet. How I didn't get up to help him.

I lay there unable to move. Trying to process what was happening. Suspended in the foggy abyss between awareness and sleep.

How was I supposed to look at him after that? He didn't say anything about it the next day. I couldn't tell Mom. I couldn't tell Lark.

I don't know if he even knows he did it. I don't even know if he remembers. Are the whites of my shocked eyes seared into the back of his skull like the bleary whites of his are on mine?

That was two days before Mom sat us on the couch for the meeting. Four days before I left. I didn't sleep the next two nights. All I could think was, what if it happens again? What do I do? I couldn't decide whether to hide my purse or leave it out for him.

Would he tear apart the room?

Was he himself at all in that moment? Was he some Mr. Hyde iteration of the man I know? Would he hurt me?

How could he not address it at our family meeting if he knew it had happened? Does my mom know? Why didn't he tell her? Did she know he was unraveling?

Water I can't afford to lose slips down my cheeks. I close my eyes. Count to five. Heave in three steadying breaths.

"WHY DOES EVERYONE FUCKING LIE TO ME?" I run at the tree again, calculating my aim according to what hasn't worked the last two times. A growl rips up my throat as I drive the stick upward to where the fruit attaches to the trunk. I feel it break through some ligament of the plant. There's an incredibly satisfying snap. My feet thump down, and two more clunks follow.

For a long second, I stare at the fallen fruit in disbelief. Then my screech of triumph slices through the ether. I dance around my bounty like a child.

"I got the fruit!" I pick up one of the large yellow-green ovals. I think it's a papaya! "I GOT TWO PAPAYAS!!!" I scream to no one.

I pop one into my bag and set the other down in front of me, grabbing the machete and gripping it the way Osprey showed me. It slices through the fruit with a juicy *shwip*.

Joy unspools in my chest like a runaway ream of yellow ribbon. LOOK AT ME PROVIDING FOR MYSELF!

I pick up half the papaya, carve out a square piece of the meat, and pop it into my mouth. It tastes like independence.

The trail has sort of ended. Now all I have to go on are the landmarks on the map. I keep stopping to compare the tiny drawn objects with three-dimensional things around me, worrying I may have made a wrong turn.

I wonder how long Wes was unhappy before he started talking to the Tea Shop Girl. Exactly how long I had been missing it. *It's humiliating* how much I agonized over how hurt he would be if I broke up with him.

I was so focused on myself and my non-feelings, I treated him . . . less than. I took his generosity for granted. I was so confused about my own life, I let it mess up the happiness of the people closest to me.

I must have been missing hints from Lark about our content. She's a hint dropper. She doesn't do confrontation unless it's absolutely essential. None of us Lennoxes do. We're a nonconfrontational family. We push through and pretend everything's fine.

I missed my dad's business falling apart.

I've been living in my own little bubble in the basement. Flouncing about, pontificating in my unhappiness, ignoring everyone else's problems with absolutely no plans for any sort of resolution.

I don't want to be like that. I don't want to be *that person*. I want to be proactive. I want to be a person who does the thing. Who helps people. I want to be someone other people can depend on.

I *need* to win this game. That is where my primary focus has to be. I need to bring back the money. I—

I go still as I emerge onto a small beach . . . a cove.

To my right, jutting out into the water, is a hulking black rock. It has to be at least twenty-five feet tall and twenty feet wide. It's pyramidlike in shape. A natural, crooked, flawed pyramid covered in indents and out-croppings that appears to be flat at the top.

I sigh. Time for another climb.

If I hadn't eaten that papaya, I don't think I would have made it up this rock. The water is rougher on this beach. It crashes against the outcrop-ping and spritzes the area in a light layer of mist every few minutes. My hands are bloody and cut up from gripping uneven bits of stone. I'm damp, and my arms are shaking as I approach the top.

My cameraman has switched to his drone. It's been flying around me like some giant alien wasp since I arrived in the clearing.

I haul myself up to the semi-flat top, throw a leg over the edge, and roll over onto the rough, uneven rock.

Laughter rumbles through me as I lie there on my back, breathing hard, staring at the sky, simultaneously exhausted and exhilarated. I crossed the island with an elementary cloth map—on my own! On a social experiment romantic-slanted *Survivor* spin-off reality show!

I have three solid alliances! If I play this right, if I keep my people in the game, I *can get to the end.* I wonder what Remy's doing with Kennedi right now. Is she one of his three matches?

I should probably talk to Remy about Osprey. Not that anything's hap-pened with Osprey, but just that we clicked. So he knows. So he doesn't feel like I'm being secretive. I want to form a solid foundation for us to build on after the show. The vague future he painted, I want that. I've always loved reading, but I find films, their design, their structure, and all the hype they create for a story endlessly captivating.

Books are so crammed full of great lines that you can't possibly remember them all. But a film—you can hold on to a film word for word, scene for scene. That's beautiful and awe-inspiring in so many ways. Words have power, and their reach expands exponentially once they've been memorialized via film. Great visuals make the words stickier. Dialogue that shines on a page can sparkle on a screen. A film can permeate the zeitgeist in such a tangible way.

Back in freshman year of high school, I had mentioned writing movies to Lark in passing after watching a crappy book-to-movie adaptation, and she'd laughed. Squashed the idea with a well-meaning but poorly thought-out comment about it not being an actual, attainable job. I'd laughed back. Told her she was right. That *I was just kidding*.

When I brought it up randomly again later that year, she dropped a more thorough hammer. Nobody actually becomes a screenwriter. They live on odd jobs, struggling to make ends meet, writing pages and pages of story that no one will ever read. I laughed again. Said, *Oh. Yeah, I hadn't thought about it. Hadn't considered the logistics.* And I realized she was right. There was no path for me to get anywhere near anything like that.

Until now. Working in that world would be fostering an actual passion. Even the prospect of reviewing movies more seriously sends little jolts of lightning running over my skin. Doing that along with someone else would be—spectacular.

Remy, Jerri, and I could start a podcast together. Or a YouTube channel or a TikTok or all of those things. It would get our production company's name out there, and we could build a community while we're getting started. I could write my first script and work our socials. We just have to come up with a great name!

The potential of it all thrums through me.

Remy is like . . . a delicious wrap. (Yes, I had that papaya, but I'm still hungry. One fruit doesn't magically erase the need for three meals a day.) He's spicy and big and full of mystery. I never know what's going to be in the next (metaphorical) bite of him I take. He can be dangerously hot and a little obnoxious, but other bites are sweet and comforting. I love unveiling his unknowns. There's so much more to him than meets the eye. And he has such a great relationship with his sister.

I love that he and Jerri get along so well. I have a running theory that guys who have strong friendships with their sisters have patient, open hearts. (Yes, I'm mostly basing this off of books and movies, but guess what? Books and movies are written by humans.)

Remy and I have fate pushing for us. The universe has spun us back together after four years apart.

The drone pulls my attention for a moment, and I remember the purpose for climbing this rock. I didn't come up here to *contemplate life*.

I twist onto my stomach. Toward the front end of this uneven boulder, tucked into a shallow crevasse, is a tiny yellow wrapped package.

It takes me a minute, but I gather my limbs back under me and hobble over to pluck it from the stone. There's a small scroll attached.

Congratulations, you have found an advantage. Unless you'd like to try for first place in the next challenge, you do not have to compete. You have earned an automatic second-place finish, meaning you will have second choice of partner for the next cycle.

I unwrap the package. Inside is a brown leather bracelet imprinted with the number 2. I secure it on my wrist.

34

Fireside

I ate my other papaya.

I've curled up on the sand next to my firepit, clutching my walking stick that I've now sharpened into a spear. I doubt I'll get any sleep tonight. I can't just close my eyes out here on the sand next to the ocean.

What if a shark man comes out and decides to devour me whole? I wouldn't even be able to attempt to defend myself before I die. If I'm conscious, at least I have a shot at poking out his eyes or bonking him on the nose with my sharp stick. I have to be my own guard dog. The camera guy's not going to protect me. He's going to film it; it's his job.

I'm shivering in my sweatshirt. I miss Remy's warmth at my back. I miss his arm around my waist. I miss our cave. I miss Kennedi making fun of me. I miss Osprey's calm, steady presence.

As much as I'm "okay" here by the fire alone, I hate being here by myself. I want a partner. I want to love someone. I want to take care of them, and I want them to take care of me. Is that so terrible? Everyone says you have to stop trying to fall in love for it to happen. It'll happen *when you least expect it.* Why can't I expect it? Why am I not allowed to want to fall in love, for it to happen for me?

Is that why I couldn't love Wes? Because I wanted it too much? I wanted my own romance so hard that it couldn't possibly work out despite the perfect setup for a childhood-best-friends-to-lovers trope?

Isn't that piece of advice kind of sexist in itself? Because women tend to look for romance, and dudes tend to be afraid of it for years, so we should pretend to be uncaring and aloof?

I care so much. I can't not care. How can I pretend I don't care about the thing I've always cared the most about just so that very thing can finally happen! It's literally nonsensical.

I want a career, too. I want to do things. But why can't I do both?

I want to spend more time with Remy. I want to know what it's like to be *with him* with him. I want to commit to one of the many career paths I'm interested in and take a risk in real life like I've been doing out here in trees and with machetes and papayas and tall rocks.

The first rays of light are breaking over the horizon. I've been wearily tending the fire all night. My joints are stiff, and my muscles are tight.

I get up, fill my pot at the well, boil it over my fire, and head off down the beach. I'm going to circle this island with my spear. Look for more food.

I'm walking as the sun rises over the ocean. I walk until the hunger gnawing at my stomach makes my legs start to quake, and I've finished all my water. I walk until I come across . . . a tiny makeshift tentlike shelter right on the sand. The top is made of woven palm fronds. Inside there are woven palm fronds covering the sand: like a makeshift floor mat. There's a blanket folded up and a single pillow.

I'm so tired.

Maybe I'm hallucinating? Did production take pity on me and set this up? I lie down, unfold the blanket, lay my head on the pillow, and sleep.

35

Intruder

DAY 10

"Orie?" The voice is soft and concerned. I stir.

"What the hell are you doing here?" That voice is not.

I blink my eyes open and sit up. Some sand comes with me, stuck to my face. I dust it off. The pillow is sitting next to my head. I've rolled off. Kennedi and Remy are hunched over, staring at me.

"Huh?" I mumble, blinking some more.

"How did you get here?" Remy smiles. I grin back sleepily, heart glowing in my chest. *Remy's here.* Kennedi clacks her tongue.

"Why are you in our shelter, Orie?" Kennedi demands.

I run a hand down my face. "I walked here . . . I just kept following the beach."

"Are you okay? Are you hungry? Are you allowed to be here? We have some coconuts."

"You didn't vote for Rick!" Kennedi snaps.

I put a hand to my head. I feel so groggy. "Can you give me a second? I must have been mid-REM cycle."

"Oh no, did us returning to *our* camp interrupt your beauty rest?" Kennedi takes her canteen and slogs a sheet of water onto me.

"Gah!" It splashes over my yoga pants, making it look and feel like I peed myself.

"Was that necessary?" Remy says.

"Yes," Kennedi affirms.

"It's okay. I deserved it," I mumble.

Kennedi, Remy, and I sit by their campfire. Their coconut is chopped and roasting in a pot perched over the flames.

"So, I guess I'm allowed to be here," I ponder aloud. "You can wander in exile. Which begs the question, who else is within walking distance?"

"Why didn't you vote for Rick?" Kennedi asks.

"Because I didn't think you were going to flip Priya and Trina so fast! That was wizardry! I thought they were going to vote me out."

"Well, I did flip them that fast; you doubted my skills, and you let down the entire female *Survivor* community."

"I'm sorry. I thought I was making the best decision for my advancement in the game. It's a cardinal rule: when someone's gunning for you, vote them out! I didn't mean to screw up your plans. I didn't think we had the vote."

"I told her to vote for Trina," Remy says conversationally.

"Yeah, I'm aware," Kennedi snarks.

"Are you two . . . not getting along?"

"We're fine," Remy says.

"What's around your wrist?" Kennedi asks, popping a darkened piece of coconut meat into her mouth.

I hold my arm up for them to inspect. "I found an advantage. I get second choice next challenge."

"Nice!" Remy nods approvingly.

"I think we need to vote out Rick. He and Leo were in love back in college, and I'm getting the feeling they've slipped right back," Kennedi says.

"Keeping Rick and Leo provides a shield for me and you," Remy tells me. "People think we're a threat. I know Jerri would kill me if I got rid of our perfect shield."

"But at this point, there's only seven of us anyway," I argue.

"We also need to vote out Osprey," Kennedi injects. "He's too level-headed; that's dangerous."

Remy nods. "I'm open to that."

Kennedi looks to me.

I bob my head. "Ugh, yeah, he's really logical, but Rick is probably the more physical threat."

"All right, it's settled." Kennedi grins at Remy. "Orie and I want Rick. Two versus one. We're all voting Rick."

Remy sighs.

I nod to Kennedi. "Okay! The next person we vote out is Rick. Remy, can I have a word with you alone for a moment?"

Kennedi narrows her eyes. "You're kidding, right?"

"It's nothing gamey. I just would really love to talk to him for a minute."

"First off, of course it's gamey; it's inherently gamey. Second, I'm attached to him via rope."

"Can I take him eight feet away, and can you sing something? Please?"

Kennedi shoots me a sharp look. I shoot her a sad girl one back.

"FINE. I'm going in the shelter." She gets up, dragging Remy along with her. I follow behind.

Kennedi starts loudly singing the *Survivor* theme.

I turn to Remy. "I missed you."

He runs a finger down my cheek. "I missed you, too. It's been so weird not being able to like . . . text."

The statement lights a match in my chest. "I was thinking the same thing!"

"Good."

"So we're good?" I say quietly.

"We're great. AP Chemistry great."

"Happy to hear that." I smile up at him. He bends down and presses his lips to mine. A tiny sun bursts to life between us.

"I can hear you kissing," Kennedi comments.

We break apart. "Are you going to stay with us?" Remy asks.

"I'm only allowed to spend the night at my beach and get water from my well, so I have to head back."

Remy hugs me, leans his lips over my ear, and breathes very faintly, "We need to get rid of Kennedi."

My stomach twists.

"She's too cutthroat," he says. "We can't trust her."

I pull back and look into his gray eyes. He's been shaving out here, using the razor in his first aid kit, I guess. He takes my hands, sandwiches them, and kisses my knuckles. Then he hugs me to him and whispers into my hair, "I want us to win."

He releases me.

Kennedi pokes her head out of the shelter. "I would like a moment, just the two of us, Orie!"

Remy goes into the shelter and Kennedi swaps out. She hugs me and pulls back. "Hey, you're forgiven. For the Trina vote."

"Oh." I frown, tears pricking at my eyes. "Thank you."

"Onomatopoeia," she says.

I grin. "Kittens." Together we throw our heads up to look at the sky and bow our necks to stare at the ground, catching each other's eyes along the way.

I start the trek back to my beach.

36

Slides

DAY 12

Wind rages against us as we line up for our next challenge. It feels like my bangs are splayed straight up over my head: electrocuted chic. Jamie's hair flies in every direction as she claps her hands, eager to get started.

"Welcome, welcome to day twelve!" She has to project over the incredibly loud breeze rumbling through the area.

Behind her is a steep slide, as wide as a house, divided into seven different sections. Each section is a different color. There's a metal bar running across the top of them all—the kind that one would sit under pre-slide. Colorful matching flags atop each slide sector writhe around in the wind.

Jamie smiles at us. "Time's going fast, isn't it? We're just about at the halfway point. By now, I know you've all made at least one strong connection."

A drop of water falls on my head. I glance up at the sky. Another drop lands on my cheek. *Great.*

"Today, you're once again fighting for immunity from elimination and first dibs at the choosing ceremony." Jamie walks along our lineup, making eye contact with each of us individually as she yells over the storm stirring to life before our eyes.

"The choosing ceremony will be a little different this afternoon. We're leaning into our romantic side today. Each pair will be taken separately to a romantic location for a lovely five-course meal. So, choose wisely; you may want to take someone you've got sparks with." She smirks at us.

The idea of going on an actual date with Remy makes my organs flutter. Today, I get to choose Remy.

Rain patters down on us in a steady, even shower as Jamie throws her arms out and tosses her head back, readily embracing the weather as she screams, "Are we ready!"

There's a general mumbling from the seven of us lined up in front of her.

"Today the challenge is simple. You'll each take a spot on one of the slide sectors. When I say go, you'll slip forward, holding on to the bar overhead. The last person left hanging from the bar wins immunity and first choice. Orie has found an advantage that gives her an automatic second-place win today. She doesn't have to participate if she's satisfied with that position. She can try for first place so she has immunity from the vote, or sit out. The order of the choosing ceremony will continue based on how you do in the challenge. Let's get set up!"

I sit on the challenge bench hugging myself. The rain's coming down harder, and I feel like the wind is actively trying to blow me away. I hunch forward, waiting on pins and needles for someone to drop. My six castmates are hanging by their arms at the top of their respective slides, faces warped in concentration.

I jerk in surprise as Remy's right hand falls off the metal bar, quickly followed by his left. He goes flying down the yellow slide he was suspended over.

"WOW, Remy goes down first!" Jamie yells. "How the mighty do fall! From first place last challenge to last place today! Kennedi, Priya, Rick, Leo, and Osprey still going strong, but that rain and this wind are *wicked*. Things are getting slipperier by the second."

A sopping-wet Remy comes to sit next to me on the bench. He reaches out and squeezes my thigh in greeting. The contact sends a jolt of heat through me.

The more I think about his instinct to vote out Kennedi, the more I understand where he's coming from. Kennedi doesn't seem to like him.

She could easily turn everyone else against him. But hopefully, we're all still set to vote Rick.

"Rick drops!" Jamie calls as Rick and his Mets hat go flying down the slide and splash into the shallow pool at the bottom.

Thunder rumbles in the distance.

Jamie bellows over the rain, "We're down to Priya, Leo, Osprey, and Kennedi. All looking SOLID!"

With a curse, Priya goes flying down the slide.

"WITHOUT WARNING, PRIYA LOSES HER GRIP! Rain really starting to pummel them."

Rick, Priya, Remy, and I huddle together, shivering on the bench. I can't stop bouncing my heels around. Fifteen excruciating minutes pass. The rain's coming sideways now, pelting us from every angle.

Leo takes one hand off the metal bar and stretches out his fingers. He switches to his other arm and does the same thing.

"Risky move taking your hand off the bar. Doing okay up there, Leo?" Jamie asks.

"Fantastic," he calls. Thirty seconds later, Leo drops.

"And Leo's out! Would you look at this? We have a showdown between our first two challenge winners, Kennedi and Osprey. Who will prevail?"

I can't be sure, because he's so far up on that slide, but I swear to god Osprey looks straight at me as Jamie says this. The message is clear: *She's going to beat me.*

A wind burst so strong I have to concentrate on staying upright shoves into us. Leo and Rick's hats go flying. Two PAs appear out of nowhere to chase them.

I watch as Jamie presses a hand to her ear, eyebrows knitting together in concern.

Osprey drops and goes flying down the blue slide.

Kennedi wins immunity.

Z hands us each a marker and a strip of parchment. Mine's already wet when I take it from him.

"Do your best to keep that dry!" he says. "Kennedi has immunity, but you can vote for anyone else. You have ten minutes to discuss before the actual elimination. Go."

Kennedi runs into me and initiates our secret handshake-dance. I humor her, hunching through the movements in the rain.

"Okay, I know you're, like, in love with him, but is there any universe in which we can vote out Remy?" she asks quickly.

I sigh inwardly and shake my head, hopping around to stay warm. "I'm not ready; I still think he's a good ally."

She nods once. "All right, Rick?"

I nod back. "Yep."

Kennedi grabs my elbows as another gust slams into us. I bend my legs to ground myself against its force.

"Okay," Kennedi says. "I'll get Priya; you get Osprey and Remy?"

"Got it. What should we tell Leo and Rick?"

"If they ask, let's tell them it's Priya."

We break apart. On cue, Remy, Osprey, and Leo break as well. Rick and Priya look up belatedly, and we all reshuffle, soaked, freezing, and exhausted. Osprey speeds over, back against the wind, hair slipping out of his bun.

"Is Kennedi gunning for me?" he asks.

"No! She's all in on Rick. We want to break up him and Leo; they're a well-cemented couple! Are you okay with that? I know you've bonded with Leo."

He nods. "I feel better voting off Rick than Leo. Leo and I have a bit of a thing." The wind pushes me into Osprey. I stumble and he steadies me. He has a thing with Leo. *Cool.*

I do my best to smile. "All right, Paperback Party out! If Rick and Leo ask, it's Priya."

I bound away from Osprey and right into Remy.

"Hey," Remy greets me with a small smile. "We going Rick today? Can I ask why are we holding on to Leo? He's better at challenges than Rick."

"Because Kennedi and Osprey are voting with us, and they've both made connections with Leo during one of the cycles but not with Rick. Rick got the short end of the stick here. He's only been paired with Leo and Priya."

"That sucks. I really like those guys."

"We'll have to hang out with them after the game!" I say.

We shuffle one last time, and I end up next to Leo and Rick. "Kennedi says—" I start.

"TIME!" Jamie roars. Her floofy neon hair has completely deflated; it sticks in ringlets against her face. "ALL RIGHT! We're going to do this quickly! Submit your votes. I'm gonna add them up."

Jamie wastes no time being dramatic today. The rain has only intensified. The sky has darkened to a deep threatening gray, the sun completely swallowed up by the clouds. Thunder roars closer. The vote ends up being two for Priya, five for Rick. Rick is escorted off the beach and onto a boat by Z. We all shout our apologies and well wishes.

And then it's time to choose.

Kennedi stands in front of the five of us left and chooses Priya. I catch her eye, and she winks at me.

I choose Remy. He picks me up and swings me around, and I feel like I'm in the first act of *The Notebook* (if that scene took place during a wild storm in the South Pacific).

Leo chooses his only remaining option, Osprey. Maybe with Rick gone, they'll be able to get to know each other better.

A pang of sadness clangs through me.

"Congratulations, final six!" Jamie belts over the weather. "It's been a long twelve days, and I'm getting live updates in my ear right now—" A PA runs out with our colored rope tethers. "Hold on, Ray, don't tether," Jamie directs. "Shit. This storm has actually been upgraded to a cyclone. We're going to have to evacuate right now."

The six of us blink at one another, shaking in the endless onslaught of rain.

"The game will be placed on hold while we're out of commission here!" Jamie instructs. "For all of your safety, we need to get you and all the crew indoors as soon as possible! We're bringing a couple 'copters around."

37

Quarantine

DAY 12

Everyone's damp and exhausted. Examining their hands. Sleeping sitting up.

The past hour has been chaos. Two helicopters landed in the clearing next to the slide challenge. Jamie loaded us all inside, and in a flurry of panic, the pilots whipped us off the small island we were on and over to the mainland. The storm should pass by morning.

They've dropped us in a windowless magenta meeting room on the fourth floor of a small Fiji resort. We're dispersed across various pieces of furniture. Zarar has asked us politely not to speak or physically interact with each other to maintain the integrity of the game.

I'm scrunched up in a ball on a pink, single-person sofa with a back made to look like a seashell. Remy's at the edge of a deep pink couch a few feet away. He looks up and smiles at me every so often before returning to his exhaustion stance: leaning over his legs, forearms resting on his thighs, hanging his head.

Kennedi's on the light pink carpeted ground, a few feet from my solo sofa, stretching. Priya's on a decorative chair, her head slumped and eyes closed, sleeping. Leo's on a light blue two-person love seat opposite the couch Remy is on. Osprey's on the floor leaning against the light blue love seat, his head propped up by a bent arm, eyes slipping shut. Effectively, we all make up a big circle around a coffee table full of beachy decorative knickknacks. Z is on a dining room chair at the head of our circle. Babysitting us.

Leo's anxious. His foot taps out a faint, rapid rhythm against the carpet. He's probably upset; he just lost his number-one ally. Now he has to go on a date with Osprey, and he's probably realized he's always loved Rick and wants to get back together and doesn't want to potentially ruin it with a very public TV show date.

I wish I could use this time to write. If only I had a notebook. Maybe I'll try to plot out an adventure-driven rom-com screenplay in my head while we're here doing absolutely nothing.

Thunder crashes over the resort. We all look up as if we could see through the many floors above us to the sky. Heavier, louder rain pounds down on the roof.

It reminds my body, with a sudden increase of discomfort, that I desperately have to pee. I've had to pee since the helicopter, but the crew have been so intent about keeping us quiet and confined, I've been afraid to say anything.

It's time to ask. I'm ridiculously excited to use actual indoor plumbing. I look toward Zarar, who's currently huddled over an iPhone, and raise my hand. After a few awkward seconds, he gets up and comes over to where I'm sitting.

"You okay?" he asks softly.

Everyone turns to look at us. Why wouldn't they? There's nothing else to look at.

"May I use the bathroom?" I ask quietly.

He nods. "Production picked this floor because there's a restroom at the end of the hall. I think they actually just finished prepping it. Hold on, let me shoot out a text to the intern working on that." Z taps out a text. Ten seconds later, his phone vibrates. "Yeah! Right down the hall, all the way at the end, on the left."

I nod in thanks, hop up, and tiptoe out of the quiet room. I smile at Remy, who's watching me with an amused expression, before closing the door. *I can't wait for our date!* A real date! With food! And real-date conversation. Off the beach!

The room they've corralled us in is at the center of a long pastel hall-way. They must have rented out this entire floor. I make a right and start my journey to the toilet. A hum of voices floats out from an open door halfway down the hall.

"Yeah, I got Lark," I hear someone say. "We're sorted there."

I stop a few feet from the door, ears perked. Lark? There are not many people named Lark.

"And I've been trying to get ahold of Jerri. I finally got Remy's mom on the phone ten minutes ago. She says there is no Jerri; he doesn't have a sister."

"What?" a male voice says.

"His only sibling is an older brother who lives in Florida: Dante Lasorsa; he works for NASA. And I asked if I could have the number to reach the grandmother he lives with in California—his mom said both his grandmothers are dead."

38

Cyclone

DAY 12

My joints have frozen over.

"Get this," the female voice continues. "She didn't even know he was out here filming the show. Apparently, he doesn't live in LA; he lives in her mother's—his dead grandmother's—house in Montana."

No. No, he doesn't. No. He lives right off the UCLA campus.

"How can that be? Didn't we vet him? What about the program he said he's in at UCLA? Someone get on calling the school, please."

"I'm on it," says a different male voice.

"He was the missed connection pull for Orie," the female voice says.

"He doesn't have any profiles online that are active, so it's hard to pinpoint any information on him," someone adds.

"We have the right mom, correct?" asks the male.

"Yeah, it's definitely her. That's how we got ahold of him in the first place. She gave us his number when we were hunting him down."

All the saliva in my mouth has vaporized.

"Shit, okay, I want someone fact-checking everything he's told us starting at day one. Diane, great, you take it. What about Priya's mom?"

"Yes, I talked to her . . ."

I force my feet to move forward, glancing covertly into the room as I pass. It's some sort of makeshift production headquarters: full of monitors and people on laptops wearing headphones. There's footage of the game up on a few screens.

I scurry past, breaking into a run, bulldozing into the bathroom door, tripping over my feet with the force of my entrance. I throw out an arm as it swings shut, panting as I steady myself against a pink-striped wall.

I don't understand.

I glance around. Someone's taped posters over the mirrors.

I fall against a sink, clutching the cold ceramic with both hands. There's a white-hot sphere of pressure building in my gut.

The dramatic part of my consciousness offers a name for it: *betrayal*.

I squeeze my eyes shut. My dad's face floods my mind. I open them again. Turn on the cold water. Throw it across my chest. My neck. My face. It soaks my sports bra. Glides down my torso. I try to focus on the temperature. On the micro-streams flowing down my stomach. I can't.

Why would Remy make up a sister?

Clips of conversation, moments of connection, projections of the future I've painted, whip through me: a flip book of our relationship thus far. Jerri's the reason he's here! *I feel like I know her!* She's got a square face like him and curly brown hair. She's five foot six. She plays on the high school soccer team. Her favorite show is *Breaking Bad* even though she was way too young to watch it. She binged it with Remy the second he was old enough to want to watch, and it's one of her biggest directorial inspirations.

I swing down into a squat, clinging to the sink for leverage, finger pads slipping, squeaking down the smooth edges. Lips quivering. Thoughts kaleidoscoping into one another.

I feel like a panel on a film strip that's been set on fire.

He does laundry with his grandma; it's one of his favorite hobbies!

This doesn't make *sense*!

I need to calm down.

I cycle through eight deep breaths until I remember I have to pee. I shut myself into a stall.

Maybe they did have the wrong mom. Or maybe she has memory loss. Or she's playing a trick. Why would Remy be lying to me? He can't be. He can't be lying to me. He can't be. This is not fucking happening.

I wash my hands. This isn't how this goes. This isn't how it's supposed to go! This has to be a misunderstanding. I should go back to the control room. See if they got through to UCLA. Listen to see if they bring him up again.

I storm back down the hall, slowing as I approach the room.

The door's been shut.

THIS ISN'T HAPPENING.

Should I knock?

I have my hand raised over the door when a thought hits me like a piano to the head. I drop my arm. *I can't knock. I can't risk getting in trouble.*

My priority has to be the game. What if they take this as cheating? What if they pull me from the competition? Oh. My. God.

I pitch one foot in front of the other until I've made it back to the meeting room.

39

Date

DAY 13

I spent the night doom spiraling.

I have come up with three possible scenarios:

Scenario A): This is all a big misunderstanding—maybe this is a mind game. Maybe the game wanted me to walk by that door when they were saying those things about Remy to stir up drama between us. Maybe they timed it so there was something that each of us heard as we were going to the bathroom!

Scenario B): Remy lied about having a sister and a grandma he lived with in California . . . because he's dealing with something so traumatic that he felt the need to invent a fake backstory to cope with his pain? Or to gain sympathy? Or to make people like him? But he still has feelings for me? He planned to keep up a wall, but the wall fell down, and this is somewhat of an innocent mistake, and now he wants to be with me and nothing else matters.

Scenario C): Remy is a sociopath. Please hold while I drown in a sinkhole of horror.

I really hope it's A. I really, really hope it's A. It has to be A.

But I'd be okay with B. Please be A.

I haven't been able to confer with anyone. I'm so on edge, I jumped up in my sleeping bag this morning when Priya put her coffee cup down too hard on the table and proceeded to trip over Kennedi and flop back onto the floor like a dead fish.

They gave us tea and coffee. It would have been heavenly had I not been worried that my new pseudo-boyfriend could be a serial killer.

If I straight-up accuse Remy of lying, our alliance could go up in flames. It could make him want to turn on me. He could try to vote me out to protect himself. My chances of winning this game would drop exponentially.

So I have a three-step plan of attack:

1. Don't actually attack—be subtle, probe with casual questions. Try to catch him in a lie.
2. Figure out if the rest of the cast has been set up to learn information like I possibly was in the hallway.
3. If signs are pointing toward Remy lying, tell another alliance mate and figure out the best course of action.

Water billows out in a *V* behind our speedboat. Remy and I are sitting in the bow. Cameras and mics are back on. The motor hums beneath us as we bounce across the ocean. Remy pensively watches the beach fly by.

The storm has passed. They're driving us to the date we were supposed to have after yesterday's challenge. We're not tethered yet. We haven't spoken yet. But we're going to speak. My stomach is eating itself in anticipation.

Our boat pulls up to the back of a romantic-looking yacht laced with fairy lights parked off the coast.

My breath catches as a PA on board escorts us up to an elaborately dressed table with candles and a white metallic tablecloth. They tell us we'll be here for four hours. In that time, we're free to enjoy the amenities. There's a hot tub on the bow. A lounge inside. A shower down in the cabin!

Apparently, we've each been left a new set of clothes to change into in the bedroom. Dinner will begin in forty minutes.

Remy gives me the go-ahead to shower first. I thank him without making eye contact.

The PA shows me to our appointed bedroom featuring an en suite bathroom. The second he leaves, I strip out of my rank yellow yoga outfit, lock myself in the bathroom, and climb into the small white boat shower.

Showering after thirteen days of ocean baths feels like being reborn. The hot water is satin against my skin. There's soap. Shampoo. *Conditioner.* The steam grounds me, clears my mind, quiets the radio static that's been blasting behind my thoughts since I walked by the control room last night.

I have to go out there and face Remy in a way that doesn't ruin my game. If he's playing me, I have to play him right back.

When I turn off the water, someone knocks to warn me that cameras will be rolling once I exit the bathroom.

Not surprising. I barely clock them anymore. I've gotten so used to people silently hovering. I wash my hopelessly filthy, smeared glasses with soap in the mirrorless bathroom sink. When I put them on, *I can see clearly again.*

I cannot believe how accustomed I've become to muggy, cloudy vision. I was so strung out last night, it didn't even occur to me to wash them in the hotel restroom.

I stagger back a step when I catch sight of a full-length mirror waiting for me outside the bathroom door. A camerawoman stands in the corner, rolling. I swallow and slowly turn my focus on the reflection before me.

Thirteen days doesn't sound like very long, but normally, we see ourselves multiple times a day, seven days a week. Thirteen mirrorless days may as well be a year.

My pale face is peppered with new freckles. I'm kind of, vaguely, tan. The blotchy red patches of skin I've grown accustomed to on various parts of my face are virtually gone. My eyes are bright, if a little wild, the blue of my irises lit from behind. They look . . . a little scary.

Someone knocks on the bedroom door, and I jump. I tighten the towel around my chest and clear my throat.

"Come in!" I say cheerily.

It's Remy. We exchange a quick grin.

"Shower's all yours," I tell him. I stiffen as he slips past me into the bathroom.

When the door is closed and locked behind him, I do a more thorough sweep of the bedroom. It's basic. Everything blue and white. Classical nautical decor. My eyes freeze on the long emerald-green silk dress hanging on a hook across the room.

I wander over to find ORIE written in careful cursive letters on the tag. The camerawoman turns away as I pull it on. The dress slides up over my skin like warm butter. It's corseted from the waist up. Once it's zipped, it manages to give my small bust a tiny bit of cleavage. A perfect fit. It drops straight down at the hips, an emerald waterfall with a thigh-high slit up the right side. The thick straps purposefully hang down on my arms, giving it an off-the-shoulder look.

When I stand in front of the mirror, I feel like Island Cinderella heading to a ball. My eyes fall to the puka shells around my neck. They look especially ridiculous with this dress, but I leave them. I don't want to give Remy any reason to question my loyalty.

There are some makeup basics on a small vanity in the corner of the room. It's all L'Oréal. They must be a sponsor. My camera lady spins around to film again as I apply some lip gloss and mascara.

Then I head up to our fancy table, sit down, and worry.

I swallow hard as Remy emerges from the cabin, clean shaven, in brand-new black slacks and a new long-sleeved black button-up shirt, a blazer slung over his shoulder, his gold cross necklace glinting at his neck. Here we go.

40

Inquisition

DAY 13

I nervously straighten my glasses. "Wow, it's like day one in Fiji all over again."

He smirks and sits down across from me. "You look gorgeous."

"Thank you," I say in a terrible random English accent.

A server appears out of nowhere to give us menus, explain the courses, and take our drink orders before setting down a basket of bread. We dig into it voraciously.

How do I open this conversation? What would me forty-eight hours ago ask? I was planning to tell him about Osprey. Build an *honest foundation* for our hopefully long-term relationship.

"So, how have the last nine days been for you?" I ask. "Any love connections forming with your other partners?"

He scoffs. "Nope. It's been dreadfully lackluster without you."

"Dreadfully? Lackluster?" I laugh. And for a moment, I'm sure it must be scenario A. For a second, I forget I'm worried at all. "Since when do you use British-y words like 'dreadful' and 'lackluster'?"

"Since I was dropped off on an island attached to a beautiful girl who enjoys words."

Fire runs down my neck, over my shoulders.

"While I was sitting on the beach with people who weren't you, I thought about all the fancier ways to say *this sucks,* so when we finally got to talk again, I could tell you, and I could use some good Orie-worthy words to do so."

I smile again, blood pooling in my cheeks. *Wow.*

"That dress is . . . the opposite of lackluster."

Brain, jellified. I wave a dismissive hand. "All right, it's not that amazing."

"It's amazing because you're in it."

He stares at me. I stare back.

Well. This is how I die. Complimented to death by Remy Orlando Lasorsa.

Get back on track; you're on a mission. "Remy Orlando Lasorsa, stop trying to woo me."

"Is it working?"

"Of course it's working." I clear my throat as the server comes by to deliver our first course: a posh salad full of cranberries and almonds. I pick up my fork and shuffle the leaves around. "I've . . . been thinking about what you said back in our first cycle, about working together. On movie stuff, maybe?"

His eyes light up. "Yeah?"

I nod. "Yeah, I was thinking, um, I'd love to work with you and Jerri. Maybe we could, like, start a movie review podcast, too. Build a community and stuff."

His smile falls open. "That's a baller idea."

I nod, chuckling. He seems so real. "Baller indeed." *Ask something relevant. Something about Jerri.* "So, when's your sister's birthday?"

"December ninth, why?"

I feel my jaw tense. "Oh, what year?"

"2005."

I wish I was better at math so I could calculate that faster. "That would make her . . ."

"Eighteen," he says.

I nod. "Of course." That checks out. Damn it. "When's your birthday?" I ask.

"December eighth." He smiles.

My stomach trips into a ditch. That's the day after my birthday.

What the fuck? *Why did I ask this?* I can't fact-check anything. IS THIS FATE, or coincidence? Or . . . is he lying? Who lies about their own birthday?

"My mom thinks that's why we get along so well. She buys into the whole astrology mindset. Why are you interested?" He quirks a sly brow.

"Uh, same reason as your mom . . . I want to make sure our astrological signs are in order if we're planning on working together long-term," I say lightly. *I know nothing of astrological signs.*

He narrows his gaze, amused. "Jerri and I are Sagittarius. When's your birthday?" He picks up his fork and pushes his salad around.

I watch, struck with the sudden urge to cry. *Why is this happening?* He's so perfect. "It's December seventh," I say.

He puts down the fork and stares. "Are you shitting me?"

I shake my head, willing my mind to stay calm.

"You are not December seventh," he jests, smiling. "You're fucking with me."

I force a laugh. "I'm not." I stuff a bite of salad in my mouth.

If he's lying . . . how would he know my birthday?

We both cut our gaze to the left as a violinist emerges from the cabin, tearing up the strings with a complex, glorious-sounding tango.

We grew up together. I've been on social media since I was thirteen. He could easily know my birthday.

Remy looks over his shoulder, delighted as the musician approaches the table. He turns his freckled boyish grin on me. "Shall we dance?" He stands and holds out a hand.

I take it, fear a cold, tight coil in my stomach, want a furnace roaring beneath it. His eyes rove over me as I place my hand in his and stand. He pulls me against him with a sharp tug. His left palm pushes hot against my lower back. Our chests brush against each other. He clutches my right hand, directing our arms into a hard ninety-degree angle, and leads us— his steps precise, staccato, clean, and measured. I follow, stunned, as I try to keep up.

"How do you know how to dance like this?" I demand. "You're too muscular to be so graceful."

He pulls me tighter, his right leg slipping in between mine, his face hovering at my ear as we pivot around each other. "Any good f-boy knows the ladies love a man who can dance."

I jerk back, my brows slanting together, and Remy laughs as he maneuvers us in a tight circle. "Relax, Orie. I wasn't good at striking up conversation, and I thought girls would like me if I knew how to move. I took classes during college." He twirls me. Once. Twice. Three times.

"At UCLA?" I spout between spins, a cocktail of dread and anticipation raging through my veins.

"Yes, at UCLA, that's where I went to college," he reiterates, smiling.

"When's your grandma's birthday?" I ask as I somehow end up with my back against his built chest.

"January second." His lips move against my cheek. His voice vibrates through me. "Just missed it."

Why am I asking about dates! Anyone can make up a birthdate! I don't have anyone's birth certificates!

I swallow as he pulls my arms up and places my palms behind his head. "Did anything, um, weird happen when you used the bathroom yesterday at the hotel?" I wisp out.

He reaches up for my elbows. "Yeah, actually."

Yes! A piece of my stomach uncoils.

His hands slide, achingly slow, down my biceps and over my shoulder blades. They press into my sides, dipping into my waist, over my hips; hot coals burning through the fabric of the dress, leaving a shimmering trail of desire in their wake.

My mind's been thrown into a food processor.

His fingers wrap around my knee through the slit in my dress. "What happened on your trip?" I breathe.

He brings my right leg up to hook backward over his waist, his fingers skating down to my calf. He takes my left hand from his neck, and we lean to one side together, left arms extending. And for a moment, I'm not me, he's not Remy—we're the dance. For one suspended second, I'm a tangle of ivy winding over a fortress.

His right palm runs over my hooked calf, and with one clean motion, I'm spun outward in a bent arabesque. I land with my right leg straight up, his hand clutching my ankle, my back arched over his forearm, breathless as the violin player's ballad ends.

Whoa.

Remy's slate eyes hold mine as he pulls me upright. Please stand by while my brain reboots.

We return to our table as the violinist begins a more tranquil ballad. The server replaces our salads with a pesto pasta dish outfitted with a vibrant assortment of veggies.

"Did you find yourself connecting with anyone else?" Remy asks, not sounding the least bit worried that I did. Amusement colors his words.

I'm going to be honest. Not too detailed. But honest. Just in case scenario A pans out, and we are, in fact, building the foundation for a long-lasting romantic relationship.

I swallow the pasta in my mouth. "Well, I think Kennedi and Osprey are both great, but you're still my number-one ally."

He smiles, swirling his wine. "Same."

I bite my lip, trying not to look too relieved. "Good."

I have to give him the benefit of the doubt, right? I have to check with everyone else. See if anyone else had an encounter in the hallway; he—

Wait. He never answered that question. I was too distracted by the dance to notice.

"Oh." I try to sound aloof. "What happened on your trip to the restroom last night?"

"Oh yeah." He swallows another sip of wine, mirth lighting his eyes. "I finally truly appreciated the wonders of indoor plumbing. I've never been so grateful for the existence of toilet paper."

41

Together

DAY 13

After dessert, Remy leans across the table to pull me into a kiss that leaves my entire body feeling like strawberry Jell-O that's been chucked in the microwave.

I don't think I'm good at this detective-ing thing. We just chatted through a five-course meal, and I feel no more sure of his character than I was when I stepped onto this boat.

I'm very confused and infatuated. I should have scripted something specific to say. Every topic I broached started with a clear intention to try to unearth information. Then Remy opened his mouth, and my solid thoughts scattered into a million pieces—lollipops dropped on the pavement, stampeded by a crowd of annoyingly attractive Italian boys. (Yes, I am always thinking about food.)

When the date concludes, the PA gives me a pair of biker shorts to pull on and asks me to dip under the slit of the dress to reattach our tether.

We get to take our new fancy clothes back to the beach with us. (Green silk dress, perfect for an island marooning.) I straight-up laugh when the PA tells us the "good news." Apparently, the producers really want us to have that *just washed up on shore after an epic disaster ruined my expensive event* aesthetic.

As we're loading back onto the motorboat for the beach, the driver hands us our island bags back with an extra little gift inside. A bathing suit. This is the actual good news. I've lived these last thirteen days as that towel a teenage boy always leaves on the floor. Kind of smelly and perpetually damp. ALAS, I WILL DRY.

It's early evening as our boat approaches what must be our new beach. As we get closer, I realize there are two people already on the shoreline. *Osprey and Leo.* And a large wooden crate.

Dang, they look good. Osprey's in a white suit with a bold dark line running through the fabric in strategic stylish places. That's gonna get ruined quickly. Leo's in a navy blue suit with a Yankees tie. Another boat pulls up near ours carrying Kennedi and Priya. They hop off into the shallow water in their formal wear. Kennedi's is a two-piece bright orange asymmetrical crop top and a long matching pencil skirt with a slit that cuts up to her thigh. Priya's in a yellow corseted dress that waterfalls at the hip and brushes the floor. They both look amazing, and, yes, a little weird with their tether emerging awkwardly around their skirts.

We all converge at the extra large wooden box on the beach. There's a note on top that reads WAIT FOR EVERYONE.

Leo picks it off once the six of us are all huddled around it. "I think this is everyone?"

We all nod.

"Everyone looks hot," Kennedi notes.

Leo opens the envelope and reads it aloud: "You're all in this together now. This is your beach till the end of the game. Celebrate. Build a shelter. Engage in helter-skelter. Congratulations on being the final six. We've thrown a care package into the mix. Enjoy! And rejoice! Your next challenge will ring in another big choice."

The care package is immaculate. There are two hammers, nails, and a whole roll of twine. There's a huge quilt! A tarp to protect us from the rain. A basket full of fruit. Three bottles of wine and a batch of eggs.

Leo takes point, directing Osprey, Remy, and me in building the shelter while Kennedi and Priya get to work on a firepit and boiling water. We only have a couple of hours left before sunset, and there's a ton of work to do if we want to have a decent place to sleep.

Remy's shirtless, hacking at a piece of wood six feet away next to Leo who's doing the same thing. They're basically having a machete-off with all the bamboo we gathered while I work on twining together the area that will become the corner of our shelter with Osprey. Osprey holds the pieces on top of each other as I weave over it with the twine in the meticulous way Leo taught us ten minutes ago.

"You look really nice, Tube Stop," Osprey says just loud enough for me to hear. I slide my eyes to his. He's looking down at the bamboo.

"You do, too," I tell him.

His hair's clean, half up in a bun, half down. He's shed his suit jacket. Now he's in a navy blue button-up with the top couple of buttons undone and the sleeves rolled up to reveal his forearms. They look . . . great. I don't remember ever caring about forearms before this moment.

"Did anything weird happen to you yesterday when you used the restroom at the hotel?" I ask quietly.

"When you say . . . weird?" he prompts, a hint of dry humor in his voice. He makes eye contact this time. We're only inches apart, and it startles me how much it startles me.

I shake it off. "Um, like, did you hear anything?"

"Anything . . . like what, the precious sound of running water?"

I suck in a flustered breath and blink at him. "You smell *so good*. Like spicy vanilla or something."

He laughs. "You know, under normal circumstances, I shower regularly."

I snort and shake my head. "When I say weird, I mean, like . . ." I glance around at the camerapeople hovering around. I can't have them hearing this conversation if there's any chance it's going to get me ousted from the game.

"Whoa! Hey, keep it tight," Osprey says quickly. I look down to find I've completely let go of the twine I was wrapping.

"Shit!" I gasp, grabbing it and yanking it taut. "Sorry!"

"What happened?"

"I'm . . ." I glance over at shirtless Remy chopping, muscles rippling in the afternoon sun. He and Leo are talking about the Yankees. I swing my head quickly back to Osprey. I almost slam right into his face. He retreats an inch so we don't smack heads. "Remy might be lying to me about weird stuff," I say so softly, I almost can't hear myself.

Osprey's brow furrows. "What kind of stuff?"

"Like . . . I'm afraid to say with . . . an audience."

Osprey throws a quick glance at Remy who's still in conversation. Kennedi and Priya are still building a firepit ten feet away with the stones they gathered.

Osprey reaches back and turns off his mic. I reach under my skirt and turn mine off.

"Tell me," he breathes.

"When I was walking to the bathroom, I overheard the crew talking in this makeshift control room. A PA or something was reporting to whoever was in charge. They were trying to get ahold of Remy's sister, Jerri, and his mom said he doesn't have a sister. So the PA asked for Remy's grandma's number because Remy lives with her in LA. And Remy's mom said both of his grandmothers have passed."

Osprey's brow furrows. "What the actual fuck?" he says quietly.

"I know. I don't know, though; maybe this is part of the game, and they're trying to stir up drama?"

"I didn't hear anything in the hallway," Osprey says.

A frown pulls at my lips. "Did Leo?"

"He didn't say anything about anything like that happening. I can ask the next time we get a second alone."

I tie off the twine and we both let go of the corner we're working on.

"I was really hoping you heard something. He talks about his sister all the time. It'd be really disturbing if she's not real."

Osprey swallows, his eyes darting to Remy again. "Aren't you two close? Can you . . . ask him?"

"No!" I hiss. "If I find out he's a sociopathic liar, he's going to try and get me out of the game. I'm tethered to him, Osprey! If he's a serial killer, I'm right there ready to be murdered. He has a machete!"

Osprey purses his lips. "I'll keep an eye on him now that we're here, see if I pick up on anything."

I reach back under the dress and flip the mic back on. My legs are sweating bullets under this fabric.

"I need to chop the skirt off this thing, or I'm gonna get heatstroke." I yank my machete off the ground.

"Are you just gonna—?"

I start sawing at my skirt from the slit.

"Yeah, you're just sawing it off, okay," Osprey says.

I can't get the back bit without potentially cutting up my legs. "Can you slice the last bit in the back?" I ask, handing Osprey my machete.

"I guess." He takes the machete and gathers the fabric in his hands.

"Whoa, what's going on over here!" I look up to find Remy standing in front of the two of us, grinning.

My mouth falls open. I glance back at Osprey, hovered near my butt with a giant knife. "Uh, Osprey's just helping me with my skirt."

"I can help you with it, no worries," Remy says.

With one swift chop, Osprey slices off the bottom half of the dress and straightens. "All good."

At sunset, Remy and I change into our bathing suits to take a quick dip in the ocean. An absurd amount of sweat has been spilled trying to throw together a shelter in three hours. We need a bath.

Kennedi and Priya tell us they're going to "join us," but they quickly move off on their own, flirting a little way down the beach. That seems to be going well!

Osprey volunteered himself and Leo to babysit the fire. They're hunched together talking up on the beach. I wonder what they're discussing. I wonder if they're falling for each other. I wonder if Osprey hit it off with him the same way he hit it off with me.

Remy takes my hand and pulls me toward him. "Hey."

"Hey." I drag my attention away from the shore.

"Is there something going on with you and Osprey?"

"Um. We're friends?" I tell him.

"Okay. I just caught a vibe."

A mild panic swirls to life in my gut. "You're my number one."

He tugs my arms, pulling me closer, and wraps them around his neck. "Good. I'm all-in on this." Our foreheads fall together.

I smile like I'm all-in on this, too, but all I want to do is ask about Jerri. If Jerri doesn't exist, did Remy grow up making sketches and commercials and scene reenactments? He said Jerri wanted to go to UCLA for film like him. If Jerri doesn't exist, and his grandma doesn't exist, and he lives in Montana . . . does he even like film?

Could this whole working-together-to-make-movies thing be a steaming heap of bullshit I've fallen into face-first?

"Can I ask you something?" I whisper.

He reaches up and runs his hand under the puka shells on my neck. "Obviously."

"What kind of classes did you take as a film production major?"

He laughs. "You debating going back to school?"

No. "Maybe," I tell him.

He wraps my legs around his waist and pulls me flush against his torso. "I think you'd love film school."

He catches my lips with his.

It's the first time his kiss doesn't turn my mind to mush. The first time I'm not overtaken by heart flutters and stomach sparklers. I'm very aware of myself as his tongue flirts with mine. Of the fact that Osprey and Leo can see us from the shore. And that he blatantly ignored my question.

I pull away, carefully arranging my face in a casual smile. "What's your favorite movie?"

Remy chuckles. "*Iron Man,* remember?"

"*Iron Man*'s your favorite movie of all time?"

"Hells yeah!" He spins us in a lazy arc through the water.

"Who directed that one again?" I ask, feigning forgetfulness. I was hoping he'd share a more obscure favorite. I know who directed *Iron Man.* Jon Favreau, obviously. I think everyone knows that.

Remy clicks his tongue. "Shit, I'm blanking . . . Jerri would be ashamed."

I nod robotically. "Oh! Judd Apatow, right?"

"Yes! That's it, shit! How did I forget his name? Fucking embarrassing." Remy laughs.

I blink at him, trying not to spiral into a panic right here in front of his face.

"What's wrong?" Remy chuckles.

Judd Apatow famously directs comedies. He's known for films like *Knocked Up* and *The 40-Year-Old Virgin*. He is not confused with Jon Favreau.

"Nothing, I . . ." I take a few steps back. I can tell you absolutely everything and anything about my favorite films. Director, writer, main cast, producer, composer, favorite lines, five-paragraph verbal essay digging into the themes.

Remy steps forward and takes my hands. "You all right?"

I am not all right. My throat feels tight. My breathing is wonky. Maybe I'm overreacting?

Is it possible he went to film school and—quote—loves superhero movies and he really doesn't know the director of his favorite film? IS IT?

"Can you turn off your mic?" I mutter.

Remy reaches back and turns off his mic. I turn off mine.

"Are you really playing this game for Jerri?"

He squints at me like I asked something preposterous. "Of course. What does that have to do with this?"

My voice breaks. "Is *your dad* an addict?"

Remy's expression shifts. "We talked about this, yes. Jesus, Orie, are you okay? Where is this coming from?" I swallow hard as he steps closer. "Orie, we have to stay strong. We're a huge threat. People are going to try and lie and turn us against each other. We can't let them. You have to trust me. We have to trust each other. Have you been sleeping?" He tips my chin up with his fingers. "Your eyes are bloodshot."

His fingers slide off my face as I shake my head. *No, I haven't been sleeping. I need you to come clean so I can sleep.*

"You can tell me anything, Remy," I squeak. "I won't judge, I promise."

Remy studies me, swinging our hands gently back and forth in the water. "I know that, Orie. I've already told you more about my family than I usually share with anyone. You were . . ." He sighs. "A little right about me when we got here. I've hooked up with my fair share of people through college and shit, but I've never opened up like this. Everyone I've been with—I mean, it was all surface-level nothing. I've never had something like this. Real.

"There's something strong here. A connection that's heavier and more substantial than I've ever felt before. I've never shared shit about my dad. I've never talked about Jerri. It's only been fourteen days, and I feel like a different person. That's because of you."

I close my eyes, and as always out here, I see my dad. My mom. *One million dollars.* My shoulders roll forward. I cannot blow the game to call out Remy on day fourteen about what may or may not be a lie. I can't push this conversation *and lose his trust.* Remy is my path to the end.

I look up at him and nod. "I'm . . . I actually haven't slept in a while. I'm sorry. You're right."

He pulls me into a tight hug. I stare over his shoulder at Osprey who's watching, arms crossed, from the shoreline.

"It's okay," Remy murmurs. "We'll have the shelter done soon. It should help with sleep."

"Okay," I say robotically.

The fire crackles gently next to us. The ocean washes up and down over the sand. The wind whistles through the trees. The night is full of soothing white noise, but none of it seems to have an effect on me. I'm wide awake, brain whirring in its usual circles now that everything Remy has told me about his life may be bullshit.

Since the shelter's still incomplete, the whole lot of us are in a clump on the quilt laid over the sand next to the fire.

In the event that Remy's lying, I need to get ahead of the narrative, and to do that I need to let America in on this. Tomorrow, I have to talk about this in my confessional. Nothing about overhearing the control people, but I need to plant the seed that I'm suspicious.

Remy's completely conked out with his back flat against the blanket. We started out semi-spooning, but once he fell asleep, he shifted to his back. Kennedi and Priya are next to us. Kennedi is facing me with her eyes closed. When I shift slightly so my shoulder stops falling asleep, they pop open.

She smiles at me. *Hey,* she mouths.

Hi, I mouth back.

She scoots a tiny bit closer so we're right up against each other before breathe-talking. "I talked to Osprey."

My brows shoot up. "You talked to Osprey?" I breathe back. "I thought you hated him?"

"We have an underlying understanding of each other. What are we going to do?" She mouths *about* and points a finger at Remy.

My mouth flops open. "Does . . ." I point to Priya. "Know?"

Kennedi shakes her head the tiniest bit. "She respects a private convo."

"Healthy," I breathe. "Is it going well with her romantically?" I smile.

She unleashes a catlike grin. "Unexpectedly, yes. She's an environmental scientist; she's so fucking smart—I'm obsessed. She's only twenty-three, Orie! You were wrong. She's getting her master's."

"I'm twenty-three, and you said I was ancient," I hiss.

"It's different with her."

I roll my eyes. "We need a nickname for . . ." I nod subtly toward Remy.

"Katy Perry," she says automatically.

I choke down a laugh.

"We need to get her album far away from here so you can get those catchy tunes out of your head," Kennedi says.

"I need to be sure before I throw out the CD."

DAY 15—PRODUCER CONFESSIONAL NOTES
ORIE LENNOX—CONFESSIONAL #12

TRANSCRIPT OF EDIT TO BE INSERTED DURING POST

ORIE

I guess there is a world where Remy is malnourished and forgot his favorite director's name and is so brain-fogged due to all the hardships of island life that he latched on the name Judd Apatow in the moment. It's a possibility. Maybe his film aspirations are more finance-based and less creatively driven?

I'm still not sleeping, and it's making it very hard to think. There's no concrete way to discern fact from fiction without access to the internet and the rest of society.

[Orie slumps and rests her face in her hands.]

42

Love

DAY 15

I'm questioning everything everyone out here has ever said. I know in the grand scheme of things, the little details people lie about in our conversations don't matter. *I just have to stay the course.* But it's absolutely maddening to be so unsure of everything all the time.

I am itching to de-tether from Remy.

The six of us file out of the jungle to stand in front of Jamie and Z for whatever they have in store for our challenge today.

I've nodded along to everything Remy's said these past few days. Kept up polite smiles. We've survived for seventy-two hours on a beach with our four other castmates, and today we'll vote another person out.

It can't be Remy. I need him here. His new potential sociopathic status doesn't change the fact I need to win. It doesn't change the fact I need to have the potential to be *chosen* by the players who win each challenge. That's how you advance.

Leo is never going to *choose* me. We've only had base-level conversations about insubstantial day-to-day things, and I voted off Rick. Leo puts up a good front, but there's no way he's over that. I don't think he trusts any of us, other than Osprey. Which has to make him my number-one target for elimination today.

Because bottom line: Remy still trusts me. We cuddled last night. He was the big spoon, and I was the little spoon who never quite managed to shut her eyes. We're still AP Chem to the end.

I can count on Remy winning things. He's good at challenges. And I can count on him to bring me to the next cycle each round. As scared and unsure as I am, it would be counterproductive to vote him out right now. I need to make it to the final four with Osprey, Kennedi, and Remy. Then we can work on getting him out.

Then, there's no chance of someone I don't have a strong bond with winning a challenge. Kennedi doesn't want to go to the end with Osprey. And I don't think Osprey wants to go to the end with Kennedi. I think, if I play my cards right, they'll both want to bring me.

Priya seems great, and I'm so happy Kennedi's found a romantic connection, but I don't have a connection with her. And Kennedi could choose her over me, if it came down to it. So after Leo, Priya has to go.

In front of us, Jamie claps three times, like a teacher quieting her class. She beams at us. "Welcome, final six! You're killing it out here! We're about to have one hell of a day!"

Z walks up, untethering our connective cords. There's an enormous rectangular area chalked off before us. At one end of it is a big . . . pool of mud. *Okay*.

At the center of the court are six tall wooden seesawlike structures. The ends that are up in the air are supporting six colorful buckets suspended from the wood via wire. On the opposite end of each plank are flags lying dormant on the ground. At the far end of the course are six tables. *Puzzle stations*. On each table is some sort of white base to build on. Whatever this is, it ends in a standing puzzle.

"Today is going to be a little different," Jamie explains. "You've all made it fifteen days. I know it doesn't sound very long, but we started this adventure with everyone in a ten-day quarantine. Each contestant was put in a hotel room, cut off from everyone they know and could know, without phones or internet, before they even stepped foot on the island. Isolation was a precursor before they even knew what this game entailed.

"Since arriving here in Fiji, they've been cut off from society, living with a bunch of people they don't know very well, scavenging for food and water, unsure of who to trust, never knowing what tomorrow's going to bring—that takes a toll on your psyche. That makes each day feel like a lifetime.

"I get anxious when I don't talk to my sister for seventy-two hours. Twenty-five days without so much as a text message from a loved one? That's hard. That can feel like an eternity. We know you're all emotionally drained." Jamie pauses, gazing around dramatically. "We understand that sometimes, it just takes a little love—"

I smack a hand up over my mouth.

"To give you the energy boost you need to finish the game. Today you won't be tethered to a fellow castmate; you'll be competing for an amazing reward and immunity from elimination *with* your loved ones."

A few of us gasp (myself included). Priya's already crying next to me.

"Let's bring out today's guests." Jamie grins. "Osprey, here's your sister, Dove."

A beautiful young girl around sixteen with long dark hair in shorts and a black tank comes running out of the trees, skipping every few feet with excitement.

Osprey's lips press into a tight line. His eyes are glassy as Dove closes in. He steps forward as she attacks him with a hug.

"Remy," Jamie starts.

Please bring out Jerri.

"Here's your friend Tom."

A guy even more jacked than Remy comes out of the jungle jogging over. He and Remy shake hands and pull each other into one of those macho-man hugs where they slap each other's backs.

Osprey and I share a quick glance. I've never heard of this Tom, but I can't muster the energy right now to care. I'm shaking waiting for it to be my turn.

Say my name, Jamie.

"Kennedi." Jamie smiles. "Here's your mom."

Kennedi, who was seemingly fine a moment ago, heaves in a sob as her mother comes running out of the jungle. Mrs. Jacobs is a gorgeous, super fit woman just like her daughter. They're both in tears as Kennedi throws herself into her mom's outstretched arms.

"Priya," Jamie says, "here's your dad."

Priya power walks out to embrace her dad, a tiny balding man she towers over.

Jamie scans the two of us left waiting without a loved one. Leo and I have rearranged ourselves to stand next to each other. Everyone else is speaking to our left in hushed voices with their people. "Orie."

"Yeah?" I blubber.

"Here's your sister, Lark."

I laugh-sob as Lark jogs out of the jungle in my exact show outfit. Clean, bright gold—yellow sports bra and leggings, polka-dot knee highs. Ponytail swinging. I go sprinting for her, tears slipping down my cheeks as I fly across the tall grass. We collide in a tangled hug.

I can't explain how wonderful it is to see her right now. To solidly know with all my heart, in my bones, that she's 1,000 percent on my team. That she loves me, and I love her, and no matter what questions I have, she'll have some sort of solid, confident answer, or advice to share.

Lark is here!

"I'm so proud of you," she says into my hair.

I grab her hand, overrun with emotion as I drag her back to the lineup. Jamie announces Leo's loved one, a smiley, curly-haired blond woman— his cousin. They're super cute, running up to each other for a double high- five jump before embracing.

Jamie claps again. "ALL RIGHT. Let's get this party started."

Z snaps on new tethers, connecting us to our loved ones. They're all sporting a harness like ours, ready to jump into the game.

"Today's elimination and choosing ceremony will take place at the end of the day. Z and I will come to your beach at sunset, so you can push those worries aside for the moment. This afternoon is about enjoying the company of your loved ones! Z, what are our contestants competing for today?"

Z steps up next to Jamie. "Today, you're playing for immunity from to- night's elimination, plus an afternoon in paradise with your loved one. The first- and second-place teams today will be flown to a beautiful location to share a picnic and spend some quality time together. The rest of you will, unfortunately, have to say goodbye to your loved ones after the challenge. In addition to the picnic, and the time with their loved ones, the first- and second-place winners will be safe at tonight's vote," Z finishes.

"You and your loved one," Jamie starts, "will be playing in the mud today."

I am vibrating. A revved-up engine idling at the starting line. I'm about to compete *with* Lark. This is the dream. This is what we've been talking about since I was eight years old. *This is the moment.* Adrenaline is rocket fuel drumming through my veins.

It's a classic straightforward challenge. We have to roll around in the dirt pit and race back to the suspended bucket, bringing with us as much mud as we can carry on our person. Dump the mud in the bucket. When the bucket has enough mud, it'll drop. Once the bucket drops, puzzle pieces will fall as well. First two teams to finish their puzzles win.

We've been spread among the seesaw-mud-bucket-holding devices. Lark and I are all the way to the left, our hands resting on the wooden seesaw beam as we stare across the field at the mud pit.

"On your mark," Jamie calls out.

"We're diving into that mud pool, right?" Lark whispers.

"Get set." We bend our knees, rearing back.

"Obviously," I say.

"Go!" Jamie says.

We explode away from the wooden seesaw, hurtling at top speed for the mud. Once we're within jumping distance, the two of us launch ourselves screaming into the pit.

The earth swallows us. It's thick, squishy, suffocating, smooth. Just watery enough to make it difficult to transfer. I scrape a path through it across my eyes so I can see. We fill our bras. Our pants. I cake my hair, piling mud atop my head like a terrible homemade poop emoji hat.

I have to fight off hysterics when I see Lark. She's mussed her hair into a gigantic mud bun piled comically high, à la Marge Simpson.

"Ready?" Lark asks giddily.

I nod, smothering the urge to giggle as we leave the pit, waddling like we've shit our pants toward the bucket in an effort to maintain a hold on our dirt bounty.

"Remy and Tom are working this SO FAST," Jamie shouts. "Somehow managing to carry colossal amounts of mud without spending too much time prepping in the pit. Kennedi and her mom and Priya and her dad are unfortunately falling a little behind. Leo and Shane, Osprey and Dove, and Orie and Lark are all coming back with their first dump! Everyone looking sewer-monster chic. Y'all make mud look good."

Laughter splits through my resolve as I catch a glance of the ten other mud people flailing toward the buckets. Just the slight shake of my stomach sends bits of dirt flopping off my body. "Crap!"

"No laughing!" Lark screeches as we reach our bucket. "Laughing is a trap." We slide the dirt piles off our heads.

Another laugh barks out of me as we squeeze out our ponytails, empty our sports bras, scoop mud from our pants. When the bucket doesn't fall, we head back to the pit and do it again.

We're on our third waddle back to the seesaw when the first bucket crashes to the ground.

"REMY AND THOMAS HAVE HIT WEIGHT WITH THEIR MUD! They have their pieces; they're clamoring for their puzzle station looking like two clay sculptures that haven't gone through the kiln yet."

Lark and I shuck our latest schlep of mud into the bucket with renewed vigor. It wobbles but doesn't fall.

"Shit!" I hiss.

"Haul ass!" Lark screams as we lunge back toward the pit.

"Everyone giving it their all today, racing to catch Remy and Thomas. Remy's got his pieces out on the table but he hasn't made ANY progress. Remy and puzzles are a lot like oil and water. Just not compatible, folks. Everyone IS STILL IN THIS!"

We clobber ourselves in mud one last time and hobble back, panting.

I drop my load in the bucket, and it immediately smashes down into the earth, the flag end of the seesaw soaring upward. Our puzzle pieces flop to the ground in a yellow bag. I snatch them up and we sprint for the table at the other end of the field.

"ORIE AND LARK MAKE WEIGHT. THEY HAVE THEIR PIECES. There they go!" Jamie screams.

I rip open the bag and dump the pieces across our table: thirty-five chunky ones. They're brown today. They'll form a tall vertical puzzle built up around the white support base nailed to the table.

"Remy and Thomas still ONLY have three pieces in place. My guys, this is embarrassing. You have to step it up or everyone's going to pass you," Jamie belts.

"Thanks, Jamie," Remy quips.

Lark fits a piece into the base. "*Here we fucking go.*"

I fit the next piece in a second later.

There's a bang behind us. "Osprey and Dove make weight," Jamie updates. "We've got three teams in this!"

"FOUR!" Leo yells as their bucket crashes down.

Lark fits a third piece; I fit a fourth. Osprey and Dove hit the table next to us. "We've got this," she urges.

"Lark and Orie working well together, obviously passing Remy and Thomas. But Osprey and Dove are here, and we know Osprey's puzzle skills are a force to be reckoned with. We might be in for another showdown."

Lark and I fit pieces eight and nine. Ten and eleven. "It's a tree," I hiss in her ear.

"Yeah, I noticed about five seconds after we started," she says with a laugh.

"Leo and Shane making progress, but it doesn't look like they're going to be fast enough—Jesus, Osprey and Dove, Lark and Orie—both teams are already halfway through."

The tree wobbles now as we wedge in each new piece. We can't force them. It's essentially two dimensional. The puzzle's getting gradually more and more unstable—it's already two and half feet high. But Lark and I are a well-oiled machine, arms twining around, supporting the structure, as the other settles a new piece and vice versa.

"THIS IS IT," Jamie yells. "THREE PIECES LEFT. OSPREY AND DOVE HUSTLING HARD TO KEEP PACE WITH ORIE AND LARK. Osprey's tree is wobbling as Dove pushes in another piece! Oh no, they lost two pieces off the side!"

My hand shakes as I lift our final piece up to the hole at the center of our tree.

"Holding," Lark shouts as she presses her palms flat against the potential pressure points in the front and back of the puzzle. I gingerly place the piece and start to tap it in. With each tap, it snags on the pieces around it. The tree wavers. We wait, it steadies, and I tap again. *Patience.*

"The sisters are sweating as they try to bring this home at snail speed. Osprey and Dove have slowed considerably as well as they work their last three pieces in. Our other teams are racing, trying to catch them. OH! And Leo and Shane's collapses. They tried, folks, too hard, too fast."

I tap the piece one last time, holding my breath.

It's in place. "It's in!" I hiss. Lark removes her arms.

It remains standing.

"JAMIE!" I yell as chills race over my body. Lark grabs my hand.

Jamie appears in front of our station. "ORIE AND LARK HAVE IT. ORIE WINS IMMUNITY! AND AN UNFORGETTABLE REST OF THE DAY WITH HER SISTER!"

Lark leaps on me, screaming. We jump together, holding hands, hugging, yelling incomprehensible things—oh my god—mud flinging about every which way. WE WON! WE WON! WE WON!

"Jamie!" Osprey yells.

Jamie's eyes snap to their puzzle. "And OSPREY AND DOVE TAKE SECOND!"

Jamie instructs Lark, Osprey, Dove, and me to come stand next to her.

"Congratulations!" Z says as he removes our tethers. "We've got a helicopter waiting for you four."

Lark and I bounce on our heels like little girls, arms hooked together, quaking with excitement.

"Everyone else," Jamie says, "please say goodbye to your loved ones."

I feel terrible for everyone who didn't win. It's such a gut-wrenching prize to miss out on.

But I am RAW JOY. I'm the phone call that school is canceled! That first bite into your favorite dessert! Reading the last sentence of a novel that really brings it home! I am the feeling you get when you realize you have a one-in-five chance of winning $1 million.

43

Sisters

DAY 15

The helicopter sets us down in an actual oasis. The four of us step out, caked head to toe in dried mud, onto a patch of bright grass next to a thirty-foot roaring waterfall that spills into a quaint contained body of water.

There's a picnic basket and a blanket decked out with a charcuterie board, sandwiches, drinks, and chocolate chip cookies. A large pile of black towels sits off to the side so we can jump in the water and clean up.

First, we feast, laughing as we exchange stories about the challenge. Dove is adorable. She's on the quieter side, but she's quick to laugh and very sweet. It's clear she looks up to Osprey in the way she drinks in everything he says.

Osprey and Lark get along fabulously; they fall down a little rabbit hole, chatting about the best biographies of last year. I ask Dove what her favorite film is and smile over at Osprey when she tells me it's *The Martian*; they watch it around Christmas every year. We giggle and discuss silly mundane things. Living, for a second, outside the game.

Osprey asks to see some AcroYoga, so after our feast, we put on a little show for him and Dove and teach them some poses to do along with us. Dove gets a kick out of it. She takes on Lark's role as flyer. I lay parallel to

Osprey, walking him through the handgrips and movements. His smiles were fleeting when we were tethered. His guard was up. But here, with Dove, he wears a constant grin. Warm sarcasm and humor coat his every comment.

Eventually, we break off to spend alone time with our respective sisters. Lark and I dive into the water, work the mud off our bodies, and climb up onto a car-sized rock to dry off. The flat black stone is warm from the sun and we lie out, enjoying the heat like mermaids in matching outfits with our hair fanned around our heads.

"So how's Dad?" I ask once we're good and comfortable.

Lark rolls onto her stomach. "Well, the program he's in is no contact for a hundred days. We're only allowed to write letters like we're in the 1800s. He's doing okay. Dealing with a lot of guilt. I've been reading a lot of books about addiction."

"Any fiction?"

She smiles. "Yeah, I have a pile I'm making for when you get home."

I stick my bottom lip out in gratitude. "Thank you. Do you think Dad's . . . upset with me?"

Lark guffaws. "Why would he be upset with you?"

I swallow, looking up at the ice blue sky. "I haven't looked at him since before I left. Or talked to him. Those two days before my flight, I treated him like . . . he wasn't my dad anymore. Like I'd never talk to him again."

The story of his drunken 4:00 A.M. appearance in my room spills out of me. Lark listens, gasping at all the right moments. It feels good to tell someone who understands. Who knows Dad and how wonderful he is.

"Oh, Orie." Lark sits up, tugging me with her, and pulls me into a hug.

I collapse against her for a moment. "I'm sorry, Lark." The words come out in a whisper.

She rubs my arm. "For what?"

I pull back and sit up so I can look into her freakishly big green eyes. "I've been so caught up in my own dumb drama, I haven't seen anything."

She snorts. "Seen what?"

"Uh, I live with Dad, and I didn't see he was struggling. I didn't catch on that something was wrong with the restaurant. I didn't realize I was leaning on you so much with work. I didn't realize I was being so . . . self-centered." I drag my hands down my face. "I love you. I never want to be a thing that's burdening you."

Lark's smiling at me like she's holding back another laugh. It's obnoxious.

"Or," she says softly, "you're still becoming a person. I know how easy it is to get caught in your own head when you're figuring out how to adult. And, Jesus, Dad is *not* mad at you. He sent along a letter for you. A PA has it. They said I can give it to you before I leave to go home."

My voice cracks. "He wrote me a letter?"

"Of course he did." Lark laughs again. "You've been doing a lot of thinking out here, huh?"

"There isn't much else to do," I say pointedly. "How's everything going with our socials?"

She bobs her head. "I miss you, obviously. But Mel and I have been doing okay."

I smile at her. "Good."

"Really?" She grins. "You didn't want us to crumble without your mad skills?"

I snort. "The fact that you think I would is upsetting."

"Eh, I never know with you."

I nudge her playfully. "I've been thinking about maybe changing the theme of my socials and angling it more toward . . ." I pause, nerves nipping at me.

"More toward . . . ?" she prompts.

I purse my lips. "Film. More toward film. Because I really love talking about movies. And I'm thinking of maybe starting a movie podcast? Where I review things and discuss them in detail."

Lark's mouth falls open for an extended moment before she comes to, blinking. "Wow. Movies. Who would you do the podcast with?"

I shrug. "I don't know. I think I would just do it. Maybe bring on guests to discuss certain things."

Lark fiddles with her hair, watching the waterfall. "Wow."

"And I've been thinking about moving out."

Lark's eyes whip back to mine. "Really?"

"Not, like, immediately. I want to help Mom and Dad get back on track and save up some more, figure out how I go from point A to point B a bit, but I think I might want to try out . . . California."

"California! With who?"

I shrug. "I don't know, probably by myself at this point, but I think I want to go. See what it's like."

"*You* want to move to California," she parrots.

I nod.

"Alone."

I nod again.

She chuckles. "Holy shit, Orie."

"Don't laugh at me. I think I want to try to find a job in the movie industry. I might try my hand at writing a script when I get home. And, like, I don't know, read up on directing. I gotta buy some books about all that, too. Maybe I'll try and write a simple short film. I want to learn more about producing, too. And editing. Basically, I want to try everything and pick the lane I like the best."

Lark microshakes her head. "Wow."

"Are you mad?" I squeak.

She lets go of a waterlogged "Nooo." Clears her throat. "No. I'm not mad. I knew someday you'd figure out what you wanted and . . . do it. I just didn't think you'd do something . . . so ambitious and far away. But that's great." Her voice goes up an octave.

"I don't know if any of that will work out. I might get out there and miss you so much, I turn right back around. And if that doesn't happen, I'm probably going to mess up every opportunity I get and come crying home, broke, after six months anyway."

Lark rolls her eyes. "Shut up, Orie, you're going to figure it out, and you're going to make whatever you want to happen, happen."

I drop a shaky laugh. "I think you're mistaking me for you."

She pushes me. "Catch me up on this game!"

I laugh. "Did you know I wasn't going to be on *Survivor*?"

"Not exactly—but they did call me to ask questions about you. They asked about crushes and stuff, so I told them about Remy."

"How did you know about Remy?" I demand.

"Um, you only constantly stalked his blank Instagram all through high school. And before that, I would catch you looking at his Facebook. Which, by the way, still only has five pictures."

I tell her about Remy, about our first three days, and then our second three. And then we switch off our mics so I can tell her about the control room. I watch as her excited expression starts to darken.

"WHAT THE FUCK!" she yells. "You need to get him out."

But then I explain how the game works. My lack of evidence. How without him, my chances of winning plummet. I map out my plan for the rest of the eliminations. I tell her about my relationships with Osprey and Kennedi. By the end of our conversation, I've brought her around to my thinking on it.

We switch the mics back on.

"I'm gonna win this game for Mom and Dad," I tell her.

She serves me a hard look. "And for you."

I roll my teary eyes. "And me."

"What are you going to call the movie podcast?" she asks, changing the subject.

"I don't know, maybe, like, MoORies."

"What the hell does that mean?"

"It's like a pun on movies. But with Orie."

"No."

"No?" I ask.

"That's not a pun," Lark says. "New suggestion."

"*Orie*-iginal movie discussions?" I pitch.

"That's worse."

"*Porie*-opcorn Films."

Lark's expression flattens. "That sounds like a porn company."

"P(uh)orie-corn is pretty good."

"No, no, it's not."

"THE M-ORIE THEATER."

"Stop trying to use your name as a pun. That sucks. And it doesn't have broad appeal to randoms. You need to find a little bit of a gimmick for how you'll discuss things and then name the show based on that. I'll have a brainstorm."

"A gimmick?" I ask, aghast.

"You need a fun angle!" she snaps.

I snort, laughing at her frustration. "What about me? I'm a fun angle."

Lark pushes me off the rock, and I belly flop back into the water.

44

Farewell

DAY 15

Lark and Dove join Osprey and me on our boat ride back to camp. I hug Dove and give Lark one last squeeze. She slips me an envelope: the letter from Dad. I stuff it into my bag.

Osprey and I share a wistful smile as we step off the boat. It's been such a lovely afternoon, and now we've got to wander back into the chaos of an elimination.

Jamie, Z, and the rest of our castmates are waiting by the campfire. They welcome us back with a chorus of hellos as Osprey and I take a seat on the log.

"So." Jamie claps. "We're down to six. These eliminations are getting more and more difficult. Today, we're making the decision a little less stressful. Today only two people will be vulnerable to the vote."

My stomach drops—and then I remember I won immunity. I'm safe. Osprey won, too. We're both safe.

But still. I have plans. I need Leo out of the game. I need to keep Remy and Kennedi in the game. Only Leo and Priya can leave if I want everything to move forward smoothly, and if they're not available to vote for, then there's no persuading people to vote for them.

"We will begin tonight with the choosing ceremony. Once we have our first two pairs, the remaining two contestants who were not chosen will be up for elimination.

"Our immunity winners will rock, paper, scissors for the right to pick first. We've been choosing in order of how y'all place at the challenge for a while now; tonight we're shaking things up."

I can't choose Remy this cycle because we were linked last round. But I need him to move to the next round. I'll need to choose Kennedi so she's safe. And to guarantee Remy's safety, as weird as this would be, I really need Osprey to choose him.

If given the choice to vote between Remy or anyone else, Remy will probably go at this point. He's a big physical threat, and everyone got a whiff of my suspicions through Kennedi and Osprey last cycle.

Osprey and I talked very briefly today about who we want to vote out. I kept throwing out Priya or Leo, and Osprey kept saying—*or Potential Sociopath Remy?* I wasn't shooting it down, but I also wasn't shooting it up. I didn't plead my case for Remy. And now it's too late.

Z points to the space in front of him and Jamie. "Osprey, Orie, step forward. Rock, paper, scissors, shoot for us, please."

I throw scissors, and Osprey shoots rock.

Jamie nods. "All right, Orie, stand back. Osprey, you're up."

I move to stand with my castmates, worry tugging a scowl onto my lips.

"Who do you choose?" Jamie asks.

Osprey scans over the five of us. I throw my head in Remy's direction, mentally begging him to choose my potentially sociopathic love interest.

Osprey closes his eyes, exhales, and says, "Orie."

45

Chosen

DAY 15

A giddy thrill shoots up my spine as my jaw drops. *Osprey picked me.*

But that leaves Remy and Kennedi vulnerable.

I shoot Remy an *I'm sorry I didn't get to choose first; I would have picked Kennedi!* look in attempt to quell any fears he has about Osprey and me being partnered. I don't want him to feel threatened. I need to keep him happy.

I move to stand next to Osprey. Z hooks us together with a yellow rope.

"Remy, Kennedi, Priya, Leo?" Jamie prompts. "We're gonna have you do a four-way rock, paper, scissors over there. Z will be refereeing. We'll go until we have one winner."

Kennedi wins.

I send a *please pick Remy* telepathic message her way as she steps up to choose, but she seems to be purposefully avoiding eye contact.

Kennedi opens her mouth—

"Wait!" I scream.

Everyone turns toward me. I feel like the rebellious rom-com love interest bursting through the church doors to stop a wedding. *Speak now.*

I clear my throat awkwardly. "Uh, sorry, can I talk to Kennedi?"

Jamie blinks at me, working through the pros and cons of allowing this interjection right here in the moment. They don't have protocols for this. First-season-of-a-show perks.

Jamie shares a look with Z. She turns back to me. "Okay. You have thirty seconds."

I lunge toward Kennedi, dragging Osprey along with me via tether, and cup a hand over her ear. It's all very fifth-grade recess, but my game plan is on the line, which means my family is on the line. It's necessary.

"Ken, can you take Remy?" I whisper frantically. "We'll save Priya! Things are going well with you two, right? I'm worried about keeping Leo in the game. He's strong, and he's holding a grudge against us for voting out Rick."

Kennedi pulls back to cut me an irritated look. "Orie, Remy's sketchy af."

I cup my hand over her ear again. "Yeah, but so far, he's been loyal af, too. We're not a hundred percent sure about anything other than the fact that he's been loyal. You can't pick Priya this week, but if you pick Remy over Leo, I guarantee we will save her."

Kennedi studies my eyes. "Remy's a big threat, Orie. This is risky."

"I think leaving an empty connection in the game with us is riskier," I tell her. "Leo could win immunity, align with Priya, move to bring in Osprey, and take out either of us. I know Remy will always align with *us* as long as he doesn't think we're against him."

Kennedi glares at me. "If Remy wins the game because of this move, I will murder you, Orie."

"Understood."

"Time!" Jamie calls.

Kennedi moves back to face our remaining three castmates, frustration etched in her features. "Remy."

Z clips a purple tether between Remy and Kennedi.

We get five minutes to discuss the vote. We save Priya and eliminate Leo.

We hug Leo and say our goodbyes before he's escorted off the island. Poor guy finished building our new shelter just in time to be kicked out of it.

"This week we have a third wheel," Jamie announces as Leo is boated away. "One member from each partnership, please step forward for a final round of rock, paper, scissors. Loser gets the third wheel."

Remy and I volunteer; he shoots me a grateful smile. *Good.* He knows I just put my game on the line to save him.

I win with paper.

"Third wheel goes to Remy and Kennedi!" Jamie announces.

Z walks over and puts a second carabiner on the open side of Remy's hip harness. He slips on a second rope and latches it to Priya.

Remy's going to spend the next three days in a Kennedi–Priya sandwich.

46

Sleep

DAY 16

My eyes creak open.

Osprey's hovering over me. He's propped up on one arm in the shelter. Behind him, the sky is bright gray, right on the cusp of daybreak. A Polaroid coming into its prime.

I . . . slept. For the first time in four days, my body relaxed enough to sleep. I meet Osprey's eyes. They're dark in the faint light. His artsy mustache has fully come in.

His hair's down, falling around his face. The darkness accentuates his thick eyeliner lashes.

Remy's on the other side of me. Priya and Kennedi managed to squish together onto one side of him despite being hooked to opposite sides of his harness.

"Up for crab hunting?" Osprey breathes. A sleepy grin curls up my face.

The two of us scour the area, turning over rocks and poking around with sharpened sticks in holes at the bases of trees and bushes without success. But we never give up; we just weave our way deeper into the forest. Surely there must be a crab within reach on this island. We go farther and farther in, poking around, finding nothing, until eventually, we emerge from the trees entirely and step out onto a different beach.

We're in a new small tranquil cove. Tall outcroppings of rock jut far into the sea to our left and farther down to our right, boxing in this small stretch of soft sand. It's empty. And beautiful. And for one reason or another, it sends a flurry of happiness corkscrewing through me.

I slide my eyes to Osprey. "Want to run?"

His lip tips upward into an understated Osprey smile. "Run?"

I grin back at him. "Just a small run!"

I toss my hunting stick to the side and take off down the sand, throwing a cartwheel in along the way. Osprey jogs alongside me so the rope doesn't go taut.

I feel so much lighter today without Remy lingering eight feet away. My stress levels have dropped 500 percent. I frolic along the waterline until I'm out of breath (it doesn't take long) and collapse onto the sand.

Osprey plops down beside me, and I let myself fall flat, assuming classic snow-angel position.

Instantly, I'm back with Remy. Melting under the sun after we finished our FML sign on our first day. *How is it possible that it's only been sixteen days since that moment? It feels like a lifetime ago.*

So much has changed. I feel like the world itself has shifted. It feels sharper, more pronounced, like I was wearing the wrong glasses, and someone came along and pulled focus on my life. Sixteen days ago, things like hating to leave my room without makeup took up so much brain space in my everyday life. Which outfit to put on in the morning. Which movie to watch next. Which song to use in our next video to ensure its success.

I sigh up toward the clouds. "Do you hate anything?"

"Wingdings," Osprey says immediately.

I burst out laughing. "Wingdings? The font?"

"Yes, Wingdings," he says passionately. "It's a horrific font. And there's, like, five hundred versions of it. Why? No one uses it. Why is it even a thing? Why was it ever a thing?"

I snicker, shaking in the sand next to him. "Osprey," I say once I've regained some composure.

"Yeah."

"Was Wingdings a spelling-bee word?"

He smiles, still sitting up beside me. "It was at the fifth-grade qualifiers."

"AH!" I dissolve into another bout of laughter.

"I didn't know what it was! I'd never seen the word before. I spelled it w-y-n-d-i-n-g-s, lost, got home, and ran to Google only to come face-to-face with the most futile, ridiculous, nonsensical font of all time!" He watches, lips pursed in amusement, as I cackle through this in the sand. "Want to do some AcroYoga?"

I suck in a breath. "Are you going to be the flyer?"

He snorts. "You're going to be the flyer."

"But I'm a base."

"I think given the opportunity, you'll fly just fine."

I get up and move to stand in front of his feet. "Mmm, skeptical."

He grins. "Do the thing. The diving thing Lark did to you yesterday."

He's referring to a move where Lark stands in front of me and basically falls, very gracefully, down onto me. I catch her at the last possible moment with my arms shooting straight out to support her pelvis, and she levels out, her back arched, arms up and flayed out behind her, her face serene like she's just casually defying gravity.

"Lark trusts me! She knows I'm going to catch her. We've practiced that move a gazillion times. It's easy, but only once you know the proper placement."

Osprey lowers back onto the sand and tucks his hands behind his head. "Show me."

My heart rate kicks up.

"Um, straighten your arms," I tell him. He extends his arms, humor tucked away, all focus now. "You're going to want them to land here." I splay my own hands across the front of my hip area to show him.

"Okay." He nods. "I can do that. Try it."

I shoot him a dry look.

"Come on, I'll catch you."

I widen my eyes. "You better!"

"Is that all I need to know? Arms straight, catch at the pelvis?"

I nod, tossing our tether out to the side. "Are you sure you can hold me?"

Osprey eyes me sarcastically through his dark lashes. I glance down at his ropey, sculpted arms. Yeah, *I should be okay.*

Lark doesn't watch me as she falls; she looks up and out, like soaring through the air is one of her innate gifts. She's the body; I'm the wings. She doesn't have to think about them catching her—they just will. So, I keep my gaze up.

Doing AcroYoga willy-nilly during a competitive reality show with a complete noob is not the smartest idea.

But trusting people is starting to scare me. And I want to tell that fear to fork off. I don't want to be that person who can't trust people. I love people.

I arch my back slightly, step forward, throw my arms, tighten my core, and fall.

The breath goes out of me as Osprey's strong hands slam into my hip bones. My next breath is a choked laugh of disbelief as I level out parallel over him.

"Hey, you're doing it!" I beam out at the forest behind us. "I'M FLY-ING, JACK," I yelp in a weird high-pitched voice. "I'M FLYING!"

"It's like that's the only movie you've ever seen."

I convulse with laughter and go flailing onto the sand.

DAY 16—PRODUCER CONFESSIONAL NOTES
REMY ORLANDO LASORSA—CONFESSIONAL #15

TRANSCRIPT OF EDIT

REMY

I wake up this morning, and Orie and Osprey are just gone.
I have no idea where they went, when they'll be back. I'm
stuck here attached to Kennedi and Priya, who both, for
some reason, have decided they don't like me.

It's the same judgy crap I deal with all the time. They don't
know me. They just pretend like they do.

PRODUCER Z

Are you worried about a relationship developing between
Osprey and Orie?

REMY

I've never been more confident about anything in my life
than I am about Orie. Maybe I sound like a chump out
here, but all I want to do is get home and make her dinner.
Be together in the real world. Introduce her to Jerri.

I know we live in different states, but my mom's house is
five minutes from her parents. We're going to make this
work.

PRODUCER Z

So, things are going well romantically?

REMY

I've never felt like this before. And it's really hard knowing
she's off with some other guy.

PRODUCER Z

Things seemed a little rocky between you two the other day in the water.

REMY

Orie and I trust each other. Things are going to get more complicated as we get deeper into this game. The other cast members are going to try and turn us against each other with lies and rumors. It's a classic *Survivor* move. We just have to stay strong.

47

The Climb

I'm skipping. *Skipping* through the jungle, greenery flashing by. Osprey is jogging along, never snagging the rope. At the edge of our secret beach, we found a papaya tree! Now our bags are stacked. We didn't find crabs, but we're still going to provide for the group.

I dig my heels into the ground, stopping short as a vast eccentric tree rises before us. Osprey grabs my shoulders to keep from slamming into my back.

"Wow," he says behind me.

"Wow," I echo.

The trunk is massive. The branches are thicker than us, winding around, curving out, and looping back up into each other, all the way up into the tree canopy. It's absolutely stunning. More than stunning, it's *majestic.*

Osprey throws his stick aside and takes off his bag. "That is begging to be climbed."

I guffaw. "You do remember the last time we climbed a tree."

Osprey leads us through a thicket of hefty branches. It's a much easier ascent than the coconut tree. Somewhere between twenty and thirty feet off the ground, we settle into a sturdy *V*-shaped crevasse where two mammoth branches converge. It's a standing settle, but I can comfortably hold the branch above me and lean into my side of the *V* while Osprey leans on the side behind him. And, as always, we fall into an effortless chat.

I learn Osprey has a favorite word—*persnickety*—because it won him his first regional competition in his freshman year.

"Everything comes back to being a spelling-bee nerd with you, doesn't it."

He snorts, titling his head. "You say nerd; I say champion."

I finally work up the courage to ask, "So, what are you gonna do, um, with the money? If you win?"

Osprey shifts against the tree. "A lot of things, I hope. Help my parents renovate and revamp our store." He pulls on a sad smile. "Business isn't exactly booming at I Like Books and I Cannot Lie. Give some to charity. Save a bunch for the future. I want to do the whole settle down, buy a house, have kids thing eventually." My heart bloats three sizes as he shrugs. "What about you?"

I want to tell Osprey everything. So I ask him to turn off his mic, and I spill my whole saga. I tell him about my dad. I tell him about the week I left for Fiji. The pressure I'm worried it will all put on my parents' marriage. He listens in his attentive, intense Osprey way, never interrupting or looking away. He's the only person I've ever met who does that. Listens so completely. It makes my skin hum.

Osprey's quiet for a long moment after I finish, arms crossed, brows drawn, eyes fixed on mine, leaning against his side of the *V.* Then he lifts a hand like he's about to perform the Pledge of Allegiance.

"May I offer some comfort?" he says.

A breathy laugh huffs out of me, and I nod, pushing away from the rough bark behind me so I'm within reach. "Sure."

I'm expecting Osprey to continue our tradition of the awkward comfort pat, but he takes a step forward and wraps his arms around me. Presses his chin against my head. Holds me tight against his chest. I bury my face in his shoulder and cling to his torso like he's the only solid thing left in the universe. Today, he smells like sweat with hints of dirt and a smidge of spicy vanilla. I nuzzle closer as his fingers comb the hair away from my face, gently scratching my scalp.

Hugging Osprey is like slipping into a bubble bath after a bad day. The squirmy, restless emotions slithering around in my chest come to a hard stop.

"You're sweaty, but you still smell good," I breathe.

His chest vibrates with a silent laugh. After a long moment, he mumbles against my hair, "You are irritatingly likable."

I disengage just enough to catch the sea green of his eyes. "Irritatingly likable?" I repeat. "Is that some sort of compliment?"

He presses his full lips together, hiding a smile as we balance together, embraced, in the heart of the *V*. "Take it how you will."

Fire arrows dance their way down into my chest as I search his eyes. They're brighter at the center ring, more of a parakeet color. They deepen to a dark basil as you move outward from the pupil. He's just a breath away. His face tips closer to mine, and I swallow as blue flames lick up my skin, searing through my thin layer of clothes. I don't move as our noses graze. Everything in me wants to close the space between our lips.

"Osprey," I whisper.

"Mmm."

"I'm not here to be seduced. I will not *be seduced*," I say, parroting the tone he used with me that day on the barbecue boat.

His laugh comes out in a rush of breath that tickles my skin, sending goose bumps running down my back. "Do I look like I'm about to seduce you?"

Our lips are practically touching now. Anticipation races over me, glitter shivering down my face, over my neck and collar bone. "Yes," I whisper into his mouth.

My breath hitches as his hand skates up the side of my neck. His fingers come to gently support my chin, tilt it slightly, fitting the planes of us together for a perfect—

There's a loud creak below us. My head snaps toward the sound. The camera guy is on a branch below us, repositioning to get a better shot. *Jesus.*

Panic courses in, swallowing up every last drop of giddy sorcery thrumming through me.

What am I doing? This is reckless. I have to maintain Remy's trust so my plan keeps running smoothly, and I can't do that if I start up a thing with Osprey. I can't jump into another potential rom-com plot until I sort out the muddled one I'm already tangled up in. This is a mess. I need to think. I need to take a beat.

I step back from Osprey, and then I'm falling. My arms shoot out as my back hits my side of the *V*, and I slip sideways, twisting and grasping for a handhold on the rough bark. Then Osprey has my elbow, my forearm. He swings me back up and around. With a gasp of relief, I find purchase with my feet. We're immediately face-to-face again in the small space between the *V*, breathing hard, our foreheads touching.

"You're really not good at trees."

48

It's Fine

DAY 16

"I'm sorry," Osprey says as I touch down on solid ground. He climbed down behind me, ready to save my life again if I misstepped along the way. "I didn't mean to over, uh—I didn't. Should we talk about . . . ?" He trails off, lacking the usual confidence imbued within his words.

I'm not ready to talk about this. "No, it's fine!" I grab my bag, brushing myself off, as he jumps the last few feet behind me.

"It's fine?" he repeats skeptically. "What, exactly, would you say is fine?"

Osprey pivots, bending to grab his bag. I glance nervously at the camera guy standing four feet away.

How do I say *I can't get romantically involved with you because I have to uphold the facade of a real relationship with a potential sociopathic liar to win this game* without sounding like a terrible person on national television? "Uh, I just mean, it's fine that we're frien—" That's when I see it.

A live, human-face-sized spider from the inner depths of hell on the back of Osprey's gray shirt.

Demon. *There's a demon! ON OSPREY'S BACK.*

I rip off my shoe, a scream of terrifying proportions tearing out of me as I pummel the spot between his shoulder blades with everything in my arsenal.

"Jesus Christ!" Osprey falls forward onto his hands.

The spider skitters to the ground, and I slam it again with my foot that still has a shoe. "*DIE, BITCH, DIE! DIEE!*" I drop to the dirt and come down on it again.

Osprey scrambles up. "It's dead."

I keep going. "IT'S HERCULEAN!" I screech. "IT'S ARACHNE'S THIRD COUSIN! IT WAS ON YOUR BACK, OSPREY!"

I don't know how long I've been shouting when Osprey grabs my wrist. I'm on my knees, smacking the spider repeatedly with my hand in the sneaker. Osprey carefully lifts the arm connected to my hand holding the shoe.

The spider is in pieces on the ground. I shudder, fear still drumming through me. A rogue smoke alarm wailing long after they've put out the fire.

Osprey pulls me against his chest. Wraps his warm, steady arms around me again. "Thank you," he says. "That one's actually poisonous. Great call. It's okay. Inhale now."

I suck in a breath. Exhale. Feel Osprey's heartbeat against my spine. Inhale. Feel his heartbeat. Exhale. Osprey's arms tighten around my waist. His lips press into my shoulder.

I feel them *everywhere.* Like his mouth hit a trip wire, triggering a set of glowing dominoes to zigzag through my limbs.

Whoa.

That's not normal. People don't feel shoulder kisses like that.

I'm so confused.

I've kind of done the same thing with Remy that I did with Wes when I was thirteen years old. I was so eager to find my person, I latched on to the first prospect of a happy ending to wander into my trajectory. Assumed it was my destiny. Became obsessed with our potential story. Conflated what I wanted my partner to be with the reality of who they actually were.

I thought I was so sure of Remy. But was I actually sure of Remy? Or was it the idea of Remy? Didn't I hate everything he had to say? Or was it funny? Or did I want it to be funny?

Apparently, I don't know how to balance being a romantic with being delusional.

"What's the plan when we get back?" Osprey asks quietly. His voice so close to my skin, it does more things to my insides.

I stare at our feet. My polka-dotted shoeless foot leaning casually against the top of his black sneaker. "Eliminate Priya at final five; eliminate Remy at final four. Come back with papayas now. Act normal."

"What's normal?" he quips.

"Os—" I'm cut off by the jarring rumble of a helicopter. We jerk our heads back, watching as it soars right over us in the direction of our camp.

Helicopters appearing out of the blue are usually not good.

Osprey turns to the camera guy filming us ten feet away. "Do you know what that's about?" His voice is laced with the same instinctive panic filling my gut.

"One second." The camera guy pulls out his phone and taps through it. "Fuck, someone's hurt."

"Who!" I demand.

He shakes his head. Repositions his camera back up.

Osprey and I share a look. We leap off the ground. I shove my shoe back on. We grab our bags and sticks and spring into a sprint.

What if Kennedi's hurt? What if Kennedi's hurt? What if Kennedi's hurt?

It pulses through my brain in time with my heartbeat. What if Kennedi's hurt, and it's Remy's doing? What if Remy *is an evil sociopath*?

What if me not getting Remy out of this game put my friend in danger?

Branches and twigs scratch our faces and arms as we leap over fallen trees and bushes, our hearts pounding, lungs screaming.

We run at full speed for what feels like fifteen minutes. At the ten-minute mark, we breeze past the water well, and we know we're getting close.

The helicopter's rumble blares again. Loud and overpowering. We break out of the forest and onto the beach as it's rising up into the air, away from our camp.

The anguished *noooo* that rips out of me is lost on the wind. My eyes dart frantically over the sand and land on Kennedi. My hand whips over my heart.

Oh my god. *Thank god.* She's on her knees in the sand, crying. Remy's there standing with his arms crossed. Jamie's there.

Priya is missing.

Osprey and I hobble the rest of the way over—adrenaline gone, energy depleted. I collapse next to Kennedi. She's hysterical.

"What happened?" I demand. I look to Remy. "What happened?" I swing my head between him and Jamie. "Someone tell me what happened!"

Remy's eyes flash with an intensity I've yet to see. "Where were you?"

Kennedi dry heaves, staring at the sand. I rub her back.

"Jamie, can you tell us what happened?" Osprey asks.

Jamie sighs. "Priya tripped over the rocks around the bonfire and fell in."

"FELL IN!" I gawk.

"Luckily, she only hit the edge of the fire. She broke her ankle and suffered some second-degree burns. She's on her way to the hospital now and has, unfortunately, been eliminated from the game."

I gasp. "Eliminated! What? How? What exactly happened?"

"Your castmates can fill you in once I leave. Right now, I have to inform all of you that the game's been pushed up. Instead of twenty-four days, we'll be running to twenty-one. The competition has intensified. There are only two challenges left before the last choice. You are now the final four." Jamie presses her lips together. "We'll give you an update on Priya as soon as we have one. She's going to be okay."

Osprey and I watch in stunned silence as Jamie gets on a motorboat and leaves camp. Kennedi's still gasping for breath, tears raining down her cheeks. I stuff my canteen in her face. "Here, Kennedi."

She takes the canteen and chugs some water.

I look from her to Remy. "Y'all, what happened!"

"He happened," she gasps.

"Kennedi attacked me is what happened," Remy says calmly.

"Are you kidding! *He* was insisting we go into the jungle for firewood when we have a perfectly decent amount already. I am not in the business of being bossed around; I just stood up to your bullshit."

"You literally pushed me," Remy says.

"I didn't touch you; you were yelling at me," Kennedi grinds out.

"I was asking why you insist on constantly being belligerent toward me. I just wanted to be friends."

"I don't want to be friends with you," Kennedi breathes.

Osprey steps between them. "Okay, let's all try to take a deep breath here."

I swallow, eyes wide, head swinging from one to the other.

Remy shrugs. "Kennedi pushed me right into Priya. Priya tripped over the rocks and fell over into the fire."

"You tripped into her and grabbed her so *you wouldn't fall,* and she tripped from the strain of holding your giant meathead ass and fell into the fire."

"I did not touch her," Remy insists, voice level as ever.

Kennedi has snot all the way down her beautiful face. "He pulled her down. He tripped her! He wanted her out! He tripped her into the fire!"

Remy's silver eyes catch mine. "I would never hurt someone, Orie, you know that. I did not grab Priya. Priya and I were friends. I was pushed into Priya. It was an accident."

"Orie!" Kennedi looks at me, desperate for validation. For me to take a side. When I don't say anything, she looks to Osprey. "*Osprey!* REMY DID THIS."

Osprey frowns. "Ken, take a deep breath. Priya's going to be okay."

"Don't tell me to take a deep breath," she whispers.

"It sounds like it was an accident on both accounts," I say diplomatically.

Remy sighs. "It wasn't an accident that Kennedi charged me right into the fire. I would love an apology."

Kennedi looks up at him, livid. "Hold your breath for that one, dick-wad."

Remy shakes his head.

I pull Kennedi into a hug. "Ken," I whisper. "I believe you, and I am horrified. Remy has to go next, and to do that, we have to play it cool until the challenge. If he knows we're all plotting against him, he'll go the extra mile to win immunity. We have to catch him off guard."

Kennedi exhales a long breath.

"I'm sorry," I breathe. "You were right. We should have let him go last round."

TRANSCRIPT OF EDIT

PRODUCER Z

What happened?

REMY

Listen, I was trying to get Priya and Kennedi up to go gather some firewood because, as I rightly assumed, Orie and Osprey were out scavenging for food. Priya was up and ready, and Kennedi refused to get off the fire bench.

I confront Kennedi about her constant agitation toward me. She says it's because she *doesn't like me.* She called me Captain America's [censored]hole, stood up, and charged at me toward the fire. I tripped, banged into Priya. Priya tripped over the stones surrounding the firepit, fell, broke her ankle, and suffered second-degree burns from the bits of her arm and leg that grazed the flames.

Kennedi started screaming. We both ran to help Priya, lifted her out of the firepit, and pulled her to the water because her leg and arm were in a massive amount of pain from where she was burned.

It was horrific. I wouldn't wish that on *ANYONE.* Kennedi wants to see me as a dickish monster, so she's projecting me as a dickish monster. I'm just a guy trying to figure shit out and help his family. I would never hurt anyone.

DAY 16—PRODUCER CONFESSIONAL NOTES
KENNEDI JACOBS—CONFESSIONAL #16

TRANSCRIPT OF EDIT

PRODUCER Z
What happened today?

KENNEDI
Priya and I were planning to hang in the ocean and have a relaxing morning, but Captain America's [censored]hole insisted we go gather firewood and replenish the water supply. When I said no, not right now, he got flustered and irritable and demanded to know why I "didn't like him."

I can't tell him exactly why I don't like him. All the sketchy potential lies Orie's been digging up are still hypotheticals, and we can't let him know that we know until it's time to slit his metaphorical throat. So yes, maybe in this moment, I tried to provoke him into showing his true douchebag colors.

I got close, I calmly insulted him, but I *did not* touch him, and yet, he went flying backward. He's putting on an act. He rammed right into Priya. He grabbed her for purchase, maybe pushed her in the process, and she tripped into THE FIREPIT.

I'll have nightmares about that moment for the rest of my life.

TRANSCRIPT OF EDIT

PRODUCER Z

Congratulations on making it to the final four. How are you feeling?

OSPREY

This game has been such an unexpected maelstrom of chaos. I was prepped for a human chess match, and I feel like I ended up in a messy reality show adaptation of ships and sailors.

The game started out slow. The first six days lasted a thousand years. It's speeding up now; we're running downhill, and we have no idea what's going to be at the bottom.

PRODUCER Z

Is there something going on between you and Orie?

OSPREY

I don't know what's going on with me and Orie. I couldn't tell you if I wanted to.

TRANSCRIPT OF EDIT

ORIE

Kennedi won't speak to Remy. Remy keeps obnoxiously bringing up the fact that he deserves an apology. We're all excited for the challenge-slash-elimination tomorrow.

PRODUCER Z

How are you feeling about Remy?

ORIE

I can't figure out what Remy wants. If he's been lying about working on movies in LA, UCLA, his grandma, having a close relationship with a sister . . . like, why? He didn't have to lie about those things to get to this point. He's smart, and he's really strong in all the challenges.

I don't get it. What's his angle?

49

Beginning of the End

NIGHT 17

I need sleep before our final-four challenge, but I can't keep my hold on it tonight.

Osprey's on my left, and Kennedi's on my right. She jumped into the shelter next to me before Remy could, just to piss him off.

The past two days have passed in a weary blur. We take a bath in the ocean as a group. Osprey stays as close as he can to land; his expression still says, *Help, I'm being tortured,* but he's able to function. That's incredible progress.

We go into the forest for papayas as a group. We walk the trail for water as a group. We're always quiet. Tense. As far as I can tell, Osprey, Kennedi, and I are on the same page. Remy cannot win the next challenge. It is time for him to go.

When Remy looks at me and smiles, I smile back. When he says things about our future film production company, I smile. When he talks about how Jerri's favorite movie is *Booksmart,* I feel sick. When he takes my hand in the moments we're standing next to each other and rubs his thumb comfortingly over my skin, I feel sick. When I catch Osprey watching Remy run his fingers over my arms or put a hand around my waist, I feel like there's a hole in my side, and my organs are leaking out of it.

My brain feels like a junk drawer full of wires so completely entangled that I can't even begin to make sense of what is what. I need an empty room with a whiteboard, bins, and labels to sort them all out. I can't do it stuck on this beach full of variables and uncertainty, battling hunger and exhaustion. It's impossible to ever fully concentrate. How do you fact-check anything when you're cut off from the internet and general society!

You have to just trust your gut.

But my gut said Wes would never betray me. That my father was a perfect, infallible human. That Remy was quite possibly the start of my forever. My gut has no grip on reality. MY GUT IS AN OVEREAGER FANGIRL WHO'S USUALLY WRONG.

50

Fire Starters

DAY 18

Z unclips our tethers as we arrive at the challenge space. It's extensive this time. Lots of different stations and phases.

"All right! Final four!" Jamie claps. "Welcome to your most elaborate, important challenge yet. Today, we have a bit of an obstacle course set up for y'all.

"It starts with a puzzle. Put it together, get my approval, move on. Between each obstacle are two question stations. These questions will test how well you know your fellow castmates.

"First, read the question. Then move to the next cubby. In front of you will be four jars, one with each of your names on it. Open the jar of the person whom the question is referring to. Pull out the package inside. Unwrap it. If there's a gold bracelet, you answered correctly. If there's a bone-colored bracelet, you answered incorrectly and have incurred a forty-five-second penalty. There will be PAs at every station to time your penalties and ensure no cheating ensues.

"More than one person may be in the question-reading section of the booths, but only one contestant may be in the answer cubby at any given time.

"The trick here is that there is a total of eight question booths, but you only need seven gold bracelets on your arms at the end to be qualified to win. Use your time wisely. You get to skip one question.

"After the first two question booths is a balance beam; cross the beam without falling and move on. Two more question stations, and then a throwing challenge. Use the provided sandbags to knock down the six cans on the table twenty feet away.

"Two more questions, and you'll hit a word scramble. Unscramble the words, get approved by me or Z, and move on. Be sure to cover your work with the provided sheet if you don't want your fellow castmates copying your answer. Two more questions, and you'll hit the final leg—fire. You'll have everything you need to make fire with flint at the final station. Build a fire tall enough to burn through the rope three feet off the ground, with seven bracelets on your person, and win immunity from today's vote."

Osprey, Kennedi, and I exchange determined looks.

Remy winks at me as we take our spots on the course. Apparently, I've been doing a good job making him believe we're still AP Chem till the end. A tiny part of me is still clinging to it; 10 percent of me is still determined to give him the benefit of the doubt. I can't rule out his statements yet, and I don't understand his motives, so I can't completely give up on him as a person.

But I can win this challenge. I can make sure he doesn't get immunity and doesn't go any further in this game. We can vote him out, and if it turns out he's not lying, we'll be able to talk everything through when this is all over.

I can't let Osprey or Kennedi go home over Remy.

Z has set us all on our marks in front of the first obstacle: the puzzle. As usual, I'm at the station all the way to the left. If I turn my head, Remy's next to me, then Kennedi, then Osprey.

Jamie stands in front of our puzzle stations. The pieces are already here in a bag, and they'll fit into a fish-shaped frame nailed down into the wood.

I CAN DO THIS.

"On your marks," Jamie yells. "Get set."

"GO!" Z yells from behind us.

I rip open the bag and dump the pieces. Only fifteen. Easy.

"Everyone doing well on the puzzle!" Jamie notes. "Osprey whipping through as usual! Orie right on his tail! Remy and Kennedi bringing up the rear."

"Jamie!" Osprey calls.

"YOU'RE GOOD!" Jamie yells.

I drop the last piece into my fish puzzle. "Jamie!"

She runs over. "Orie, you're good!"

I sprint away, right into the open question stall. The question is printed on a poster lying flat atop a small table.

Who had the highest GPA of their high school class?

I run to the answer cubby next door.

Our four names are carved into four opaque jars. Remy wasn't first in our class. Osprey was a spelling-bee champion, but he's said nothing about being valedictorian. Kennedi left during her last semester, but she was on track to be valedictorian before she left. I open the Kennedi jar, pull out a small cloth bundle wrapped in twine, and rabidly unwrap it.

Gold bracelet. I squeal, shove it onto my arm, and sprint to the second station. Osprey's running away from it. We nod to each other as we cross paths. I swing myself into the second question stall. A second later, Kennedi appears beside me.

Whose parents are divorced?

"It's me," Kennedi spits.

"Amazing. The other one's also you."

I whip around to the answer area, open the Kennedi jar, grab a bundle, and move out so she can grab hers. I unwrap the bundle and shove the next gold bracelet onto my arm as I sprint for the balance beam.

The beam is cake. It zigzags back and forth for about twenty feet. Osprey jumps up on his while I'm halfway through, and he's caught up to me by the time I get to the end. We both leap off at the same time.

"Shit, Osprey," I breathe as I sprint for the next question.

I can hear Jamie narrating from down the field, but I'm too in the zone to pay her any attention. No distractions. That's the only way to beat Remy.

Who's not currently based on the East Coast?

It's not me, Osprey, or Kennedi. I swing into the answer cubby, grab a bundle from the Remy jar, and unwrap it. Gold. That's three. I shove it on and sprint for the other booth. Osprey and I crisscross past each other again.

"This one's Remy," I hiss as we pass. He does a double take as he flies by.

Kennedi's jumping off her beam. She's only twenty seconds behind us. Remy's sprinting to one of the question booths behind the beams. He must have gotten a question wrong. Holy shit. YES.

Kennedi runs up behind me again as I read the next poster.

Whose sibling is currently engaged to be married?

"Me," I breathe, swinging into the answer cubby. I snatch a bundle from my jar and sprint for the throwing challenge. Four gold bracelets.

This station's going to be the most difficult for me. Osprey's a few seconds ahead. I watch as he misses with his first throw. I pick up a sandbag and chuck it. I miss the target by about a five-foot margin.

Great.

"*FIRST PANCAKE,*" Osprey yells from down the line. He chucks his second one and hits the cans. Only the top one of six falls off.

The cans are heavy.

I take a breath, wind up like I've watched pitchers do on the rare occasion my dad's watching them on the TV outside my room, and throw.

I just barely nudge the one on the edge of the little six-can pyramid. *Closer.*

"Osprey with one can, Kennedi with one can, Orie with zip!" Jamie booms.

I pick up another sandbag, focus, and throw—a frantic "ARGHHH!" tearing out of me. The sandbag smacks into the middle of the pyramid. The top can wobbles and falls.

"Orie with one down! Osprey's halfway there with three. Kennedi with two!"

I throw two more duds.

"Osprey with four! Kennedi with three! Y'all have gotta pick it up—Remy's on your tail."

I throw another dud, and Remy pulls up next to me. He throws one sandbag and knocks over two cans.

Crap. Kennedi knocks over another can. Remy knocks over a third can.

"Shit," Jamie narrates. "Remy coming back right now like it's nobody's business. He's been here no more than thirty seconds and he's knocked over half his cans."

I chuck another sandbag with all my might.

Another can falls. Four left.

"REMY KNOCKS TWO MORE; he only has one left. Kennedi and Osprey with one left as well. We've got a challenge, people!

"Orie making slow progress—AND REMY'S GOT IT! HE'S ON TO THE NEXT QUESTION BOOTH. Wow, after a wrong answer, he's pulled out into first place. OSPREY HAS HIS LAST ONE DOWN! KENNEDI HAS HERS DOWN! DAMN, THERE THEY GO!"

I'm panicking now. I still have three left. I'm in last place. I take a deep breath, wind back, and throw this thing with my whole body. Another can goes over.

"And Remy gets ANOTHER FORTY-FIVE-SECOND PENALTY! Damn, that's gotta hurt."

I hit another.

"Kennedi and Osprey working together, it seems; they've both bypassed Remy now, and they're on to the word scramble! Orie with one can left! It's still anybody's game. Don't give up!"

I throw two more duds before I smash the last can, screaming in triumph as I sprint on to the question booth Remy isn't doing his penalty next to.

Who played the lead in their sixth-, seventh-, and eighth-grade plays?

That has to be Kennedi. I swing around to the answer cubby, grab a Kennedi bundle, unwrap it. GOLD. "FORK YEAH!" That's five. I run for Remy's question area.

"Time!" the PA calls. Before I can even make eye contact, Remy sprints off like a bat out of hell for the word scramble. He's not even going to bother trying this one again.

I throw myself into the booth.

Who skipped second grade?

Well, Remy got it wrong, so it's not him. Kennedi . . . is a genius, but she's eighteen, so that wouldn't make sense. Know-it-all Osprey definitely fits the bill. I snatch a bundle from the Osprey jar.

GOLD. *That's six.* I force the bracelet up my arm and sprint to the word scramble. Everyone's still working. It must be difficult. *Thank you, universe!*

I slam into the word scramble table, catching myself against it with my hands. The wood has square indentations for letters to make up a three-word phrase. There's an array of letters set up in a line below the indentations.

_ _ _   _ _ _   _ _ _ _ _ _

T C M Y N U C O M O A I

Two three-letter words.

YOU jumps out at me. I pull the letters down onto one of the three-word spots.

YOU _ _ _   _ _ _ _ _ _

T C M N C O M A I

"Osprey thinks he has it! His hands are flying across the board, shuffling things around."

"Jamie!" Osprey yells.

"Yes! OSPREY MOVING ON!" Jamie approves.

Osprey pulls the provided sheet over his phrase and runs for the last two questions.

Concentrate. I stare at the letters. There's another three-letter word. *WHAT IS IT?*

COM keeps leaping out at me. That's not a word. Stupid internet.

Ton. Tan. Tam Tac. Tin. Cat. You Cat? Can! Can!!!

I throw the letters next to "you." YOU CAN _ _ _ _ _ _ .

T M C O M I. You can ticomm? You can Tommic. Commit. COM-MIT.

YOU CAN COMMIT—HOLY SHIT.

I arrange the letters on the board.

"JAMIE!" Remy calls Jamie over before I can.

"REMY HAS IT!" Jamie yells.

Remy throws the sheet over his board and runs off. *Goddamn it.*

"Jamie!" I wave her over to mine.

"Orie thinks she has it!" She jogs over to my board and shakes her head. "But she doesn't!"

"WHAT!" I blurt staring down at it. This has to be it! "You can commit!" Those are the words. It has to be "commit"! IT'S IN THE GAME SLOGAN.

"Wait, is it—?" I swap the order of the words "you" and "can."

CAN YOU COMMIT.

"Jamie!" I yell again.

Jamie races over. "ORIE HAS IT!"

Kennedi's head snaps up. I motion to my board and run for the questions without throwing the sheet over my answer. We need all hands on deck to beat Remy Orlando Lasorsa.

Kennedi's riddled with panic; I can see it in the way she's hunched, holding her arms in front of her, reading my board. She's the most confident eighteen-year-old I've ever met, but this game and Remy are taking a toll. He's stealing all her focus.

"Remy and Osprey have all their bracelets; they're working on fire!" Jamie announces.

"Fuck!" Kennedi yells behind me.

I sprint into what will hopefully be my last question.

Who's the oldest contestant left in the game?

Me! I throw myself into the answer cubby, snatch an Orie bundle. Unwrap it. It's—bone white.

Noo. I stare at it in disbelief. *No, no, no.*

"Orie incurs a forty-five-second penalty right before that last obstacle! It burns! Osprey and Remy are out there shaving magnesium, but no sparks yet."

A PA starts a countdown next to me. A gust of wind blows my bangs around my face, and I shove them back. Remy told me his birthday was the day after mine.

Remy lied.

This is it. *This is hard confirmation that Remy lied*—Kennedi sprints up next to me.

"Who is it?" she breathes.

"Remy," I wheeze.

Kennedi grabs a Remy bundle and sprints off for fire.

"REMY HAS SPARKS," Jamie calls out. "Anything can still happen. He has to nurse that flame; he has to turn it into a healthy three-foot-high roaring fire to burn through the winning rope.

"Now Osprey has sparks! Remy's feeding his with coconut husk. Osprey's maneuvering his, creating a tepee with his wood. Kennedi joining in, putting together her materials and shaving magnesium."

"TIME!" the PA screams out.

YES, BITCH. I snatch the Remy bundle from the jar, unwrap it as I'm sprinting to my fire station, shove the gold thing onto my wrist, and drop to the ground.

I CAN STILL DO THIS. They've outlined a circle where my fire will go in the dirt. Suspended three feet over the circle, via wooden stakes, is the rope I need to burn through. Fire materials are in a pile to my right. I grab the coconut husk, throw together a small tepee with some of the sticks. Snatch the machete. The flint.

Thirty seconds later, I've got something going.

Jamie's screaming narration to my right. I'm nursing my spark into a fire, hovering over it as the wind blows. Adding stick after slightly bigger stick. Careful not to smother.

I ration my coconut husk because it burns fast and hard. I'll need to use it strategically. I watch, fists clenched, as my baby fire blooms into a small, steady flame. *There we go.*

I glance over at Remy's. It's bigger than mine, but I'm gaining. Osprey's fire is about my height. Kennedi's struggling to get a flame going. Her eyes are wild with panic as she strikes the flint again and again to no avail.

"Remy's fire continues to grow as he feeds it increasingly large pieces of wood. Osprey's slowly gaining momentum. Oh, whoa. Orie's already got a fire as big as Osprey's. But Remy's fire's already crackling like hell."

I increase the size of the wood I'm adding to my tepee, giving the flame room and the fuel to grow. It's not as big as Remy's, but it's coming. I toss a chunk of coconut husk on, and it explodes upward, greedily devouring the material, expanding on contact out over my larger pieces of wood.

Remy looks over and smiles at me encouragingly.

Don't look at him. Don't get distracted!

"Remy's fire is reaching out for that rope; the tips of his flames are caressing it!"

"No!" Kennedi screams, still attacking her flint.

Jamie's voice jumps up an octave. "AND KENNEDI HAS A SPARK! SHE HAS SOMETHING! But here comes a gust of wind."

I scramble around to the other side of my fire like a deranged goblin, making it just in time to guard it from the incoming onslaught of wind.

It's almost licking the rope. I add the biggest pieces of wood.

"KENNEDI'S FIRE GOES OUT IN THE WIND! OSPREY'S FIRE FLICKERS OUT CONSIDERABLY; he has to build that back up again. Remy and Orie are RISKING THEIR LIVES FOR THESE FIRES, HOVERING OVER THEM LIKE HELICOPTER PARENTS."

I'm sweating bullets. My chest is beet red. I ease back as the wind dies down.

"Remy's fire's roaring; it's at the rope!" Jamie yells.

I throw everything I've got on my fire. All the coconut husks. Sticks, hair, twigs, feathers. The flames surge upward.

I have to win this. *I can win this.*

"ORIE'S IS RIGHT ON REMY'S. SHE'S FEEDING HER FIRE LITERALLY EVERYTHING IN HER ARSENAL. Her flames are licking at the finish, but it doesn't have the same ferocity as Remy's. The wind's throwing her flame slightly to the left instead of straight onto the rope. It's burning unevenly! But hey, it's still burning. The question is WHO'S GOING TO BURN THROUGH THE ROPE FIRST?"

Kennedi slams into the ground next to me, clutching all of her remaining coconut husks, and she chucks it all onto my fire. The flames erupt toward the rope.

"COME ON!!!!" she screams as my flame flickers upward and sideways, burning different parts of the rope. "*COME ON!!!!!*"

The two of us stare at the darkening spot on my rope. *Come on. Burn.* Kennedi clutches my arm, nails digging into my skin. *COME ON.*

There's a *crack* to my right. Our heads snap in slow motion to Remy's station as his fire soars past his broken rope.

My ears ring as Jamie announces his win, a haze rolling in over my reality.

No. No, I had him. I had him. I HAD HIM.

Kennedi's cursing next to me. I look back over at my own fire just as the rope snaps.

Eight seconds later. Eight. Seconds.

Fire is mine. That's my thing. I'm so good at fire.

I'm in the air. Remy's picked me up, his arms wrapped under my hips under the harness.

Apparently, not good enough.

Remy swings me around. "WE DID IT, OR!"

Remy's birthday is not December eighth. Which means he knew my birthday was December seventh.

I pull on what must be a smile and throw out my arms as my insides shrivel to ash along with everything else I threw on that fire.

"*You* did it," I correct.

There's a snap as Osprey's fire burns through his rope.

51

Brutal

DAY 18

Remy won.

We can't vote for Remy.

Everything's ruined.

I should have won that. That was mine. That was what I trained for my entire pubescent life. I don't want to vote for anyone else.

I'm tearing up as Remy slides me down his chest and places me in front of him.

"What's wrong?" he asks quietly.

I sniffle up my intense disappointment. Try to level out my voice. Camouflage it with sadness. "I just love everyone here, and I don't want anyone to be eliminated."

Remy hugs me to his chest. "It's going to be okay; they both know it's a game. They'll forgive you."

But will I forgive me?

Jamie claps for our attention. Z comes to stand next to her.

"All right," Z says, "you all know the drill by now. You have ten minutes to chat, and then we vote. You cannot vote for Remy, but you can vote for anyone else. Good luck."

Kennedi sprints over toward us, but instead of pulling me aside like I expect her to, she grabs Remy.

Osprey comes to me. "I think Kennedi's gunning for me. Who are you thinking?" He focuses his eyes on my chin.

"I don't want to vote for either of you."

"But you have to."

"I don't want to vote for Kennedi." I swallow. "But I feel like she's still so young, and the game is taking a mental toll. She just turned eighteen. She's missing her senior year right now."

"She's a super overachiever. I think anything she does in life she's going to excel in, she's so freakin' smart. I love her. I hate this so much."

Osprey meets my eyes. "Are you sure it isn't me? Just tell me if you're voting for me."

"Osprey, I'm not voting for you. Paperback Party holds firm. I've voted with you every single elimination. I'm not going to stop now."

He nods, emotion welling in the creases on his forehead, the tight lines around his mouth. "We should have invented our own secret handshake. For paranoid moments like this."

I reach out, jerk my arm up and down, and pat his shoulder. He smiles and does the same.

"Kennedi's going to be fine, Tube Stop; she's about to be the number-one parkour athlete on the eastern seaboard."

I nod. "This just sucks."

Kennedi comes barraging toward us. She drags me to the side, away from Osprey. "We're voting Oss, right? He's a threat to win the game, Orie. He's been lying low, not upsetting anyone. He's good at everything. We have to get him out."

I pull Kennedi into a hug. She pulls away. "Don't hug me! What are you doing!"

I'm crying now.

"No, don't you dare cry. You're not voting for me. Womentopia, Orie!"

"Kennedi, you have so much going for you at home right now. You're killing it at school, and in the beauty pageant world, and, according to Osprey, the parkour community. You're on the up and up; this isn't even going to be a blip on your success radar. Go finish senior year."

"Orie! Shut up. Don't vote for me. Vote for Osprey!"

I shake my head. "Osprey and Remy are voting for you, Kennedi. You're so young to have to be dealing with all this."

"Please, YOU'RE, LIKE, FIVE SECONDS OLDER THAN ME, ORIE. I'm so mad at you right now. I knew this was going to happen once Priya was gone. I knew it."

"You're a threat, Kennedi. You're cutthroat and kind and caring and charismatic. You could sway any jury to your side, no matter what the situation. I love you, but I have to play the game to win, too.

"This is my best play right now. You would beat me in the final two. You are the most persuasive, persistent person I've ever met."

Kennedi stares me down, water welling up in her eyes. "If you let that bitch over there win, I will never forgive you."

"I'm going to do my darnedest."

"Do better than that," Kennedi says. She launches away from me. "I gotta go try and convince Osprey and Remy to vote you out."

Remy walks over. "Kennedi," he says. I nod, wiping my cheeks.

52

Non-Musketeers

DAY 18

Kennedi went home. I feel like a traitor.

I am hooked to two boys. One on my left and one on my right.

I want to be alone.

I want to eat alone. I want to pee alone. I want to sit and stare out into the distance while I question all my choices, and I want to do it alone.

We returned to a picnic basket full of fruit and sandwiches, a variety of cheeses, bacon, bread, and three bottles of wine with a card that read CON-GRATULATIONS FINAL 3 laid out at our camp.

Body Update:

1. We are all starving, so this food is a godsend.
2. I haven't pooped since my night at the hotel. *How many* nights ago was that? It feels like an eternity. That was day twelve. It basically was an eternity. It's day eighteen. Six days ago. And now I'm tethered to a creepy man-boy I've had a crush on for eight years, and a boy I'm in . . . something with.

3. This might be when it finally happens ("it" being me dying of constipation).

4. I've stopped being attracted to Remy. The charge I've been feeling so strongly has completely died.

5. I'm deeply attracted to Osprey.

6. I've started losing muscle mass. I worked so hard to build that up. So many protein shakes. So many early-morning training sessions.

7. I'm always thirsty.

Mental Update:

1. Upon receiving this congratulations package, I realized I still haven't read my father's letter. I miss him. I'm afraid of what he might say, but I want to hear his voice, and reading his voice is the next best thing. I'm going to open it before our final challenge.

"I have to take a piss," Remy says, stirring Osprey and me from our various reveries. "Any of y'all have to? Orie, you gotta poop?"

I glare at him as he stands up. We're still mid-picnic. "Remy, I told you I never poop."

Osprey and Remy both snort. Osprey and I are sitting in the sand slowly working through the food. I'm stuffing a piece of bread dressed with an enormous chunk of brie down my throat.

"Can it wait till we finish eating?" Osprey asks cordially.

Remy grabs a bottle of wine and unscrews the cap before plopping back down. "All right." He takes a swig. "Can you believe one of us might win a million dollars?"

Osprey and I exchange a quick look. "No," I say quietly. "It's surreal."

"Shall we play another round of truth or dare, 'never have I ever' mashup? We've got the booze for it." Remy puts on a weird British accent. "Osprey, what do you think, 'never have I ever' truth or dare? Orie and I played the first night of our first cycle out here; it was a blast."

Osprey shrugs. "Sure, man."

We're two rounds in.

"Truth or dare," I ask Remy.

"Truth." He smiles at me. His eyes are already glassy. Wine hits quick when you've been scavenging to ingest one meal a day.

"When is your birthday?" I challenge.

"What do you mean? I told you December eighth, day after yours."

"Yeah, and I got it wrong in the challenge when I said I was the oldest." That cost me *the game*.

"No, no, I'm a year older than you. My parents held me back from school a year so I'd be better at sports. It's kinda fucked up. They wanted me to be bigger than the other kids so I'd have an advantage. But my birthday is December eighth."

I'm silent for a moment, scrutinizing him. He has an answer for everything.

I need to get off this island so I can actually figure this out. Every time he explains something, my head goes spinning off my body into the atmosphere, running through everything I've ever known to prove or disprove his statements.

"All right," Remy starts. "Osprey, truth or dare." Remy passes him the wine.

Osprey has his game face on. There's no emotion in his eyes as he watches Remy. His hair's pulled back in a tight bun today, making those cheekbones look sharp as knives. I want to trace them with my fingers. "Truth."

Remy pulls his legs up against his chest. Orange light drenches his innocent-looking freckled face as the sun starts to set. "Have you and Orie kissed?"

"Remy," I groan.

Osprey takes a sip from the wine bottle. "No, Remy, we have not."

Remy smiles, his eyes sparking. "You should; she hasn't kissed many people."

"Remy!" I snap. "What the hell."

"I can tell she wants to give it a go." He continues, "This way, you both get it out of your systems."

Osprey sizes him up. "What is this, some sort of test?"

"Remy, you're cut off," I tell him.

He picks up my foot that's closest to him and starts massaging it.

"Okay, you don't have to do that," I say. He shifts closer until he's behind me and pulls me into his lap against his chest. Presses his lips into my hair. Fingers the puka shells around my neck. My eyes flick to Osprey.

"Remy, what are you doing?" I ask as calmly as I can manage. I'm afraid to yell at him. I'm afraid of what might happen if he gets angry.

"He doesn't care," Remy murmurs.

"I care," I say softly. I crawl out of his lap.

Remy watches me. "I thought you said you two are just friends."

"We *are* friends." I hug my legs up to my chest.

"I think we should take that bathroom break," Osprey says, standing. He holds out a hand to help me up.

53

Closing In

DAYS 19–21

The next three days stretch and condense depending on the activity we're engaging in.

I feel like I'm being peed on every time Remy reminisces about our first three days on the island in front of Osprey. Osprey never brings up our time together in front of Remy.

We ration the fruit from our picnic so we don't have to go searching through the jungle for constant sustenance. Now that the end is nigh, we all want to conserve our energy for the final challenge.

We spend a lot of time just lying in the shelter. Talking about food. Talking about movies. In my head, I brainstorm movie-centric podcast titles. Outside my head, I make a game out of chatting about our favorite movie-star classics.

First, our favorite Julia Roberts film: *Runaway Bride* for me, *Erin Brockovich* for Osprey, *Ocean's Eleven* for Remy.

Then Tom Hanks: *You've Got Mail* for me, *Cast Away* for Osprey, *Big* for Remy.

Brad Pitt: *Mr. & Mrs. Smith* for me, *Ad Astra* for Osprey, *Inglourious Basterds* for Remy.

When one of us can't think of any film to say for a specific star, that person gets a point. The more points you have, the worse you're doing at our structureless game. I secretly figured it would add fire to my *Remy is lying about wanting to make movies* theory.

But my plan kind of backfires because Remy knows a lot of movies, and I end up enjoying our conversations immensely and growing even more confused.

A dynamic develops between the three of us. A weird one, but it's civil. By the morning of day twenty-one, my very last brain cell has morphed to scrambled eggs.

Even Osprey pulls me aside at one point while Remy is chopping wood to question if we possibly miscalculated. If all the "lies" were us projecting. If Kennedi was exaggerating. And I tell him I've been wondering the same thing.

Because I have to admit it's weird that I would catch a discussion about a call to Remy's mom exactly as I'm passing the control room on the way to the bathroom. It could have easily been a plant to create drama.

And his story about being older than me makes sense. He was an athlete throughout high school. I didn't consider that he could be an entire year older than me. That would make him twenty-four. Kennedi could have been exaggerating about Remy's role in Priya's accident to get us on board with voting him out.

We have no actual proof that Remy's lying about Jerri's existence, other than the fact that Jerri wasn't here for the family visit. But what if she had something important going on at school? Or in life? What if she was sick? What if she just couldn't make it?

If Jerri is actually real, this entire lying theory unravels.

We have no real proof Remy didn't study film other than the fact he didn't know the director of *Iron Man*. But he still *knows* movies.

What if all this time Remy wasn't lying? What if I've warped a whole new reality around a conspiracy theory planted by production? What if I accidentally turned everyone against him for no reason?

"What's the first thing you're going to do when you get home?" Osprey asks the night before our final challenge. The three of us are sitting around the fire sharing a meal of three roasted coconuts.

"Hit the gym. Jesus, it's been too long," Remy says.

"Really, Remy," I say dryly.

"Ay, don't judge. I miss the gym. Those people are my second family, and I'm losing all my mass."

Osprey and I chuckle. But also, wasn't I just worrying about losing my mass two days ago? Am I still going to be able to lift Lark when I get back?

"What about you, Orie?" Osprey asks. Osprey doesn't call me Tube Stop in front of Remy.

"Hug my mom and dad. Demand my dad's braised short rib red wine stew, slip into a bubble bath with the latest rom-com book my mom's brought home from the office, and then watch a movie in bed on my computer with a steaming hot cup of Irish breakfast tea with a spoonful of sugar and oat milk." I close my eyes. "Mmm."

"Damn, that sounds good," Osprey says dreamily. "It's high time I pick up a rom-com, expand my reading horizons. Which would you recommend I start with?"

A smile pops onto my face. "Oh! You gotta go Christina Lauren! *The Unhoneymooners* for sure! What's one of your favorite non-rom-coms? We can start a Paperback Party book club!"

"Have you read *Project Hail Mary* yet?"

"No."

He grins. "That's your assignment."

"What about me? Do I get an assignment?" Remy smirks.

I tilt my head. "You read both those books, Remy Orlando Lasorsa, and see which you like better."

Remy has his back against the fire bench. He's sitting on the sand next to my legs. He reaches out and gives my foot a compassionate squeeze. I don't know what to think about this Remy. The Remy from the last three days has been almost back to my original cycle Remy. Calm. Cute. A little obnoxious.

Again, I am so confused. In those random moments, remnants of that initial attraction ricochet through me.

"What about you, Oss?" I ask, picking back up the conversation. "What's the first thing you want to do?"

"Family game night. Ask my dad to make dinner on the grill. Go out for ice cream afterward. Curl up with a book in bed."

"Mmm, what games do you play? We don't do game night, but I wish we did. We do *family reading nights.* It's almost embarrassing. Kennedi would tell me we're embarrassing. I miss Kennedi."

Osprey laughs. "When I have kids, I am *so* enforcing family reading nights. Do you all just sit there reading different books, or do you all read the same thing so you can discuss?"

I snort. "No! We all just sit in the same room reading different things."

Osprey barks out a laugh. "That's amazing. That's like when the whole family's in the car, and everyone has their earbuds in listening to different shit."

Remy laughs. "That's me and my family always."

I find myself staring wistfully into the fire. "I'll miss this, though. Being completely unplugged. It has its cons, but there is a certain peace that comes with being rendered utterly clueless to what everyone else is doing every second of the day."

"Mm-hmm," Oss agrees beside me.

"You're forced to live in the moment," I say quietly. "Every hour feels so much more significant. You feel time *harder.* It just slips away when you have all the distractions of the normal world."

I glance sidelong at Osprey. He's staring, unabashedly smiling at me. Like I'm—I don't know, something impressive. A cool elephant. A nice ghost. A tree? *A good tree.*

I grin back, a flush burning fast and hard up my neck. "What?" I ask self-consciously.

He shakes his head and looks away at the fire. "Nothing. I'm going to miss it, too. But I am excited to sit down with a burger the size of my face."

I laugh.

"I'm excited to get back to training," he continues. "I'm excited to sit in the armchair tucked in the corner of my parents' store with a cup of tea and whatever exciting new release I've missed."

"I'm excited for fucking electricity," Remy adds.

"I'm excited for TOILETS!" I throw out.

Osprey smiles. "I can get behind a toilet."

Remy throws up a fist. "FUCK YEAH, TOILETS!"

54

Last Dawn

DAY 21

I'm up at dawn with the boys. We watch the sunrise one last time. At some point, I remove myself from our huddle to finally read my dad's letter.

I swallow down a rush of emotion as I extract it from the worn envelope I've had sitting in the bottom of my bag. It's on a folded-up piece of yellow legal pad paper. Dad must have done multiple drafts because it's written in ink, and there are no cross-outs. It's flawlessly penned. If I handwrote something like this, I would have made a million mistakes, changing my mind about the wording of this or that a million different times along the way, scribbling all over the margins. *This is neat.* Purposeful.

ORIE,

I AM SO EMBARRASSED.

I WILL BE ETERNALLY SORRY THAT I LET YOU LEAVE THE COUNTRY WITHOUT APOLOGIZING FOR THE OTHER NIGHT. YOU DESERVED AN EXPLANATION.

IN SO MANY WAYS, THESE PAST FEW MONTHS, I HAVE LET YOU DOWN. I LET LARK DOWN. I LET YOUR MOTHER DOWN. I LET MYSELF DOWN.

I'M SORRY FOR PUTTING YOU IN SUCH AN AWKWARD, TERRIBLE POSITION IN THE MIDDLE OF THE NIGHT. FOR SCARING YOU TO DEATH, AS

I'M SURE I DID. FOR GOING THROUGH YOUR PURSE?! I WAS OUT OF CASH, AND OUT OF MY MIND, SOLELY FOCUSED ON KEEPING MY LIQUOR STORE CHARGES FROM SHOWING UP ON THE CREDIT CARD BILL.

AT FIRST, WHEN I WOKE UP THE NEXT DAY, I DIDN'T EVEN REMEMBER IT HAD HAPPENED. IT CAME BACK TO ME IN FLASHES THROUGH THE MORNING. I PUZZLED IT TOGETHER IN MORTIFYING PIECES. I THREW A HAND OVER YOUR MOUTH IN THE MIDDLE OF THE NIGHT. GOD ONLY KNOWS WHAT YOU THOUGHT IN THAT MOMENT.

I'M SO SORRY. I CAME CLEAN TO YOUR MOTHER ABOUT MY RELAPSE THE NEXT DAY.

I HOPED YOU WOULD NEVER HAVE TO SEE THAT SIDE OF ME. I NEVER WANTED YOU TO KNOW THAT PART OF ME. BUT I THINK KEEPING IT FROM YOU GIRLS, ULTIMATELY, ONLY AIDED IN MY INEVITABLE DOWNWARD SPIRAL THIS SUMMER.

I'M LEARNING (THE HARD WAY) THAT THE HEALTHIEST WAY FOR ME TO HEAL AND STAY HEALTHY IS TO BE OPEN. SECRECY IS OIL ON A SLIPPERY SLOPE.

PLEASE KNOW, I LOVE YOU. YOU AND LARK HAVE KEPT ME ON TRACK, INSPIRED ME, FUELED MY SOBRIETY, FOR SO LONG.

LARK TOLD ME THAT, AS I EXPECTED, YOU'RE KICKING ASS OUT THERE.

I'M SORRY TO HEAR ABOUT WES (AGAIN, LARK TOLD ME), BUT I'M GLAD YOU TWO HAVE DECIDED TO GO YOUR SEPARATE WAYS. I KNOW HOW HARD THAT MUST HAVE BEEN. I KNOW HOW MUCH YOU WANTED HIM TO BE YOUR PERSON. SOMETIMES YOU GROW OUT OF A RELATIONSHIP. PEOPLE EVOLVE IN DIFFERENT DIRECTIONS AT DIFFERENT SPEEDS. HE WASN'T MAKING YOU HAPPY, AND WE'VE ALL JUST BEEN WAITING FOR YOU TO REALIZE IT.

LARK TOLD YOU ME YOU'RE ACTUALLY ON A <u>SURVIVOR</u> SPIN-OFF SHOW WITH A ROMANTIC TWIST? THAT SOUNDS RIGHT UP YOUR ALLEY.

I HOPE YOU FIND EVERYTHING YOU'RE LOOKING FOR OUT THERE. I HOPE YOU KNOW I'M IN YOUR CORNER NO MATTER WHAT HAPPENS. I AM HONORED TO BE YOUR DAD.

I KNOW YOUR TRUST IN ME HAS PROBABLY BEEN SHAKEN. MAYBE IRREPARABLY SO? GOD, I HOPE NOT, BUT I UNDERSTAND IF IT HAS. I UNDERSTAND THAT WHAT HAPPENED COULD REALLY MESS WITH YOUR

REALITY. I UNDERSTAND THAT YOU MIGHT NOT WANT TO LIVE WITH US ANYMORE. I WILL UNDERSTAND IF THAT'S THE CASE. BUT I HOPE WE CAN MOVE PAST THIS.

I CAN'T WAIT TO HEAR ABOUT YOUR ADVENTURES. AND WHILE I'M WAITING, I'M GOING TO WRITE DOWN MINE, SO I KNOW I DON'T FORGET ANYTHING WHEN WE FINALLY GET TO TALK.

I'VE GOTTEN BACK INTO BIRD-WATCHING HERE AT THE RECOVERY CENTER.

RECOVERY IS HOW I GOT INTO BIRD-WATCHING IN THE FIRST PLACE. I STARTED IN MY EARLY TWENTIES, WHEN I FIRST GOT SOBER. I FOUND SO MUCH PEACE IN THEIR BEAUTY, THEIR FOIBLES, THE INTRICACIES OF THEIR INTERACTIONS. THEY TAUGHT ME PATIENCE. HOW TO BE STILL. HOW TO APPRECIATE WHAT'S RIGHT IN FRONT OF ME. THEY TAUGHT ME ABOUT HOPE. AND IN SO MANY WAYS THEY PREPARED ME FOR YOU (AND YOUR SISTER).

HOPE IS THE THING WITH FUCKING FEATHERS. THERE'S NEVER BEEN A LINE OF PROSE SO INCREDIBLY RELEVANT TO MY LIFE. I'VE NEVER REALLY EXPRESSED HOW JAZZED I WAS WHEN YOU GOT INTO EMILY DICKINSON. I TEARED UP THE DAY I SAW "I DWELL IN POSSIBILITY" SCRAWLED ACROSS YOUR BACK.

ALL RIGHT, I'M REALLY DIGGING INTO DEEP WATERS HERE. I'LL SAVE IT FOR MY LEGAL PAD AUTOBIOGRAPHY.

IN THE PROLIFIC WORDS OF MILEY CYRUS, I CAN'T WAIT TO SEE YOU AGAIN.

YOU'LL ALWAYS BE MY FEATHERS.

ALL MY LOVE,

DAD

I read it five times. I've never been sent a real, handwritten letter before. He's never told me about the birds before. Or Emily Dickinson. I hold the legal pad paper to my heart, trying to absorb all the emotional support from the page via skin-to-paper contact (like some weird, love-hungry, feeds-on-handwritten-letters-only vampire).

Then we all get up, pack our things, say goodbye to camp, and head to the final challenge.

55

Final Stand

DAY 21

The three of us have been placed on a grassy clearing at the top of an intimidating, aesthetically pleasing cliff. We've been positioned before what appears to be a row of torture devices. Z moves through us, removing the tethers.

Three larger-than-a-human-sized square wooden frames are arranged in a shallow horseshoe. Each frame has two pegs sticking up on the bottom line of the square, and two foam handholds hang from ropes that have been nailed to the top two corners. It's clearly an endurance challenge. It looks horrific.

The sun's almost directly overhead as Jamie walks out to join us in the clearing. There's a black crew tent set up about a hundred feet away, off to the right among some trees so it's out of shot. Jamie comes to a stop in the space between us and the torture frames.

"Hello, final three!" She smiles. "It's your last day; are we excited?"

We chorus an enthused *yes*.

"That's what I like to hear!" She claps. "Before we begin, we're going to have you all take a seat." Jamie glances over her shoulder toward some crew members hovering off to the side of the set. "Can we bring out the bench?"

Two PAs hurry out with a wooden bench and place it directly behind the three of us. We sit.

My heels bounce against the ground. This is it. I'm in the final three. I really could . . . win this. I really could help my family.

"As I stated at the beginning of the game, this is a social experiment about relationships. Testing extreme compatibility in romance and friendship against different backdrops, against money, in various situations and seeing how they play out. I told you there'd be some curveballs. Today, we're gonna throw you one.

"Right now, I'm going to give y'all an opportunity. A chance to make a big decision that could change the course of the game. You have come as far as you can survival-wise, and the relationships you made with your castmates have gotten you here. So today, if you so choose, we don't have to do this challenge." Jamie gestures to the torture setup behind her.

"Right now," she continues, "if you so choose, we can end this game. All three of you can be crowned champions of *Attached at the Hip* season one." She pauses to make separate eye contact with each of us. I stare back at her suspiciously. "Instead of potentially one of you walking away with the million dollars, the three of you would all leave here with three hundred and forty thousand dollars, about seven thousand dollars per person more than one million divided by three."

I raise my hand. Jamie nods at me. "But you said one or two people could win at the beginning of the game."

She nods. "Yes, one or two people can still win. And right now, we're opening that up to three. Or we play the final challenge, and the winner will choose one person to take with them to the finale. Those two final players would then present their case for the million-dollar prize to all of America." She pauses again, letting that sink in.

We'd plead our case *to America. Not to the people we've eliminated.* We have to convince the viewers we deserve this, *not our castmates.*

"You have three minutes to decide what you'd like to do. You can take the money now and win the game together, but the decision has to be unanimous." Jamie smiles. "Go."

Osprey, Remy, and I curve into a huddle on the bench, staring at one another for an extended moment, waiting for someone to speak first.

When no one does, I decide to go for it. "I think we should split the title and take the money."

Osprey nods. "I'm up for it." We turn to Remy.

Remy shifts toward me. "Orie, we can't. I could see if it were splitting it between the two of us; that'd be different, but three ways? That's not enough to cover what I need it to cover. I don't think that's going to be enough to cover your family's issues, either."

I sigh. "Probably not completely, but it's enough to make a big dent for all of us in whatever we need the money for! And if we don't split it, two of us might not get anything!"

Remy doesn't respond.

"Remy," I press, "three hundred and forty thousand dollars is still an unbelievable amount of money, and we're making it in thirty-one days! That's huge, and we all get the title! The first season! That's so cool."

Remy shakes his head. "Sorry, no."

I blink at him. "No! Just no?"

"You're going to be happy I said no, Orie, when you realize that's not nearly enough to solve your problems."

"Remy, come on. Look at those things." Osprey nods to the torture devices. "It's gotta be at least a hundred degrees out right now."

Remy looks up at Jamie. "We're going to do the challenge."

Osprey and I exchange an exhausted, hollow look. I drop my head in my hands.

"Okay." Jamie claps. "Let's get you three set up."

The balls of my feet are balanced on square wooden pegs about three feet apart. My arms are stretched out above me, clutching the handles dangling off the ropes nailed into the corners of the wooden frame. I'm in the center torture frame between Osprey and Remy. We're in full star positions, arms and legs extended. I keep imagining I'm about to be pulled apart. It's not helping my nerves.

Jamie folds her hands together. "The rules are simple today: The last person standing in position, feet on the pegs, hands on the handles, wins.

You let go of a handle, you're out. Either foot leaves the pegs, you're out." She turns to face the camera. "Everyone's in position. It's noon, and this challenge is on."

Drones buzz as they hover over us. Three different camerapeople are scattered around on the ground.

The pegs are already hurting my feet. Sweat drips down my forehead. The sun beats down on my neck. I close my eyes. Hang my head.

Remy didn't want to split the money with Osprey. Just another red flag to add to my collection.

I slide my eyes to Osprey on my right. His hair is pulled back tight at the nape of his neck. He gives me his *you can do this* nod. I nod back. Close my eyes. Redirect my focus elsewhere. I go back to the beach. Sit with my father's letter.

"You've been up there for forty-five minutes."

Jamie's voice brings me back. I open my eyes. I can't feel my hands. I don't dare move them. When I rock on my feet, I find them full of pins and needles.

"This is for the million dollars. How are y'all feeling? You're probably going to be up there a looong while."

Panic nips at my numb toes. Urges me to move them. Massage them. Wiggle.

I glance over at Remy, and he smiles at me. *Smiles.* I turn to Osprey. His eyes are closed. I exhale again and close mine.

When I get home, I'm going to start a movie podcast. Time to brainstorm an angle.

"Four hours," Zarar says.

I gasp back into myself. I've been running through a list of all my teachers from kindergarten on, rating them on a one-to-five scale.

"You've all been up there for four hours!" Z continues. "That's a feat. You should be very proud of yourselves."

I lift my chin. I feel weak and feathery, hollow. Burnt. Thirsty. The sun has been relentless. Where are the clouds? I spent forty-five minutes earlier trying to manifest a cloud through telekinesis.

I've been trying so hard not to think about my body. Concentrate on the endgame. My parents already lost the restaurant. They could very likely lose the house. I just have to hold on. *Keep going.*

"You gotta be thinking about who you're doing this for right now," Zarar says. "You gotta be thinking, 'Why did we choose this over three hundred and forty thousand dollars?'"

"I'm definitely thinking that," I croak out.

"I feel fine, Zarar," Remy says. "I could go twenty-four hours like this."

Next to me, Osprey rolls his neck like one might roll their eyes.

"Orie, who are you playing for right now?"

The word "Dad" wisps out of me. "Mom . . . Sister. Me. I had to prove to myself that I was capable of things. Succeeding on my own." My head falls forward against my chest.

I feel like an empty juice box. An empty Capri Sun pouch.

"Osprey, how 'bout you?" Z asks.

I slide my eyes his way.

"Playing for my family. They're all home, watching on the couch, on edge, rooting for me. Playing a survival game has been my dream since I was ten years old."

Z nods. "Remy?"

"As always, my sister, Jerri. I got you, girl."

Jamie stands up from the bench where she's been watching.

"Anyone thinking of throwing in the towel anytime soon? It's gotta be scalding up there."

"I'll never let go, Jamie," I mumble.

She points to me, smiling. "Never let go!"

"Six hours," I hear Jamie say. "Wow."

I've just been counting. I've run out of things to think about. I'm up to 3,428.

My hair is soaked against my neck. Sweat drips down my back, my chest. My legs have started to quake. I feel nothing.

"Orie is shaking. But Osprey and Remy are still looking solid as ever. You okay, Orie?"

"I'll never let go," I mumble again. I can do this. I've. Come this far. I'm going to do this.

"Orie. Your head's lolling a bit. Are you with us?" Jamie asks.

I try to say yes.

"Orie!" That sounds like Osprey.

The world blinks out.

56

Fallen

DAY 21

My arms are on fire. Pain shoots up through my legs. They're cramping. Everywhere. Water's . . . dripping into my ears? My eyes jerk open.

I'm on my back.

No. *No, no, no, no, no.* I open my mouth to object. It comes out as a bumble of nothing.

Osprey's hovering over me . . . I'm in Osprey's lap.

No! Osprey's in the challenge. Is the challenge over?

"Drink," he says. "It's okay."

I gurgle down some water. It's sweet. Gatorade? Liquid IV? Pedialyte?

Jamie's face hovers over me. She's holding an umbrella. But it's not raining? I look down at my arms. A medic is taking my pulse. My blood pressure.

I open my mouth. "Jamie, I want to keep going."

"I'm so sorry, babe. You're out. Osprey's out. Remy won the challenge."

My eyes bulge as the medic slides an oxygen mask on me. I knock it off with a limp hand. "No, no, I'm out, but Osprey can still play."

"Osprey jumped off to catch you, babe. You fainted and fell off the perch."

No. No. Noooo. Water I don't have in my body floods my eyes as they slide up toward Osprey.

"Osprey." I heave in a labored breath as more cramps rack me. "That was so stupid, Osprey. That was so stupid."

"Just relax, Tube Stop."

"I can't relax when you're being stupid."

A flare of humor sparks behind his sea green eyes. "We have each other's backs; we don't do crack. Does the covenant mean nothing to you?"

I hold his gaze, my chin quivering, until Remy hobbles into view. "Or, you okay? Is she all right?" he asks the doctor taking my pulse.

The doctor nods. "Dehydration, and she's extremely pale; the sun's taken a harsh toll, even with sunblock. She needs shade. Give us ten minutes. We'll get some more fluids in her, and she should start to feel better."

Jamie stands before us. The sun has finally dipped below the horizon. Torches have been lit around the challenge arena, giving the wooden frames an extra medieval aesthetic.

I'm on my feet again. I can't believe I fainted. I blew the final challenge. I ruined Osprey's shot at the challenge. I ruined everything.

"Remy, please step up over here." Jamie directs him to stand in front of us. "Congratulations, you've won yourself a spot at the final two. How does it feel!"

"It feels fantastic, Jamie."

She nods toward me and Osprey. "It's time to choose. Who do you want up there with you? Who else gets to make their case for the million-dollar prize?"

Remy smiles. "I gotta bring Orie, my main babe from day one!"

Jamie spins toward me. "Congratulations, Orie! You're in the final two! Your relationships and survival instincts have carved a path for you all the way to the finale!" She turns to Oss. "And I'm so sorry, Osprey, that means you, unfortunately, are the eighth person eliminated from this season of *Attached at the Hip*. You did an amazing job, and you have been a joy to watch. Z is going to escort you to a boat we have waiting. You can say your goodbyes."

Osprey looks at Remy. He lifts a tired hand in acknowledgment. "Good game, man."

Remy nods from his spot next to Jamie.

I turn and wrap Osprey in a hug. "Oss, I'm so, so sorry."

"You have nothing to be sorry for. I don't regret anything. I had an amazing time." He pulls back and smiles at me. "I'll see you in the real world, Piccadilly. I'm rooting for you."

I have to smash my lips together to stop them from quivering. "Kennedi's going to be so mad I fainted."

Osprey laughs. He picks up his bag and waves as Z escorts him away.

Remy comes to stand next to me. He takes my hand and squeezes. I try to be excited. But the moment feels thick. Heavy. Uncomfortable.

"Orie. Remy." Jamie throws her hands out excitedly. "You are our two finalists! This, of course, is the last day for you here on the island. Now you're going to go home, we're going to edit the show, and we'll all come back together for our live finale where you'll present your case to America for a million dollars. Start to think about what you'll say. How did you connect, commit, and conquer this game full of friendship and strong potential romantic relationships?

"During the finale, your castmates will have the opportunity to back either of you, live, as their choice for the winner. And then America will vote to choose our champion. If it's a fifty-fifty split, you two will be splitting the money. If there's more than a one-percent margin, then we will have a million-dollar winner. If you're really a match, and you care that much about each other, then it won't matter who wins. You can split the prize outside the show if you wish.

"A couple ground rules: during our three-month hiatus, there is no interacting on the internet or in person with any of your castmates; it violates our NDA to make in-person or private contact during the break. After the finale airs, you're free to do whatever you want. The isolation from each other while the show is airing is, of course, part of preserving the integrity of this social game.

"We've booked you both on the next flights home. Tonight, you'll each have a room at a hotel right next to the airport. Thank you so much for being on the first season of the show. It's been amazing. There are eleven episodes, and then our live finale. They'll start airing soon! Our first episode drops in two weeks on Valentine's Day! We'll talk more in three months. The finale will be May second!" Jamie finishes.

"Damn," Remy breathes.

I squint at her. "So Remy and I can't talk or see each other for the next three months? That's ninety days."

"Wow, you really didn't read any of your paperwork." Jamie grins. "If y'all can't make it ninety days, I don't think you can make it a lifetime."

57

Over

DAYS 22-23

I'm devastated for Osprey.

Remy and I are given hotel rooms to shower and change into different clothes. We have a few hours to nap before a production assistant knocks on both our doors.

Outside the airport entrance, the PA hands us back our phones. I stare at my cold blank iPhone for a moment before pocketing it. Panic seizes my gut at the thought of turning it on. Returning to the real world. Facing the reality of everything I've missed these past thirty-two days. All the missed comments, messages, DMs, emails.

I'll wait until I reach the gate.

Remy and I have flights that are thirty minutes apart, but our gates are different. Our airlines are different.

The PA shakes our hands in farewell before leaving the two of us standing outside in the night. I stare into the slate gray eyes I once thought were so genuine.

"Don't be nervous," Remy starts. "Whatever happens, we both win. We'll just split the money like Jamie said. What we have is real. We did it."

A weight falls into my stomach. "I can't believe we're not going to see each other or speak for ninety days."

"I can't wait to see your gorgeous face up on the TV every week once this starts to air."

"What are you actually going to do first when you get home? Laundry?" I ask, forcing a smile into my cheeks.

"You know it. I'm gonna give Grandma a call as soon as I get past security." He puts a finger under my necklace and runs it over the puka shells.

"Oh—do you want your necklace back?" I scramble to unscrew the latch.

"Orie, no, keep it. Wear it. Think of me and know I'm thinking about you. I'll be in the shadows of your socials, watching, getting excited about whatever you're doing."

I try to laugh.

"I might even post some stuff myself. Retire from lurker life."

I blink at him, anxiety slicing across my chest. "Oh yeah?"

"Yeah. You've inspired me." He grins.

I've inspired him. To Instagram?

"You gonna work on a script? Can I look forward to reading something the next time we see each other?"

I squint at him. "We'll see, I guess."

"Come here," he says. I take the tiniest step forward, and he pulls me into a kiss. I feel nothing. He pulls back, looking pleased with himself. "I'm gonna miss that macaroni outfit."

"You're basically in your island outfit." He is. New black slacks and a new black button-up.

"The ladies love this look."

I groan. He slips his hand into the back pocket of my jeans and pecks me again.

I step away. "I guess I'll see you in three months."

He smirks. "I guess so. Good luck, Or."

"Good luck to you, Remy Orlando Lasorsa."

At the gate, I don't find much as I scour the internet for anything on Remy. There's the Facebook he hasn't posted on since senior year of high school. His blank Instagram. He doesn't have Twitter. No pictures come up on Google when you punch in his name. He doesn't have a LinkedIn. I can't find Jerri anywhere. I can't find his parents, either, because I don't know their names or what they do. Neither he nor his sister is on YouTube or TikTok.

It's infuriating. How does a person in modern society have absolutely no internet presence?

Mom, Lark, and Lark's fiancée, Mel, pick me up at baggage claim at 9:00 A.M. New Jersey time. Mel's holding a sign that says WELCOME BACK! CONGRATULATIONS! Lark's clutching my tea order from the Tea Shop and a Jersey Mike's sub that I told her I was craving back during the family visit.

My family interrogates me on the drive home in Mom's turquoise blue Prius.

"How did you end up doing?" Mom asks, absolutely bursting with curiosity.

I swallow the chunk of Italian sub in my mouth. "I can't say."

"Did you win any challenges?" Mel asks.

I snort. "You'll have to wait and see; aka, I can't say."

"Did you find love!" Lark claps her hands.

"Y'all, I cannot say."

"What's the first thing you want to do when we get back to the house?" Mom asks.

I gulp down a large sip of my lukewarm tea, watching the greenery pass by the window on Route 287. "I want to make an appointment to get my license."

"You do!" Mom asks excitedly.

"*You* want to get your license?" Lark asks pointedly.

"Yes. Maybe you could practice parallel parking with me tomorrow, Lark?"

"Really?" Lark says.

"How's Dad? Is he coming home soon?" I ask.

"Sixty-eight more days," Mom says. "He's so excited to see you. Maybe you could write him!"

"You up for coming back to the Instagram?" Lark asks hesitantly.

"Yeah, I have a few things I'm going to be working on these next few weeks, but I can do AcroYoga stuff in between. You have stuff lined up?"

"No retreats or anything, but I've got some sponsorships."

"Yeah, send me the posting schedule. We can divide them up. I'll handle half the editing/posting duties, so we can divide and conquer."

I head to the house next door and knock.

Mrs. Diaz comes to the door. She greets me enthusiastically with a big hug and effervescent excitement about my reality show endeavors.

"Is Wes home?" I finally ask.

"Yes! I think he's filming downstairs. Let me grab him."

She must know we broke up. I wonder if she knew we weren't going to last like, supposedly, my entire family had. Apparently, I was the last one to realize what was right for my own life.

After a minute, Wes comes to the door looking disheveled but in an undeniably cute way. Sweats, messy hair. Still not attracted to him.

"Or," he breathes. "Wow. You look different."

"Run-down and malnourished?" I ask.

"I mean, yes to malnourished, but, I don't know, you're not wearing any makeup."

"Oh." I touch my face.

"No, I mean, like, you look good. You always do. But you're, like . . ." He looks me up and down. "I don't know, wearing yourself differently."

I cock a brow. "That sounded creepy."

"Sorry. I'm sorry." He casts his eyes down and runs his hands over his face. "Like, about everything. I've relived that day at the airport on a loop since I dropped you off. I'm sorry I told you about her that way. I should have been up front sooner. I'm sorry."

"Yeah, well." I smile. "I hadn't been feeling us romantically for a long while, and I should have said something sooner, too."

He closes his eyes and nods. It's a nod that says *I understand exactly how you were feeling*. "It's pretty weird to step back and acknowledge something's not working after being a dynamic duo for your entire life."

"Yeah. But I think we'll be better off this way." I shift awkwardly.

He lifts a shoulder and lets it fall. "You don't have to stand outside. You want to hang out?"

I shake my head. "Oh no, I don't think we should do a casual hang—I just got home and I—I had a quick question."

He leans against the doorframe. "You could have texted me the question."

You know what's batshit? I didn't even think about texting. I knew Wes was right next door, and I could walk, so I did.

"You and Remy Orlando Lasorsa were on the swim team together; you used to carpool and stuff, right?" I ask.

"Yeah . . ."

"How well did you know him?"

"Um, we were friends, but, like, the kind you don't really hang out with outside of the thing you're mandatorily doing together, you know? He was cocaptain of the team with me senior year. I've never actually been inside his house, but it's up in that hilly development on the other side of town. He worked at a coffee place in West Caldwell next to that little church. We mostly talked about swimming and the team and that kinda stuff."

"Could you give me his home address?"

58

Premiere

13 DAYS POSTGAME

I'm back to working out. Watching movies before bed. Reviewing them on my Instagram stories. Grinding out routines with Lark. Helping her edit and craft posts. I'm reading a book on screenwriting. I already read two about addiction. I'm taking a masterclass on podcasting. I passed my driver's test today.

I am the poster girl for productivity. I'm trying really hard to feel good. Because I really don't.

I feel like my personality's been put on mute . . . and I can't find the remote control to switch the volume back on. I'm claustrophobic and anxious. Trapped in my own thoughts, unable to share or talk about anything that's actually weighing on me because it all has to do with the game. Everything that comes out of my mouth goes through a five-step mental filter.

I feel the pull of mistrust everywhere I go. In the tiniest, most ridiculous interactions. At the gym when the receptionist tells me about a new show he's loving, my gut screams, *He's lying.* When I ask an employee at Barnes & Noble where to find a screenwriting book I read about online, and they don't have it in stock, it snaps, *She just doesn't want you to have it.* I'm stuck in this constant state of vigilance where I'm perpetually talking myself down so I can interact civilly with strangers on the most basic human level.

It's finally Valentine's Day.

I was originally planning to watch the *Attached at the Hip* premiere alone, because I wasn't sure if I'd be ready to relive the game experience with an audience. But Lark and Mel wanted to throw me a watch party, so I reluctantly agreed.

Now, as I take a seat on Lark's tan couch between her and Mom—my heart pounding, pits sweating, mind racing—I know I'm not. *I'm not ready to relive this with an audience.* My throat feels tight. Mouth dry.

Mel turns off the lights as Jamie comes on screen to explain the game's premise.

Lark reaches out to take my hand, and then, for all intents and purposes, I black out. My eyes stay trained on a small orange stain in Lark's carpet as I try to quell the rising static in my head.

I register Lark exclaiming random things next to me from time to time.

"You asked them to call you Piccadilly! Why? That's not a nickname!"

"Okay, I love Leo and Rick. Shipping it."

"YOU WON THE SOS CHALLENGE!"

It's not until the rain starts on screen that I manage to wrangle my anxiety enough to come back to the moment on the couch with my family.

On screen, Remy and I are in the cave. The edit shows bits of our journey among snippets of all the other couples struggling in the storm.

You can't actually see Remy and me, but they show the cave from the outside, light flickering from the opening, and they play the audio from bits of our conversations. Of "never have I ever." Everyone in the room goes quiet, eating up the juicy relationship-building moments.

Lark inhales a sharp breath when I ask Remy if his dad has a gambling problem.

I squint at the screen. *That's when I asked Remy to turn off the mic. Right after that.*

But the audio cuts to me saying *My dad has a serious gambling issue.*

The conversation continues. As I share that *I just found out my father's a gambling addict and an alcoholic. He just relapsed. Lost his restaurant. Rehab.*

Parents in a ton of debt. There's overlay: pictures. From my Instagram. Of me and my family slow zooming over the screen as a visual aid over my voice. Snapshots of me and my dad.

I feel like someone shoved me into oncoming traffic and a truck plowed into my chest.

What the.

What the actual.

A cold, paralyzing helplessness spreads over me as I struggle to make sense of what we just saw and heard.

As the logic of it solidifies.

As I realize how they must have captured this.

Remy.

Remy.

Didn't.

Turn.

Off.

His.

Mic.

They didn't even air me asking him to turn it off.

I fumble off the couch, hysterics threatening my ability to breathe.

"Orie, it's okay," someone's saying as I grab my purse from the floor. Mom.

"Orie, don't go—don't worry about it!" Lark's voice.

"Orielle, please stay. It's all right!" Mom again.

I walk out the front door and into the cold February air, trying to catch my breath as tears gush out of me.

I unlock the door to Mom's Prius, fall into the driver's seat, drop my head against the wheel.

WHAT THE FUCK. WHAT IN THE FUCKING FUCK!

WHY! WHY WOULD HE LIE ABOUT TURNING OFF HIS MIC. WHY WOULD SOMEONE DO THAT. WHY?

The passenger door opens and closes. Lark's in the car.

"I need to be alone right now." My voice comes out waterlogged and weak.

"Orie—" she says empathetically.

"I'm going to go home, Lark."

She sighs. "I—okay. I'll see you tomorrow." She gets out of the car.

An hour later, my mom appears in my bedroom doorway to insist she's not upset with me for sharing all our issues on national television. How she's sure Dad won't be, either.

And if that's true, it's great. They're understanding and wonderful.

But I am seething.

My Twitter is being flooded with memes:

Me yelling at a calm Remy to stop yelling.

Me calling Remy's pecs boobs.

Me telling him I don't poop.

Commentary is pouring in on my socials.

OMG I SHIP YOU AND REMY SO HARD.

LOL PICCADILLY AND LEISTER SQUARE YOU'RE WEIRDER THAN I THOUGHT YOU WERE

I love, love too. I hope you get your happy ending with Remy! You two are adorable

PETITION TO MAKE MACARONI A PRIMARY COLOR

They're using the ship name RemAdilly. We sound like an arthritis medication.

As soon as it's available, I stream the premiere alone on my laptop, this time more cognizant of what's actually happening on screen.

Didn't-turn-off-his-mic Remy is charming as ever.

I can't stand it.

Past me fawns all over him. And I can't stand it.

All I can think about is Osprey watching the show. Osprey seeing #RemAdilly on socials. Osprey listening to the Remy-crazed version of me on screen. Listening to me tell America I'm on page eleven of my own real-life rom-com script. I want to reach through my laptop and shake her.

I want to call Osprey. Or Kennedi. Or even Leo.

And I can't. I can't break the damn NDA. I can't do anything to put winning the prize money in jeopardy.

I open Instagram and tap into Remy's page.

The show ended three hours ago. He's already shot up from twenty-three followers to ten thousand. There are six posts that have gone up since I checked the account at the airport and found it blank. As promised, the first is a shirtless mirror selfie at the gym. #CrossFitLife. Then he did a "leg day" reel.

The next picture is him in a UCLA sweatshirt out in front of a statue on campus: *Getting back on track with school after a month-long hiatus for an epic adventure.* Then there's a selfie of him holding four coffees outside a Starbucks: *Intern life.* A shot at the beach—shirtless—holding a script, reading in his beach chair. A network-given picture of him in Fiji before the game, and, finally, a reel cut from his entrance interview.

I scroll down to the UCLA one again and zoom in. I tap the page to see if he tagged anything. My heart skips a beat as I read the account name hovering over the grass. @VeryJerri11.

I stare at it for a long, livid moment before I tap.

The account is private. It has twenty-five followers. It's following 150 accounts. A young girl with shoulder-length brown hair is laughing in the profile pic with her head turned to the right. The photo's too small to discern any real details. I type her handle into Google. Nothing relevant comes up. Anger is a hulking, living thing, breathing down my neck as I pull up Google Maps.

I can't break the NDA. But I can prep the most compelling argument humanly possible to bury Remy at the finale.

59

Mission

15 DAYS POSTGAME

"I'm sorry, what do you mean you're going to Florida!" Lark asks, aghast, from the doorframe.

"I'm doing something."

"Should I come with you?" Lark asks. "Do you want company?"

"No, I have to do this by myself."

"When is your flight?" she demands.

"I'm driving; it's cheaper."

"DRIVING! ALONE! With what car? You just got your license!"

"Dad's car! I have to do this myself. First, because I have to. Second, because of the NDA. I'll be fine."

"What about stops?"

"I have it all planned out." I toss her my notebook. "I finished our edits for the new Alo yoga sets. I emailed them this morning. We don't have any more sponsored stuff for two weeks, right?"

She nods.

I zip my suitcase and pop up to give her a hug. "Love you. I'll see you in a week or so." I yank my bag off the bed.

Lark follows me out of the room. "You're leaving *right now*?"

I heft my suitcase up the steps.

60

Returned

"Have you seen the ratings for the show?" Lark exclaims from the door-jamb. "I just saw an article saying it's the most-watched CBN premiere they've had in years, and they were even higher for episode two!"

"I saw. It's mind-boggling," I answer robotically. I'm sitting on my bed with my laptop.

I got back from Florida two days ago.

Remy is all anyone wants to talk about on all my socials. People are talking about the show all over the internet. I haven't seen this many people excited about a new reality show since the first season of *Love Is Blind.*

On-screen Remy kisses the audience's ass in his confessionals, leaning into our showmance, babbling about how much he misses me while he's tethered to Priya. It's taking a significant toll on my mental health.

"Orie." Lark's voice is strained. "Please, talk to me. Let me help. How can I help?"

I shrug halfheartedly because I don't know. I don't know how she can help. "I think . . . maybe I need to get out of here."

"Here, your room?"

"I want to do a trip to London, and I've been watching the airline prices. But even with a good deal it would still be a significant chunk of change, and I know we can't afford to waste any money right now."

Lark comes to sit on the edge of my bed. "If you go, can I come with you?"

I grip my laptop harder. "I can go by myself."

"I know you *can* go by yourself," Lark says softly. "But you don't have to. Do you want to do all these things by yourself? Was the road trip helpful? Did you find what you were looking for?"

"I found it." I feel brittle as she moves closer, like the slightest movement will crack me into a million pieces.

"Orie." She places a hand on my arm.

I shrug her off. "Aren't you the one who told me I was too dependent on the people around me for everything? That I couldn't do anything alone?" I ask pointedly.

Her mouth bobs open and shut. "O—"

"I DO EVERYTHING ALONE NOW, LARK." I heave in a great breath, thrown by the volume of my own voice. "I just drove down the entire coast by myself. Have you noticed? Does it even matter to you? You haven't said anything. You haven't said you were wrong!

"I don't *like* being alone all the time, if that's what you're asking! At home, I already felt lonely all the time with Wes, and with you, whenever we weren't doing AcroYoga.

"When we're doing yoga, we're connected. But as soon as we're apart, you're this superior being who yells things from the sidelines but never gets on the field with me."

I flail my hands dramatically. "You go out of your way to *not* connect with me on anything other than our work stuff. Would it be that hard to go with me to a movie every once in a while when I ask? Read a book I read so we can talk story together? I've literally warped my whole life to connect with you."

"I didn't realize—"

"And now I met these people that I formed these intense bonds with— two specifically—that I have these really incredible relationships with, and I can't talk to them for months. And I can't even talk to you about what happened with them!

"And Mom's extra busy with work because of the freelance projects she's taking on because of all of Dad's debt, and I'm here and I want to help, but I JUST HAVE TO WAIT AROUND on eggshells for ninety days, hoping I win this money so I can do my part.

"And Dad's not here, and I can't make myself write a letter because I just want to talk to him in person! I can't put the words down. I don't want anything I say to be permanently preserved in a letter right now. I can't trust that it won't come out wrong when I'm so all over the place emotionally.

"Dad's the only one in this family who goes out of his way to do things with me that I like and he doesn't." I stare at Lark for a moment, catching my breath. Her eyes are saucer-wide, but she doesn't speak.

"That's what people who love each other do, right?" I urge. "That's why when I met Remy, I was instantly ready to try CrossFit. It's why I try every weird thing Dad puts in front of me and ask him how he came up with the recipe. It's why I specifically read all the books Mom brings home that she's already read. Not just because I trust her judgment, *Lark,* or because I'm too lazy to find ones I'll like another way, but because I can go upstairs after I finish one, and she'll be there to gush about it with me because I know she loved it, too.

"That's why I stayed with Wes for so long despite not actually connecting with him as an adult on, like, anything. He still tried, at least a little bit. He still went with me to stuff. He at least pretended to be interested in the things I talk about. He doesn't just boss me around and stand on his pedestal telling me what's wrong with my life without ever offering to get involved. He was involved.

"I want to go to London and do a bunch of stuff and go to a bunch of places I read about in one of my favorite books that, again, you have never touched. And, yeah, it would be fun to go with someone, but not someone who will be scoffing at all the random things I want to do, not getting excited about all the obscure shit I'm going to get excited about!" I collapse backward onto my pillow, breathless. Silent tears fall in rivulets down my cheeks.

"Orie," she says quietly.

"What!" I yell, all worked up.

Lark's voice cracks. "You're waiting to see if you won the money?"

I suck in a tight breath and vehemently shake my head. "No! I didn't say that. Don't remember that."

Lark presses her lips together. "That was very eloquent." She scoots so she's fully on the bed. "Orie," she says nervously. "Let me bend for you now. I want to be better. Give me the books. And listen." She heaves in a breath. "I've got brands rolling into our business email left and right with the show doing so well. Let me play manager. See if we can get a yoga gig out there—maybe they'll cover the expense." She holds my eyes with her enormous doelike green ones. They're bleary, like she may actually be on the verge of tears for once. "I'm sorry for making you feel alone. I'm sorry you felt alone even when you weren't. *I see you.* Okay?"

I slide off the bed, tears clouding my eyes as I wander out to the living room, and pull *Accidentally Abroad* and *Flailing Through the Freefall* from the bookshelf.

"Do you know 'I see you' is from *Avatar*?" I ask quietly as I reenter my room. I point to where *Avatar* sits on my favorite DVDs shelf.

She grins. "Yeah, that is why I said it. It's Mel's favorite movie, so I've seen it."

I drop the books onto the mattress next to her.

She catches my arm and tugs me into a hug.

61

United

30–39 DAYS POSTGAME

It only takes Lark twenty hours to book us a covered AcroYoga retreat gig in London, and she finishes both the novels I threw at her last week before we touch down in the UK.

We teach a London workshop in the morning, and afterward, we explore the city, eating the food and hunting down the places they talk about in my books. Since Lark is so fresh on the stories, she's able to point out a bunch of stuff I've forgotten over the years.

It's surprisingly wonderful.

We film an AcroYoga flow in Hyde Park. We explore all the London bookstores within walking distance of our hotel. We stop in front of classic London landmarks, set up our tripod with the camera on a timer, and bust out some artsy AcroYoga moves.

And it all helps. For a few days I forget about the eggshells I've been living on. Lark doesn't even bring up the show until we're sitting in bed the night before our flight back to New Jersey.

"Hey, you know that girl Jamie?" she asks.

I bark a laugh. "'That girl'? You mean the woman who hosts and produces the show I'm on? Yeah, I know."

"She's the one who called me, back before you left for Fiji. She wanted to know everything about you. She worked really hard to make sure you and everyone out there had really solid love matches. I thought she was, like . . . I don't know, a casting person or someone. Not the host."

"Okay . . ."

"I've just been thinking, you know, as I watch the episodes, about what I said about you not being able to be alone." Lark clears her throat. "And how much you took it to heart.

"I don't know *everything* that happened out there. But I can tell you're not feeling great about it. And I just hope, I hope you don't skip out, or run away from any potentially really wonderful relationship because you're still trying to prove something about yourself to me.

"Because you're very capable, and I think you know that now, and I'm really proud of you. I just want you to be happy. And you've really started shifting gears to work toward *your* specific happy, career wise, and that's amazing. Um, but you don't *have* to do it alone—*just to do it alone.* Does that make sense? Like, you can do life alone if that's what you want, but, like, if you're holding back on the one thing you've wanted your entire life—cough, fairy-tale love, cough—"

I snort.

"Because I said you are codependent." She shakes her head. "Don't. Please don't do that. That fairy-tale love connection only comes around once in a blue moon, so if you did find it out there from Jamie's intense matchmaking research, please grab it. Don't let it slip through your fingers."

I stare at her on the bed across from me for a long moment.

"You've only seen three episodes," I say dubiously. Our trip has put us behind. Episode three ended with Osprey choosing me as his next partner and Quintin going home.

"Orie, I was there on day thirteen." She narrows her giant eyes at me. It makes me feel like one of those plastic see-through backpacks.

"What are you saying, Lark?"

"If you've started to feel anything that resembles a fairy tale, pounce."

"Is that what you did with Mel? Pounced?"

She grins. "Uh, duh. She lived down the hall from me sophomore year. If I hadn't pounced, who knows who would have started dating her."

I roll my eyes. "What exactly do you mean by pounce? It sounds so aggressive."

"I mean *ask them out*. Tell them you'd like to give romance a go. Do it in your own Orie way. Just *say something*."

"We're NDA contracted or whatever not to speak until the finale."

"Then pounce at the finale."

I sigh, falling back against the hotel pillows. "I feel like all men turn out to be horrible, backstabbing, lying liars. And I'm afraid if I let myself fall for another one in any capacity, they'll just turn around and ratify that belief."

Lark snorts. "All men aren't horrible, backstabbing, lying liars . . . Are you referring to Wes or . . . ?" She gestures to the TV in the room that's not even on.

"I mean, even Wes emotionally cheated."

Lark nods. "He's human. You were in an unhealthy relationship for a long time, and it took a toll."

And then there's Dad.

62

NP

71 DAYS POSTGAME

I pull up Osprey's parkour-filled Instagram. The boy can basically walk on air.

Torturing myself via Osprey's Instagram has become a morning ritual. Seeing him through the lens of the show edit has only made me like him more. He's cynical and a little too logical when he gets to talking about the game, but he's so kind to everyone he's partnered with. And he visibly softens when he's on screen with me.

I miss talking to him. I daydream about *running my fingers through his hair*. Pulling out his hair tie. Touching his pirate mustache. *Is that normal?*

I relive that moment in the tree, wondering what would have happened if that damn camera guy didn't make that stupid noise *all the time*.

There're so many things we haven't talked about yet. I don't know his favorite days of the week, or his favorite episode of *Friends*. Or what kind of toothpaste he uses. Or whether he read the Twilight Saga or scoffs at it, or just saw the movies. Or when he decided to grow out his hair. Or if he's ever broken a bone—

I sigh and tap out of his profile.

There's a big slice of *Attached at the Hip* viewers shipping us. When some fan thread found out my full name was Orielle, there was an explosion of memes from *The Notebook*'s "If you're a bird, I'm a bird" scene with our faces superimposed on the characters.

Remy has been posting up a storm the past nine weeks. He's been live tweeting every episode. At first, the overwhelming theme of his feed was: how great the two of us are together, and how much he cares about me. He flooded his Instagram with snapshots of us in very couple-y positions on the show. There's one from that rainy day in the ocean that looks like the cover of a romance novel.

Once we hit the episode where I was partnered with Osprey, little by little, Remy's tone changed. Twisted. He started calling me a heartbreaker. Worried I wasn't loyal to him anymore. That I was leading him on. Victimizing himself.

On-screen me has now vocalized her suspicions about his many lies. During one of my confessionals, they spliced in the clips of him actively *not* turning off his mic when he said he would. The show is leaning into the mystery of it all. The drama of his potential duplicitous nature. It's making *Attached at the Hip* even more of a viral sensation. The internet loves a potential conspiracy, and it *loves* to take sides.

On his socials, Remy has an answer for everything. He can reframe any narrative. He has baby pictures of a very young child he claims is himself and an even younger girl he claims is Jerri. He swears he turned his mic off despite blatantly not doing it on screen.

But so many people are still rooting for him. *Rooting for us.*

He's hot and charming, and he's garnered a group of adoring fans who drool over his every word. His follower count has blown up to three hundred thousand. There are so many fucking shirtless selfies, it makes me want to barf.

I throw my phone across the bed.

We're picking up my dad today.

Dad's waiting outside the facility with his bag when we pull up in his white Prius. He looks like he always looks, clean cut. Salt-and-pepper hair, casual shirt, Levi's.

"You drove here!" he exclaims when I pop out of the driver's side.

"Yeah, I finally got my license." I smile.

"Hell yeah." He holds up his hand for a high five. I smack it before wrapping him in a hug.

"Post-island Orie's been makin' moves," Lark says behind me.

I pull out of the hug. "I've been afraid to write and ask you if you've seen the show," I admit quietly. We're only three episodes away from the finale.

He and Lark pull out of their hug. "Why have you been afraid to ask me? Of course I've been watching it! Highlight of my week has been watching you kick ass out there."

He brings Mom into an embrace. They kiss and hug for an extended period of time. Lark and I fiddle with our phones and get back into the car. Lark takes Mom's spot, hopping into the passenger seat.

"You're gonna make Mom sit in the back?" I ask.

"She'll sit with the love of her life; it'll be fine."

I snort as Mom and Dad slide into the back.

"Dad would like to propose getting family tattoos to mark a new chapter of honesty between the group of us here," Mom announces.

Lark looks over at her. "Can Dad speak for himself?"

He laughs. "I would like to propose a family tattoo to mark this new chapter of candor among us. I love you all, and I appreciate everything you are. We're going to get through this. I don't want any of you to stress about the money stuff. Your mother and I are going to figure it out. Orie, you kept talking about doing the show for us; we didn't want that. If you win, we want you to use that money for your future."

Lark and I share a look.

I twist in the seat to look at them. "Firstly, Dad, I'm so, so sorry I talked about the relapse and all of the fallout on the show. I really thought the mics were turned off."

"Orielle, please hear me when I say, it's okay. I'm not hiding anything. I don't want to hide anything anymore. It's part of your story. It makes sense you would talk about it."

"Secondly." I swallow back the knot of emotion in my throat. "I sure as heck am going to use that money to help you if I win. You've only been helping me do literally everything with *your money* my entire life."

"Orie—" Mom starts.

"End of discussion there, thank you," I say, turning around and putting the car into drive. "Are we getting these tattoos now or after brunch?"

We go to brunch. Dad tells us about his time at the center, the people he met there, how much he's been thinking of us. He asks me if I got his letter, and I tell him I loved it.

He tells us about his childhood. For the first time, we hear all the nitty-gritty specifics of his trauma, the details of his mistakes. Our grandpa was an addict. He passed before we were born. Mom and Dad were high school sweethearts, but during his senior year he started to lose his grip on his own health. He asked Mom to marry him three years later when she was in college. She wouldn't say yes until he got the help he needed.

So he did. He enrolled in cooking school while doing photography on the side. He forged a path. He's had a misstep here or there along the way, but he's been going to AA and Gamblers Anonymous (GA) meetings every week since we were born, and it's changed his life.

I feel an unexpected sense of kinship with his story. With his loneliness. His guilt about letting people down. His shame. Tears well in my eyes as I flash to different moments on the island. Moments when I helped Remy. When I betrayed Kennedi. Moments when Osprey opened himself to me and I closed off.

Hearing Dad talk so freely about his failures, admit to them, own them—fills me with a sense of pride and empowerment I've never experienced before. I'm so . . . proud of him. And my mom, she's been there by his side through almost all of it; holding down the fort, leading with empathy and kindness like she does in every aspect of her life.

I want to be her when I grow up.

I've felt so much shame these past months around my relationship with Remy: how readily I believed his lies; how long I gave him the benefit of the doubt.

But . . . that part of me is Mom. I love that part of myself. I always want to choose compassion over cynicism.

"I can't believe you went to those meetings every week, and we never picked up on it," Lark says next to me.

He shrugs. "You thought I was going in to work."

"Where were you actually going? An abandoned cafeteria somewhere?" she asks.

"No." He laughs. "The nearest meetings here are at that church up in West Caldwell. They're great. An addict owns the café next door. They bring over coffee and leftover pastries every Tuesday night for GA."

We find street parking outside the tattoo parlor. Dad brings us into a little huddle before we go inside.

"What are we getting, Dad?" I ask.

He beams at us. "I feel like some iteration of 'Nobody's Perfect' feels appropriate."

"Nobody's Perfect?" Lark says blandly.

Dad holds up a hand. "Hear me out. Whenever you two fuck something up, or in the rare instance when your flawless mother stumbles, and those negative self-berating thoughts come storming in, I want you to look at your silly tattoos and think of how nobody's fucking perfect. And that's what makes us beautiful." I widen my eyes at him, and he pauses. "And yes, I'm aware I just blatantly referenced two pop songs from your youth. They're very catchy and send great messages.

"But in those moments of despair when you mess up, you need something to interrupt the doom spiral! That's what this will be. Your comedic relief in the times you forget you need it. You see the tattoo, stop. Remember that whatever's happened, it's going to teach you something, make you wiser, and you're going to use that new info to build a stronger, happier life."

Lark tries to share a skeptical look with Mom, but Mom's all smiles today. She's so proud of Dad. Love billows off her like wind. She's his biggest fan.

"Profound," Lark deadpans.

"I figure we can all choose from three options. Option one—" He holds up a finger. "Minimalist—just an 'NP,' which can double as the classic 'no problem.' Brush it off. It's great. Two." He holds up a second finger. "The actual phrase, 'Nobody's Perfect.' Or three, the clever twist on the phrase: 'Pobody's Nerfect.'"

At this, my sister audibly scoffs. Predictably, Mom and Lark decide to run with "NP." We let them go in and get theirs done first.

Dad turns to me while we wait. "What are we doing?"

I smile. "Oh, 'Pobody's Nerfect,' for sure."

His face lights up like a kid's on Christmas morning. "Really? Even though it's silly and completely 'off brand' compared to all the actual profound statements you already have on your back?"

I laugh, gesticulating with my hands. "Dad, the ridiculousness is part of what makes this profound."

He beams at me again.

"I'm sorry I didn't write you," I say quietly. "I was—"

"Don't apologize," he cuts me off. "You had every right to take your time processing. It's been really wonderful watching and hearing about you coming into your own."

I shrug. "I made some big mistakes in the game."

Dad puts his arm around me and pulls me to his side. "Whatever it is, nothing's permanent. You'll make it right."

I fiddle nervously with my hands. "I have to give a presentation at the finale. And I'm petrified that I'm going to mess it up."

Dad pulls me in front of him and puts his arms on my shoulders like we're in a huddle on the sidelines of a soccer field. "Can I tell you something?"

I raise an eyebrow. "If it's another *Hannah Montana* or One Direction quote, then, no."

He smiles. "Life is short. You've seized the crap out of it these past few months. Does it feel good to be doing things, even if you're messing some stuff up along the way?"

I bounce my head up and down. *Yes*. I've done more in the past four months than I've done in the past four years.

"In the end, it's not about messing it up or knocking it out of the park, it's about getting up off the couch and doing it in the first place. Trying. Growing. You've already done it. You're doing it. You can't mess it up. Not really." He gives my shoulder an encouraging squeeze. "Life's what you make it, so let's make it rock."

"STOP THAT, DAD."

ATTACHED AT THE HIP WEEK 11 END CAP: TRANSCRIPT

Jamie Federov and Zarar Jafri

JAMIE

Thanks for tuning in tonight to *Attached at the Hip*! The drama at the end of that final challenge was heartbreaking. Let us know on socials who you were rooting for.

And as always, I want to remind you our live show finale is coming up, and the power to crown the winner of the million-dollar prize will shift to *you at home*.

ZARAR

Next week, we'll get to catch up with our cast, and our two finalists will present their case for why they deserve to be crowned our season one *Attached at the Hip* champion.

JAMIE

Plus, we have so many questions! Are Remy and Orie together? Will they split the million-dollar prize? All that and more—next Friday LIVE at 8:00 P.M. Eastern. Come be a part of the fiery results! There are more twists and turns to come in this hot mess of a season.

63

Live

93 DAYS POSTGAME

I'm very, very sweaty. I've bypassed wet-carrot status. I'm an oversteamed slice of yellow zucchini. I have a dish towel in my purse that I keep whipping out to dab my forehead.

Remy and I were given an earlier call time then the rest of the cast. I arrive an hour earlier than that early call time.

A PA meets me at the front of the building and escorts me to a dressing room complete with a couch, TV monitor, and vanity. I'm only alone in there for a moment before three different glam people hustle into the tiny space and descend upon my damp hair and slick face.

I'm alone again when the dressing room monitor finally flips on. I keep standing and pacing, too worried about wrinkling the gold silk cowl-necked dress I'm wearing to sit for any extended period of time. *The show's about to start.*

They're keeping Remy and me in separate holding rooms so all of America gets to watch our live reunion.

On my phone I tap open my Instagram drafts and hover my finger over the post button.

A countdown comes up on the monitor: 10. 9. 8. 7. 6. I concentrate on breathing exercises as Jamie's face appears on screen.

She opens the show with the official *Attached at the Hip* finale intro. Then, it cuts to Z as he announces our eight other cast members in order of when they were eliminated. One by one, they come out and settle in on a small set of bleachers on the righthand side of the soundstage. I suck in a breath as Osprey and Kennedi walk out. They're seated right in front. Third and fourth place. They both look stunning. Kennedi's in a short, elaborately beaded lavender dress, and Osprey's in a fitted three-piece emerald green suit.

Zarar and Jamie take a seat on two red stools positioned between the bleachers and a small bench where Remy and I will sit once we're brought out.

"Okay!" Zarar announces. "We're going to get our final two out here momentarily, but first, we've got a surprise for our eight other castmates!"

The audience cheers.

Jamie smiles. "As we all know, because I've said it a zillion times on the show, this game is a social experiment that explores human relationships. And although the final winner is in your hands, America, the cast will now get to crown an ISLAND MVP among themselves who will win a whopping hundred thousand dollars tonight."

A roar erupts from both the crowd and my castmates. I squeal from my dressing room couch.

"I know!" Jamie beams. "The network is loving the response to the show, and they loved our colorful cast, so they've given us an extra prize to award tonight. So." Jamie turns to the cast. "You'll each get a vote. The contestant with the most votes wins *Attached at the Hip* MVP. Before you ask, you are allowed to vote for yourself. But if there is no majority, no one gets this money. So, keep that in mind as you're scribbling."

Z doles out markers and parchment.

"While they're doing that . . ." Jamie smirks as the camera pushes in on her. "Let's take a look at some highlights from our first season."

I look away, scrunching my hands open and closed. I hear the moment when Kennedi and I sang Enya to use "the bathroom." The editors used that sound bite over a shot of trees in the second episode. Kennedi and I were so enchanted by our group poop plan, we forgot to turn off our mics. It's become a meme as well. I glance up as the montage shows a touching moment where Rick asks Leo if he'd be willing to give their relationship a real second shot outside the game, and despite being hurt by whatever happened with them in the past, Leo tearily agrees. There's a mini montage of Osprey slaying the challenge puzzles. Remy and me dancing on the yacht date. Kennedi calling Remy Captain America's asshole. Osprey giving me a head massage in the ocean. Kennedi winning the slide challenge. Priya slicing *off* the head of a snake in the jungle during the cycle she was with Remy. Rick and Leo crafting their amazing shelter. Trina and I losing our shit during the gross food challenge. Kennedi and Priya kissing next to the fire. Me slo-mo diving for my fleeting pet chicken. The moment where Osprey and I fall off the coconut tree. (That's also become a meme.)

I grin to myself. I think Osprey's got this award in the bag.

"All right, we have the votes, folks." The screen dissolves back to Jamie. They cut to a close-up of my eight castmates, all wide-eyed and hopeful—*oh my god.* Osprey's hair! When he walked out, I thought I just couldn't see his bun, but HE CUT IT. It's short. And he looks—well, hot. "And our *Attached at the Hip* season one ISLAND MVP is . . ." There's a drum roll as Jamie holds us in suspense. "With a four-to-three-to-one vote: OSPREY SUZUKI, you're going home with a hundred thousand dollars today!!!!"

Happy tears flood my vision.

"Come over here, Oss!" Z calls. Jamie and Z stand to give Osprey a round of applause, and I hop up to do the same, slapping my free hand against my forearm.

Osprey and his new hair are in complete shock. My other castmates are standing around him, clapping. Slack-jawed, he rises and walks over to where Jamie is clutching a prop-sized check.

He gazes around, at a loss for words for a moment. "Wow. This is unexpected, thank you! And thank you to my castmates, wow. Thank you. So much. Wow."

"Unsung hero of the show!" Jamie says. "Challenge beast Osprey Suzuki! We were honored to have you on this season; it wouldn't have been the same without you facing your fears and cajoling Orie into participating in all the climbing-induced hijinks."

Osprey's cheeks heat to a bright red. He takes the check, embarrassed but smiling. "It was an amazing experience, thank you." He drops his head and makes his way back to his front-row spot on the bleachers.

There's a knock on my door. I jump two feet to the left and fall into the wall.

"Come in!" I squeak, frantically tapping the post button on the Instagram draft.

"All right!" Z says on the monitor. "It's time to bring out our final two!"

A PA sticks her head inside my dressing room. "Can you come with me, Orie?"

We power walk through dimly lit areas until I'm on the far-left wing of the soundstage. My palms are slick. I wave my hands around, airing them out. I try to heave in a big breath. It doesn't work. I purse my lips and try again.

"Here they are—it's their first time seeing each other in person in three months—Remy Orlando Lasorsa and Orie 'Piccadilly' Lennox!" Jamie announces us.

Music blasts from the speakers as I step out into the light. I freeze momentarily as the roar of the live studio audience fills the room. I gape at them as I hobble toward center stage, my eyes welling up from the sheer force of the audible support.

I stop walking on the *X* I was instructed to and gaze out at the crowd, thunderstruck. Some of them are saying my name. Some of them have . . . posters with my name. Someone takes my hand and gives it a sharp tug. I snap out of my stupor in time to realize Remy has also walked onto the stage. *Remy is tugging me to him.* He's trying to initiate a dramatic reunion kiss.

I duck my head and tuck my chin just in time to cleanly avoid his lips and hug him instead. He pulls back to look into my eyes. "It's great to see you, heartbreaker."

I force a laugh, my organs quivering nervously in my chest. After everything he saw and heard me say and do on the show, he still wants to kiss me? The entire second half of the season was me wavering back and forth on Remy. *Does he think kissing me after all that is going to win him votes?*

"You okay?" he asks, his face split into a charming grin.

I nod. "Yeah, just nervous. Live crowd. Scary. Missed you," I choke out.

Remy takes my hand and brings me to our bench. I allow it, my eyes saucer wide as I scan the crowd again. I find my family in the front row. They all shoot me reassuring smiles. I let go of Remy's palm and lace my hands in my lap as we sit.

Across the way, Kennedi grins at me. When I find Osprey's eyes, he gives me the smallest encouraging nod.

"Welcome, you two!" Jamie sits back on her red stool. "I'm going to remind the audience how this works tonight. You're about to hear both Orie's and Remy's arguments for the million-dollar prize. Then, we'll have the cast get up and stand behind the contestant they think you should back. These eight people have firsthand insight on our finalists that we might have missed, and that's worth taking into account.

"And then, you at home and in the audience, YOU will vote for our winner! This is in *your hands*! If the vote is only separated by a one-percent margin, *they will* split the money. If there is any more than a one-percent margin, the majority winner will be crowned the first-ever *Attached at the Hip* champion."

Jamie shifts to face Remy and me. Remy's got his hand on my knee now. I'm not sure what to do about it. If I push it off, everyone will race to interpret the move in four hundred different ways.

Music plays, the studio lights tilt down, and a spotlight falls on us. "Remy and Orie," Jamie says seriously, "are you clear on how this will play out?"

"Yep." Remy grins, squeezing my knee.

"Yes," I say, concentrating on breathing. Steady. Steady breaths so I can speak. I can do this.

"All right, you'll both get your chance to present. Please do not interrupt while your opponent is pleading their case, okay?"

We agree. The lights go wild again before settling in on Jamie, Remy, and me once more.

"Remy, you're up first. Go for it," Jamie instructs.

Remy smiles out at the audience. He's in a typical Remy outfit. Black suit. Black button-up underneath. Black tie. He props his legs open and leans forward.

"All right! Hey, everyone! I'm so excited to be here, so honored to be sitting next to this beautiful competitor. I went into this game with an open mind, and I came out of it with a relationship more real and more genuine than I've ever experienced before. This was about forming strong bonds, and I did. I was loyal to my alliance. My number one, AP Chem, was Orie. We dodged everyone else along the way and made it to the end. I'd call that a massive triumph.

"As for why I should win over Orie, I mean, she was cute and a fun watch. A fun partner. But let's face it—she would have had a hard time getting to the end without my physicality. That first challenge was won because I lugged and chopped all that wood for our sign."

My eyebrows shoot up.

"I got us into that cave in the rain."

You've got to be kidding me.

"I won the food challenge, and I got her to the final round by eating her spider as well as mine."

I didn't ask him to eat that damn spider.

"I had great relationships with Priya, Leo, and Rick outside of our AP Chem alliance. And I formed a great relationship with Orie's other main alliance, Osprey, before the end of the game. I connected with a lot of the cast. I was committed to Orie the entire time even as she questioned my kindness and my family troubles. She went behind my back and turned the rest of the cast against me, and still I stuck by her. I have protected her. Cared for her. And I forgive her because I understand what a game like this can do to your mental health. I conquered every challenge, winning the final one after a six-hour stretch."

Rage sears down my spine.

"I opened my heart," he continues, "which is something I really struggle with. I don't know how this one next to me is feeling right now about us because she keeps her cards tight to her chest these days, but I've . . . I've fallen for her. These last three months have been miserable without her smile in my life.

"And yeah, that's it." Remy straightens and glances at Jamie. "I'm so grateful to be here. I hope I can bring this home for Jerri."

There's an *aw* from some of the crowd. Jamie, Z, and our castmates clap politely.

"All right, Remy. Thank you," Jamie says. "Okay, Orie. You're up."

I blow out a slow breath before turning to the camera lens. "Okay. I'm going to start by just pointing out a few quick things from that speech that made Remy sound delusional.

"We all watched the show. I pitched the idea to have our SOS sign say FML and to make the letters out of trenches that we proceeded to set on fire. It was a group effort. If I hadn't given the idea, we would not have won. Second, I found that cave; that's why we had shelter. I used our care package crate to step up into it. Third, him eating that spider during the food challenge did nothing for me. It was an empty gesture. No one chose me, and I ended up in exile." There's a roar of encouragement from the audience.

I scan the crowd, smiling out at everyone, before returning my attention to the lead camera. "I created three extremely strong bonds. One with Remy, one with Kennedi, and one with Osprey. I cared immensely about all of them. I knew from being a *Survivor* superfan that one should always say yes to an alliance and figure out who to turn on, as necessary, later in the game. But I didn't want to turn on anyone, so I did my best to get all these people with me to final four. And I did. Despite the fact that half our cast was gunning for Remy after cycle two, and they started gunning for Kennedi after that."

There's another roar from the audience.

"I know I wasn't the absolute strongest competitor here, but I got second place quite a bit, and that was enough for me because I had formed strong connections to get me the rest of the way. I didn't need immunity.

"I loved the romantic twist of this show. I fell into it with open arms. I grew up hoping my life would play out like a fairy tale, obsessed with romance and finding my happily ever after. I've been trying to manufacture my own since I was thirteen, and failing miserably. But for the first nine days of this game, I thought I'd found it in Remy. He said all the right things, and even the things he said wrong, he somehow made endearing." There's a swoon-filled giggle from the audience. "And we had so much in common.

"But you all saw him say and do questionable things on the show. The moment with Priya's accident. The moments where he didn't turn off his mic during conversations I trusted we would keep private. And, over the past three months, I did some investigating into who Remy actually is, and I, well, I made a mini documentary about it. It just went live on my Instagram, @OrieLennox. You can watch it right now—"

"Whoa, hold on," Jamie cuts me off. "Can we get the video she's talking about up on screen here?" She presses a hand to her ear before looking back to camera. "Don't touch that dial—we're going to get that for all of you right now. Orie, do we have your verbal permission to air this video?"

I whip my head from Jamie to the massive screen on the wall behind her and nod. "Uh . . . well, yeah. Of course." There's a general chuckling from the audience that quickly fades to silence as the lights dim. The screen, currently sporting the *Attached at the Hip* logo, goes dark for a moment.

Then I appear on camera in my backyard.

My sweat levels shoot back up. I should have strapped an emergency deodorant stick to my thigh.

Past Me
So I grew up in the same town as Remy, and we went to high school together. But we never got to know each other. My high school boyfriend, Wes, was on the swim team with him.

A photo of Wes's senior swim team comes up. It slowly zooms in on Remy next to Wes. An arrow points out the boy who is clearly Remy.

We switch to a view of my town through my dad's windshield as I drive to Remy's house.

Past Me [voice-over]
They used to carpool, so I got Remy's home address from my ex-boyfriend and headed over to visit Remy's parents' house. As you know if you watched the show, Remy doesn't currently live with his parents; he lives in Los Angeles right off the UCLA campus with his grandmother.

The shot switches back to me in the yard.

Past Me

When I rang the doorbell, Remy's mother came to the door. She agreed to answer some simple questions about Remy on camera for the show. As I walked through her house, I saw Remy's face in various portraits on the walls.

We cut to the B-roll I grabbed of these school and family portraits on my iPhone.

Past Me [voice-over]

This was for sure his parents' house. But you might notice, strangely, I saw no pictures of Jerri, the sister he continually referenced throughout the entirety of the twenty-one-day game. As I sat down on the couch in front of his mother, I was relieved that I would finally get to set the record straight once and for all. Is Jerri real?

The camera is set up over my shoulder to capture Mrs. Lasorsa. You can tell she's Remy's mom. She's in her late fifties, very pretty. She has a freckled square face. She and Remy have the same nose and gray eyes.

Past Me

So I couldn't help but notice the big family portrait on the way in.

A snapshot of the family portrait I'm referencing comes on screen again. It's a posed picture featuring Remy's parents, Remy around age eleven, and an older boy with darker brown hair.

Mrs. Lasorsa

Yes! It's nice, isn't it! Got it done back when Remy was in middle school.

Past Me

Where is Jerri?

Mrs. Lasorsa

[sighs, exasperated] Someone else from the show called a little while back asking the same thing. He didn't even tell me he was going on any show. I didn't believe them at first. We don't have a daughter.

There are gasps from the live studio audience.

Mrs. Lasorsa

He has an older brother, Dante. He's wonderful! He's down in Florida—we miss him so much. He's an astronaut for NASA. Hasn't gone up yet, but he's doing important work.

Past Me

Do you have a photo you could share of you and Remy more recently?

Mrs. Lasorsa taps through her phone until she finds one. She holds it up for me. I flip the phone toward the camera. It's an early-twenties Remy on the couch with her in an ugly Christmas sweater.

Mrs. Lasorsa

That's a few Christmases back.

Past Me

When's Remy's birthday?

Mrs. Lasorsa

[smiling] May thirtieth.

We cut back to me in the yard.

Past Me

If you remember on the show, Remy told me his birthday was the day after mine, December eighth. And that his fake sister's birthday was December ninth.

The audience mutters a chorus of *what the fuck* and *hell*.

On screen, we return to the interview with his mom.

Past Me

What was Remy's major in college?

Mrs. Lasorsa

He started off doing engineering at the community college here. He didn't like it, though. Dropped out when my mother died out in Montana—that's where I'm originally from. He moved out there to live in her house. Originally, he had volunteered to get it ready to sell, but he got a job out there. Decided he wanted to stay.

Past Me

So he didn't major in film? He isn't getting his master's in film production at UCLA? He's not interning for a producer out there?

Mrs. Lasorsa

What? No. Remy does not have the self-discipline you need to get a master's. He barely made it through a bachelor's degree before he lost interest.

Past Me

Oh, he told me about majoring in film at UCLA when I met him.

Mrs. Lasorsa

[face scrunches up] Well, he was fibbing to impress you, girlie. I'm sorry to burst your bubble.

The film cuts back to me in the yard.

Past Me

But he wasn't just fibbing. He was aware that I loved film from following my Instagram for years. That "fib" was designed to catch my attention. It's extra sad because he already had my attention, lies or no lies.

We cut back to the interview.

Past Me
May I ask what Remy's occupation is?

Mrs. Lasorsa
He's an exterminator. He works for some pest company out there in Montana.

Past Me
To recap: he doesn't live in LA, doesn't go to UCLA, doesn't have a sister, wasn't born in December, doesn't have a film degree, isn't getting his master's in film production, and isn't doing an internship with a big Hollywood producer.

Mrs. Lasorsa
No, none of that.

Past me
One last question. I'm so sorry if this is crossing a privacy line. But my father is an addict, and Remy told me his father was an addict as well. Is that true?

Mrs. Lasorsa
An addict? Why would he say that? Christ. What kind of addict?

Past Me
Gambling.

Mrs. Lasorsa
What! The only thing that man's addicted to currently is the couch.

We cut back to the yard.

Past Me
It was a disturbing visit, and to be absolutely 100 percent sure everything checked out, I got his brother's address from Mrs. Lasorsa and went on a road trip to talk to him in Florida on a lunch break.

The camera's set up, pointed across an outdoor cafeteria table. I'm sitting next to Remy's handsome older brother who we saw in various home pictures.

Past Me

Thanks for sitting down with me.

Dante

Yeah, sure. So, Remy's my younger brother. He's always kind of been the quieter kid, one who stands in the corner at family parties. Uh, but he loves fitness. Super into CrossFit. Lives in Montana where there's apparently a thriving Cross-Fit community. Yeah, I see him at Christmas. We're not very close. I was always busy with school and sports, and then my degree, so we didn't hang out much once I hit, like, age fourteen.

Past Me

Did you know he's on a reality show right now? The first episode premiered last week on CBN.

Dante

No kidding! No, he didn't tell me. That's cute. We really went in opposite directions, didn't we? He always loved reality TV, obsessed with, like, *The Challenge, Big Brother, Survivor,* and all those random dating show ones.

Past Me

Are your grandparents alive?

Dante

No, all have passed, unfortunately. He lives in our grandma's old house.

Past Me

When's his birthday?

Dante

Remy's is May thirtieth.

Past Me

When's yours?

Dante

December ninth.

Past Me

Wow. Okay, thanks, Dante! So Remy never was enrolled in UCLA?

Dante

No . . . I went to UCLA. That's where I got my master's in aerospace engineering.

We cut back to me in the yard.

Past Me

Remy Orlando Lasorsa lied to me about his entire life. His sister and her predicament don't exist, so I don't know how he actually plans to use the prize money. He gaslighted me at every chance he got in an attempt to dismiss my questions about his identity.

The video goes black. The audience remains silent.

Jamie clears her throat. "Our team has been fact-checking Remy since halfway through the taping of the season when we couldn't get ahold of Jerri for the family visit, and we can confirm everything in this video is true."

I turn to the crowd again. "The deception was ongoing, cruel, and unnecessary. I connected with the *Attached at the Hip* audience, committed to my alliances, and conquered the physical aspect of this game. I did the coconuts, made fires, found fruit—I survived by myself for three days. I made friends that I will stay connected with for the rest of my life. I made love connections. I wanted, and was willing, to split the money at the final-three challenge so we'd all go home with something because Osprey played an amazing game. He's so deserving of that MVP award; I'm so happy it exists. My name is Orie Lennox, and I would love your vote."

The audience erupts into cheers.

Remy glares at our host. "Am I just supposed to sit here and not respond after she came at me with an attack tape?"

"Do you feel the need to say something, Remy?" Jamie asks.

"This is all ridiculous. I don't know what possessed Orie to do something this unhinged. Hiring actors to create a smear campaign against me is crossing a line. That was all a bunch of calculated lies."

Jamie looks at the camera. "Our team has already checked on everything in the video; it is true."

Remy turns to the nearest camera and looks down the barrel. "I told you, it's not—"

"He made a fake Instagram account for his sister. It's tagged in his fake photo on the UCLA campus," I say tiredly.

Remy looks from me to the camera, aghast. "A *fake* photo on the UCLA campus? Really? Do you hear yourself right now? It's sad."

I turn to the audience. "He found out my dad was an addict because he worked for the café next to the church that hosted the GA meetings, and they would bring over coffee every Tuesday. He did not go to those meetings with his dad."

Remy bites his lip like he's about to cry and looks out at the crowd. "I had to say my dad's the one with the gambling problem." He shakes his head, apparently chagrined. "But in actuality, it's me. There's a stigma against addicts, and Orie never would have wanted to work with me if she knew I was actually the one with the problem. I'm the reason Jerri's lifelong dreams are on the line."

The audience gasps again.

"What!" My face twists into a knot of utter disbelief. "There IS NO JERRI!" I growl. "Why should we believe anything you say? The only true thing you ever told me was that you did CrossFit."

"Everything I told you is true. But go ahead, keep rambling. It only helps my case."

"Is your favorite color even macaroni?" I blurt.

Laughter bubbles up from the crowd.

"Listen," Remy says. "Even if I had lied about all that—" He gestures to the screen behind Jamie. "Which I didn't. But if I had, that also was great gameplay. All the things Orie's claiming are 'lies'—"

"They are lies," I insist as I stare at a spot on the ground.

"All those things she's claiming are 'lies,'" Remy repeats, "enabled us to connect on a deep level and form a bond that got me all the way to the final two. That's great strategy. You *were all* rooting for us. I connected with all of you in the audience, I connected with my castmates, and I conquered the physical game. Any way you look at this, I am more than deserving of your vote tonight."

A close-up shot of me goes up on the screen, eyes wide with indignation, teeth clenched.

"What she's alleging isn't against any rule," he continues. "She's basically pushing the argument that she was *my* pawn in this game. I never claimed that. I've been honest with her this entire time. But that's the narrative Orie is pushing. It's almost like she wants me to win. Orie Lennox was dependent on me through the entire game, and I won the final challenge and brought her to the end. I am the only reason she's sitting up here right now."

My vision goes red. Fuck.

Fuck. Fuck. Fuck. I glance over at my family. Lark's knuckles are bone-white as she death-grips her phone and armrest.

"I was no one's pawn," I spit. "And all of you watching saw that. I'm the reason Remy stayed in the game this long. So that he could help *me* get to the end. If anything, he was mine. If I hadn't convinced Kennedi to choose him in exchange for protecting Priya from the vote, he would have been gone before final five."

Remy laughs like I said something hilarious.

"Okay!" Jamie claps her hands. "Cast members, please come stand behind the contestant you'd like to back as most deserving for the million-dollar prize."

All of my castmates come line up on my side of the bench. The audience cheers.

"The cast is unanimously backing Orie here." Jamie smiles to the camera. "Now it's time to hear from you, America, because although they get to show their support, you're the ones who actually vote! This is your moment. Call or text the numbers on the screen right now for either Remy or Orie. You have ten minutes to get them in!" The screen behind her switches to a horizontal bar graph with REMY and ORIE both at 0 percent. "We're going to cut to break, and we'll be right back to watch your results coming in live!"

64

The Vote

93 DAYS POSTGAME

"And we're back." Jamie sits on her stool next to Zarar. The screen behind her has reverted back to the game logo. "There are five minutes left to vote. Remember, you're giving someone a million dollars here. If the vote is separated by a one-percent margin or less, the prize money will be split between the two contestants. If there is a majority of over one percent, we have a clear winner."

"All right," Zarar says. "Let's see where we're at." The graphs comes up on the screen. My stomach breaks into a thousand pieces, and each one of them explodes outward, leaving my body at a different exit point. Gasps pepper the room.

Jamie does a double take. "Forty-nine point five percent, Orie; fifty point five percent, Remy?"

"The fuck!" an audience member yells.

"Come on, everyone out there!" Osprey says nervously. "You need to vote!"

I blink at the graph, my eyes burning with fresh tears. I've been recognized a lot this week. A lot of people have wished me luck. Others have been less pleasant, screaming things like *You don't deserve Remy, you fickle bitch.*

"This is uncomfortably close," Jamie says.

I watched the Reddit threads while the show was airing. I saw the conversations about my Remy theories evolve over the weeks. I never had any hard proof. So eventually, all the red flags I waved were overlooked and forgotten. I became the paranoid hysterical girl who couldn't let anything go. I never thought in a million years those threads were speaking for the majority.

People pointed to Kennedi's freakout about Priya being pushed into the fire and called her melodramatic. On camera, they caught the incident at an angle that makes it look like both Remy and Priya did simply trip.

There is a set group of people who think Remy is a sociopath. I've been checking that thread every week. But there's another group who believes everything Remy says and thinks I'm a tactless jerk for second-guessing his every comment.

How could she question something so personal about his family as addiction. He's clearly had a hard childhood. He's such a catch and she's pushing him away.

"It refreshed!" Jamie yelps. "Things are even closer now: we're at fifty percent for Orie; fifty percent for Remy! Three minutes left to vote."

Osprey squeezes my shoulders behind me. I don't know when she grabbed my hand, but Kennedi's clutching it. "Breathe, Orie," she says. "It's not over."

But it feels over. What will we do if I don't win this? I thought I had it with the video. I had actual proof. People don't care about my proof? Is he too hot for people to care? He hired some actor to play his sister! HE'S NOT GOING TO DO ANYTHING NOBLE WITH THE MONEY— DON'T THEY GET THAT? HE'S A FUCKING LIAR!

"While we're waiting, we're going to grab some live reactions coming in from social and our audience. Zarar is out there with his mic."

The camera switches to a shot of a five-year-old girl. "I think Piccadilly should win because she's really brave and smart." The audience lets out an *aw.* My tears finally spill over.

"I have a tweet," Jamie announces. "@WillReeto87 says 'CROWN OSPREY KING OF EVERYTHING. Reply for a good time.'" The crowd chuckles.

An older man in the audience comes on screen. "Remy played an extremely elevated game. You don't see stuff like that every day. He got to the end, he was so slick, and I admire that." *Oh my god.*

Jamie clears her throat. "@boblovesBOOS says 'Remy played the game hard, he was creative and innovative. Class act.'"

Buried alive. That's what this feels like. I'm being buried alive.

I thought I gave a good speech.

"Breathe, Orie," Kennedi says again.

On screen, Zarar holds the mic for a teenage girl; she takes it from him aggressively. "If Orie doesn't win this, I am going to lose my faith in humanity. I thought Remy Orlando Lasorsa was cute, and now he's dead to me. DEAD."

"She knows what's up!" Kennedi points approvingly. The girl fades to black on the monitor, and the *Attached at the Hip* logo appears.

Jamie straightens on her stool and lifts her mic. "All right, I'm hearing we have the results, so, audience members, please, take your seats."

My castmates remain standing, huddled behind me. Kennedi's other hand comes to grip my biceps. Osprey's still gripping my shoulders.

My lungs are full of sand.

"There is more than a one-percent margin," Jamie starts. "We have *a* winner. The champion of season one of *Attached at the Hip* and winner of the one-million-dollar prize . . . with fifty-five percent of the vote . . ." Jamie pauses. The lights go up and down again.

The audience has gone dead silent. I'm going to pass out.

"Orrrrie Lennox!!!!" Jamie belts. Loud, upbeat music kicks on. Confetti guns erupt on either side of the stage. It's raining silver and gold.

Kennedi's trying to yank me up off the bench, jumping up and down screaming.

"Orie, you won!"

Osprey squeezes my shoulder from behind. "Congratulations, Tube Stop!"

What? I can't move—I'm full of sand. My castmates, Jamie, Z— everyone's hovering. Smiling. Standing. Everyone is standing.

I won. I won? The audience is deafening. Tears of shame are still trickling down my cheeks. But I won. I have to stand up.

I do. I rise, and Remy steps right in front of me, blocking my view of everything else. He pulls me into a tight hug. I know next to me Kennedi is scolding him, but her voice slides away as Remy's lips find my ear.

"It might feel like you won," he breathes, "but I got what I came for."

"Get off of me," I mutter.

"I'm really glad it was you on the other end of my rope that first day. It made this all so much easier." I stiffen in his arms.

"Imagine my luck when a girl I followed religiously from high school with 700,000 followers showed up drooling over me on a romantic spin-off of *Survivor*."

My heart thumps too hard against my rib cage. People are yelling around me. I don't move.

"I know you're upset." I feel him smile. "But your audience loves me." My head's going to blow off.

I wrench myself from his grip, glaring into his shiny silver eyes. He's wearing a shit-eating grin, still standing less than a foot away.

"You know what's sad, Remy?" I breathe. "The closest thing to a friend you're ever going to have is your fake sister."

His lips stretch wider, but I don't miss the way his eyes tighten. "You keep telling yourself that, Or."

"It's Orie," I snap.

A large hand clamps down on his arm. And then security drags Remy Orlando Lasorsa away. He has the nerve to wink at me as he disappears through the exit door.

A weight slumps off my chest.

I gaze around, my surroundings coming back into focus. The music's still blaring. People are yelling. Confetti is still falling. I *won*.

Jamie appears next to me, offering an empathetic smile. She extends her hand, and I take it, a new round of tears pooling and falling down my cheeks.

She leads me to the front of the stage. "You did it," she says firmly. The crowd is still clapping. *Still standing*. "Not hypothetically. Or in theory. Actually."

I choke on a wet laugh as Jamie lifts my hand, and the cheering intensifies.

My family rushes the stage, and a real smile finally cracks across my face. For a euphoric fifteen seconds, I'm engulfed in their arms. In their *joy*.

I did do it. I did it. They pull back as Zarar emerges holding an over-sized million-dollar check with my name on it. He hands it to me, and I take it, giggling now.

Actual full emotional whiplash.

"There you have it, people!" Jamie cheers. "*Survivor* superfan since age eight, Orie 'Piccadilly' Lennox is our winner! THAT'S OUR SHOW! We'll have these amazing peeps back in a month for an official reunion to see what's shaking, who's dating who, and which missed connections have been mended! Let's give our winner another round of applause!"

The audience explodes again. A laugh barks out of me as "Roar" by Katy Perry starts up over the speakers. I let Lark hold my check as Kennedi grabs my hands and pulls me back toward the rest of the cast, yelling the lyrics. They're congratulating and hugging me, and Osprey's here, and we're all dancing, and I can't stop crying.

It's by far the best moment of my life.

65

After (Party)

93 DAYS POSTGAME

I am overwhelmed. My castmates and all their families and friends and other people associated with the show swirl from pocket to pocket of mingling humans, drinking and eating in this beautifully lit room full of cocktail tables and excitement. Mom and Dad are doing the rounds, talking to all my castmates. They're currently engaged in an enthusiastic chat with Kennedi and her mom.

I haven't *really* spoken to anyone yet. I've said thank you about a hundred times to a hundred different strangers who have come up to congratulate me.

Adrenaline spikes through me when I spot Osprey and his family among the procession. I beam as they step up to greet me, and heartily congratulate Osprey. A million questions burn on the tip of my tongue as he quickly thanks me and leads his family off to another area of the room. I blink at his retreating silhouette. *What was that?* Could he be dating someone now? Is that why he hasn't talked to me for more than fifteen seconds at a time all night?

Before I can move to follow him, another stranger steps in front of me. *"Oh my gosh, congratulations!"*

I take a quick moment to thank them and excuse myself before dashing after Osprey. His parents are chatting with Priya's parents. I tap him on the back, and my heart lodges itself in my throat as he turns around. This is it: *pounce.*

"Hey!" He looks at me quizzically. "What are you doing over here? You've got a whole lineup waiting to talk to you."

"I-I want to talk to you. How have you been? Can we exchange numbers? I . . . I miss you." I said it. I said it. I said it.

"Give me your phone," he says with a small smile. I hand it to him. He punches something in and calls himself.

"You seem weird," I tell him.

"You always seem weird," he tells me.

"Do you, um, I read the assign—"

My sister and Mel walk up with a glass of wine for me, accompanied by Leo and a woman who looks very familiar. "Hey, Or, I think you're going to want to talk to these two," Lark says as I take the offered glass of wine.

I turn back to Osprey—to find he's disappeared into the crowd. What the hell. I pivot back to Leo and his cousin. She starts to say something, but I completely cut her off.

"YOU'RE *THE* SHANE PRIMAVERI!"

She laughs. "Yeah, hi!"

My head swivels to Leo. I point from him to her. "I could not believe when the family episode aired that I hadn't clocked you in person. I was in the presence of my favorite author and I was too distracted by my damn sister I see EVERY DAY to notice! I LOVE YOU." I lunge forward and wrap Shane in an aggressive hug, before immediately thinking better of it and pulling back. "Sorry!"

She laughs. "Don't apologize! Hugs are fantastic! I'm so happy you liked my books!"

"I cab believe you're here! CAN'T. I *can't believe you're here, not cab*! Your duology means so much to me, I—"

I twist and point to the lamppost on my shoulder and spin back around as she squees with glee. We chat about the show and other books we love for a glorious eight minutes before a new stranger takes her place. I smile and thank the new people, and smile and thank the new people—the next thirty minutes are a blur of happy faces and kind words, and I have absolutely no complaints.

At some point, Jamie appears and whisks me away. She drags me across the room toward an older man, maybe in his late forties.

"Hey, Grier!" she greets him casually.

He turns from the conversation he's currently engaged in. "Oh, hey!" Jamie introduces me. "This is Orie."

"I'm aware," he says, reaching out to shake my hand.

"Orie, this is Grier Federov, my dad. He and I produced the show together. He's also an Oscar-nominated writer/filmmaker with a spot for a new intern with your name on it opening up next month as he shifts projects."

Grier smiles. "Yeah, I'd be happy to have you! I hear you're interested in screenwriting?"

Holy crapinoli.

"Yes! I think I am! And I'm also interested in a lot of the other parts of filmmaking: producing and directing, editing—and just being on set."

"Well, we have a place for you on the team as an intern-slash-PA for my next project if you want it," Grier says kindly.

"Or, if it interests you more," Jamie says, "I can bring you on as an intern production assistant for season two of *Attached at the Hip*. You've got brand-new exclusive insight on the show that could really help shape our next season. I start prep next month. You can help me with casting!" Then she adds in a whisper, "Mine's a real paid gig."

Grier injects again. "I'll have a draft of the script to work on with my team by June, so we'll be starting in about two months."

I blink at the two of them. *Is this real life?* I don't know what to say. Literally. I glance from Grier to Jamie, my head swinging from one to the other in shock.

"You don't have to decide in this moment!" Jamie laughs. "Take a few days, think about it, and let me know. Here, give me your phone so you have my number."

I hand Jamie my phone. She punches at it rapidly. *Jamie's giving me her number!*

"Take a second, no rush. Just let Jamie know sometime this week." Grier smiles at me before returning to his prior conversation circle.

"All right." Jamie hands me back my phone. "It's time for the speech."

She picks her drink up from the nearest cocktail table and bangs her little appetizer fork against it.

"What speech?" I ask.

The room joins in with the clinking.

"The winner's afterparty speech."

"Winner's? Wait, what?"

Jamie drags me to the front of the room where there's a microphone waiting on a stool. She flips it on, hands it to me, and steps back.

"What, Jamie!" I look around at the guests, all of whom are moving in this direction, crowding around me. A PA comes out of nowhere, puts down a wooden box, and whispers for me to stand on it.

I step up onto the box, looking out at everyone, focusing on no one. "I-I wasn't told I was supposed to be giving a speech. Um. So, I'm not prepared. But, hi, I guess, I'm Orie. Um. I kinda stumbled into this *Survivor* spin-off journey trying to prove a point to my sister. But I ended up, uh, proving one to myself.

"I think a lot of us do this subconsciously . . ." I pause, scanning the crowd again. I spot Osprey way in the back. And Kennedi standing with Priya. My eyes stop on my dad beaming at me, right in the middle of all the guests. I smile back. "We put ourselves in neat labeled boxes to make sense of who we should be. We wall ourselves off from what *we think* we can't do to try and protect ourselves from getting hurt. From failing.

"I've come to realize . . . that what we're really doing in those moments is putting a ceiling on our capacity to grow. To learn. Evolve. We're holding ourselves back. Pushing against those self-imposed limits, breaking them down, has been so incredibly satisfying. Before I started this, I had so much anxiety about even the smallest confrontation. I didn't trust in my own ability to adequately take on any mild or significant challenge. Today, I managed to fluently confront Remy Orlando Lasorsa on national television." I cough a laugh. Chuckles and cheers ruffle through the crowd. "I won a survival show!" I blink, glancing down for a moment at my not-numb hands.

"I want to . . . run wild into the world. I want to say things instead of holding them in! I want to try everything! And chase after experiences I thought were too swift for me to ever catch." I scrunch my shoulders up to my ears, a smile eating up my whole face. "We can all do so much more than we give ourselves credit for. We just have to step out of those neat little boxes to realize it.

"Thank you, Jamie, for casting me. Thanks to my sister, Lark, for insulting me enough to push me onto this path. Thank you to all my castmates for your encouragement and companionship, especially Kennedi and Osprey. Thank you to everyone involved, and my wonderful parents. Thank you!"

The room applauds as Jamie raises her glass with an authoritative "To stepping out of the box!" I laugh as the whole crowd repeats her toast, cheering, "To stepping out of the box!" and clinking their glasses.

The moment I step off the makeshift stage, another group of people descends to chat. I smile and nod politely. Greet everyone. Thank them. Greet another group and thank them as I crane my head as inconspicuously as I can manage, trying to locate Osprey.

Where is he? I pull out my phone.

Me
You still here? I see your parents but not you
Osprey
Needed a second away. In the empty dressing rooms.
Be back in a bit.

I speed walk to the side door and slip out of the party.

66

Paperback (Party)

93 DAYS POSTGAME

I wander down the hall to the soundstage. It's empty now. I don't want to make a racket clacking across it in heels, so I take them off, tiptoe to the other side, and scurry over to the far hall where the dressing rooms are.

I find Osprey behind the fourth door. He's lounging on a couch, one leg out across the cushions, one on the ground, reading a weathered-looking paperback.

He looks up in surprise as I step in and close the door. "Whoa, hey." He puts down the book and scoots up so he's not taking up the entire sofa.

He's shed his blazer and is now sporting the fitted green vest that was underneath, which is over a white dress shirt with an emerald tie. It's an A-plus look.

I settle on the far end of the couch with my back against the arm and pull my legs to my chest. "Hey," I say belatedly. "What's up? I feel like you're, maybe, avoiding me?"

"No, I just . . ." He shrugs. "I'm not good around big crowds. I get drained pretty quickly. Too many conversations, too many humans talking at the same time, overload of strangers."

"What happens at your parkour competitions?"

He laughs. "There are not this many people at those competitions.

And, I don't know. I'm in my element there. I have a purpose. Here, I'm just floating, you know?"

I nod. "Yeah. You cut your hair." For some reason, I reach out like I'm going to mime touching his old hair. I drop my hand.

He laughs. "What was that?"

"I don't even know. I was going to, like, push back your old hair, but it doesn't exist, so."

A grin appears at the edge of his lips. "You don't like the short hair?"

"No, I like it. It looks good." I swallow. "You dress much cooler outside the island."

His head falls forward as he laughs again. "Uh, so do you. Where are the polka-dot socks, huh? Where are the glasses? Your face looks so different without them."

I laugh and cover my face, a tad self-conscious for a second. "Is my face better with glasses? Should I retire the contacts?"

"No, it's just different! You look good. You look really good both ways! It's just jarring to see you all gussied up after living on an island for a month."

"So you prefer my beach-rat look."

"Do you prefer mine?" he challenges.

My face heats. "I like you both ways."

He purses his lips and presses them into a line. "Same."

"It's so strange," I say quietly. "Living so intimately for such an intense, short period of time, and then being away from each other for ninety days. I feel like I don't know how to act. Are you trying to keep your distance? I don't smell, right? Are the anxiety sweats overpowering my deodorant? I reapplied, like, an hour ago."

He grins and shakes his head. Fiddles with the edge of his vest for a moment. "You smell great. I just—this is, you know."

"No, I don't know," I share.

He blows out a breath. "I like you a lot, and it's not going to go anywhere, so I need to keep my distance so I can get over it." He tells this to my feet.

My heart dips. "I don't want you to get over it," I say softly. "I don't want to get over it. Why should we get over it?"

"Because," he says solemnly. "The show is over . . . and I went all in on you, and you went all in on someone else."

I swallow back the torrent of emotion gathering in my throat. "Our lives aren't over because the show is over. Our story doesn't have to be over."

"Orie, long distance never works," he mumbles.

I slide my legs down off the couch and scoot closer. I drop a hand onto his knee. "We're not long distance," I say. "We're both right here."

His eyes fall to my hand and trace up my arm. "You got a new tattoo?"

I nod. "Yeah." I got the family tattoo on the inside of my right biceps so I'd be able to read it when I need it, like my dad intended.

"Can I see?"

I nod again. Osprey sits up and shifts closer, his foot moving along the inside seam of the cushions, so I end up in between his legs. I lift my right arm to show him. A wave of his spicy vanilla scent washes over me as he reaches out to hold my elbow.

"Pobody's Nerfect?" He smiles, amused.

I grin. "Pobody *is* Nerfect."

He snorts.

"Osprey . . ." I start. He lifts his head, and I catch his eyes. They look like liquid emeralds today. Open. Vulnerable. "I am so sorry I hitched my wagon to Remy's. I created an entire false reality of who he was in my head. I was so desperate to escape the reality of what I was actually going through with my ex, and afraid to come to terms with my failed relationship, that I threw myself into the illusion of a perfect match." I glance down at the couch for a moment, worrying at my lip as my stomach takes a nosedive. "I'm pretty sure there was an *actual perfect match* waiting six days away."

Osprey's brows rise, but he doesn't interrupt. He holds my gaze intently. A low hum vibrates under my skin.

"When I met you," I continue, "I kept telling myself I only liked you as a friend because I didn't want to fall into a love triangle. No one wants that. It gets so complicated. Everyone always gets hurt. But I most definitely had a crush. And that crush grew into something ridiculously dramatic by the end of the show.

"All I thought about when I was watching the episodes air was you, Oss. *Osprey is watching this—what is he thinking? How is he feeling? How is he coping?* All I've wanted to do these past ninety days is talk to you."

"Perfect match?" Osprey repeats slowly. He tilts his head, the shadow of a smile on his lips. "I seem to recall you very recently preaching *pobody's nerfect?*"

I scoot a smidge closer. "Well, *nobody's perfect* in the way that everyone makes mistakes. But people can be perfect for each other in an imperfect way."

Osprey's full grin clicks into place. "What are you saying? That the internet is right about us? You're a bird, I'm a bird?"

We're right up on each other now. My bent leg's pressed into his thigh. The rest of me is inches from his face. "I mean, if we're gonna get metaphorical, we are."

A shiver helicopters up my torso as his hands settle on my waist. They slide over my obliques, and the blue flames flare up, dancing over my abdomen as he leans in. Our foreheads meet as his thumbs come to rest firmly in the crease between my hips and thighs, hitting a trip wire I didn't know was there. An influx of gold dust rolls through me.

Slowly, I shift so our mouths align. Twist my arms around his neck. He pulls me closer, and the leg I have on the couch slips around his waist.

Anticipatory glitter spills over me as his mouth hovers over mine. We sit like that for a moment, breathing. Skin pulsing. Heart hovering at the edge of the cliff in my chest.

I suck in a shaky breath. "You planning to ever actually kiss me?"

He laughs, moving his lips across my cheek. He kisses the corner where my neck meets my ear. I inhale an embarrassing amount of air as it scorches a trail down to my center. *How did an ear kiss do that? How?*

"What if," he says slowly, "it breaks the spell?"

My head falls back as his mouth moves down my neck. "What spell?"

"This spell. The one where I can't take my eyes off of you." His teeth clamp gently over my clavicle, and I feel *it*. The Katy Perry song. I am *the firework*. I didn't know what I was talking about before. That was just an ember, a spark. A fraction of this feeling.

Osprey's hand slips the spaghetti strap down off my right shoulder. "The one where you're actually all I ever fucking think about."

He presses a kiss to my shoulder. "All I want to learn about. The spell that makes me feel like my body is vibrating on a different plane when we touch."

I shift against him. He sucks in a sharp breath as I close more of the space between us. I snake my hands into his hair on both sides of his face. It's thick and silky and wonderful. I trace my thumb over that pirate mustache. Down his lip. "Pretty sure I'm under that same one."

His hands glide down to wrap around my knees.

"If it breaks the spell." I skate my fingers over his shoulders, down his back. "Then we let ourselves get over this." I pull at his shirt until it's free so I can slide my hands under it, over his skin. His grip tenses around my legs.

"We need to test it for science," I inform him as desire cascades through me, a tidal wave of pressure against my skin. We are as pressed up against each other as much as two people with clothes on can be. Living, breathing puzzle pieces.

His gaze flicks up from my mouth to my eyes. "Tube Stop, I'm feeling very seduced."

"Shut up, Osprey."

He tilts forward, his mouth finally meeting mine. Lips parting, I tug him closer. His hands skim under the dress, back up my legs. My insides swirl into a molten euphoric tizzy as we dissolve into each other.

He tastes like cherries and whiskey and words, and I feel completely and utterly out of control as I acquiesce to this magic radiating between us. We're horizontal, and Osprey is everywhere. Everything is fireworks. My blood has been spiked with shimmering gold confetti.

"Or?" The door creaks open. "Oh my god!" It slams shut.

We freeze.

"Sorry!" the voice sounds again. Lark.

"Hey, um, in the middle of something," I try to say calmly.

"Sorry, sorry, sorry, sorry. As you were. Mom and Dad wanted to know if you were ready to leave. I'll cover. Don't, um—just, it's fine." Her footsteps retreat.

We're in a compromising position, but we're clothed, so. It is fine? Our eyes slide back to each other. I snort, and his head drops forward with a laugh. Another burst of gold dust tornadoes around my torso.

I shift us so we're on our sides. "What's the verdict? Spell still intact for you?"

He mashes his lips together, unsuccessfully hiding a smile. It pops back up after a second of eye contact. "Spell holds firm. You want to get back to the party?"

I sit up, twisting to put my feet on the ground and fix the straps of my dress. "I'm happy here at the paperback party."

"Oof, you're going to have to stop calling us that." *Us.*

I am way too excited about that "us." He slides behind me, framing my legs with his. Presses his lips to where the quote collection starts on my shoulder. The kiss ripples through me.

"Can I call us Ori-sprey?" I ask.

"That sounds like a pest repellent."

I twist my neck to catch his face over my shoulder. We kiss again. I feel it everywhere, like points of light, tiny fusion reactions moving through me, roaring, expanding.

The kiss breaks. We gaze at each other. "Circle of trust," I say slowly. "Kissing you feels like becoming the sun."

He holds my eyes as I rotate in his arms to stand, so I can admire his pretty, geometrical, sharp face and boyish grin and pirate-liner lashes from above. His hands glide down my sides as he looks up at me. "Your bangs grew out."

"Yeah, thank the gods. They were the worst."

"It's nice to see your whole face, your eyes . . ." He tapers off.

"What?" I grin down at him.

"They're so fucking bright. You were hiding those things behind the glasses so you wouldn't intimidate the crap out of everyone."

I hold my pinky to my mouth like Dr. Evil. "So what if I was. I needed to be approachable, Oss!"

His smile gleams and fades. "What happens when we leave here, Orie?"

"I don't know, but we'll figure it out when we leave here."

"I'm leaving for my last parkour championship tomorrow. Last one before I'm gonna, quote, *retire*," he says quietly. "From the competition side of things, at least. It's down in Florida."

"Whoa. I didn't realize that was happening so soon. Um, I have a bunch of press stuff this week with Jamie, and I have to figure out some internship things, but, I mean, we have phones, Osprey. When do you get back?"

"Ten days."

"Okay, that's nothing."

"Okay."

He says okay, but sadness washes through his eyes. His nails skate up the backs of my thighs, sending a flurry of blue flames up into my core.

I kneel on the couch over him, and we fall together again. A little more frantic, a little more desperate to make the most of this moment— the illogical fringe worry that this may be the only time we get to do this looming over us.

67

After the After

I stare into space on the way home. A car hired by the network brought me into the city earlier, but I'm riding home in my dad's Prius with my parents, Lark, Mel, and my check.

Mom twists around in the front passenger seat. "Maybe you should have rented a hotel room if you have to be back in the city by noon for all that press stuff."

"Jamie asked her if she wanted a room at the hotel they're staying in, but she wants to sleep at home," Lark answers for me. "They're going to send a car for her at ten."

I'm glad Lark is on top of things because my brain feels hazy, struggling to process everything that happened tonight. Trying to sort through all the upcoming decisions only I can make.

I need to talk to Lark in private. I need to figure out how to make things with Osprey work. We have to be able to make it work.

He's worried about "long distance" from Delaware to New Jersey. Here I am ready to ride the wind to California to try to chase a career in film or TV.

I feel like a million things just fell on top of me at once. I'm too tired right now to pick them up and arrange them into something discernible. So, I stare out the window in a spinning heap of happy confusion.

I had the most amazing makeout session of my life with Osprey.

Osprey. Osprey. Osprey.

I've been offered two internship opportunities in LA.

I just won. A million. Dollars.

I can help my family.

"I'm giving you the money, Mom, Dad," I tell them from the back seat.

"No, you're not," Dad says.

"Yes, I am. I'm not budging on that," I say firmly.

"No," Mom says.

"Are you in danger of losing the house right now?" I snap. "Yes or no, don't lie to me."

"We might, but sweetheart—" Mom starts.

"No, I meant it when I said I wanted to do this for you two. *I mean it.* I'm giving you the money."

"If you insist on helping . . . then fine, but you're not giving us all of it," Mom snaps back.

I huff. "How much are you out? You must need almost all of it! You can have ninety percent."

"That's way too much, sweetheart, no," Dad says.

"Then eighty percent," I say.

"Orielle, stop it." My mother is crying.

"Stop what? You raised me, you paid for my college education, you PAID for fire lessons. *Come on.*"

"We can't accept that much money from you, Orie." Dad's crying now, too?

"Fine, seventy percent. I'm not going any lower," I growl. "You're accepting the money. I love you. Take my freakin' winnings, goddamn it!"

I shoot Lark an exhausted look at the sound of them weeping in the front seat, only to find Lark weeping, too. Mel has her arm around her; Lark's head is on her shoulder.

"What the hell is going on here!" I cry.

When we get home, I ask Lark if she'll come downstairs for a few minutes before she and Mel head to their apartment. I tell her everything that happened with Osprey. Everything about the internships.

"This is not a few-minutes'-long conversation, Or. Let me shoot Mel a text. I'm just gonna stay over."

Lark and I curl up facing each other in my bed. "First things first—which internship calls to you?" she asks.

"Both of them do!"

"Do you want my thoughts?"

"Obviously. My mind is mush, Lark! Do you have some pro-cons?"

"I think *I* would do the film one. He's an Oscar-nominated writer; he doesn't always have a new film project in motion that you can hop onto. This is an amazing opportunity to learn from one of the best. With *Attached at the Hip,* I mean, it did really well. It's probably going to have a lot more seasons. And being their first winner and knowing the producers, I bet you could always slip back into that world in one form or another if you wanted.

"Plus, you're trying to get your podcast up and running; you want to be able to write on the side. You want to be able to make new connections and get guests on the show. If you have a base in LA, you can do that. But you can't juggle all that if you're heading out to Fiji again in September with Jamie."

"This is why I love you."

She laughs. "Because I make decisions for you?"

"No! Because you're, like, a human computer. You sorted through all that in ten minutes as I was telling it to you. I was caught up in the emotional part of the decision, and you were able to pinpoint the logical choice instantaneously! That's a gift, Lark. I've realized lately that logic is always my last thought cycle. I'll get there, but it takes a long, agonizing time to reach that corner of my brain."

She rolls her eyes, but she's smiling. Pleased with herself. "At your service, my champion."

"I agree with what you said. And I would say something if I didn't."

She pulls my blankets up over her shoulder. "Good."

I snort. "What about Osprey."

"What about him?" she asks suggestively. "You pounced!"

I roll my eyes. "What do I do?"

"What do you want to do?"

"Something bananas," I tell her.

She laughs. "Do you feel *it*?"

I frown, trying to sort through my scattered emotions. "Is it insane if I say I do? Because I do. You know when people say, *When you know, you know*? I'm always like, *But how do you know? You don't know!* But I think I know. There's this feeling in my gut of rightness. Of safety. And happiness. And everything good all at once . . . I know that sounds melodramatic."

"It doesn't sound melodramatic, Or. I'm engaged. I felt it." She smacks my arm lightly. "I know what it's like."

"Well, other people are going to think my plan is rash and foolish, and melodramatic."

"Who are these other people you speak of?" she asks with a smile. "You said it yourself in your speech tonight, you have to chase your passions. Go wild. Don't box yourself in by what other people might think of your plan. You've been playing it safe your entire life. If you're falling for this guy, then jump and see what happens. Follow your happy and see where it goes. Run after the fairy tale. That's the only way you're ever going to catch it."

I loose a long sigh. "But how do I trust that this is *the it* when my gut has been so, SO wrong in the past?"

Lark squints at me. "Has your gut actually been wrong, or have *you* been wrong? Did you think it was romantically right with Wes?"

I squint back at her. "No, I was thirteen, and he liked me, and I wanted my fairy tale."

"Exactly. Did you think it was right with Remy?"

"*Yes*," I groan, running my hands down my face.

"Did it feel like it does with Osprey?"

I glare up at the ceiling. "No . . . it was different."

"What made you think it was so right with Remy?"

"The things he liked. The family things we connected on. The way he made me feel wanted."

"But you didn't actually connect on those things, and he didn't actually like most of the things he said he liked. They were all lies."

My throat feels tight. "Yeah."

"Why does it feel right with Osprey?"

"It just does . . . He sees me. He knows exactly what I mean when I say things. We grew up on the same stories, and he, like, speaks that same language without even trying to. He's pushy and empathetic, and gentle, and logical, and everything I'm not, but at the same time, he loves stories and appreciates them with the same meticulous care and passion that I do. And he's so smart. I love how smart he is. And when we're together-together, I feel like I'm experiencing firsthand magic."

"Or, Osprey jumped off that last challenge and threw his spot to make sure you didn't get hurt."

"I know," my voice squeaks. "Who does that? Who does that for some-one they just met twenty days ago?"

"Someone you can count on," Lark says.

"Someone worth knowing," I whisper.

"I vote jump."

68

Epilogue-ing

109 DAYS POSTGAME

I got a car. My own Prius. A yellow one.

I follow the GPS down I-95 South to Delaware. Osprey got back from his last competition a couple of days ago, but he's been busy helping his parents reorganize the bookstore. He'll be there working with them all week.

His schedule was jam-packed when he was down in Florida, so we only texted once or twice a day.

A can't wait to see you again. Or How are you? Or Thinking of you. A picture of a book I'm reading. A picture of what he's reading. A quote I really like. His thoughts on said quote.

Then he got home, and he called. And we've talked for an hour each day since. About arbitrary things. Fun things. Life things. Every new thing I learn about him makes me like him more. Every random tiny detail makes my heart swell.

His first screen name was BookReadingLover5. Not "book lover." Not "reader" or "I love reading." BookReadingLover FIVE. Is that not the cutest thing you've ever heard?

He keeps his movie tickets in a scrapbook and writes what he thought of the movie next to it. He bullet journals every day and starts each bullet journal entry with something he's grateful for that day.

We've chatted about a million little things, but not us. Not the elephant in the room. Not about my internship. Our tentative plan was to meet up later this week when he and his parents would be nearing the finish line with the store so we can figure out what we're doing. What this can be.

I parallel park in front of I Like Books and I Cannot Lie at noon, two and a half hours after leaving my parents' house. It's on an adorable little small-town-feeling block, sandwiched between a Marshalls and an Instagrammable acai bowl shop. The words I LIKE and & I CANNOT LIE are small across the window, and the word BOOKS is enormous.

I text Osprey. How goes it today?

He texts back a minute later.

Osprey

Slow, parents out getting lunch. We just have the upstairs left to do! Currently browsing for a new read. Did I ever tell you I finished the assignment? I need a new rec.

Me

I finished mine too! Time for a Paperback Party Parley

Osprey

Do we really want our book club to be called PPP

Me

TIME FOR A PUH.

Osprey

I exhale a slow breath and get out of the car.

When I push open the door, it jingles lightly. A smile breaks across my face as I take in this little corner of bookish heaven. The first floor is a warmly lit narrow maze of bookshelves. There's some movement from above. My eyes snap toward the spiral staircase off to the right that leads to a loft. I dart toward the back of the store so I'm out of sight from the balcony.

In the very back-left corner of the shop, I find the YA section. I squat down at the sight of a little handwritten recommendation card. It's in front of *Divergent*. I bite back a smile. It's dated 2015. *This book changed my life. Epic, inspiring—you won't be able to put it down.—Osprey.*

"Hello?" Osprey's voice travels from the front of the store. Footsteps come in my direction.

"Hello?" he says again, closer now.

I stand up and turn around. "Hi, I was just browsing."

Osprey stops short. Laughs. Runs a hand over his hair. I smile at him nervously.

"What are you—hi!" He strides over and pulls me into a tight hug. "You're here! And you're all—" He pulls back.

"Gussied up?" I'm wearing a long dress covered in sunflowers and a white jean jacket. Not that fancy.

He's in a white shirt with a thick black stripe across it and black cargo shorts.

He runs his hands down my arms. I close my eyes as the usual pleasant shiver runs through me. "You look beautiful."

I purse my lips together, feeling shy. "Thank you." This is feeling crazier by the second.

"Are you going somewhere? Is this a pit stop?" He studies me for another moment. "Why are you nervous, Orie? What's happening? Is everything okay? Is this a depressing visit?"

I grab his elbows. "No, I'm nervous because I have to tell you things."

"Bad things?"

My eyes fall to his lips. I'm back on that dressing room couch with him and the magic.

"What are you thinking about right now?" A smile curls up his face.

I blow out a breath, smiling back. "Nothing! Stop trying to read my mind." I step around him, and he follows.

"I can't," he says haughtily. "It's both a blessing and a curse. And why I'd be super good on *Survivor*."

I laugh, wandering around a bookshelf aimlessly, needing to keep moving so the anxiety doesn't pool.

"Can we talk somewhere? Is there a couch somewhere private-ish?"

He nods. "Yeah, let's go upstairs."

I peer out over the balcony, at the flat tops of all the shelves below. "Have you ever parkoured in here?"

Osprey smiles, pleasantly surprised by this question. He takes my hand and intertwines it with his. "Of course. Got in trouble back when I was fifteen. Knocked over a bookshelf and caused a domino effect with three more."

He leads me over to an old, worn leather sofa tucked in the corner among the upstairs shelves. I'm chuffed to find the romance section on the shelf across from us. *It's a sign.*

Or not.

Or it is.

Osprey squeezes my hand as he settles in next to me. "Are you sure this isn't bad?"

I drop my purse on the floor and take my zillionth deep breath. "It's not bad, just wild."

"All right." He closes his eyes and nods. "I'm ready. Hit me with it."

"So I . . . I got an internship in LA." I dive right into the details: Jamie's dad, his new film, how he wants me there in two months.

"So, I'm going to fly out to California next week to look at apartments." Osprey's brows start to rise. "No, calm down!" I scold. "I was thinking. I was just thinking that after this whole experience, I, more than ever, want to carpe diem and just do things that feel right. And moving to LA to chase a job that makes me happy feels right. And you *feel right.* And I know you said you wanted to go into stunt work after you were retired from parkouring, and a lot of your work is through Instagram, and you could do that anywhere like me. And the stunt work is out there, you know? That's where everything is happening, and I thought . . .

"Maybe we could both move out there and chase our dreams together, but, like, live in separate apartments, and, like, date like normal people. Who live in the same state and are trying to do the wild things they want to do. And I was thinking maybe you would want to come out to California with me next week and just check out the vibe and where the good places to live are and, you know, just have fun. Jamie said she'd be happy to give us a list of area recommendations."

He cocks his head. "You told Jamie about this plan?"

"No! I just mentioned that I was going to look out there, and she was going to give me the list, but I wanted to ask you if you'd want to join . . . me." I drop my head in my hands. Oh my god. This is ludicrous. We've never even gone on a date. I sound ridiculous.

"Orie. I, um . . ." he struggles.

Oh my god. My stomach plunges into my uterus. I can't look up. I can't look at him. "I'm *so* sorry!" I focus on a dent in the tan-and-black carpet. "I don't know what I was thinking—this is so stupid! I'm trying to be romantic, but I'm coming off as insane! I'm just super-dumb in like with you, and the alternative is not seeing you, and I hate that. I hate that idea. I just want this to keep going."

He hasn't said anything in a minute, so I risk a peek to see if he's left the couch. He's still here. And he's . . . staring blankly at the shelves.

ALL RIGHT. This is mortifying. I stand and start toward the steps. He doesn't say anything, so I stumble down them. I drop my keys pulling them out of my jacket pocket and drop them again after I pick them up. Outside, I can't find the unlock button on the fob. I relock the door three times trying to get it open.

I finally get in the car. Still no movement in the shop. This is the most embarrassing thing I've ever done.

I put the car in drive and pull out onto the road.

I'm halfway down the block when I catch him in my sideview mirror sprinting down the sidewalk. *Oh god.*

He's not going to let me go without discussing how embarrassing this was. Carpe diem-ing is horrifying—why didn't Lark prep me for how embarrassing this would be!

I pull into the next open spot and step out of the car, gnawing at my lip. Dear god. Why does Osprey look so attractive running? Running makes everyone else look like a cartoon character.

He stops in front of me, barely out of breath. "Orie. *Jesus.* You forgot your entire purse." He pulls the thing off his body and hands it to me.

Like this could get worse. He's delivering my purse. He's not even here to talk to me.

I turn to leave, and he catches my arm. "Hey, stop trying to leave, will you?" His voice is warm and sweet.

I slowly turn to face him, cringing.

"Orie." He huffs a silent chuckle. "I am dumb in like with you, too. Like, super ridiculously."

"You are?" My eyes are watering from overwhelming embarrassment.

"Yes, and I am feeling the same way postgame. I want to just do things. I want to be happy, and right now, you're the brightest point of every day for me. I didn't know when I would actually work up the courage to get out of Delaware. It's a big deal to leave my family."

"I know. Me, too."

"But this is probably the best time to try to do movie things, right after the show's finished airing."

I nod.

"Fuck," he says. "This is so ridiculous."

I shrug my shoulders up, and let them fall. "I know. I decided to just jump."

He cuts me a dry look. "Are you setting me up for a *Titanic* reference right now?"

"Not purposefully, but it does work really well if you're feeling it."

"What happens if we don't work out?"

"I didn't say live together! Just go out with me! I'm just asking you to date me. It's not *that* wild."

"You want me to move out to California to date you."

"And follow your stuntman career dreams! You were going to move out there! I'm only giving you a push!" I drop my head, crossing my arms. "We only live once, and . . . I . . . I want to run into my fears, and pounce on good things, and chase them."

"I think you're describing a day in the life of an outdoor cat."

I deflate, flopping my forehead against his chest, sad laughter wracking through me.

He grabs my chin and lifts it, his green eyes bright with adrenaline. "Hey. I don't know what page of the rom-com script we're on . . . maybe it's only five, or, like, nine? But I want to see where it goes."

"I think we're at page seventeen."

He grins. "Why seventeen?"

"Crazy shit happens on page seventeen. I've been reading about it; it's a thing."

He takes my hands and pulls them out to our sides, stepping in so we're face-to-face. He's quiet for a long moment before he says softly, "'You jump, I jump,' remember?"

I blow out a breath. "Oh, that was good; sidestep the obvious *Titanic* setup but slip it in the next time it works."

He presses forward, leaning me against the car. "I thought so."

"So, are we going to California . . . together?" I ask giddily.

His head dips back in disbelief. "I can't believe you came all the way down here to ask me out—of state."

I beam, a thousand fireworks going off in my chest all at once. "I can't believe you said yes—you're out of your mind! We barely know each other, and think about the age gap! Have you thought about how much older I am than you? A full one and a half yeeeeaars—"

He cuts me off with his mouth, and I go molten with him pressed against me, tangling my hands in his hair, pulling him tighter, drinking him in, reveling in the flaming-baton-twirler sensation in my stomach. My fingers drop, skating down his back before this kiss breaks.

"Irritatingly likable." He takes the keys I have clutched in my hand and locks the door. "All right, you're coming with me." He tugs my hand behind him down the street.

"Where are we going?"

"On a date."

I narrow my eyes. "A date?"

He raises a playful brow. "Oh, are you not familiar with the concept? It's what normal people do to get to know each other romantically. Involves a meal, sometimes a movie. Usually comes before asking someone to follow you across the country?"

I frown and shake my head. "No . . . Osprey, I'm, like, ninety-nine percent sure a date is a weird fruit."

He keels forward in a boneless silent annoyed laugh.

And this is how my real-life fairy-tale happily ever after starts. Not with an elevator meet-cute or an accidental coffee collision at Starbucks. There's no dicey bet or mysterious might-be-handsome email pen pal who turns out to be the owner of the gigantic bookstore down the street. It starts with an idiotic joke about fruit.

AND I WILL TREASURE THAT JOKE FOR THE REST OF TIME. I will tell my grandkids. I will write it into my first screenplay. We will tell the story at our eventual wedding where we will give dates as funny party favors. Maybe I'll engrave it on our tombstones, and from afar, it'll look like a giant essay text followed by an annoying one-line response.

Fingers crossed, knock on wood, this one works out.

I am chock full of hope. (Because we both have feathers.)

Acknowledgments

Book three. Hot damn. I wrote a *Survivor*/stranded on an island/game show book, something I've been wanting to do for years. Probably since the magical year 2000, when I both read *Harry Potter and the Goblet of Fire* and watched my first season of *Survivor*.

I got to rewatch forty-two seasons of my favorite show over the quarantine as "research" for this book. If you haven't seen *Survivor*, and you enjoyed this tale, I reckon you will also enjoy *Survivor*.

Starting this book was a struggle, as every book has been in its own special way, but somewhere around the forty-thousand-word mark I fell head over heels for the story. The characters. The game. The ships. The family dynamic. To put it frankly, I had *the best time ever*. When I was in my *AATH* mind palace, I was flying. I really hope that joy translated to y'all on the page.

I have so many humans to thank today. First, JL Stermer, for being so encouraging when I told her I wanted to write a *Survivor* book back in 2018, and again in 2020 when I started to flesh out the idea. Thank you to my agent, Suzie Townsend, for the incredible feedback and unwavering support throughout the editing and publishing process. Thank you, Sophia Ramos and Kate Sullivan, for your integral notes and early feedback on the first act! Thank you to the entire kickass team at New Leaf. Thank you to my fabulous, insightful editor, Eileen Rothschild! Thank you to Lisa, Lexi, Kerri, and the whole team at Wednesday Books!

It took some deep reflecting on this story and some of the themes running through it for me to realize I have made an ERROR. I haven't thanked Katarina Schwan in either of my two previous novels. I always say *Twilight* was what gave me the confidence to even believe I was capable of writing a book. But in reality it was *Twilight* and *Kat Schwan*. Kat, you were the first nonteacher who made me believe I might be good at this. Your enthusiastic feedback on those early college short stories has served as Patronus fuel to combat imposter syndrome, time and time again throughout the last fifteen years. Thank you, thank you, thank you for being so open and kind.

Thank you to Kat O'Keefe, story wizard, who pulled me through the darkest, most unhinged, most confusing parts of the drafting process of *AATH*. Thank you for reading the raw rough draft. For all the feedback. For answering all the frantic Voxer messages at random hours of the day as I tried to untangle a story idea or plot problem and talking me down from so many story cliffs. I don't know how I would have gotten this all out without you.

Thank you to Dr. Katie McCormick-Huhn, who always has a genius fresh take on the plot questions/issues I throw at her, and the most encouraging, positive commentary. I don't know where I'd be without your two cents on every aspect of this novel. For real. Thank you for making the time in your scary, overwhelmingly busy law school schedule to read this draft and help me through all my big story road blocks.

Thank you to Natasha Polis, for listening to me tell stories about these characters for extensive periods of time on the phone. For recommending I rewatch *The Mummy* and *Romancing the Stone* when I was stuck on the fire scene, to help me nail down the perfect tone.

Thank you to Abby Barnett for being such an amazing beta reader and getting back to me with pivotal feedback when I really needed it.

Thank you to Tiernan Bertrand-Essington for providing me with such spectacular, thoughtful notes!

Thank you to Dr. Jenna Presto for reading this baby before it came out and sharing your notes and thoughts despite reading being not quite your favorite thing!

Thank you to John for picking up my midnight phone calls when I was in massive book three plot panics. The first when I had the idea for Remy's character and the other when I was trying to figure out how to write the challenges—you helped make this book so much cooler.

Thank you to Cynthia Yee for recommending *FBoy Island,* which ended up being an indispensable source of unexpected inspiration during the drafting process.

Olivia and Paulith, thank you for the endless supply of entertainment, sibling support, and inspiration. I think this will probably be your favorite book of mine if you get around to reading it.

Julia Friley, Kristina Marjieh, Jesse George, Holly Springhorn, Caroline Springhorn: thank you for all the love, emotional support, and enthusiasm for whatever part of the writing process I came to you to gush or vent about.

Mom and Nana, thank you for all the love and support throughout this process. Thanks for hanging out with me for various endless phone calls' worth of anxiety times.

To the *Those Forking Fangirls* listeners and Patreon community—I'm so grateful for all of y'all's kindness. Hanging out with you on a weekly basis is an absolute delight. I feel so, so lucky to have y'all in my life. Thank you so much for all the love and support.

To my polandbananasBOOKS subscribers/viewers/YouTube family, from the bottom of my heart: thank you. Thank you for sticking with me through the years. Thank you for all the comments and encouragement across all my "Trials and Tribulations of Writing a Book" videos where I drafted this novel. I can never truly express how much I appreciate y'all. Thank you for sharing your lives with me. For sharing your time with me. Thank you for preordering my books. For making it possible for me to be here right now, writing the acknowledgments for my third novel. I'm here because you decided I was worth listening to. And I am so incredibly grateful, and lucky to have so many wonderfully compassionate, kind humans in my corner.

Bookstagram/BookTok/BookTube/Book bloggers—thank you so much for any and every post supporting something I've written. I appreciate it SO MUCH. Y'all are integral to helping a story find its audience. Thank you for helping me. (Also, you're the absolute coolest. Your creativity inspires me on the daily.)

Jeff Probst, thank you for spearheading my favorite show. *Survivor* has motivated me, taught me, inspired me, and entertained me for twenty-three years now. Cheers to many more!

BOSTON ROB AND AMBER—KING AND QUEEN OF THE SHOWMANCE REALM. YOUR LOVE STORY IS EVERYTHING. Growing up, season eight was my holy grail. Thank you for being so inspiring and so much fun to watch.

Reader! Hi! Thank you for picking up my book! I'm so glad you're here. I hope this story brought you at least a quarter as much joy to read as it brought me to write. If this is our first time chatting, my name's Christine. I love reading books. And writing them. I've been making videos about them on the internet for thirteen years now on YouTube under the name polandbananasBOOKS. If you want to chat more you can always catch me there. Or on Instagram @xtinemay! I'd love to keep in touch! <3

xoxo,
2023 Christine